Children with Invisible Faces

A Suspense Thriller

Steve Jaffe

A Weaver of Tales Press Edition
www.aweaveroftalespress.com

A Weaver of Tales Press
Palm Desert, CA. 92211

First Edition Copyright © 2009 by Steve Jaffe
ISBN 978-0-9819410-1-1
2nd Edition Copyright © 2026
ISBN 979-8-9903969-3-7

Acknowledgements

I must first thank my wife, Nancy, for her ongoing support and meticulous editing, both with her "red pen" and her insightful suggestions. Without her encouragement, I would never have finished this book.

Fiction Books by Steve Jaffe

The Conglomerate

The Invisible Terrorist

The Propagandists

The Architect's Manifesto

The Plantation

The Faces of Doctor Richards

Check them out at www.aweaveroftalespress.com

Introduction

During the 1970s and 1980s, I traveled extensively throughout Guatemala. I had read many State Department bulletins aimed at Americans traveling to that country with small children. The warnings were strong and frightening: American children are at risk of being kidnapped in Central America.

When I came up with the idea for this story, I began researching problems within foster care agencies across the United States and discovered some troubling facts.

- *Recent reports from some states are also concerning. In Georgia, almost 1,800 children in state care went missing between 2018 and 2022, according to a new analysis by the National Center for Missing & Exploited Children as part of a U.S. Senate panel's ongoing investigation into Georgia's child welfare system. More than 20% of those were likely trafficked.*
- *As of early 2025, recent data shows that 390,000 children are in foster care across the United States. This number is based on verified reports from the Child Welfare Information Gateway and reflects trends seen in late 2023 and early 2024.*
- *Under federal law, state social service agencies must submit a report to the National Center for Missing & Exploited Children, a nonprofit organization established by Congress in 1984, when a child under their care goes missing. They are also required to notify law enforcement, who report missing children to the National Crime Information Center.*
- *A recent audit published earlier this year by the U.S. Department of Health and Human Services found that across 46 states, state agencies failed to report an estimated 34,800 cases of missing foster kids. These cases include children who ran away multiple times. The average age, according to the National Center for Missing & Exploited Children, was 15.*

- *After the high-profile disappearance of a five-year-old foster child in Florida in April 2002, it was discovered that the child had not been checked on for sixteen months. An investigation showed that hundreds of other missing foster children were unaccounted for and were assumed either to be runaways or to have been abducted from state care.*
- *Recent reports from some states are equally concerning. In Georgia, nearly 1,800 children in state care disappeared between 2018 and 2022, according to a new analysis by the National Center for Missing & Exploited Children as part of a U.S. Senate panel's ongoing investigation into Georgia's child welfare system. More than 20% of those were likely trafficked.*
- *Nationwide, roughly 2% of foster children are considered "runaways".*
- *Many cases of missing foster children have raised concerns that our foster care system is overwhelmed due to the highest national caseload in history.*
- *Reports of thousands of missing foster children are absent from the national media...WHY?*

The grave situation involving our American children gave rise to the story of The Pied Piper and the Children with Invisible Faces.

Prologue

Guatemala City, 1990

The horrifying tales—the whispered, unspeakable rumors of children snatched and slaughtered for their organs—were met with widespread disbelief. Instead, dominating dinner conversations, coffee shop chats, and prime-time radio were the exponentially rising global child abductions.

Infant disappearances, occurring in alarming clusters, vanished in the blink of an eye. These crimes targeted even the most idyllic vacation spots, shattering the illusion of family safety. The motive was not financial gain, but a dark secret that the authorities desperately tried to hide.

Innocent children and trusting souls disappeared without a trace, leaving behind heartbroken parents whose cries for justice were ignored, met with weak excuses, and lacking any real leads. In their desperation, some authorities accused the grieving parents, turning them into scapegoats and making the investigation even colder.

This escalating crisis sparked a firestorm in the international press, fueled by the American media's relentless craving for sensational stories. Meanwhile, the US government stayed notably silent, trying to bury its head in the sand.

Infant abductions have plagued Guatemalan authorities for decades. Highly organized, brutal human trafficking rings have operated with chilling efficiency, targeting resorts offering childcare services as prime hunting grounds.

Complicit staff, deeply embedded in these criminal networks, allowed kidnappers ample time and space to escape with their victims before anyone even noticed they were gone. Parents, returning from leisurely outings—such as scuba diving, snorkeling, or bus tours—were often the first to realize the horrifying truth: their child was missing.

The local police were severely unprepared and overwhelmed, struggling to launch effective investigations. The crisis only drew significant international attention when American children vacationing in Guatemala, a country once regarded as a safe haven for US citizens, became victims. This prompted immediate action from the President of the United States, unleashing the full investigative power of the FBI.

Tensions simmered inside the White House. President Hollister, his Chief of Staff, and Press Secretary were extremely anxious. Looming re-election prospects called for a decisive response to the escalating crisis in Guatemala. This situation had sparked a national firestorm. The President, frustrated by the lack of cooperation from the corrupt Guatemalan regime, demanded action.

The FBI and CIA had a prime suspect: Frederick Ramirez, a notorious kingpin of human trafficking who wielded immense power and influence, protecting him from accountability. Even whispering accusations against him would provoke swift, brutal retaliation. Disappearance was a common outcome for his enemies.

The FBI painted a chilling picture in Guatemala. They discovered that Frederick Ramirez's human trafficking cartel had shifted to the lucrative, untraceable trade of infant organ harvesting.

Under immense pressure, the Guatemalan President reluctantly agreed to a joint operation to capture Ramirez. The stakes were high for him, as revenue from the travel industry had almost completely stopped, crippling the economy. American tourism had dropped by fifty percent.

The immediate priority was to calm the public's fears and rebuild trust. The administration had to determine whether this was a horrifying truth or just a scary urban legend, hoping to cast it as the latter. It was a grim fairytale for tourists to dismiss as a macabre sideshow in a land rich with ancient superstitions and lively folklore.

This carefully crafted story, however, relied on successfully neutralizing Frederick Ramirez. His reign of terror and his criminal empire were about to end, as long as the complicit Guatemalan government cooperated.

The fate of Ramirez and his cartel hung precariously in the balance. The FBI's elite team of agents, Jack Seymour, Robert Evans, and Ted Blanchard, was tasked with capturing him at all costs.

Chapter 1

For three decades, Frederick Ramirez projected an image of civic virtue, standing as a pillar of his community during his clearer moments. His philanthropy, given to the very people he had brutalized, was a distorted display of goodwill. He supplied his town with financial support, helping thousands of Indigenous families—a generosity that only superficially secured their loyalty.

Ironically, Ramirez truly saw himself as kind and righteous. This belief was unfailing. He would stroll through the busy marketplace in Belize, sure of widespread admiration. He justified his terrible acts, like the abductions and buying children from poor parents, as acts of compassionate help.

Like his father before him, a massive ego drove his distorted justifications. He thought that sending these unfortunate children to work in exploitative sweatshops worldwide, owned by ruthless crime bosses, was actually a significant improvement over their miserable lives. He was a master of his dark trade, a kingpin of human trafficking who accumulated billions — a giant of wickedness.

Complete, unwavering loyalty meant everything to Frederick. Failing to meet his strict standards led to swift, ruthless punishment. He had a loyal network of intermediaries who constantly protected him from authorities trying to bring him down.

He trained Enrique, his only male heir, in his father's brutal methods. He needed to make him strong so that one day, he would inherit his reign of terror and the twisted admiration it earned.

Frederick's legacy of bloodshed and intimidation was beaten into him by his father. The Ramirez Cartel, led by his grandfather Enrique, maintained an oppressive hold on international human trafficking, illegal adoptions, and prostitution rings.

The elder Enrique had an uncanny talent for navigating the perilous political terrains of nations involved in this modern-day barbarity. He took advantage of impoverished countries where desperate parents willingly sacrificed their children for a small amount of money, tragically believing they were securing a better future for their sons or daughters.

This belief, sometimes correct, often led to an even more horrifying existence. Bribes, generously given to law enforcement and corrupt officials, facilitated their operations, silencing opposition through carefully planned intimidation. The cartel's secret influence was so deeply embedded within these compromised governments that Interpol and U.S. law enforcement agencies were almost powerless, with their efforts blocked at every turn.

Enrique Sr., the patriarch, had a warped moral code regarding child trafficking. He firmly refused to knowingly hand over minors to the exploitative cartels involved in prostitution and child pornography.

Enrique Sr., a devout Catholic, attended Sunday Mass with his wife and son, Frederick, as a ritual of piety. This warped morality, however, was deeply ingrained in his son, fostering relentless expectations of unwavering obedience.

Young Frederick absorbed these lessons, but his fragile mental state worsened due to relentless abuse and beatings with a belt. The family's sinister enterprise continued until Enrique Sr., in a final, horrifying act, murdered his wife before taking his own life.

After his father's death, nineteen-year-old Frederick decided to reshape the cartel and create new, profitable ways of exploiting it. Now the only owner, he ruthlessly restructured the organization, adapting to the harsh realities of the underworld to keep its dominance.

A terrifying inheritance haunted the Ramirez men—a crippling mental illness that worsened with each generation. Each father, fully aware of this dreadful legacy, passed it on, believing there was no other way.

Divine retribution, it seemed, manifested in every Ramirez man by age eighteen. Then, at forty-five, a cold, ruthless pattern set off a spiral into madness. Paranoia took control, leading to the murder of loved ones and ultimately, suicide.

After taking control of the family's criminal empire, Frederick married the stunning Rosa Guzman. She bore him a son, Enrique, a dark tribute to his father, continuing the cycle of inherited depravity. Like a malignant tumor left untreated, it was passed down from generation to generation.

From a young age, Enrique's separation from his father was apparent. He sought comfort and affection only from his mother. His migraines worsened whenever his father was near.

Rosa desperately tried to shield him from this harsh reality, repeatedly reading children's stories to soothe his troubled mind. *The Pied Piper of Hamlin* became his obsession. The story fed an idealistic self-image. Enrique wanted to be a modern-day savior of children, a liberator from the suffering caused by his father.

Fueled by his mother's unwavering support, Enrique fostered a strong belief in his ability to redeem himself, imagining a future where he could rescue all the children, including himself, who suffered from his father's cruelty. He withdrew into a fantasy world, dreaming of a secret sanctuary where he could escape and flourish with all the children he saved.

This peaceful vision, however, was shattered. Frederick, following his father's lead, began his son's indoctrination into the family's ruthless business. The same belt that had left scars on his father now marked Enrique's back, instilling the inhuman values of the Ramirez legacy.

Gentle and compassionate, young Enrique could not stand up to his physically abusive father. Even his mother's strong influence eventually diminished.

When Enrique turned sixteen, Rosa noticed her once innocent child was slipping into the dark world her husband controlled. She sensed the urgency and acted quickly. She created a story about increased educational opportunities in the United States, which she argued were essential for his future in the family business.

This ruse allowed her to send him to Los Angeles to live with her sister. However, this exile hid a vital secret she kept from her husband. Enrique had started psychiatric treatment, including medication to control his bipolar disorder.

Rosa's doctor reassured her that Enrique's bipolar disorder could be managed with medication, promising a fulfilling life as long as his stress levels stayed low. That summer, Enrique's return home led to a secretive act by his mother. Hiding his lithium from her husband, Rosa begged Enrique, her face showing desperation, to keep his medication a secret from his father.

Clasping her hands around his head, she pleaded, "My love, you have a chance to break this cycle, to become a man better than your father and his father before him. The power to choose is yours. Either yield to this illness or conquer it by sticking to your treatment. Your father's days are numbered; when he's gone, we'll finally live a normal life."

A rare, radiant smile lit up Enrique's face as he hugged his mother, sealing his promise with a kiss. "I can do this, Mama," he said, full of hope. "The doctor said a few years on this medicine will rebalance me, and I'll be normal. That's what I want for both of us. I love you so much."

But Enrique's brave effort to stay balanced was broken. His father wouldn't let him go back to Los Angeles at the end of summer break, ending his much-needed treatment.

Frederick's discovery of lithium in Enrique's dresser triggered a violent outburst and a brutal attack on Rosa. Enrique's physical abuse resumed.

Deprived of his medication, the transformation happened swiftly. The once innocent, optimistic young man was dragged into the depths of his illness. Each horrifying act of violence—watching his father commit kidnappings and murders—dulled Enrique's senses and left him emotionally numb.

Although Rosa desperately tried to protect him, Frederick, embodying the malevolence of his father, ultimately succeeded. On Enrique's nineteenth birthday, he received a gift from his father that would permanently alter his life.

* * * * *

Enrique, a statue of chilling stillness on the office couch, with eyes like glacial pools of resentment, waited for his father's commands and orders. The mission would be a quick, brutal abduction in Santa Catarina, a village seventy kilometers beyond Guatemala City. His first solo job seemed simple enough.

Yet, as Enrique would learn painfully, simplicity is a cruel illusion, especially within the complex horrors of human trafficking. Terror gnawed at him, a fear that far exceeded the usual worry.

His father's recent descent into savagery chilled him to the bone. The damp stain of blood, a grim testament to the beating, still clung to his shirt. A macabre reminder of his mother's desperate attempts at healing.

Since his forty-fifth birthday three weeks ago, Frederick had slipped into a crippling depression, unleashing unprovoked anger and violence toward his son. A profound and frightening change had taken place, not only within him but also within Enrique. From the veranda, his mother's crying served as a mournful counterpoint to his grim departure.

She pleaded for her husband to delay this mission. Her pleas were met with a brutal slap, cruelly silencing her maternal concern. Enrique could only offer a helpless shrug and a fleeting, silent kiss, with a whispered, "I love you," that hung heavy with unspoken sorrow.

His eyes showed the profound sadness he carried, a desperate vow to himself that this would be the end of his mother's tears. Fate, however, had a more painful truth in store.

Chapter 2

Enrique's 19ᵗʰ Birthday

The howling wind, like a dragon's breath, kept rattling the shutters on the ranch house. It drowned out the brutal belt whipping Frederick Ramirez had been bestowing on his son Enrique for the last thirty minutes. Each loud snap sounded like a firecracker, *pop, pop, pop,* as each snap of the belt echoed throughout the house. Each blow from the oversized brass buckle added more cuts to the old scars on the young boy's back, causing a red sheet of blood to blanket Enrique's pale skin.

Sound for sound, the clatter created by the wind as it whipped each shutter with explosive force matched perfectly with Frederick's rage. He had become an orchestra conductor, animated by his bloodied belt. Enrique's father appeared lost in a distant place, staring blankly out the window in his office, his arm in perfect harmony, never missing a beat to lessen his cruelty, not even when Enrique's old scars ruptured, splattering blood on the surrounding furniture and carpet.

Today, on Enrique's birthday, there was no cake, no party, and no friends to celebrate with—only his final beating, which his father gave him. Another Ramirez son was about to take over the family business. Each job and every child taken away provided food on their table.

For Enrique's birthday gift, Frederick was sending him on his first snatch-and-grab with his cousin Mario, another sociopath brought up in the

Ramirez environment. Frederick would not join them. He had become weak and unstable, and his illness was about to peak.

The young girls Enrique was forced to abduct today were very valuable to an Arab Sheikh. They needed to be delivered safely and unharmed.

"Failure tomorrow is not an option," Frederick said in a calm, even tone. "You're now a man," he told him in a low soothing voice as each blow from the belt landed on his son's back. "After today, your mother won't be permitted to coddle you."

Before the lashings ended, Frederick's clothing was crimson, and his face was splattered with his son's blood. His arm felt like a sack of potatoes, twitching at his side and limp from exhaustion. He was done. He walked over to his desk, his eyes unblinking, staring blankly as he sank back into his chair, unaware that his son was unconscious and covered in blood. Now everything was in place.

This particular beating on this day was a tradition, a kind of rite of passage for another Ramirez son to become a man.

* * * * *

Rosa gently held Enrique in her arms after his beating, his body marked with bruises and bloody welts. The coldness of the Spanish tiles pressed against her bare feet as she kept him close. The weight of her son, unconscious but heavy with the sins of his father, bore down on her.

The flickering light bulb cast long, distorted shadows, with dust motes swirling in the still air. Enrique's breathing was shallow and ragged, a fragile echo in the suffocating silence of the night.

Your father... he's dying," Maria whispered, her voice hoarse with unshed tears. Her words carried the weight of a lifetime of regret. "The Ramirez cartel... soon, it will be nothing more than a ghost story. We have enough money to live ten lifetimes. You can use it for good, Enrique. Make amends. Do something for humanity."

She sensed the slightest flutter in Enrique's chest, a reaction to her words. A flicker of life appeared from the battered figure she held. The hope that grew in her chest was delicate and easily shattered.

Enrique's eyes snapped open, their usual dark intensity heightened by pain and a hint of something else, something chillingly cold. He looked at his mother, her face marked with worry and grief.

He tried to speak, but instead a groan escaped his lips. It was a sound born of pain and inner chaos. "Mother," he finally managed, his voice a strained rasp. "Please stop."

Rosa flinched. The desperation in her gaze starkly contrasted with the coldness of Enrique's eyes. She had expected tears, pleas, and remorse, not this.

"I hate him, Momma. I despise everything he's done." The pain in his body seemed to fade behind a strange conviction, temporarily hardening his gaze. "Don't talk of such treason," he hissed, his words sharp and edged with the threat of unspoken violence. "Don't you dare speak of ending it in front of him. I'm not sure I could protect you." His words revealed a confession, offering a terrifying glimpse into the twisted loyalties and chilling ambition simmering beneath his pain.

The office seemed to tighten around them, with shadows growing darker and more threatening. Rosa's carefully thought-out plan, her hopes of redemption, fell apart in the face of her son's chilling declaration. The light bulb flickered again, casting a harsh, revealing glow on the scene.

Mother and son are locked in a silent battle of wills amid the stench of violence and the shadow of a dying empire. Rosa's hope, a fragile ember, is slowly being extinguished, replaced by the chilling realization that the legacy of the Ramirez cartel might extend far beyond its leader's imminent demise. It lives on now in the chillingly indifferent heart of her son.

Chapter 3

Guatemala, Central America, July 1999

The moment had arrived. Four cartel suspects were in the custody of Guatemalan authorities. Three FBI agents, observing through a one-way mirror, saw a brutal scene.

A man, only in his underwear, was strapped to a metal chair under a single, harsh light bulb. The yellowish beam harshly reflected off his battered face, highlighting the fresh crimson blood mixing with the dried, caked blood from earlier attacks. Three feet away, another prisoner sat, exhausted and terrified; his ordeal was about to begin.

The interrogator, a storm of fury, relentlessly struck the bound man with a broom handle. His frantic demands for the location of Frederick Ramirez's next abduction echoed in the sterile room.

Special Agent Seymour had intelligence confirming these men were tied to the Ramirez cartel. His intel confirmed these men possessed crucial information about where and when a kidnapping would take place. After five more brutal blows, the man's head sank onto his chest.

"You're a worthless piece of shit," the interrogator shouted at the man. He jerked the man's head upright, only to let it fall again. A cruel laugh erupted as he casually drew his weapon. With chilling dispassion, he executed the prisoner with a single shot. The lifeless body crashed to the floor, sprawling at the feet of the petrified second captive.

Rookie FBI Agent Robert Evans, his outrage boiling over, lunged toward the door, desperate to intervene. Special Agent Seymour grabbed his arm. "This is how they interrogate kidnappers in Guatemala. Our instructions are clear: non-interference."

"That's bullshit," Evans exploded. "We've just witnessed a cold-blooded execution, and you expect me to stay passive?" Evans, a rookie agent bound by the strict principles of his oath, felt betrayed. His idealistic view of the FBI as a beacon of justice was shattered by the harsh reality before him. He demanded accountability from his colleagues; anything less was unacceptable.

Seymour's arm wrapped around the young agent. "Maintain focus," he commanded softly but urgently. "Remember our goal: Frederick Rameriz, the head of the snake," he said, emphasizing with a sharp tap against the glass, "These men are responsible for the abduction and murder of countless innocent children, leaving devastated families behind." His breath hitched, raw emotion almost spilling over. He steadied himself, his voice dropping to a whisper. "Are you a man of faith, Agent Evans?"

Evans furrowed his brow. "What relevance does my spirituality have?"

Seymour's patience wore thin. "Everything. Such depravity calls for retribution. An eye for an eye. Letting the other prisoner realize he's going to face the same fate as his friend will produce the desired result."

"Does the Director know what's happening down here?" Evans asked.

"He knows but looks the other way. He's a politician who doesn't need any new scandals under his watch. Now, let's get back to this prisoner," Seymour ordered, as he pointed at the fluids pooling about the prisoner's feet. "Observe his bare feet wallowing in his urine and the blood of the body in front of him. He knows that if he doesn't cooperate, he's next."

Evans took a few controlling breaths before responding. "Jack, I didn't sign up for murder."

Remember our mission. We must catch Frederick Ramirez red-handed and return him to the United States. We need solid evidence; otherwise, he'll go free. There's always a cost in the fight against such evil.

Evans pulled away from Seymour's grip, moving to his seat with a face full of anguish. Seymour's words were hateful; his moral sense couldn't accept such cruelty. As a rookie, he was helplessly forced to watch.

Special Agent Blanchard, a seasoned veteran hardened by years of witnessing horrors, shrugged. He held the American legal system in disdain. He'd seen too many guilty murderers evade justice. The scene before him, with its brutal starkness, barely registered. He casually took another bite of his steak sandwich, unfazed by the gruesome sight. "It gets easier, kid," he mumbled through a mouthful of food.

The interrogator glanced at his watch. His gaze hardened as he pivoted to the next prisoner. Waving his pistol in the air, in a low whisper, he spoke. "Tell me what I need to know now," the interrogator's voice was chillingly calm. "I'll just as soon end you, you worthless piece of garbage, and display your remains to your accomplices. One of you will talk. It matters little which."

The gun barrel pressed firmly against the prisoner's temple. The man's pleas for mercy were immediate, his confession a torrent of information about Ramirez's upcoming planned kidnapping.

* * * * *

The next morning, Jack Seymour held an urgent meeting with Blanchard and Evans. The seriousness of their upcoming mission to rescue three girls from a village in Santa Catarina, seventy kilometers outside the city, required complete unity.

Seymour's voice reflected anxiety as he said, "Failure to capture Rameriz now jeopardizes our nation. Our children, our families are at risk." He added grimly, "American children are vanishing in this wretched country, and it has to end today."

Blanchard rolled his eyes and barely paused before biting into his Pan Dulce, a Guatemalan sweet bread. He noticed Evans wasn't buying what their leader was saying. "Rookie," he scoffed, "adapt or return to your desk at the Hoover Building. Field work operates under a different, harsher code."

Evans, still shaken from yesterday's interrogation, burst out in disgust. "Damn it, both of you! I didn't sign up for sanctioned brutality and murder. We're becoming indistinguishable from the monsters we hunt."

Before Seymour could respond, Blanchard kept talking. "Sometimes, we must descend to their level. Mercy is futile. Only retribution resonates with such depravity. The complete annihilation of Ramirez and his entire network would bring me immense satisfaction and a profound sense of security. These individuals harbor unforgiving grudges. Failure to eliminate the serpent's head, along with its entire brood, guarantees a venomous strike. My future, my potential family—their safety is paramount."

Seymour, raising a hand to silence Evans's impending retort, responded, "The statistics are horrifying. Over four thousand children have disappeared across Central America in the past three years, all linked to the Ramirez Cartel." He looked steadily at Evans, choosing his words carefully. "Our role is advisory. Intervention in Guatemalan law enforcement is forbidden. This nation has a two-century history of silencing dissent through political disappearances. Criminals are no exception. Let's stick to our mandate and return to our carefully refined system of justice." His final words were spoken with thinly veiled contempt.

* * * * *

The three FBI agents followed a military vehicle carrying fifteen secret police officers armed with automatic weapons. They were heading toward a Mayan village called Santa Caterina on Lake Atitlán. They left the paved highway and traveled down a rough country road that led to the small town inhabited by indigenous people.

The Guatemalan secret police were ready to reveal their methods for dealing with a notorious murderer. The remaining prisoner said that this operation would capture both Frederick, the cartel boss, and his son Enrique, who would face a baptism by fire.

The FBI team, mainly there for observation, had not received any explicit orders from the Director to arrest either Frederick or his heir. Still, the subtle cues from the Guatemalan police indicated they also had no real intention of making arrests.

Seymour, very aware of the tension among the Guatemalan officers, had a chilling feeling that they would show no mercy.

Chapter 4

The small village of Santa Catarina had been hit by a tropical storm, signaling changes that would forever transform their town. It was a humid, rainy afternoon when Enrique Ramirez and his cousin Mario Castro parked their car on the pothole-filled dirt road where his father had told them to go. It was the best spot to wait for the school bus.

Enrique looked at his orders one last time. They were clear. His father was specific: snatch three young girls, avoid getting caught, and get them back to Belize Harbor before sunrise to board the cargo ship.

The rain was now pounding against their car even harder. The sound brought Enrique back to his last whipping. The dirt street had turned into a fast-moving river, but it couldn't match the way his blood surged through his body from his racing heart.

Enrique was nervous, mostly scared he would mess up. His cousin Mario looked calm and relaxed. His eyes were tightly shut as he listened to a cassette of the Doors, his favorite American rock band.

Enrique's nerves made him breathe quickly, causing the windows to fog up. It wasn't easy to see out the left side of the car. Neither of them noticed the unmarked van parked diagonally across from their position.

Enrique nudged Mario's side when he saw the school bus turn the corner. He pulled the earphones off his cousin's head. "It's time," he said, his voice unsteady.

Mario jumped out of the car when he saw the bus stop at the corner. He pulled the hood of his raincoat forward, covering his Yankee baseball cap; they were his favorite baseball team.

Enrique had followed right behind his cousin. As if he had been sprayed with a fire hose, the heavy rain soaked through his corduroy jacket.

The tropical storm had turned into their ally.

The streets were empty. All the windows of the lively adobe homes around were tightly shut. No one could hear the girls cry out or see anything.

"This is going to be so fucking easy," Enrique shouted over the pouring rain, his confidence high as he slapped his cousin's back.

The three young girls, dressed in their school uniforms with their raincoat hoods lifted over their heads, did not hear the pounding footsteps approaching them. Enrique slipped a silk hood over one of the girls' heads and, with his pistol, struck her. Her body went limp.

He lifted her effortlessly, tossing her over his shoulder like a sack of potatoes. He craned his neck to check on his cousin as he jogged back to their car. "Everything's going perfectly," he told himself.

Just then, he tripped over the high, slick curb. He fell forward, twisting under the weight of the girl. They both hit the road hard; her head bounced off one of the cobblestones lining the street.

Enrique heard a dull cracking sound, like an eggshell breaking. At first, he was unaware of the blood gushing from the girl's head. He lifted the limp body, feeling her warm blood on his hands. Panic blanketed his body. He prayed she was not too damaged, or his father would kill him. There was blood everywhere. He looked back toward Mario and smiled. He was glad to see his cousin was not having any problems. He was bigger, stronger, and knew he could handle the remaining two girls.

Enrique opened the trunk and dumped his prey. He watched as Mario knocked out one of the girls and then chased after the other. His eyes widened in disbelief at what happened next.

* * * * *

Special Agent Robert Evans couldn't believe what he had just seen. "Aren't we going to stop them?" he asked, bewildered.

Seymour shook his head. "Our orders are only to observe. Do not engage," Agent Seymour said. "Frederick Ramirez's not here. We need the big fish," he added a bit too patronizingly. "We'll follow them to Frederick."

Evans shook his head. "This is total bullshit." Before anyone could stop him, he burst out of the back of the van, running toward the two girls who were in trouble, his weapon in his right hand, the safety off.

"Shit," yelled Seymour. "I knew working with a rookie would be the death of me." He bolted out the door with Blanchard. He had to back up Evans before he got himself killed. The Guatemalan secret police followed.

Captain Diaz looked upset as he chased after the three FBI agents. He grabbed Seymour's arm and forced him to stop. "What the fuck is your man doing?" he barked. "You're not supposed even to be here."

"I guess it's hard watching a crime being committed. He's doing what he's been trained to do," Seymour said unconvincingly, with a shrug.

Captain Diaz shook his head in disgust. "You're here as a courtesy. You mess this up, we might never get another chance at Frederick Ramirez. If he even suspects the FBI was involved…you…even your families are not safe. Your director will be hearing from me." Once he finished scolding Seymour, he signaled for two of his men to follow him. They were in hot pursuit of Enrique Ramirez.

Jack Seymour rushed toward his two agents, stunned by what he saw. "Fuck," he yelled. Evans was on the ground, struggling with Mario, while Blanchard appeared to be trying to get a clean shot.

"This is not happening," Seymour moaned.

* * * * *

Enrique was in shock. Out of nowhere, six men jumped from a van, their weapons drawn, and rushed quickly toward the girl Mario had knocked out. The men split up. Three of them, dressed in dark blue raincoats with "FBI" stenciled in bold yellow letters on their backs, were closing in on his cousin. The other three, whom he recognized, belonged to the Guatemalan Secret Police.

He knew their reputation. His body shuddered. He was more afraid of them than of his father. He saw them split up; one officer lifted the fallen girl and took her to the van, while the other two headed toward him.

He read the letters aloud. "FBI," Enrique mumbled. "They can't be here in Guatemala. My father paid a lot of money to keep them away from us."

Panic overtook him. The other three officers moved in. Enrique drew his gun from his waistband and shot. The first Guatemalan policeman fell, clutching his knee. The other man slammed onto the cobblestone street. He lay still.

Enrique's mind was racing through everything rapidly. His pounding heart overwhelmed his thoughts, making it difficult to think clearly.

Should he help his cousin? Should he run?

The idea of his father's anger influenced his choice; it felt more severe than what he was dealing with at that moment. Little did he realize how accurate his initial instincts would prove to be.

His mouth dropped open, and his eyes bulged in disbelief. Two FBI agents tackled Mario, with one wrestling him on the muddy dirt road.

Enrique stood frozen, unable to move. He jumped when he heard the first burst of gunfire. Mario lay still in the muddy water, which had turned red around his twisted body. He had two choices: stay and fight or run and live.

What he did next didn't make any sense, but he did it anyway to save himself. He was terrified. He wished he had never been born as the son of Frederick Ramirez.

Without hesitation, he fired four rounds into each tire of the police van and drove off in his car. He U-turned out of town, never looking back.

Three shots shattered his rear window, with one grazing his forearm as he sped out of the village.

When Enrique reached the Belize harbor, the girl in the trunk was already dead. She had bled out. He didn't want to go home. He was three girls short of completing his simple assignment. He had nowhere else to turn, no one to rely on but his friend Luis Rodriguez. He believed he could handle the mess he had created.

* * * * * *

Early the next morning, Luis Rodriguez, Fredericks' head of security, and his brothers arrived at the cantina Enrique often visited when his problems became too much to handle. As expected, they found him drunk, with two beautiful young girls draped in each arm. They were giggling as they cuddled him.

"Luis, come here. Meet my new girlfriends. Aren't they beautiful?" he said, slurring his words. He had his left hand inside one of the girls' sundresses, gripping her firm breast, while the other girl was kissing him on his neck, her hand inside his pants.

Luis didn't look happy. He snapped his fingers at the two women, signaling them to leave right away. "Get the fuck out of here," he yelled. "Enrique, your father's very upset with you. Have you listened to any news since yesterday?"

"No news, just drinking and fucking. A dying man's last request before he's executed," he said, laughing.

Luis tossed a newspaper at Enrique. "Read the headlines," he growled.

Enrique tried to focus, blinking a few times, shocked by what he was reading. "Mario's alive? He was lying in the street. He wasn't moving. There was so much blood." He continued reading, feeling enraged. "Those mother fuckers had to have tortured him to get him to confess." He put the paper down, his head dropping into his cupped hands.

Luis spoke. "You need to read more. It gets worse."

Enrique bit his lower lip, struggling to understand what had happened to Mario. "What does this mean? How could my cousin be hanged in front of the main church?"

The FBI agent in charge, Jack Seymour, stated that the Ramirez Cartel was involved. Mario must have confessed. The FBI knows about your father's activities.

Seymour, with the help of our secret police, aims to bring you and your father to justice. Then, Seymour's statement about the Ramirez Cartel sparked outrage among the grieving families.

Luis could not contain his anger. "It was Jack Seymour's words that set off the angry crowd and got your cousin killed. The police opened the doors and let the angry parents drag your cousin out, beating him severely before hanging him." Luis took a deep breath before he continued. "I have to get you home now. It's not safe," ordered Luis, pulling Enrique out of the booth.

Enrique's face was pale. "What's my father going to do about all of this?" he asked nervously.

Luis bit his lower lip and shook his head. "I don't know. All I know is that he's ordered me to get you back to the ranch immediately."

Chapter 5

The ranch house had come to life again as it awaited Enrique's return. Frederick paced his office like a caged lion. He scowled when he saw his son. The expression on his father's face, the dead black pools in his eyes, conveyed it all. Enrique was about to receive the worst beating of his life.

"What happened yesterday?" Frederick asked, his words slurred. He swung the thick black belt with the large, bloodstained buckle over his head. In his other hand, he held a pair of pruning shears.

Enrique stammered, his words caught in his throat. He considered fighting back, but it was only a thought. "We were ambushed," he replied nervously. "I got away, only by the grace of God. I shot two of the scumbags responsible. I think I killed one of them?" He tried to hide his trembling voice, but he failed miserably.

Frederick shook his head. "You ran scared. You left your cousin, my sister's son, to be captured by the FBI. The girls' grieving parents hung him," he bellowed. He tossed his son the front page of the Periodico, Guatemala's leading newspaper. "Read what they are saying."

"I've read it. They're lying. It didn't happen like they say. I would have been captured. I, too," Enrique told him. "I would be dead right now," he shouted at his father.

"You should have stayed and killed those FBI scum. Then, kill the police they were with," Frederick yelled, his face had become knotted with loathing toward his son.

"I didn't want to die," Enrique argued, realizing that his father didn't care whether he was alive or dead. He tried to reason. "You need me to run the fucking family business. Believe it or not, I was thinking of you. We can get other girls for the Sheik."

Frederick was silent, digesting what Enrique had just said. "I don't like losing. Your actions were embarrassing to me, and all the Ramirez's before you. How are we going to regain the respect we need to keep the business afloat?" he said, pressing his hand hard against his temple, trying to deal with a migraine.

For the next hour, Enrique endured a beating that continued until he lost consciousness. He didn't know how long he had been unconscious. A small pool of blood had formed beneath his head on the tile floor. His ear throbbed. He gently pressed his finger against it, wincing from the sharp pain.

He lifted himself off the carpet and staggered toward a mirror. He stared in horror at what his father had done. His father had cut off half of his ear.

"Father, you're a bastard. You and your hideous lessons," he murmured.

He called out for his mother, but the house was dead silent, an unnatural stillness. He hurried from room to room, suppressing his emotions, not wanting his father to punish him again.

He suddenly stopped, his eyes filled with disgust. On the floor in his parents' bedroom lay his mother, naked, in a large pool of blood where part of her skull had been. His immediate thoughts turned to the police.

His mind raced, trying to figure out who had killed his mother. "Did the police... no, it was those bastard FBI agents... they followed me home?" he stammered.

He called for his father, but there was no response. He cautiously knocked on the door to his father's den. Once more, there was no answer.

He turned the doorknob carefully, making sure the door opened slowly, just in case his father was busy working. He had felt his father's wrath many times for interrupting him unannounced.

Again, terror consumed him. Lying face down on his desk with a gunshot wound to his left temple was his father, his pistol resting on his desk covered with Frederick's blood.

In less than twenty-four hours, young Enrique Ramirez turned nineteen, failed at his first snatch and grab, and lost his entire family. As he stared at his father's body, his anger overtook him. He spat on his father and then punched the lifeless shell of his brutal father, cursing him for the life he had given him.

Enrique sat quietly in his living room, gazing into the distance at the central courtyard. His mother's beautiful gardens, enclosed by a ten-foot aqua blue adobe wall, seemed just as sad as he felt. His mother was gone forever, taking with her the vibrant colors she had added to his world. In his lap rested the belt that had belonged to his family for generations, along with the bloodied scissors that had mutilated his ear. The belt that had left a lasting impression was gone with three snips from the scissors. He picked up his severed ear, a testament to his horrible life.

"Never again will you harm another person," he said to the weapon that had scared him.

His father's head of security, Luis Rodriguez, who worked at the ranch with his brothers, hid when Frederick went on his murderous rampage. He stood by the double wooden doors to the living room, his fists clenched on his hips.

"We need to go. The police are coming to arrest you and your father. They can't find you here," Luis said sternly. "You might have been recognized yesterday."

Enrique looked up, his eyes red from crying. "Go?

Luis grabbed Enrique's arm and pulled him up, holding his friend's head. "I'm your family now. My brothers are your family. We will run the business as you see fit. I will give you the same loyalty I gave your father, this I promise."

"I don't want anything to do with the fucking family business again," Enrique cursed. "I want to kill those fucking FBI agents and make their families pay for what they've done to me."

"I suggest you do it another time," Luis said, leading him outside to his father's Mercedes.

Inside the car, Enrique kept looking at the newspaper article and the faces of the three FBI agents who changed his life. He specifically focused on the man in charge, Special Agent Jack Seymour.

"Luis, the Ramirez family died today. Never speak the name Ramirez again. My father said that life is a game; it doesn't favor good or evil. Play it well and win at all costs. Today, I will become the Pied Piper. He will now make a name for himself, but not like my fabled hero."

Luis looked confused. "The Pied Piper?" he snickered. "Isn't it a story about a man in a clown suit who punishes a town after they don't pay him for getting rid of their rats? I don't see the point of you turning into this fairy tale," he laughed.

Enrique initially appeared hurt, then suddenly erupted in rage, as if he was about to kill Luis. He grabbed him by his shirt and lifted him off the ground. "Never talk badly about the Pied Piper. If my mother believed in him, that's good enough for me. It's time for the world to feel the wrath of the Pied Piper. My father's business will now have a new purpose. We will focus on trafficking young children. Too many parents, like my father, are unfit parents. I will give these children a better life."

Enrique's eyes were black pools of hatred as he stared at Luis. "I need to have Enrique Rameriz die today."

Off in the distance, Luis noticed four military helicopters coming their way. "It's time we leave."

33

* * * * *

Four helicopters swooped down on the Ramirez ranch like predatory hawks, kicking up a dust storm. Within seconds of landing, twenty-four heavily armed commandos from the Guatemalan army were on the ground. Following closely behind were Agents Seymour, Blanchard, and Evans, unarmed. They were there as a courtesy to report to their government that Frederick Ramirez had been captured.

The situation worsened when FBI Director O'Brien learned about Evan's emotional outburst that threatened their operation. He knew some form of disciplinary action was needed, but not until their mission was finished.

When the commandos were a hundred yards from the ranch house, they came under fire. They were sitting ducks and retreated toward the helicopters for cover.

Captain Diaz ordered his team, along with the three FBI agents, back onto the aircraft. The bird lifted, banking left, and swooped down over the Ramirez house. Without hesitation, Captain Diaz issued the orders, and the two machine guns mounted under the belly of the chopper tore into the wooden frame structure. Within just one minute, the house looked like a piece of Swiss cheese.

He ordered his remaining men on the ground to storm the house. Five minutes later, he received the signal that the house was clear. Once again, the three FBI agents headed toward what they hoped was Frederick Ramirez begging to be arrested. What they found was something much worse and deeply unsettling.

The bodies of Frederick and Rosa Ramirez were dead, their flesh torn apart by the large-caliber bullets from the helicopter's machine gun. Three men, their bodies riddled with bullets, were still holding their automatic weapons outside the master bedroom; all were dead. In what was believed to be Enrique's bedroom, the body of a young man with part of his ear missing, his face a bloodied mess, was found.

This wasn't how Agent Seymour envisioned ending the Ramirez Cartel's grip on the children of the world. The President wanted a trial so the world could see what happens to criminals who believe they are above the law. Now, they have a martyr and a vacant business that the next powerful crime lord would likely take over. As far as Seymour was concerned, nothing had changed.

* * * * *

Enrique lowered his binoculars and smiled. "Good. A fitting way to give birth to the Pied Piper," he said somberly. He hated having to put more bullets into his mother, but he knew she'd understand what he needed to do to stay safe. Pedro, a young Indian field worker, had received early retirement, which Enrique wanted to handle.

Enrique shot the young, orphaned boy and cut off half of his ear. He left his severed ear, hoping the FBI agents would believe he had died that day.

Frederick's remaining security detail disliked being left behind to guard corpses; however, they faced a choice: either go and risk death at the hands of Enrique or stay and protect the ranch house.

As Enrique, the Pied Piper, gazed at what remained of his home, he felt a surge of power enveloping his body. He had a plan. He had finally discovered his purpose in life and was ready to make all the fathers around the world who abused their children pay a steep price for their cruelty. But first, Special Agent Jack Seymour had to pay for the pain he had inflicted on the Pied Piper.

Luis and his brothers stayed behind to distract the military. They escaped through a tunnel that Frederick had built at the ranch for this very purpose. They returned to Enrique before the house was torn apart. "Let us go now. They are too close for my liking," Luis told Enrique, pulling him into the car.

Chapter 6

A week after the Guatemalan mission, one of President Hollister's aides escorted Special Agent Seymour into the Oval Office. He found his boss, FBI Director Peter O'Brien, and Attorney General Alexander Flood sitting together on one of the couches, engaged in a heated discussion.

Seymour could immediately tell that O'Brien had been defending his men against the attorney general, using his slick debating skills to frustrate the attorney general.

"You can't put the entire blame on my people," O'Brien barked. "Could you have sat back while an innocent child was being battered and thrown into a car trunk?" He took a deep breath. "I don't think so. This wasn't a job for the FBI; we're too nice and follow the law. Where was the CIA during all of this? Murder and torture are out of their playbook."

Flood shrugged, showing no interest in what the Director had said. "They had orders... well, two out of the three followed them. I want Evans fired, and Blanchard and Seymour on probation until the hearing. We lost a great opportunity to show the world that the United States won't tolerate human trafficking, especially involving young children."

O'Brien chuckled. "You're just mad that you can't be on TV for the next two years, turning the Frederick Ramirez trial into a media circus. So don't try giving me orders. I only take them from the President."

Just when the timing seemed perfectly coordinated, O'Brien finished his argument as President Hollister entered. The President settled into his chair behind the firm desk, motioned for Seymour to sit, and picked up a pair of reading glasses. Pressing his intercom button, he told his aide that he did not want to be disturbed for the next thirty minutes.

President Hollister extended his hand across the desk to shake Agent Seymour's. He looked at the other two men and scowled. "I could hear you two arguing like children. I've already told you both it's over, and as far as I'm concerned, the mission was a success. I'm preparing for a press conference where I want to personally thank Agent Seymour for the job well done. When this meeting ends, I expect you both to be on the same page. We need to move forward. The country is counting on me for leadership on the human trafficking issue, and I plan to give them what they want."

O'Brien nodded, but Flood appeared to have something more to add. "Mister President, I'm not sure we've resolved this child trafficking issue. We still can't account for thousands of missing foster children, and the press continues to believe they are being taken out of the country. I'd wait a little longer so I can provide you with a more current update," he recommended.

"I don't want to talk about this anymore," President Hollister told him. By the end of the day, the Ramirez Cartel will be history. The past can guide us as we move forward in the fight against global terrorism. Now, Agent Seymour, are you ready to be thanked in front of a few million people today?"

Seymour forced a smile. He, too, knew that the human trafficking problem had not been curbed or, for that matter, resolved. He didn't like having his name and face plastered around the world. Being recognized for what his team had accomplished made him uncomfortable. "It would be an honor, sir," he replied humbly.

* * * * *

President Hollister was articulate, emphasizing all the gruesome details of what Frederick Ramirez had done to thousands of families worldwide. "The world will not mourn the loss of this psychopath or his son. Right up to the end, these two despicable human beings were attempting to murder more innocent children, but were stopped by the brave and heroic efforts of FBI agent Jack Seymour and his team. I am proud to call him a true American hero. He will be heading up a special task force that will monitor missing foster children across the United States and globally. With agent Seymour standing watch over our children, the United States will be a little safer for our young citizens."

President Hollister hoped he had satisfied his Attorney General and FBI Director with his brief speech. He wanted to move on to more urgent issues and put the human trafficking and sale of infant organs behind him. The official press release further downplayed the problem in Central America.

From: U.S. Department of State – International Information Programs
RE: The Myth: Infant Organs Are Not for Sale in Guatemala

The FBI, working with the Guatemalan government, has finally determined that the kidnapping and sale of human organs is nothing more than a rumor that has turned into an urban legend. It is nothing more than folklore to scare children, like other famous fables.

It would be nearly impossible for a third-world country to achieve this feat. Extracting organs is a highly delicate and complex procedure that requires a transplant surgeon and support staff, including an anesthesiologist, attending surgeons, and operating room nurses. The organs must be transported as quickly as possible, typically by helicopter or airplane, to the hospitals where the transplants will take place. Furthermore, before transporting any organ, special preservation solutions must be infused into it.

The Guatemalan government is unaware of any individual capable of performing this surgery in their country. The Ramirez Cartel, which at first had been believed to be trafficking in human organs, has been tragically dismantled through the dedicated work of Special Agents Jack Seymour, Ted Blanchard, and Robert Evans.

* * * * *

Blanchard looked at Evans, shaking his head in disbelief. "Let's get the fuck out of here before I throw up."

Evans wasn't as upset as Blanchard was. "This is a good thing, for me, at least. I thought I'd get fired for the dumb stunt I pulled. I hope Jack wants us as part of his new team?"

"I'd rather be working on major crimes, not looking for missing children. It will make you older before your time," Blanchard said despondently. "I hope you're wrong," he said, punching his partner's arm hard.

Chapter 7

Enrique Ramirez's anger was boiling over. He couldn't believe the lies President Hollister had spread about him and his family. Even though some of it was true, he felt furious, especially when he saw the hero's welcome that agent Jack Seymour and the other FBI agents received from the American people.

Luis, we're going to wait before punishing that bastard Seymour and his family. He needs to feel on top of the world first, so his life can crumble around him later. I want his guard down before I strike. Let him enjoy his family for a while, let him believe he's safe, and then he can face what all the families face when they bring shame to the Ramirez name.

Luis remained silent, holding his remarks to himself. "Let's not focus on Seymour for now and rebuild the Ramirez cartel," he advised.

"I know. I must first reconnect with my father's brokers. They need to know that there's a new boss, the Pied Piper, who will be running the Cartel from this day forward. We need to do it quickly and with prejudice toward those who don't want to cooperate," Enrique told him. "Also, I am legally changing my name to Miguel Guzman in honor of my mother. That was my mother's maiden name.

"Enrique,' Luis interrupted. Before he could continue, he was scolded.

"It's Piper to you and your men. Don't forget it," he said sternly.

Luis nodded. "Piper, it will take at least six months to be back up and running. I've called a dozen of your father's closest brokers, and they have already started doing business with the Russians."

"Take your brothers and show them that their choice is unhealthy. Make examples of those who turn their backs on me, and be sure to leave a note, nailed to their chests, signed by the Pied Piper. They will soon fear the wrath of my new cartel. I will not negotiate. Whoever does not return to us must die, but not before they see what I will do to their families. Their contracts are now with the Pied Piper, and I will not tolerate any breaches of the old agreements they had with Frederick Rameriz."

* * * * *

Over the next few years, the Pied Piper became the most feared crime boss in Europe and Africa. Deceiving his father's brokers and giving no hint that he was Enrique Ramirez suited his new identity. He held all his meetings wearing a multicolored jester's suit and mask.

The man known only as The Pied Piper was more ruthless than Frederick Ramirez had ever been. He had become a ghost, swooping down on his prey and vanishing before anyone realized he had been there. Aside from the callous and sadistic notes, the Pied Piper was a man everyone came to fear.

It wasn't his brutality that scared his enemies. Instead, it was the sadistic punishments he inflicted—his strange talent for making their sons or daughters vanish without a trace. It didn't take long for his father's clients to accept him and become loyal to their new boss, the Pied Piper.

As his reputation grew worldwide, he focused on Central and South America. He discovered it was easier to scare cultures that believed in the supernatural.

The Pied Piper's method was his ability to take children, no matter how well-guarded they were at home or school, leaving only a typed note signed by the legendary hero. Sometimes, his puzzling approach, which involved a jester's costume and flute, only added to the mystery that puzzled authorities worldwide.

He had become the perfect criminal, concealing his identity from his contractors and possessing the skills of a forensic expert, leaving each crime scene without any evidence linking Enrique Ramirez to his new alias, the Pied Piper or Miguel Guzman. He took pride in making no mistakes.

He made a promise to himself that he would never mess up like he did that ill-fated day with his cousin Mario. His notes, the messages he left behind, carried an arrogant tone, bragging to the local authorities that he was unstoppable.

He was about to turn twenty-one, sharpening his skills and confident that as he grew older, he would become the most skilled criminal in history. On the second anniversary of his mother's death, it was time to take revenge on FBI Special Agent Jack Seymour and President Hollister for killing her.

He prepared to execute his revenge across the United States. President Hollister would be the first of many to learn the price of speaking ill of the Pied Piper.

Piper spoke with an eerie calm. "Luis, have you secured our broker in California?"

Yes. Her name's Sally Palmer. She's a greedy DCF bitch and can be controlled easily.

Piper smiled and nodded, lost in thought. "Ashley Seymour, I believe, is having her first birthday in a few days. I have the perfect gift for her: a better family after her parents' untimely death."

Chapter 8

Carlsbad, California, 1993

Jack Seymour took his young son, Eddie, to another hero's award banquet at the La Costa Resort and Spa in Carlsbad, California. The resort was a mile from their home. However, Seymour wanted the honors to end so he could go back to his job of tracking down the notorious Pied Piper. It was important for his son to hear a speech from a young man named Miguel Guzman.

Miguel Guzman inspired millions of people worldwide. He had risen from obscurity with his Medical Ship of Hope, a floating hospital that traveled to every third-world country, offering the best medical care to impoverished children. Jack Seymour believed it was vital for his son to see firsthand that good people do exist.

Eddie was a precocious ten-year-old who absorbed all the current events he could from television and the daily newspaper. When his father was home, he thrived on debating with his father over each morning's news before school.

Recently, Eddie had become troubled by a man known as the Pied Piper and the evil deeds he had been committing against children. His father wanted to show his son that not all men are malevolent and that if you invest your energy and intellect into helping others, you can achieve meaningful results.

After receiving his key to the city of Carlsbad from the mayor, Sally Palmer stood up, gave a brief introduction, and then invited Miguel Guzman to speak.

Guzman's speech was short, but his words kept everyone on the edge of their seats.

"I am very proud to share this podium with such a great American hero, FBI Agent Jack Seymour. The wonderful work he and his team are doing to catch the Pied Piper has touched my heart. I cannot fully help all the needy children around the world if a man like the Pied Piper is allowed to run free, hurting helpless children. To show my support, I am offering a five-million-dollar reward to anyone who can help Jack Seymour and his team find the Pied Piper and bring him to justice."

Guzman raised his arms above his head, prompting the crowd to rise to their feet and cheer. Internally, he wanted to strangle the man who murdered his mother.

After the speech, Jack Seymour introduced Eddie to Miguel Guzman. His son seemed more impressed with the philanthropist than with the key to the city his father received.

"Mr. Guzman," Eddie gushed, "thank you for helping children," he told him.

"You're welcome, young man," replied Guzman, extending his hand. "And who might you be?"

"Edward Seymour. This is my dad. He's a hero like you. He's trying to catch that mean man...the Pied Piper," Eddie said.

"I'd like to see him captured, too," said Guzman, grinning.

"Can I keep the reward if I help capture him?" Eddie asked sheepishly. "Maybe you could work with my dad and help him?" he asked innocently.

Jack Seymour interrupted his son, aware that Eddie would not stop talking. He could tell Guzman wanted to leave. "Mr. Guzman, it was a pleasure meeting you. Keep up the good work. Now, Eddie, say goodbye.

You have to get some sleep. We have a big day tomorrow, celebrating your sister's first birthday at the San Diego Zoo."

Guzman again extended his hand to Eddie. "It was a pleasure talking to you, young man. Maybe when you're older, you can come work on my ship and be part of helping children like I do?"

Eddie blushed. "Thank you so much for the offer," he said politely. "But I promised my dad I would become an FBI agent. An agent like him and help find the children the Pied Piper took away from their families."

Guzman's mood shifted. His face tightened. "Wonderful. Nice goal, young man. Maybe our paths will cross again someday." Before Eddie could reply, Guzman turned and walked away.

Jack wrapped his arm around his son and began walking toward their car. "It's time to go now. Let's start thinking about Ashley's birthday."

Chapter 9

Today was Ashley Seymour's first birthday and her first big outing. Her brother Eddie had been planning the trip for two months. He acted as if it were his birthday, rushing around their Carlsbad house every day, excited that his sister was going to the San Diego Zoo.

"Dad, we have to get going. I want Ash to see the animals being fed," he yelled. Then, it's the bird show, and if it's not too crowded, she can watch the pandas, but we'll all have to be very quiet. After that, the polar bears should be swimming," he said without taking a breath. He had the zoo's schedule in his hand and needed everyone to cooperate.

"We will be going in due time," his father said. "Just calm down. You need to learn to relax."

Eddie was on a tight schedule and hurried out to check on his mother. "Timing is everything when it comes to enjoying the zoo," he mumbled, rushing up the stairs to Ashley's room.

Eddie had always been a smart and cheerful child. As a toddler, he followed his mother around, begging her, whenever she had time, to read him stories. He loved the Brothers Grimm most of all because of their frightening tales of children in danger. He didn't have a favorite. As he got older and began to understand what his father did for a living, he couldn't wait for his dad to come home and share stories about the FBI.

Day after day, week after week, he was like a sponge, soaking up every detail and case his father shared. At age ten, it was all he talked about. He wanted to be an FBI agent like his dad. After watching the video, he had his mother tape a segment about his father receiving a commendation from President Hollister for his heroic work in Guatemala. Eddie never missed a chance to brag about his father at school.

Jack Seymour loved being a father, and while he was a gentle disciplinarian, he never missed an opportunity to tell his son how much he loved him. When Ashley was born, unlike older siblings who felt neglected when a new sibling arrived, Eddie was just the opposite. He would rush home from school every day to help his mother.

Most days, he would read to his sister stories he made up about their father's heroics. When he wasn't telling stories, he kept her giggling nonstop. No sister could have had a better brother.

Eddie wanted Ashley's first birthday to be special and unforgettable. Even though she was only one year old, he knew she understood what all the excitement was about. He made her a one-of-a-kind first birthday card with silly drawings to make her laugh, but most importantly, he made sure to write on the card how much he loved her.

He made a promise to himself that on Ashley's birthday, from now on, he would make a card for her and express how much he loved her. Along with this promise, he also vowed to always protect her and be her brave big brother forever.

"Dad, Mom, we've got to get going. It's almost 8:15, and we need to be at the zoo by nine when it opens! We have to go now!" his voice squeaked.

Betty Seymour had just finished bathing Ashley when Eddie stormed into the bathroom. "Eddie," his mother said calmly. "I need you to find a spot downstairs to sit and relax. Read a book or watch some cartoons. Us girls will be ready when we're ready," she smiled warmly. "You'll just have to start getting used to not always being on time when pretty ladies are in your life."

Eddie rolled his eyes just as Ashley stuck her tongue out at him. He turned, frustrated, and muttered to himself, "Women, they just don't get the big picture." He went off looking for his dad, grumbling aloud, "Ashley's going to miss feeding time. By the time we get there, she'll need to be fed. Boy oh boy, this will never happen when I'm an FBI agent."

Jack Seymour had been on the phone with Quantico for nearly an hour. FBI Director O'Brien had informed him of a person of interest, Sally Palmer, who might be linked to the Pied Piper. He wanted her watched, her phones monitored, and a list of all her known associates. Jack was about to call his team to schedule a meeting for tomorrow when Eddie burst into his office.

"The women are not cooperating, sir. Can you do something? Can we get the FBI to move them along?" he said seriously, with his fists resting on his hips.

Jack tried to hold back his laughter. "Look, son, women are like watching a pot trying to boil on a stove. The more you stare, the longer it takes. When you're older, you'll see that the wait is always worth it."

"I'll never understand women," Eddie said, turning and storming out of the room. "We're just going to be so late. Everything's going to be ruined," he whined.

Chapter 10

Two Southern California Edison vans were parked on La Costa Avenue, between El Camino Real and the San Diego Freeway. They were there to redirect traffic. Inside the vans were the bodies of the utility workers. The Pied Piper's men, dressed in yellow and orange gear, stood nervously as they waited for their orders.

Piper argued with Sally Palmer and her brother-in-law, Earl Mathews. Luis stood nervously to the side, checking and double-checking the route they believed the Seymour's' Ford Aerostar would take to the zoo.

Luis did not like working with Sally Palmer, especially her brother-in-law, Earl Mathews. He performed best when he was in control of the job, but now someone else was going to handle this delicate operation, and he didn't like it.

Earl Mathews, from what Luis could tell, was a bit of a loose cannon and might end up getting all of them killed. He knew giving him any responsibility was a mistake. He had shared his concerns with Piper, saying that he and his brothers could handle it more effectively, but he was overruled.

Just to be safe, Luis parked an extra utility truck at the bottom of Levante Street to reroute Jack Seymour along the planned route. He wanted to prevent them from going south on El Camino Real.

The ambush was planned for La Costa Avenue, between the freeway and the vegetable stand at Saxony, a mile southwest of El Camino Real.

49

From there, the remaining stretch of road would provide the seclusion needed for the ambush.

The entire operation had to bear the Pied Piper's mark. It could not appear amateurish. It needed to strike fear into the hearts of everyone close to Jack Seymour. If it succeeded as Piper intended, it would send a loud and clear message to President Hollister that his arrogance toward the Ramirez family would not be tolerated. The man President Hollister had praised and portrayed as a hero in front of millions of Americans would face his revenge.

Luis knew that to satisfy Piper's thirst for revenge meant Jack Seymour had to witness his wife being murdered first and then see his children taken from him and placed into the world of the Pied Piper.

Jack Seymour needed to realize how his actions that day in Guatemala impacted the people he loved.

Luis knew Piper's plan was a solid one. It didn't include a moron like Earl Mathews. He had gotten distracted by hearing Sally Palmer pleading with Piper.

"The Seymour girl would be better off with me. My sister needs a child," she begged. "It's a perfect ruse since she just miscarried. I can create an untraceable story that would not alert the authorities."

"Why should his daughter get off so easily?" Piper asked.

Palmer couldn't stop staring at the ridiculous mask Piper was wearing. She tried not to sound patronizing when she responded.

"You're the Pied Piper. Jack Seymour, I know, is a bastard. His task force has been making my life difficult for the last ten years. Having him believe his daughter and son will be placed in the corrupt system he's been trying to change will be more painful than what you have planned. You want to save all the children of the world from bad parents, so what better way than to place her in a good home with my sister?" Palmer held her breath while Piper thought.

Maybe you're right. Let's see how your brother-in-law handles himself today. Then maybe, just maybe, I'll let you have the girl. However, I want the boy to disappear into your foster care system, then back into mine. I don't need Jack Seymour's son coming after me when he's older. I know all too well how vengeance can motivate a young boy.

"Perfect," she replied, pulling Earl aside. "You heard him. If you want your wife to stop being the whining bitch she's been, then don't screw this up. He's going to be a good customer for us."

Chapter 11

Eddie was about to learn that wishes can be mixed with evil, turning happiness into regret. He and his sister were finally headed to the zoo. He felt relieved.

When they reached El Camino Real, they were diverted north toward La Costa Avenue. "No," he shouted. "This is going to make us even later," Eddie complained. "It's always stop and go on the freeway from La Costa to Manchester," he grumbled.

Jack rolled his eyes and turned his head toward Betty for help.

"Eddie, we need you to relax. Everything's going to be all right. Do me a favor, please, entertain your sister so your father can pay attention to the traffic," she said softly, reaching back to rub his thin leg gently.

"But"—he tried to say, but his mother put her finger to her lips, and he knew it was time to be quiet.

Ashley's face lit up as her father began singing "The Wheels on the Bus," her favorite song. Her previously calm expression reflected her brother's joyful energy once the familiar melody filled the air. Eddie's enthusiastic singing further fueled Ashley's excitement, adding a lively spark to the otherwise tense scene.

Meanwhile, their father, his usual sharp FBI instincts dulled, failed to recognize the unusual nature of the utility workers' diversion. He let out a tired sigh, conceding Eddie's point; their delay was now unavoidable.

As they neared La Costa Avenue, the man in an orange and yellow vest signaled Seymour's van to exit traffic with some erratic hand signals and allowed them to take the La Costa Avenue route to the freeway. It seemed a bit odd to Jack that the cars ahead of him were directed straight on El Camino, except for him. He received the signal to turn left. He sighed with relief, not looking forward to another complaint from Eddie. The road was empty in both directions. Jack sped up and joined in the singing. It had been a long time since he had felt happy and relaxed.

When the Seymour's Ford Aerostar sped past a black Mercedes ML350 idling in the dirt parking lot at the vegetable stand, Luis pressed the accelerator hard and was immediately behind the Ford Aerostar.

"Slow down. You're too close," Piper said quietly.

Piper pressed his two-way radio to his lips, telling Earl it was time to initiate the accident.

Earl's big white pickup crossed the double-yellow line like a freight train running out of control. He was heading directly toward Jack Seymour's vehicle.

"What the hell is he doing?" cried Luis. "This is not how we told him to stop them."

What happened next was neither expected nor planned. Luis slammed his foot on the brakes, causing their vehicle to skid to a halt.

* * * * *

"Shit." Eddie heard his father scream.

His mother turned quickly and adjusted her seat belt, but it was already too late.

Eddie, his eyes wide and unable to speak, watched helplessly as a white Ford pickup truck with a heavily reinforced front bumper—something you'd see on a tow truck—sailed over the center divider. It was just a white line to keep oncoming traffic in its lane; however, this truck was set to cause trouble.

The pickup corrected its course, and instead of going back to its side of the road, it stayed on the Seymour's Lane. Earl Mathews was heading straight toward them without slowing down.

Eddie watched in panic as his father first looked to his right, where a large dump truck, keeping pace with their van, was blocking Jack from changing lanes.

Eddie saw his father contemplating other options, but the worry on his face told him otherwise: time had run out. Everything from that point on felt as if it happened in slow motion.

Eddie's eyes locked onto the truck driver's face, surprised that there was no fear—only an evil grin.

Earl was tightly strapped into his seat with his NASCAR safety harness, as his truck, with death seemingly etched into it, was ready to hit his target. Everything had been happening too fast for Jack Seymour to brake and lessen the impact force. The pickup struck the Ford Aerostar head-on at nearly fifty-five miles per hour.

The front of the van, hitting the heavy metal bumper, crushed the Ford Aerostar as if it were a toy. Eddie froze, paralyzed by the sight of his parents pressed against the dashboard. They were strapped in their seats. He saw the airbags expand, then heard them pop like punctured balloons.

A hot, sticky fluid splattered across Eddie's face and clothes as glass shattered around him. He heard Ashley screaming. What happened next was unbelievable. A ladder attached to a rack on top of the pickup truck suddenly went airborne. Like a missile, it smashed through the windshield on the passenger side.

Ashley was frozen in silence as she stared at her mother's severed head. It had become cradled between her two tiny legs.

Eddie felt the bile lodge in his throat. He looked in disbelief at the frozen, horrified look on his mother's loving face. The ladder was still moving towards Ashley. With the quickness of a Superhero, he grabbed

Ashley's head and pushed her down right before the ladder crushed her tiny body and exited through the rear window.

Her screams became more intense. Her tiny face rested inches away from her mother's open eyes, as the brain stem bled on her petite legs and shoes.

What seemed like an eternity in Hell finally stopped. Ashley's crying had turned to shrieks and gasps for air. Eddie could not look at his mother's severed neck and blood-soaked blouse where her smile once lived. He covered his sister's eyes with her blanket. Then he leaned forward toward his father.

His father was bleeding from a deep gash on his scalp, but that was the least of his injuries. The steering column had penetrated the airbag, impaling itself deep inside his father's chest cavity.

"Dad, I'll get you out," Eddie said hysterically. "I just need to get Ashley out first," he cried, as black smoke started to flow in from under the dashboard.

In a low whisper, Jack Seymour tried to talk to his son. "Edward, take care of your sister. I'm not going to make it."

Eddie could hear the last of the air inside his father's lungs flow out of the hole in his chest. "No!" he screamed, his eyes fixed in terror, as he watched his father's last breath escape.

"Daddy...Daddy, don't leave me," he said softly, shaking his father's shoulder.

The side door was forced open, and a man dressed in a clown costume tried to pull Ashley away from Eddie's arms. He failed. Then another man pulled Eddie out of the van, cradling his sister.

Everyone ran away from the twisted metal just as the van exploded. Eddie was thrown into the air, holding Ashley and screaming for his father. He craned his neck just in time to see the Aerostar engulfed in a black ball of flames. He hit the ground hard, never letting go of his sister. Dazed and in shock, he stared at the melted remains of the vehicle that buried his parents.

"I'm sorry, son, there's nothing you can do for them now." Eddie looked at the man with a calm voice and a confused expression on his face. The man in the silly clown costume was cradling Ashley against his chest, trying to soothe her.

Eddie leapt up and hurried to his sister, pulling her away from the man's hold. "I'll hold her," he snapped. Something about the man's eyes looked familiar. He had seen him before, but his sister's screams pulled him back to his main goal: protecting Ashley.

"Ashley, it's just the two of us. I'll take care of you, I promise." He knew he was now the head of his family. He had to keep his word. He promised his father.

Before Eddie could react, another man with big, strong hands yanked Ashley away from him. The man started running toward an ambulance with Ashley screaming.

Eddie called out, searching for help, but all he saw was the man in the colorful costume jump into the back of the ambulance. The man dressed like a jester handed Eddie a note.

Eddie unfolded the piece of paper and read the confusing words:

> Eddie:
>
> One day, you'll understand why this game had to be played today. Your father made a terrible mistake, and I'm sorry you'll be the one to suffer. Trust that your sister will be in a better place than the foster homes you'll face.
>
> Yours Truly,
>
> Pied Piper, ER

When he looked up, everyone disappeared. He stood there, alone, watching the burning tombstone that housed his parents.

Off in the distance, sirens were blasting as fire trucks and police cars sped toward the accident. What felt like an eternity to Eddie had only been minutes when three police cars pulled up beside him. "Son, you all right?" the officer asked.

"They took my sister," he screamed, pointing west. Then his mouth dropped open, and his eyes widened with shock. He saw the man who killed his parents. "That's the man who hit us," he yelled, pointing at Earl Mathews.

One of the officers turned and said, "We know. It was a terrible accident. The man made a horrible mistake," patting Eddie's head.

"What about my sister? She's been taken," he sobbed, pointing at the ambulance off in the distance as it approached the freeway onramp.

"They must be taking her to the hospital, where we need to go now." He led Eddie to the backseat of the patrol car.

Eddie turned to watch the tall, muscular man who killed his parents talking to a man in a dark brown suit. The man wasn't taking notes anymore, just having a jovial conversation with Earl Mathews.

Eddie stared. I'll never forget your face, he promised, gazing out from the small rear window of the police car. As they sped away, he took one last look at what used to be the family car. "It's my fault," he sobbed. "We should have just had a party at the house."

Fifteen minutes later, Eddie was taken to Scripps Encinitas Emergency Room. He asked the nurse who was attending to him where his sister, Ashley Seymour, was. "I need to see my sister now," he shouted.

The nurse had a puzzled expression. "We have not admitted an Ashley Seymour this morning," she told him.

"I saw her get into an ambulance," he explained. "She must be here."

Before Eddie could say another word, Sally Palmer, the Director of all San Diego's foster care agencies, introduced herself. "I'm Sally Palmer.

You must be Edward Seymour," she said in a calm, soft voice. "I'm so sorry for what happened today to your parents, but I am here to ensure you are well taken care of. I have a nice home in Carlsbad with a husband and wife who are looking forward to being your foster parents."

"I want to know where my sister, Ashley Seymour, was taken. I need to be with her. I made a promise to her before the Pied Piper, wearing a clown costume, took her from me." Eddie held the note he had been handed. He wasn't sure he could trust her and slipped the note into his pocket.

"I was only told that you were the only child in the car," Palmer replied. "I'll investigate after I get you to your new foster home."

Eddie could tell Sally was lying. He checked to see if his wallet was still in his back pocket. He felt relieved that it hadn't fallen out during the crash. He knew he had his father's partner's business card.

Chapter 12

Settled into his new foster home, Eddie was directed to his bedroom. His foster mother's parting words, an abrupt instruction to shower and rest before the five o'clock meal, were a stark contrast to the turmoil brewing within him. Fresh clothes lay untouched in the wardrobe; his mind was elsewhere. He spotted a telephone, a lifeline to a shattered world.

Immediately, he contacted Ted Blanchard, his father's partner. His voice, choked with grief, delivered a devastating report. "Ted, it's Eddie Seymour," he gasped, the words tumbling out in a torrent of anguish. "A horrible accident…on the way to Ashley's birthday celebration at the zoo…Mom and Dad…they're gone…murdered. Ashley…a man, dressed as a clown…he took her." Tears streamed down his face.

Blanchard was stunned into silence. No reports, no alerts—nothing indicated a catastrophic event, let alone the death of a fellow agent and his spouse. His initial reaction was a hesitant question, born of disbelief and concern: "Eddie, are you safe?"

"I think I'm okay. Just a little scared," Eddie declared, his voice hardening with a chilling resolve. "But I need you to find Ashley. Bring my sister home. And apprehend the monster who killed my parents."

Blanchard's thoughts spun wildly. "Eddie," he began slowly, the gravity of the situation settling upon him, "explain…why do you suspect foul play?"

Eddie struggled to find his words. "The man who crashed into us after the accident was talking to the man in the clown costume. I think they know each other," he told him.

Blanchard's mind was racing as he tried to come up with a plan. "Don't show the note to anyone but me. I should see you tomorrow," he told Eddie.

* * * * *

Agent Robert Evans arrived at Palomar Airport the next morning, where FBI Agent Ted Blanchard met him. A fog of unanswered questions and unsettling mystery surrounded the tragic murder of the recently honored FBI agent Jack Seymour.

Blanchard drove Evans to The Crossings golf course for a breakfast briefing. He needed to dissect the events of the previous day. The lingering unanswered questions weighed on him.

Blanchard was the first to speak. "Have you figured out why Seymour's death wasn't immediately reported to the Bureau?"

Evans shook his head. "I've suspected for some time that there's a mole in President Hollister's inner circle who is collaborating with the Pied Piper," he declared, his voice low and urgent.

"What about the Director? Can he be trusted?" Blanchard wondered.

Evans sucked in a deep breath. "Director O'Brien is a straight shooter and would never turn his back on the bureau. He's just hampered by the President and his upcoming reelection bid."

Blanchard couldn't control his temper. "That's bull shit. The Bureau doesn't investigate crimes in a partisan manner."

"Everything in Washington is politically motivated," Evans replied.

Blanchard threw his arms in the air, frustrated with everything that had happened to his friend. "I find it strange that the Carlsbad police are indifferent about the deadly accident and Eddie Seymour's whereabouts. Why wasn't Earl Mathews arrested or even charged with reckless driving?

He wasn't even detained for twenty-four hours while they investigated the accident."

"I agree," Evans admitted. "We're dealing with a powder keg, and we need to tread carefully."

Blanchard fell silent, deep in thought. "That note the Pied Piper gave Eddie Seymour… it unsettled me," he finally said. "Its vague wording at first was puzzling. Then I figured out what the initials ER stood for. The Pied Piper was sending us a warning from Enrique Ramerez. The bastard must have faked his death. Now he's seeking retribution for what we did in Guatemala."

"Then our pursuit of the Pied Piper requires a drastic recalibration," Evans declared.

* * * * *

Two hours later, Agent Blanchard visited Eddie Seymour's foster home to check on his safety and retrieve the note he had. FBI Agent Robert Evans stormed into the District Attorney's office, his anger barely contained.

Evans was furious with the Carlsbad police and the District Attorney's ineffective investigation. Their failure to act regarding Jack and Betty Seymour's death, Ashley Seymour's kidnapping, and the eight Southern California Edison employees found dead in their trucks was unacceptable. The Pied Piper's taunting notes were ignored.

Evans unleashed his fury on District Attorney Patterson. "What are you concealing? Why isn't Earl Mathews incarcerated for this premeditated catastrophe?"

District Attorney Patterson responded calmly, "Our investigators concluded Mathews lost control of his vehicle. Interviews with Mathews concluded it was a regrettable accident."

Evans' voice dripped with sarcasm. "Regrettable accident? Was a breathalyzer test given? Apparently, it was not considered necessary," he sarcastically accused her. "Didn't the Pied Piper's notes clearly suggest it was a premeditated assault on an FBI agent and his family? A one-year-old child is missing, her brother secreted away in foster care."

Patterson's demeanor changed. "All that you claim is accurate. However, this case has been, without explanation, reassigned to your FBI Director. He unilaterally declared his agency now controls the investigation." The District Attorney's voice grew more assertive. "Get your facts straight before making unfounded accusations against me and my police department."

* * * * *

Six months after the tragic death of his parents, Eddie Seymour was finally placed with his father's longtime confidant, Dr. Philip Harding, despite Sally Palmer's vehement protests. Palmer, arguing that the young boy needed compassionate care from his foster parents so he could recover fully. President Hollister quickly dismissed her pleas.

Meanwhile, the Pied Piper had become an urban legend, a legendary figure in the underworld. The FBI and Interpol were hopelessly outmatched, always two steps behind him. He remained an elusive phantom, kidnapping children at will, leaving only his arrogant taunts as a chilling signature.

Enraged by Palmer's failure to secure Eddie, the Pied Piper exploded with rage, demanding the boy's swift inclusion into his malicious trafficking operation. Palmer argued that the task was nearly impossible without risking open warfare with the FBI. The Piper's reply was chilling: *"My planned revenge against the Bureau would surpass any direct fight; it would be a masterstroke of calculated vengeance"*, he told her.

The search for Ashley Seymour had stalled and grown colder. The Pied Piper's increasing abduction of young girls pushed the FBI into a frantic, unproductive chase. Nonetheless, Agents Evans and Blanchard remained dedicated, pursuing every lead in hopes of finding the missing Seymour girl by investigating other cases.

* * * * *

Six months after FBI Agent Seymour's assassination, Miguel Guzman, from his Belizean estate, delivered a powerful statement during a press conference. His message resonated with force:

"A courageous American hero, who prioritized national security above his own family, was gone. I am increasing the bounty for the Pied Pipers' capture to ten million dollars, and pledging an additional five million to the President's new task force that's dedicated to ending the Pied Pipers' reign of terror."

Guzman's distraction was causing a flood of false sightings, which kept Evans and Blanchard from focusing on their investigation. Hunting for Ashley Seymour remained their number one priority.

Chapter 13

Seventeen years later, the legacy of the Pied Pipers' reign of terror had transformed from a chilling urban myth to an undeniable, devastating reality. The number of child abductions attributed to him had surpassed 10,000, each one a tragic testament to the failure of international law enforcement and the FBI to thwart his nefarious activities. The Pied Piper, once a mysterious figure veiled in shadows, had become an unstoppable force, his name synonymous with fear and despair.

The elusive nature of his operations and the global scale of his network proved insurmountable for even the most dedicated investigators. His ability to evade capture and continue his heinous crimes with impunity fostered a deep sense of powerlessness among those tasked with stopping him. The question lingering in the minds of law enforcement and the public was no longer if he would strike again, but when and where.

Inside his Capitol Hill office, Senator Jarvis was reviewing his notes for a committee meeting with Sally Palmer, the Director of the newly formed Federal Foster Care Program. Sitting next to her was the newly appointed FBI Director, Robert Jenkins.

Director Jenkins was reviewing the report that his Deputy Director, Robert Evans, had prepared. It was not very flattering about the senator's performance or Palmer's new program. A new rumor regarding child abductions and the sale of baby organs had resurfaced.

Director Jenkins was the first to speak. "This is off the record," he said cautiously. "Deputy Director Evans has a man inside one of the child trafficking cartels that we believe is working with the Pied Piper," Jenkins told them.

Jarvis had a surprised expression. "Who is this agent?" he asked.

"Only Evans and I know his name, and it will stay like that until the Pied Piper is captured," Jenkins told him. "This is the closest we've come to finding out where or when the Pied Piper would strike again. Senator, you can no longer whitewash the problems this country is facing. Too many children are going missing, especially under your watch," the Director acknowledged. He glanced at Sally Palmer.

Palmer interjected herself into the conversation. "Can we at least know which cartel he has infiltrated?"

Jenkins leaned forward, his elbows on Jarvis' desk. He gave Sally Palmer a threatening look. "Nathan, we've been friends, fraternity brothers, but I can no longer keep you updated on our investigation to stop this maniac. We have spies inside the Senate and House, and the safety of my agent is paramount."

Jarvis seemed lost in thought, processing what his friend had said. "Don't you think I care about these children? Don't you think I want to stop the Pied Piper?"

Jenkins shook his head, biting his lower lip as he searched for the right words. "Bottom line, no." He started reading from Evan's report. "Just in 1999, 1,680,900 foster children were runaways or, as some prefer to call them, throwaways. Only 21% were ever reported to police or social services. In 2004, three million children were reported neglected, and 872,000 were confirmed victims of child maltreatment. These are old numbers. Do you want me to keep going?" Jenkins said sarcastically.

"Don't you speak to me in that tone," Jarvis scolded.

Jenkins rolled his eyes. "Your committee hasn't done anything other than to make President Webster look good for his upcoming re-election bid. Since the President was elected, it's been three years, and more and more children are missing, possibly dead, their parents brutally murdered. For the first time, my task force has an opportunity to put an end to it. It's only a matter of days, and I'll have enough evidence to connect all of the dots that link the Pied Piper's brokers to him. I will end his reign of terror once and for all."

Palmer interrupted, her tone very defensive. "I admit that children go unaccounted for, but that's normal in foster care. I have stats showing that since I joined, the number of missing children has decreased by seven percent," she said proudly.

Jenkins slammed his folder on the senator's desk. "Are you not listening? You're wearing blinders if you think you're doing a great job. We're still missing hundreds of thousands of children, mostly in the cities with the largest ports. So, I don't buy your bullshit," he retorted.

"Peter, Peter, Peter," Jarvis said patronizingly, trying to steer the meeting back to why they were having this meeting. "You do what you need to do. But until I see some concrete evidence that this country has a problem, I won't trigger any alarms that could hurt President Webster's re-election bid. We don't want to give the Democrats any reason to attack his chances. He's the only president in the last eight years who has a solid grip on controlling the terrorists. That must stay his priority. I hope you still believe that only a Republican President can keep all Americans safe?"

Jenkins stood, grabbing his file, his face twisted with disgust. "I've got a meeting with my Deputy Director. This discussion is not over." He turned and stormed out the door.

Palmer looked shaken by what had just happened. "Do you really think he'll connect us to the Pied Piper?" she whispered.

Shit, Sally. You know better than to talk like this in here. Jenkins might be my best friend, but he'd still bug my office if it helps him catch the Pied Piper. We'll discuss this tonight when we see Doctor Kane.

Chapter 14

Some things are never forgotten, and those particular thoughts raced wildly through the mind of Special Agent Edward Seymour of the FBI. While he sat anxiously in the Senate Chambers, his frustration erupted like a fireworks display. President Webster was addressing the chamber. The President had labeled the Pied Piper an urban legend.

President Webster addressed the House and Senate, dismissing all reports about the Pied Piper as exaggerated conspiracies. The President wanted the White House press corps to move on to another topic.

Unfortunately, Seymour knew better. He had firsthand knowledge that the bastard did exist and that all the terrible kidnappings around the world and within the foster care system were the work of one man and a single crime ring. He had seen the man in the silly costume take his sister seventeen years ago.

It had felt like an eternity since the Pied Piper abducted Ashley, the day his parents died in a fiery car crash. He was too young then to understand the significance of her abduction or how his parents' deaths were connected to the Pied Piper. For years, he kept dreaming of finding his sister safe and unharmed, praying he could have the family he had once had.

He never gave up searching for Ashley. But after seventeen years, he needed closure so he could move on with his life.

The anniversary of her abduction always coincided with her birthday. It was a day he regretted. If he had only had a birthday party at his home instead of going to the zoo, he would still have his family. It was another unforgivable decision he kept tormenting himself over each year.

Later in the day, Eddie faced a tough choice as Ashley's eighteenth birthday approached. He was twenty-seven, a handsome man in great shape on the outside; however, inside, he was an emotional misfit, spending all his youth obsessed with finding the Pied Piper and avenging his parents' deaths. He had become a loner, fixated on finding his sister and unable to pursue a romantic relationship.

Crazy images, familiar ones he'd seen in his dreams for the last seventeen years, flashed through his mind. He tried to keep himself together, but the scars ran too deep. He began to drift back to the day he became an orphan.

Like an endless movie, constantly looping and restarting, the image of seeing his parents' battered and bloodied bodies had shattered an innocent boy's outlook on life and his emotional stability forever. He has always felt responsible for his parents' deaths and his sister's kidnapping. Nothing would ever change that.

Eddie matured that day, realizing that God's sense of humor sucked. How a man like the Pied Piper was allowed to live, and his parents die, made no sense. God's sadistic prank that day was relentless when He allowed Ashley to be kidnapped. He looked up at the panel of Senators, unable to focus.

The Senate Chambers had vanished. He was fully immersed in his ongoing nightmare. He shuddered in his seat; his shirt was drenched with sweat as the smell of burning flesh once again invaded his nostrils. He was again feeling the searing heat on his skin from the fire that entombed his parents.

He could hear his father's final breath as he grabbed his sister and carried her out of the blazing inferno.

His body jerked. He once again heard the air-splitting explosion that lifted him and Ashley, hurling them away from the liquid inferno that had consumed their parents' coffin.

The most painful part of his memory involved two men—one in a white jumpsuit and the other wearing a mask and dressed in a clown's costume.

He can still see himself standing there, arms outstretched, trying to stretch enough to grab his sister and bring her back, tightly swaddled and safe from harm.

He attempted to cry then, but his tears had evaporated, just like his family. He unfolded the note he had carried with him since that day.

Eddie:

One day, you'll understand why this game had to be played today. Your father made a terrible mistake, and I'm sorry you'll be the one to suffer. Trust that your sister will be in a better place than the foster homes you'll face.

Yours Truly,

Pied Piper, ER

The note and a picture of his sister with his parents were the only possessions he cared about from that day onward. Burying his sister's memory didn't end the game. He knew that someday he'd get his retribution, and the Pied Piper would be lying dead at his feet.

The banging of a gavel brought him back to the present.

Ashley's eighteenth birthday was in three weeks, and he refused to give up. He wanted to celebrate her day as he had for the last seventeen years, but he was exhausted, his emotions numb from all the leads that had led to painful dead ends.

He read the last birthday letter, the birthday card he had promised to write each year. He would now add it to the seventeen others gently placed inside a small urn.

One tear formed at the corner of his eye, which he quickly swatted away. He never cried and today would not be the day to start. He still had his job working with the FBI's "Operation Innocence" task force.

"Operation Innocence," the brainchild of Deputy Director Robert Evans, had attracted his attention a few years ago. When state agencies couldn't track the thousands of foster children who went missing, rumors started to spread that it might be the work of the Pied Piper. What better scheme could a crime ring have than kidnapping unwanted, discarded children from a broken system that didn't care?

The situation was alarming. It was spiraling out of control, and Evans stepped up to take action, while the Select Committee on Children, Youth, and Families remained inactive. In September 1986, the Ninety-ninth Congress created a committee to address the most critical issue in child welfare: ensuring their protection and support. Like all legislation crafted by Washington's leaders, it failed miserably.

Deputy Director Evans asked Seymour to attend today's Senate Committee hearing to listen to two important people speak.

Eddie argued that it was a waste of his time, but Evans won the heated debate.

Seymour despised political committees. It was a spectacle, first for the senators to appear favorable to their constituents, and with the committee mostly made up of Republicans, it also benefited President Webster's reelection effort.

The committee chair, Senator Nathan Jarvis, a friend of FBI Director Jenkins, seemed to infect the committee with his toxic fumes, causing the other senators to become stuck in a stagnant atmosphere.

Agent Seymour anxiously waited for the first speaker to address the committee, knowing it would be another pointless exercise that made headlines for fifteen minutes before fading away until the next meeting. Bored stiff, he re-read a fax from Deputy Director Evans.

> *To: Operation Innocence Task Force*
> *From: Deputy Director Evans*
> *RE: Pied Piper Results*

The Pied Piper is now taunting the FBI in California, Florida, Oklahoma, and Washington State. Over 1,323 young children are unaccounted for within their foster care agencies. I am concerned that the number could become more alarming as Texas, D.C., and New York have yet to report their figures to us. We have just received substantiated information that the Pied Piper is winding down his operation. The bottom line is, we need to find him now!

Pay close attention to your surroundings. The Pied Piper has escalated to a new level of brutality. He is now targeting individuals personally and has gone after the FBI. Agent Sam Waters and his wife were killed last night. His two young daughters are missing. A note signed by the Pied Piper was found. He has threatened that if we don't back off, more FBI agents will be harmed. You cannot pursue the Pied Piper without first getting approval from my office. We are taking this threat very seriously.

Eddie laughed silently. "Making it personal now," he muttered. "Evans, you need to stop going by the book and get down to the Pied Piper's level," he muttered, then pulled out his wallet again and looked at the worn note the Pied Piper had given him. He read it slowly before putting it away. His rage was now percolating.

"He made it personal seventeen years ago," he said quietly. He folded the fax Evans gave him and slipped it into his jacket pocket.

His eyes narrowed into little slits as he listened to Senator Nathan Jarvis introduce his first speaker. Seymour hated the Senator. He was scum; however, as a fraternity brother of the Director, expressing his opinion of the senator could have jeopardized his career.

Nevertheless, Agent Seymour's dislike for Jarvis was well known, and he was not afraid to discuss it with his boss, his father's friend Deputy Director Robert Evans, and anyone else willing to listen.

The first person to testify was Assistant Secretary for Immigration and Customs Enforcement, Gregory Carlson. What he had to say was a waste of time. He was there to put on a show for President Webster and to support Senator Jarvis.

Gregory Carlson had nothing new to say. Garbage in, garbage out. Everything he said had been stated months earlier. Everyone knew there were over five hundred known crime rings worldwide, their main illegal activity being the trafficking of young girls for prostitution and slavery.

"Evans was crazy for sending me here," he muttered as Carlson reiterated the president's message.

After Carlson finished, the Director from the State Department's Office to Monitor and Combat Trafficking in Persons caught Seymour's attention.

Director Brian Patterson, a heavyset man in his forties, leaned toward the microphone and cleared his throat. "I won't sugarcoat anything today. Somewhere between eight hundred thousand and nine hundred thousand women and children are trafficked across borders worldwide, including up to twenty thousand persons into the United States." He coughed while pouring himself water from a perspiring water jug, paling in comparison to the beads of sweat on Patterson's furrowed brow.

Senator Jarvis, an irritable and unpleasant man by nature, appeared more obnoxious than usual. He rudely barked at the director.

"Can you get some control over your emotions? We don't have all day."

Patterson swallowed hard, lowering his head as he read his notes. His voice cracked. "We all know that prostitution, slavery, rape, and illegal adoptions are occurring at an alarming rate. However, a larger issue has surfaced. We are witnessing an increase in American women, young girls, and even infants being trafficked around the world. American citizens are being forcibly taken and sold to crime lords as far away as Japan. Children are the most vulnerable, with some cases involving murder for their organs."

That revelation elicited a wave of gasps from the audience and the Senate panel.

Director Patterson continued, "We believe these heinous acts are being carried out with the precision of an auto theft ring that finds it more profitable to sell car parts than the entire vehicle. I don't believe I need to clarify what my example means." His sarcastic comments were directed at Senator Jarvis.

Agent Seymour had never imagined such a scenario for his sister. His heart began to pound, drowning out Senator Jarvis's protests to restore order in the chamber.

Patterson continued reading from his notes. "The United States has always believed that the sale of infant organs is a myth to scare children and their parents, but I have information that refutes these old assertions. In New Delhi, the Premier has accused a group of doctors, lawyers, middlemen, and politicians of operating a thirty-five-million-dollar racket in the illegal sale of kidneys in northern India."

Patterson saw Jarvis raising his gavel, but he spoke louder, not ready to be interrupted. "While this problem has been going on for some time, just last week, after raiding a medical clinic, the Indian police discovered over fifty infant kidneys. Interpol has uncovered more of these hideous crimes against young children in Bosnia, Sydney, Berlin, Kiev, and most recently, Washington state. There is a serious problem out there and…" he paused, catching his breath. "Senators, you need to do something immediately."

Seymour could no longer listen. He stumbled out of the crowded room, passing Miguel Guzman, a man from his past who would be the last person to speak that morning. He hurried toward the men's room, his breakfast threatening to come up. He knew who Director Patterson was talking about: The Pied Piper.

Inside the bathroom stall, eighteen years of pain spilled out of him like an erupting volcano. Thoughts of his sister, her young, innocent body violated, fiercely swirled in his mind. He always wanted to believe that Ashley was one of the lucky ones— the pretty baby, safe and adopted. He was breathing heavily, splashing cold water on his face, when his cell phone rang.

He knew the caller's ID. What does he want? he scowled silently.

He answered curtly. "Yeah, boss, what do you need? Sure, I'll be there in thirty minutes," he said, sounding annoyed.

When Agent Seymour returned to the Senate chambers, Guzman was wrapping up the information he had on the Pied Piper. It was the last sentence that got Eddie's attention.

"The Pied Piper is real, and each of you should take your heads out of the sand and hunt this despicable man down."

Even though it had been seventeen years since Seymour met Guzman, he was still impressed by the man's devotion to helping children around the world. He remembered the man's offer to work with him, which seemed tempting now. But he had made a promise to his father, and he was someone who kept his promises.

Chapter 15

Miami Harbor, Pier 69

Evil manifests itself unexpectedly, changing lives in an instant. The four men and one woman sat anxiously in a dark warehouse, waiting for the Pied Piper to arrive. Beneath their chairs lay a large, thick plastic tarp.

The only sounds they heard were their hearts pounding wildly. Four burly men, armed with AK-47s, stood watch over them.

Three years ago, they were simply ordinary DCF case workers from various states along the Eastern Seaboard, each with a different ethnic background. Recruited by Sally Palmer, they had now become criminals, selling unwanted foster children to the Pied Piper. They bought into the propaganda spread by the man they knew only as Piper, believing they were providing the children they cared for with a better life. Yet the large cash payouts eased their guilty consciences.

Whether they genuinely believed they were doing some good within the often-troubled foster care agencies they managed didn't matter. The Pied Piper thought it, and he established all the protocols that kept the missing children off the FBI's radar.

Piper only wanted children who had no family, no relatives, and no life that anyone would care about. The more invisible the child was, the better.

Most foster children are placed into homes so quickly that current photos aren't taken, making it harder for authorities to identify them. Those were Piper's rules, and no one questioned him.

Previous meetings had always been one-on-one. However, this unplanned conference left them uneasy. None had ever dealt with or seen Piper's brutality; they had only heard the gruesome rumors. They were the shepherds, gathering information from the various foster homes they managed about the kinds of children the Pied Piper wanted. They never wanted to know what happened to these innocent children after they were dropped off. For them, it was better not to know.

Al Kim Tong controlled Chinese foster care agencies in three Chinatowns: Manhattan, San Francisco, and Chicago, while Louie Luca managed the corrupt ghettos of New York. Both men were ruthless, which is why Piper worked with them. Sean McCarthy had a strong influence on the Boston DCF system but couldn't be trusted because of his short temper when upset. And Leo Washington, the worst of the lot, controlled the market for unwed mothers in Washington, D.C.

There was a booming market for embryos and newborns, and Tong easily made a living by brokering his unwed mothers. More mothers were found dead in alleys and inside dumpsters, their bodies still warm from giving birth. It was a necessary outcome to satisfy one of the Pied Piper's top clients, Dr. Thomas Kane.

Then there was Mary Lynn Rose, the stunning East Coast madam by night and DCF director by day. She managed high-class call girls for influential men, all of whom wanted to avoid being burdened with an unwanted child. It was believed that she possessed an extensive journal capable of sparking some of the worst scandals in United States history. Her special book helped keep her safe.

The grinding sounds of the large cranes unloading air-conditioned cargo containers from the semi-trucks filled with crying children echoed throughout the warehouse.

Trucks have proven to be the safest form of transportation on the East Coast. Inspection stations, when necessary, could easily be bypassed with a little bribe on old country highways that became obsolete when turnpikes replaced the traditional shipping routes.

Piper preferred his brokers to be efficient and organized. Each unmarked truck had a crew of four that rotated shifts every six hours. Two men were always in the cab, while two remained in the cargo area, with one sleeping and the other caring for the sedated children.

Rule number one: Don't get caught. Rule two: Use whatever force is necessary to protect the cargo. It was a rule he remembered every time he touched his severed ear. It served as a lasting reminder of his father's anger when he failed during his first mission.

Piper left no room for error. Each team was thoroughly equipped. Rule three: The human cargo had to be tagged. Each ID bore a barcode with the child's vital statistics and, most importantly, the contractor's details, indicating who would be paid for their efforts.

The technology was cutting-edge, encrypted through the network managed by Pied Piper. He had records on every child kidnapped worldwide, dating back to when he took over the family business. This information was stored on his computer and backed up in a CMS ABS Plus backup system.

* * * * *

Piper arrived late at the warehouse. Tonight's meeting aims to send a strong message to the FBI, especially to Deputy Director Robert Evans. He had never forgotten that Evans was part of the team responsible for his severe beating by his father and his mother's death.

He believed that by murdering agent Jack Seymour and kidnapping Ashley Seymour, he had made his point about wanting to be left alone. Robert Evans, along with his ex-partner Ted Blanchard, didn't seem to understand that killing an FBI agent and his wife was only a warning to leave him alone. Tonight, Deputy Director Evan was about to face the Pied Piper's revenge once again.

Piper had known for quite some time that his days in business were numbered. Evans was finally closing in on discovering his brokers across the United States. Piper had decided to shut down his operation and disappear within a year or two.

That was part of the reason for tonight's meeting. He needed to show his brutality while also instilling fear in his brokers so they wouldn't turn against him.

Retirement was something he had promised himself and his men a long time ago. It was finally going to happen, but not before a few loose ends were tied up. He still had some old scores to settle with Evans, Blanchard, and the son of Jack Seymour, Special Agent Eddie Seymour.

Waiting in the dark to meet his brokers, Piper watched the parade of children boarding his ship. Like sheep heading for the slaughterhouse, they marched up the unlit gangway, reminiscent of a scene from "The Children of the Corn," yet they posed no threat to anyone. He was the monster in charge.

He listened carefully as the nurses and doctors preparing them for the long journey shouted profanities at them. He yearned to see their terrified eyes, reflecting the fear that showed they knew they were going to die. However, inside the warehouse, he had other pressing matters that demanded his attention.

Piper smiled, watching his brokers squirm nervously in their cold metal chairs. He wanted Sally Palmer sitting here, but he still needed her for a bit longer.

"Perfect," he muttered. He was a faceless murderer to the FBI and a ruthless business partner who incited fear with his unpredictable moods. He adjusted his mask and smoothed out the wrinkles on his silk, multicolored costume with his hands. Then, before stepping into the room, he pulled his jester's hat down over his severed ear. He was now ready to perform.

The warehouse creaked and moaned as the pier slowly swayed with the rising tide. The dock was crying out like the frightened children who were now trapped on a ship. Just like the legendary Pied Piper, the children were safe inside his cave.

Without warning, a panel of high-wattage floodlights exploded like a thousand flashbulbs. Terror carved itself on the brokers' faces. They rubbed their eyes with one hand while using the other to shield themselves from the blinding light. They knew Piper had arrived.

"Welcome, my friends," Piper said; his bellowing tone had an eerie jovialness that reeked of lunacy. "Tonight, will be the last business dealings you will have with me. You will be allowed to find new associations if you choose to continue in your line of work." He paused. The room had become jarringly quiet. Then, without warning, Piper's voice shifted to a callous anger that resonated throughout the empty warehouse.

"There's a traitor within our ranks," he said coldly, his tone harshly accusatory. "The Pied Piper punishment is the only deterrent. Tonight, I'm going to show you what happens to those who defile the loyalty you've all promised to me."

Like guilty children waiting for the principal at school, they began to fidget in their seats, each glancing at the others to see who the traitor might be. Piper's men formed a semi-circle behind the nervous group, their automatic weapons ready.

In the past, I trusted the people I did business with. However, I cannot accept what has happened." Piper's tone shifted again, returning to a slow, steady, calm voice. "I hope this is very clear to all of you?" he paused, taking a few short breaths. "Tonight, a traitor will be dealt with, and each of you will help."

Piper watched as Mary Lynn sat in the middle, and Louie Luca at the end of the row suddenly jumped up, with apprehension on their faces, their feet slipping on the clear plastic drop cloth.

"Ah, do my friends have something they care to share?" he laughed. "You seem guilty. Confession will cleanse the soul, I've been told." He waved his hands, signaling for them to sit down. He shook his head slowly. "Neither of you are my problem, at least not now," he chuckled.

A shuffling of feet startled an already nervous group. They watched anxiously, their eyes wide, as a man was dragged out of the darkness. He was thrown to the ground in front of them, slipping on the plastic carpet. His hands were bound behind his back, and duct tape was wrapped around his ankles.

One of Piper's crew, dressed in military fatigues and holding an M-16 rifle, pulled a black hood off the helpless man. His face was already bloodied and badly beaten, making it clear that the torture had begun earlier.

They all gasped when they saw the FBI badge dangling around the man's neck. They realized that the Pied Piper was about to murder an FBI agent.

Piper was a master at controlling others. This impressive dominance was gained at an early age. He understood that the fear his father instilled with his belt had become his ally.

Fear cripples faster than any weapon man can invent, his father had drilled into him; those words were permanently etched in his mind and beaten into his body. His mother's love and her ability to soothe him with her favorite fables gave him the motivation to reinterpret the Pied Piper story. Just as religion reinterprets its Bible to fit the times, so did the man known as the Pied Piper.

"Loyalty has been my only requirement," he said calmly. "Is that too much to ask? Never mind," he waved his gloved hand, a gesture indicating not to respond. "It is measured by me and me alone." Piper paused; the only sounds filling the air were the wheezing breaths the FBI agent struggled to suck in through his broken nose.

Piper appreciated these simple moments before the stench of death filled his nostrils. It was only rivaled by the terror in his victims' eyes, a hopeless look of resignation that granted him the power he so desired.

"Each of you tonight will renew your vows to me. This Pig thought he could infiltrate and expose us. His arrogance, his boss's arrogance, will be in for quite a surprise when he arrives at Hoover Building later this morning."

Piper's demeanor had become excited once again. He rushed his words like an eager child. He was oblivious to the fact that the horrified group did not understand what he had been saying.

"No one, and I mean no one, plays games with me. I hold the keys to the gates where the games are played. I set the rules, and this man did not follow them," he sighed heavily. Then, his demeanor changed once again.

With a loud, deep, foreboding voice, Piper shouted, "Are we ready to rumble? Are you ready to take your vows?" He said, holding back a giggle. He grinned as he watched the four nervous brokers nod their heads.

"Now stand," he shouted. His shifting moods were coming on faster, rambling like a drug addict whose fix was wearing off.

Each of the brokers felt the cold barrel of a rifle pressed into their backs. They stood together, each with a Heckler & Koch MP5 with a full magazine. They had been pushed toward the terrified FBI agent.

Piper, in a low monotone, spoke with an eerie calm. "Now kill this man and be on your way. Once your weapon is emptied, you can leave."

The brokers failed to notice the tripod, perfectly positioned at the scene, ready to record them while killing the FBI agent. It was a digital video camera operated by Luis Rodriguez, Piper's head of security.

"Now do it or join him," he threatened, his mood shifting impatiently. "It's not like any of you haven't killed before."

The first shot pierced the agent's shoulder, slamming him onto the cold concrete floor. He started to wiggle across the surface like a wounded caterpillar when the second shot hit his thigh. Within seconds, a symphony of explosions tore through his body. Then, as suddenly as it started, the roar from the guns stopped. The warehouse fell silent, except for the frustrated clicks from the empty weapons.

The plumes of smoke coming from the hot barrels curled and floated upward toward the ceiling like gray ribbons, while the bright floodlights shone down on the terrified group. Piper had been laughing; his grim voice echoed off the metal walls.

"You've all done well tonight. Now go home and prepare your last orders." Piper had started clapping as he watched his executioners briskly exit the building.

Waiting for them were five black limousines, staffed by their security team. On the back seat was an envelope with their final orders.

His men had started placing the guns in plastic bags, each labeled with the murderer's name and fingerprints. The guns were then put into a large plastic storage container, along with the videotape, which would become part of Piper's files, his so aptly named loyalty insurance policy.

"It's time we go. We have a lot of work ahead of us before we leave port, he told Luis." He walked over to the dead body and fired three bullets into the agent's head. "That's for Evans, Blanchard, and Seymour," Piper muttered. His eyes were void of emotion.

"Luis, I want his body propped against the front doors of the FBI's Field Office in downtown Miami. I'm just sad I won't be able to see the look on Deputy Director Evans' face when he returns to work this morning. Be back before we set course for sea."

Chapter 16

Piper walked slowly up the gangway, deep in thought. He had been mumbling words incoherently. The violence inside the warehouse sparked an emotional struggle in a man desperate to stay human. He covered his ears as he walked past the screams of frightened young children, all crying for their mommies.

As he passed the hysterical children, he inserted two foam rubber plugs into his ears, but the infants' wailing still seeped through. He knew that soon the cries would fade once the sedatives took hold.

He lit up a cigar, drawing in the first warm smoke into his mouth. His heart had not stopped pounding from the adrenaline rush he had gotten seeing the FBI agent's dead body ripped apart by the heavy caliber rounds.

The thick plumes of cigar smoke surrounded his face as he moved through the first of many hatches towards the bridge. He needed to confirm that the harbor pilot, one of many loyal workers who, for a fair price, signed off on the ship's manifest without hesitation. This simple act guaranteed safe passage until they reached international waters.

As he stepped onto the bridge, he saw the surprised look on the man's face. He had forgotten to wear his mask, but it didn't matter because this was going to be the last business he handled with that harbor pilot. Piper could see it in the man's eyes; he knew he was going to die.

"Please don't kill me. You know I will never tell..." he was interrupted.

"No loose ends, you know that. No second chances. Please, no begging. Just die like a man. I need a safe retirement. I owe it to my wife and men; you understand…right?" he said calmly. He had learned at an early age never to leave himself exposed. Keep your friends close, your enemies closer, his father would say. If you're not sure of their loyalty, kill them.

His father had another twisted philosophy ingrained in him. Give the people around you something to live for, or they will become the most dangerous. Suicide bombers had been Frederick's favorite example of his point. *"They have nothing to lose and everything to gain by becoming martyrs. They are the most hopeless of the hopeless, as well as the easiest to manipulate,"* Enrique heard inside his head.

His father would go on, "The moment the world recognizes that the way to stop suicide bombers is to give them more than they have, then and only then will it stop. Men, women, and even children will not kill themselves if they have something to live for. Remove hopelessness, and you remove control."

"Good-bye, my friend," he said to the harbor pilot.

Herman, Luis's brother, had grabbed the man's arm and, with his other hand, jabbed the barrel of his gun into the man's ribs. The harbor pilot craned his neck, catching a glimpse of Piper, who smiled and shrugged. The knowledge that death was just moments away made Piper smile.

After the harbor pilot was taken care of, the doctors and nurses sedated their patients. Piper made it a habit to visit the operating rooms and the cargo cells that held the quiet children selected to live a little longer.

His ship, a converted World War II military floating hospital, served as the perfect cover for his operation. The hull's exterior, along with the visible bulkheads, was painted bright white. Between the two smokestacks, a large neon sign hung, reading: M.G. Enterprises, reinforcing the convincing ruse.

Inside, the metal walls were painted a deep purple, the color of success, while all the ladders and hatch doors were a bright emerald green, reflecting the money Piper earned on each voyage. The decks were made from scratch-resistant, highly polished stainless steel and were carefully maintained, especially in each of the three operating rooms. Everything inside had to be sterile, or the organs could become contaminated, and he would not get his payment.

Large drains were installed in the center of each operating room, equipped with powerful fire hoses that spray disinfectant to eliminate any traces of blood, DNA, and bone chips left after each procedure.

Piper made sure his crew practiced emergency drills every week, sharpening their skills to cover their tracks if the Coast Guard ever boarded them. Although he had never been stopped, he knew he had to be ready. Like a pit stop at a NASCAR race, their teamwork was perfectly coordinated, and they sterilized each operating room in under five minutes.

In the sealed holding cells where the chosen children waited, tiny nozzles in each corner of the ceiling were ready to release cyanide as a last resort if the authorities boarded the ship. Piper had all his bases covered. The ocean he had known for some time had become the perfect place to dispose of discarded body parts: chum for the hungry sharks.

As he passed the first operating room, the surgical saws squealed nonstop. Only highly qualified surgeons removed the organs and placed them in advanced organ transport equipment. This ensured they could be flown away on the waiting helicopter at the back of the ship.

As he climbed the ladder to the next deck, he noticed the holding cells filled with older children, some already paid for by their new adoptive parents. The remaining children were sleeping peacefully, destined for a man crazier than himself, Doctor Thomas Kane.

Each child had been sedated and was sound asleep, except for one nine-year-old girl huddled in the corner of her cage. She was special. It was just another punishment for Deputy Director Evans.

Their eyes met briefly. Her gaze, unlike any Piper had ever seen, was fixed on him. "Sleep, my child," he said softly. "Soon you'll be in a better place." Then, she buried her head between her knees.

The young girl, just before falling asleep, tried to memorize the handsome man's face and store it in her bucket of frightened memories. As the sedative took effect, it lowered a dark, unfamiliar curtain. Her real nightmare was about to begin.

Piper finally returned to his quarters, preparing for the difficult transition his mind had to endure as his lithium tablets took effect. He had always been a master of disguise. For many years, he managed to shed his evil persona and appear as a normal, unassuming businessman. Unfortunately, each time he traveled back to his safe world, a part of him was left behind.

He and Luis had known for a long time that it had to end, or he would remain stuck in the dark chaos he inherited from his father, ultimately destroying himself and the people he loved deeply.

* * * * *

Luis returned fifteen minutes before they were scheduled to set sail, reporting that Piper's orders had been carried out precisely. All the brokers and their security teams, along with their limousines, were piles of melted metal. Piper's best friend and security chief then dropped the FBI agent off at the Hoover Building's entrance.

Luis spoke, a hint of caution in his voice. "I fear we've crossed the line tonight. It's going to be tough to slip in and out of ports, especially in the United States. The Coast Guard has been on high alert since 9/11. Killing a second FBI agent will make our lives more difficult. If they see this as a terrorist attack, well, I can't even begin to tell you the shit that will follow us."

Piper, his eyelids drooping, replied, his words slurring as the medication took effect. "They will be busy looking for the people on the tapes," he laughed. "By the time they find what remains of their bodies, we will have disappeared off the face of the earth. We have just a few more months to wrap up everything. The final game for Deputy Director Evans is almost complete. Then it can finally be over. I promise this time."

* * * * *

Mary Lynn Rose had heard the explosions and knew at that moment it was time for her to call in some of her IOU's and disappear. She just had to pick the right person.

She gave the head of her security detail a pat on the shoulder. "You've done well tonight," she said nervously. "I just hope Piper doesn't realize that one of the limos was a decoy."

Chapter 17

Deputy Director Evans arranged a meeting at Miami's field office with his undercover agent, Chuck Andrews. It was a pre-dawn meeting when the building was empty except for two security guards. His agent had critical information about the Pied Pipers' next shipment.

"Damn it," FBI Deputy Director Robert Evans cursed in disgust. "What's happening to our wonderful Capitol?"

Another overlooked person wrapped in a burlap-striped blanket, one of many homeless individuals, sat slumped against the front door of Miami's FBI field office for Human Trafficking. "I've gotta stop coming to work this early," he said, shaking his head.

Today, more than any other morning, it annoyed Evans to handle the matter while he waited for his agent.

Chuck Andrews was one of the best undercover agents, having spent over eight years in the field without his cover being compromised. Evans understood that this current assignment was the agent's most dangerous yet. He was coming in from the cold for good; his last task was to catch the Pied Piper in the act.

Evans checked his watch as he neared the front door. He wasn't too worried about his agent missing the meeting. He had skipped meetings before but today made him feel more anxious.

Special Agent Chuck Andrews had shared the details of the child exchange location and time the night before through encrypted emails.

Evans had summoned his team to Miami, hoping this lead would finally help catch the sociopath who had evaded him for twenty years.

Andrews' encrypted message sounded more hopeful than before. After twenty-six months, his agent had finally made it onto the Pied Pipers' "A" list of brokers and was about to close his first deal.

Last night, Pier 96 was cordoned off. A sufficient number of FBI agents, DOJ agents, and a Miami SWAT team were ready to capture the Pied Piper. However, like previous attempts, something had gone wrong.

While Evans and his men waited, the pier and the red warehouse turned out to be a dead end. Nothing moved. Bile rose in his throat at the thought that his agent's cover had been blown, but he knew how skilled Andrews was and tried to ignore the hairs on his neck standing up.

The disappointment, which was really more of an embarrassment to "Operation Innocence," was about to make Director Jenkins furious. Evans had assured the Director that his sting operation would finally put an end to twenty years of terror.

Evans was unaware that Director Jenkins had left the Hoover building earlier that day to share the good news with Senator Jarvis and the unpleasant Sally Palmer.

Now, Evans had no agent, no arrest of the Pied Piper, and once again, the FBI and DOJ were clueless.

A cold chill ran down his spine. He believed he had taken better precautions this time. Only he and Director Jenkins knew about Andrews's undercover operation. He wasn't sure how he would handle losing another agent. Evans tried to stick to his strict protocol and meticulous attitude, but following the rules wasn't producing the results he wanted.

As he approached the sleeping man, the smell of someone who hadn't showered in a long time made him gag. "How do they live like this?" he muttered, his hand covering his mouth and nose. The frayed blanket wrapped around the man's feet and torso formed a hood that hid his face.

The nape of his neck had stiffened like porcupine quills; his heart pounded fiercely, blood rushing to his brain. The smell started to register. It was not just neglect or the odor of not showering. It was the stench of death, and a brutal one at that.

Kneeling, he spotted the bloodstained FBI badge, and the color drained from his face. It took all he had to keep last night's dinner down. He knew immediately that his worst nightmare had once again reared its ugly head.

He checked for a pulse but didn't expect to find one. He saw the note nailed to Agent Andrews's bullet-riddled jacket.

Evans's blood was boiling as he read the arrogant words the Pied Piper had written. For the first time, he hated his job. He loved catching the bad guys, but the man who called himself the Pied Piper was not fit to live.

To my dear friend and worthy opponent, Deputy Director Robert Evans:

When will you learn that I cannot be touched? I've tolerated your arrogance for many years since I killed Jack Seymour and his wife. I have friends everywhere.

Seymour and his family sacrificed for your past mistakes, and now the rest of your team will suffer because I am fed up with all of you.

How many more of your men will you sacrifice to capture me? Our little game of cat and mouse will soon be over. Time is running out, and soon I will be just a fleeting memory, but not before you, Blanchard, and young Seymour lose everything dear to you all.

We have one last game to play. Follow the music, and you'll find me, but don't get caught up in my melodic siren; you, too, will go away forever. Your encrypted emails never worked. Better luck next time... hurry, hurry, before it's too late.

Respectfully yours,

The Pied Piper

P.S. Inside the black bag, you'll find a small gift to ensure you don't leave empty-handed or embarrassed in front of the American public.

Evans tried to control his emotions, but the overwhelming feeling of helplessness that engulfed him was just too much. He brushed away a tear and reported that an officer was down.

Chapter 18

Inside Deputy Director Robert Evan's office, he read the note for the fourth time. He had only been able to watch the video of Andrews' murder once.

Special Agent Ted Blanchard and his partner Elliot Burns waited for their distraught boss to speak. Agent Seymour and his partner, Agent Ronald Jamison, sat on a worn leather couch with their arms crossed.

Evans exhaled. "We lost a brave and dedicated agent last night. I never should have risked his life," Evans admitted. "I don't know why this crazy son-of-a-bitch wants to punish us specifically?"

Agent Blanchard was stunned. His boiling anger interrupted Evans. "Agent Andrews knew his assignment would be risky. That's part of the job we all accept. I just don't understand how that fucking Pied Piper can keep flipping us off and not leave a trail. No one's that clever unless he's getting help from the inside," Blanchard complained.

Special Agent Edward Seymour jumped into the conversation. "I don't get why the murder was videotaped or why he gave us the names of the people who are in the film. And, fuck, now he's threatening all of us?"

Evan didn't reply, staring straight through his agents.

"Robert, say something," Blanchard barked at his friend.

"He's tying up loose ends. He's terminating all of the people connected to him," Evans replied. Last night at the far end of the pier, four limos were blown up. We believe they were his brokers in the video he sent. He's smart. All his business associates, if they don't know it by now, will soon realize that their usefulness has expired. If we don't stay alert, he'll find us. He's very good at being a ghost. We need to draw him out soon, or we will never find out who he is. It will remain the coldest unsolved case in FBI history."

Agent Elliot Burns, his face grim, coughed out a question. "Did Andrews report back to you since going undercover? Do you have anything we can follow up on?" the Agent's voice cracked. He had graduated from the academy with Andrews; they were good friends.

Evans's eyes kept blinking, his head shook wildly, and then he responded. "He was in so deep that communications were at first impossible. Then, early yesterday, he sent an encrypted email that it was finally going to happen at Pier 96. I don't believe in coincidences. I...," he looked at Blanchard. "I'm beginning to agree with you that we have a mole."

As the words slipped from his mouth, he realized the answer to his own question. Only two people at the bureau knew about Andrews's undercover operation or the Pier 96 location. He knew that Director Jenkins had told the President and Attorney General Jerome Mulligan about Andrews's assignment. Right now, he had three suspects.

He handed Agent Seymour and his partner their next assignment. "Shouldn't be too difficult? Just observe and then call for backup. No hero stuff, you understand," he barked. "There's another lead to the missing children in the San Diego DCF agency." "Please be careful," he said.

Agent Seymour nodded. What's one more assignment? he asked himself.

* * * * *

Later that day, Evans drove to the warehouse that the Pied Piper mentioned in the video. He had to find out where his agent was murdered; it would make it real for him. He needed to smell the Pied Piper, get his scent, and, like a bloodhound, track him down and blow his brains out.

93

The concrete floor was visible only in patches as small rays of sunlight filtered through the salt-stained windows, battered by the persistent marine layer that was part of everyday life in Miami. The plastic tarp remained in place, with the blood only partially dried since last night's shooting. The warehouse measured approximately eighty feet wide by one hundred fifty feet long, with large front doors to accommodate sizable trucks and trailers for the substantial volume of cargo moved in and out last night.

Yesterday, it wasn't cargo that was hauled out but his agent's body. The Pied Piper didn't just kill special agent Chuck Andrews; he humiliated him like a maniac that needed to be put down. Evans usually kept his emotions outside of work, but he could no longer hide how he felt about the murderous pig: The Pied Piper.

Evans jumped at the sound of his cellphone ringing. He looked at the caller ID—it was his assistant, Alice Dickerson. "What else could go wrong now?" he muttered.

"You know I didn't want to be disturbed," he barked. "This had better be important."

Alice understood her boss's moods and temperament. She knew how to speak to him when he was upset. She didn't know how to start this conversation. "Just remember, I'm only the messenger," she said cautiously.

Evans took a deep breath. "Not another agent?" he asked.

"Agent Burns' niece, Michelle Arnold, was abducted five days ago in New York, right in front of his sister and brother-in-law's eyes. You're not going to like this, but Sally Palmer's connected."

"Sally Palmer? Why am I just hearing about this now?"

It was a Manhattan DCF case. Burns' sister has been a long-term drug user. Her husband was accused of abusing their little girl about five weeks ago. That's how Palmer got involved. The dysfunctional family fell under the new federal foster care guidelines," she paused, waiting for Evans to react. When he didn't, she continued. "Everything's sketchy right now. The parents had just gained visitation rights, and while in their custody, the girl went missing. I have the file being faxed over as we speak. NYPD, even our field office in Manhattan, has no leads. It's got the Pied Piper written all over it, but there's no note.

"Does Burns know?"

"Not that I am aware of."

"I'd better tell Blanchard first. He'd want to tell his partner." He snapped his cell phone shut.

Evans, for the first time in his career, felt helpless. Things were moving too fast. How many more of his agents would suffer? He knew he was running out of time, and now he had to find an agent's niece. "When will I catch a break?" he moaned.

Chapter 19

It had been three weeks since the brutal murder of Special FBI Agent Chuck Andrews. The FBI task force hadn't fully recovered from losing one of their own.

Special Agent Edward Seymour sat next to his partner, Ronald Jamison, in their black Ford LTD on a side road just off Interstate 8, five miles east of El Cajon. They had a tip that the Pied Piper had a shipment taking the back roads toward San Diego harbor.

Seymour hoped to finally confront the Pied Piper and serve as judge, jury, and executioner for what he had done to his family. "I hope to come face-to-face with this Pied Piper clown and give him the justice he deserves."

Seymour scanned with his binoculars, searching for his target. The sporadic white headlights from the large trucks were hard to focus on, but he had only one person in mind. He would recognize the scumbag who abducted young children when he saw him.

Tonight would mark his fifth and final operation in as many weeks, aimed at saving children but failing to capture the Pied Piper. He planned to resign the next day. He recognized the need for a new career, or he would fall into an irreversible depression. Coping with so many shattered lives, especially those of young children, had become increasingly complex. The years of pain and sorrow from losing his parents and sister to the Pied Piper had worn down what little of his soul remained.

His adrenaline raced through his veins as his eyes locked onto his target. "We got our Jack Rabbits," he elbowed his sleeping partner. They were large semi-trucks constantly jumping on and off highways, bypassing weigh stations, and using the cover of darkness to travel back roads. "Jack Rabbits" was a perfect description of their movements.

Agent Jamison belched and rubbed his eyes while the scent of chili dog and onions filled the car.

Seymour had to roll down his window. His free hand covered his mouth and nose. "That's foul," he barked. "Use a fucking breath mint."

Jamison stretched his six-foot-five frame. His long arms reached the rear seats. He yawned loudly. "Give me a break. If I have to sit here night after night with you, I'll eat whatever I want," he burped once more.

Seymour's face twisted in disgust as he ignored his partner. He might be a slob, but he was the only person Seymour trusted to have his back.

"Look there," Agent Seymour pointed. "Two jack rabbits moving north."

Jamison was alert and prepared for action. He brought his transmitter to his lips. "This is Papa Bear. Two Rabbits coming your way." He quickly checked his map to confirm only one road paralleled Interstate 8. "We've got the southern position. See you in ten minutes," he said to the El Cajon police unit waiting on the old highway bypassing the weigh station.

"Roger that," came the reply.

Seymour and Jamison were now rushing north toward the human cargo they hoped was safe. Eddie set his binoculars down between himself and his partner and checked his gun. His heart pounded.

He didn't notice the black SUV following the trucks with its lights off.

"Number six," said Seymour excitedly. "I hope we're pissing off that motherfucker Pied Piper. I want him to get angry. He has to make some mistakes eventually, right?" he rhetorically stated. He hadn't told his partner yet that tonight would be their last working assignment together.

Jamison made a sharp right turn, heading east. Without thinking, he turned off his headlights. A quarter of a mile later, they came to a stop. They laid out a dozen spike strips a hundred yards ahead, spaced at twenty-yard intervals. They moved back to their position and watched.

Thirty seconds later, tiny headlights appeared on the horizon. With each passing second, they grew larger and larger. The sounds of diesel engines filled the air. They had been in this position before and knew what to expect. The popping of the tires sounded like tiny explosions, followed by the air brakes squealing like a wounded animal.

Agent Seymour patted Jamison on the back. "Let's go save some children," he said excitedly.

What happened next shocked both agents. The first truck did not apply its brakes after its tires popped. It kept driving straight toward their car, which was angled across the two-lane road. Both agents were like deer caught in headlights. They stood there frozen.

Seymour shifted to his right and fired his weapon, aiming just above the front grill, dead center at the truck driver. He emptied a full clip and, in what felt like slow motion, released the empty clip, watching it fall to the ground as he snapped in another full magazine. He cursed at his partner as he saw him dive into a drainage ditch on the opposite side of the road.

Agent Seymour stood in shock as the truck swerved out of control toward the very spot where his partner had taken cover. The semi-truck jackknifed, the cab buckled in the ditch, and its cargo container screeched to a halt, parallel to their car.

Seymour dove to his right in a perfect shoulder roll, then rose to his feet with his gun aimed at the out-of-control truck.

For what felt like an eternity, the sound of metal bending, tearing, and screeching finally came to a stop. Then, without warning, their Ford LTD exploded, engulfing the truck's cab and the entire area where his partner had taken shelter.

Seymour's first instinct was to rescue the children in the cargo container. He ran toward the rear doors, shaken. To his surprise, the back door had snapped open. He looked inside; it was empty, and then a cloud of black smoke engulfed his body.

"What the fuck?" he muttered. He spun around, startled by the air horn from the second truck that had stopped before the spike strips. He radioed his backup team, but they did not respond. Then he heard a male voice that he did not recognize.

"I will tell Evans that his arrogance has cost him more agents," the voice boasted.

"Tonight, you will die, and your reign of terror will finally end," Seymour yelled back at him.

"Agent Seymour, your overconfidence has caused me too much aggravation," the voice said emotionlessly. "You've been disrupting my business for too long now. You're just like your father," he bellowed. "Tonight, you will pay, just as your father did."

"You're a sick mother fucker," Seymour cried out.

The Pied Piper howled with laughter. "Oh, and by the way, your sister, whom you buried in that mock funeral, is still alive with her new family. To think she will never meet her brother, Special Agent Edward, or should I say little Eddie Seymour. Do you still have my note I gave you right before your family car became an inferno?" The voice then turned into a macabre snicker.

Seymour could not believe his ears. His heart was pounding hard against his ribcage. *Ashley's alive?* He tried to shout, but the burning truck drowned out his words. Without warning, the first bullet entered his shoulder, shattering bone. Then a second bullet entered his thigh, his pant leg beginning to feel wet and sticky. He fell backwards into the black smoke that had started to billow into the clear night sky.

He crawled toward his partner, feeling his way like a blind man, dragging his weak body and leaving a crimson trail. The pain in his shoulder and thigh felt like a million volts of electricity with each beat of his pounding heart.

When he reached the ditch, he lost his dinner. His partner was lying crushed under the front tire of the truck. Ronald's eyes were wide with shock.

He kept crawling like a wounded animal searching for shelter. He found a round metal drainage tunnel opening and squirmed into the damp ditch. Like a wounded dog, he dragged his bloodied body as far into the metal cave as possible before passing out. Just before darkness overtook him, he heard another loud explosion that made the shelter shake and burn hot. Unable to move, he could only pray it would be over soon.

* * * * *

Piper told Luis to drive the SUV closer to the fire. "Find Agent Seymour," he shouted. "I don't want him alive. He's done enough damage."

Luis and his brother Herman searched the area unsuccessfully. In the distance, they heard sirens and saw the flashing lights of fire trucks and police cars rushing toward them from the west.

"Piper, the explosion should have killed him. He's nowhere to be found. We must go now," he said, pointing toward the flashing lights that were quickly approaching.

Piper refused to move. He needed to be sure Seymour was dead. "We have to keep looking," he demanded.

Luis grabbed his friend's arm. "He's dead. If the explosion didn't kill him, then the two bullets I put in him definitely did. We need to go now," he said firmly.

Piper was back in the SUV. The second truck had already turned around on a dirt side road, and they were heading back the way they came. They passed a police car with the four police officers' bodies twisted on the side of the road, two notes nailed to their chests.

Piper smiled at his work. "Did they think I wouldn't discover what they were doing?" he said, flipping the dead bodies the bird. "I want our cargo delivered in three days to the pier in San Diego."

Luis nodded and hurried back to Palomar Airport in Carlsbad, where their plane was waiting.

* * * * *

Agent Seymour wasn't sure how long he had been unconscious. He listened carefully to the commotion above him. Cold water from the fire hoses filled the tunnel, cooling him down.

As the blood continued to drain from his body, the drainage ditch began to flood. He pressed his transmitter, coughing desperately for help.

Not since the day his parents were murdered and his sister abducted had he felt this hopeless. His throat felt like sandpaper as he cried out. All he could hear was his inaudible, raspy voice echoing in his metal coffin. He was cold and weak, feeling an eerie blanket of sleep envelop his body. He gave one last plea for help before his eyes fluttered shut.

Chapter 20

Miami Harbor, Pier 93

Twelve unbearable days had passed since Michelle Arnold was taken from her parents once again. This time, she wasn't in a foster home but behind a metal cage on a large ship. Trembling uncontrollably, she stayed curled into a tight ball, her slim limbs pressed close to her torso.

A relentless cold engulfed her, causing uncontrollable shivering as she pressed her forehead to her knees. The muffled voices of men, their foreign and chilling accents, confirmed her horrifying realization that she was far from home and her parents' safety.

Michelle was still groggy as she found herself in an eerie, unsettling place. She was used to fear, having moved through many foster homes in Manhattan that were cold and impersonal.

This time, it wasn't the monsters under her bed that scared her. It was the screams of the other children, cries that made her heart race. She tried to calm herself by taking slow breaths to clear her mind. It was something her mother had taught her.

Having endured a childhood filled with isolation, harsh treatment from unfamiliar people, and the upheaval of moving through five different foster homes, nine-year-old Michelle saw this new turn of events as entirely distinct from her past experiences. Hope for reuniting with her parents had been cruelly crushed.

After her admission to a Manhattan ER, she had been left in the care of foster parents who were indifferent to her well-being, their primary concern being the money they earned. Now, subjected to yet another strange punishment, Michelle realized she was not going to another foster home but to a place much more dangerous. Her mind drifted back to how new her foster home was, the one Sally Palmer had assigned her to.

Her latest nightmare started on a beautiful spring morning when her father, the brother of FBI agent Elliott Burns, was playing soccer with her at the park. She fell, as she had many times before, while chasing a soccer ball and tripped over one of the many protruding roots of the maple trees that wove through the sparse grass where she played.

Michelle loved sports, especially soccer, karate, and snow skiing. She had learned that playing hard often resulted in bruises and a few fractures over the past two years.

That day, she fell hard and twisted her ankle. She tried to hold back her tears, but the pain was worse than she had ever felt. As her father ran over to comfort her, she couldn't stop screaming for help. Other fathers, mothers, and joggers all stopped what they were doing to focus on Michelle's call for help. The news had recently been reporting many abductions in Riverside Park, so everyone was on high alert.

They quickly surrounded Michelle's father, creating a circle around the crying girl and yelling at him to leave her alone.

"I'm the girl's father," he yelled in panic. "Let me through, she's hurt and needs medical attention." He pushed through the crowd, bent down, lifted Michelle, and held his frightened daughter in his arms.

Before he could react, a burly man in shorts and a tank top grabbed Michelle and pulled her away, which only made her cry harder.

A woman in a bright pink jogging suit began running her fingers through Michelle's hair, trying to get some answers. "Is this man your father?" she asked, scowling.

The pain intensified, and her gasping screams made it impossible for her to respond. Two police officers arrived and entered the circle. They attempted to calm everyone down, but the shouting from the angry mob had gotten out of control.

"We saw him trying to abduct the girl," one man said. "He was carrying her and fondling her butt and upper chest," another woman screamed. If someone had a rope, Michelle's father would have been lynched without question.

Michelle's dad tried to explain to the police officers that he was her father. He showed the officers his driver's license. "I'm her father, for God's sake. She needs to have her ankle looked at," he said nervously as the crowd kept yelling stuff like pervert, kidnapper, and other crazy accusations.

One of the officers, noticing that Michelle's ankle was swollen, called an ambulance and told Mr. Arnold they would continue interviewing him at the hospital. The other officer turned Michelle's father around and placed handcuffs on him.

Alex Arnold was surprised. "Is this really necessary?'

"It's procedure. I'll remove them when we get you into the squad car," he said in an unemotional tone.

Michelle's father, his face pale, tried to reason with the officers. "This is crazy. I was trying to help my daughter. She got injured running after a soccer ball. Just ask her…" He inhaled deeply, trying to contain his anger and frustration.

Michelle was already on a gurney as her father was shoved into a police car. She was pushed into an NYFD EMC van, crying and begging for her father to be with her, but no one listened.

"I need to go to the hospital with her. Can't you idiots see that she's scared?" Arnold said, his tone had become belligerent.

"That's where we're all headed. If what you're saying is true, then you have nothing to worry about," the police officer who handcuffed him said.

Michelle had finally calmed down by the time her father arrived at Manhattan General. Her father noticed the somber expressions on the faces of the doctors and nurses. Their glances seemed to lack concern or compassion for him. Although he couldn't hear their hushed conversations at the nurse's station, he sensed that it wasn't good.

Michelle's eyes darted back and forth like laser beams locked onto a target. First, they flicked to her frightened father, then to the group dressed in green hospital scrubs, police uniforms, and one commanding woman who had taken charge of the scene. Immediately, the young girl sensed that something bad was about to happen. Fingers were pointed at her father.

"I just hurt my dumb ankle," she told herself. *"What's the big deal?"* she thought. *"I never cry. Why today?"*

The woman in charge introduced herself as Sally Palmer, the director of a newly established, federally funded foster care program. She was responsible for overseeing special child welfare cases across the country. Her shiny black hair was pulled back tightly into a ponytail, causing a wind-tunnel effect on her face. She resembled a mortician, dressed in a black suit and black stiletto heels. However, her tone towards Michelle's father was far from calm and friendly.

"How long have you been abusing your daughter?" Palmer Michelle's father. She had been waving X-rays in the air as she kept accusing him.

Sally Palmer disliked coming to New York, but she had just received an encrypted message from Piper saying he wanted Michelle Arnold. How likely was it that it would happen this way? This was a favor for the Pied Piper—another high-stakes request she had to fulfill.

"I've never abused my daughter," he said defiantly. "I love Michelle and would never hurt her."

Palmer looked at the doctor and motioned for him to speak. She had started to sway from side to side, her arms crossed tightly over her chest.

Mister Arnold, Michelle, as far as we can tell, has had a lot... um... let me say this better," he looked nervous, his head down as he examined the x-rays. "There appears to be an abnormal number of old fractures on her arms, ribs, and legs. If she were a boy, I might understand, but I've never seen this many injuries on a girl, unless it was from abuse.

Michelle had started to cry. She knew exactly what they were accusing her father of doing to her. She knew they were all lies. She needed to defend her father and propped herself up on her elbows. She started shouting over the loud voices, "I fall a lot," she pleaded. "My daddy loves me. He's never hurt me. You don't understand," she said, unable to hold back her sobs.

Sally Palmer stepped in between them and said, "Until my department can conduct a full investigation, your daughter will be placed in temporary foster care."

Alex stood up, a fire burning in his eyes. "What about sending her home with her mother? I'll stay in a hotel until this thing is sorted out," he pleaded.

Palmer shook her head as she read the police file. "It says here that your wife's an ex-drug addict," Palmer said, pointing at the papers in her hand.

"How the hell..." Alex stopped himself. "She's been clean for five years. This is bullshit," he said, ready to strangle Sally Palmer. He regretted showing his rage as the police officer twisted his arm, re-cuffing him. "Her brother's an FBI agent. Call him. Special Agent Elliott Burns," he begged. "He'll vouch for us."

Sally Palmer puffed out her chest, biting her lower lip, concern evident on her face. "Michelle's safety is our only concern now. I don't care if she's the niece of the Pope himself. She's not going back home with you or your wife. If everything checks out, she'll be returned in a few days," Palmer said, her tone cold as ice.

That day, Michelle's life changed. Nothing had gone back to normal, and she was once again far from home.

Chapter 21

Another scream pulled Michelle back to her current situation. She nervously fidgeted while waiting for her turn to be examined. The hell she had gone through before today seemed mild compared to what she felt was about to happen. She had heard the cries all morning coming from behind the gray steel door marked in red letters: Exam Room.

Michelle heard the same screams days earlier, along with the squealing of saw blades. She tried to block out the wailing from each child who went in before her, but the cold metal walls echoed the cries like a bell chamber inside her ears.

After a few minutes, the screams faded into muffled whimpers, only to start again when another child entered the exam room.

No one left the room after entering. She hoped there was another exit, but her frantic thoughts convinced her otherwise.

Squeezing her eyes tightly, she couldn't hide the images of pain and torture she imagined had been happening during her twelve-day ordeal. Her resolve was fading as hopelessness took over her body.

A tall, trunk-like man, his face grim and unsmiling, stood by the door. His cold, piercing eyes made Michelle shiver even more. The giant stood watch, ready to pounce on any fragile child who tried to run away.

"What do they think we can do? she wondered. Michelle tried to convince herself it was all in her imagination, but what she had seen so far felt too real for her mind to believe otherwise."

It was almost her turn. Desperation, mixed with anguish, consumed her. She felt weak, unable to move or think clearly. After watching fifteen toddlers, children Michelle's age, and small babies carried in by nurses go into the exam room and not come out, she knew she had to try to escape. "But, where? And how?" she wondered.

The guard gripped a large rifle firmly, his knuckles turning white. She felt that he was aware of her thoughts. Michelle's imagination was like a runaway train, uncontrolled and rushing along the tracks, destination unknown.

The guard became alert, his body stiff. He was ready to stop a massive attack from the small army of crying children who couldn't defend themselves. Michelle Arnold looked away, squeezing her eyes shut, hoping that when they opened, her nightmare would be over.

The sad, lonely life she hated in Manhattan haunted her thoughts. That life seemed perfect compared to where she was now.

Inside the polished, purple-colored room stood four women opposite the guard. They were all dressed in white, wearing nurses' uniforms that made them appear kind and caring, with soft voices at first. However, as they attended to the other children, their comforting moods abruptly ended when a rough-looking, unshaven man carrying a rifle stormed into the holding cell, shouting something in Spanish that appeared to upset the women.

Michelle had learned at a young age to be seen, not heard. Be invisible for her emotional survival. She observed the women's reactions; they too seemed scared.

One of the nurses ran over to one of the other cages, pulling a terrified toddler by the nape of his neck, like a mother lion rounding up one of her cubs. She jogged over with the toddler, opened a large metal door, and handed the child off to another man in a white coat. The nurse's face was sad and drained of color.

The room Michelle noticed had no windows or clocks. She had no way of knowing if it was day or night or how long she had been gone from Riverside Park. The room kept rising and falling like a teeter-totter.

A loud squealing noise hurt her ears. It reminded her of someone using a power saw. Then she realized that the high-pitched wailing sound was coming through the wall next to her cage. She heard a man's voice, deep and foreboding, laughing after the machinery stopped. With the side of her head close to the cold metal bars, she tried to listen.

"Take what's left of the body; the fish need their meal," the gruff voice shouted. Michelle slid away from the bars, terrified, hoping she had misunderstood.

With her eyes tightly closed, Michelle remembered her reunion with her mother and father a week before her abduction. The kind judge had granted her parents temporary custody. To celebrate, they took her to her favorite park.

In the distance, her mom and dad argued on a bench, their images lively and vivid, unaware of what she was doing. She wished with all her heart they would stop fighting and see how happy she was, pumping her legs and making the swing go so high.

She remembered the words of the stern-looking woman in a dark suit who had spoken to her parents. She recalled that her name was Sally Palmer, and she had given her parents an ultimatum. "If you want your daughter back permanently, you'll have to prove to me that you are fit parents."

Michelle knew when adults lied. She could tell that Sally Palmer was dishonest with her parents. She remembered how hard she prayed they would not anger the mean woman. She did not want to go back to foster care.

"Mrs. Arnold, if you want to have full custody of Michelle, you'll have to enter a twelve-step program," Palmer demanded.

"Lies! My parents are wonderful to me," Michelle complained to herself. *"Why can't she leave us alone?"*

Michelle did not understand any of the issues that Sally Palmer ranted about. Her parents consistently protested.

They begged Sally Palmer to let them provide blood, urine, or anything else to prove they weren't the kind of people she claimed they were. Unfortunately, the mean, controlling witch refused to let it happen.

After her father proved he was not abusing her, Palmer seemed to find other things to complain about, never letting up. She remembered hearing her father threaten to report Palmer's lies to the authorities. Still, the attorney appointed by New York City's Public Defender's Office appeared to side with Social Services and Sally Palmer.

No one seemed to believe her parents. Neither the courts nor the police, and not even the Social Services-appointed psychiatrist, Dr. Waverly, appeared to believe them. While the doctor promised Michelle he'd fight to help all of them, nothing happened—at least not quickly enough. He was just another adult who lied.

As the arc of the swing reached its peak, she gazed at the small boats cruising up and down the Hudson River. Michelle was enjoying a fleeting moment of serenity as she continued to pump her legs harder and harder.

The swing moved gracefully—a perfectly weighted pendulum. She felt a tingle in her stomach as she launched off the swing and landed hard on the ground.

She could not remember when either of her parents had played or even made her laugh. They argued constantly. Now, the fighting centered on whose fault it all was. When they were not arguing with each other, they were battling with Palmer.

Off to her left, she noticed a man in a colorful costume playing a melodic tune on a long wooden flute. She was captivated as he strolled closer. Michelle felt a strange sensation envelop her body, causing her eyes to close as she continued pumping her legs on the swing.

She heard the jester's shoes crunching on the loose sand. Without warning, two strong arms stopped her mid-swing, and before she could open her eyes, a damp cloth was pressed over her mouth and nose. She caught a strange, sweet scent, and the pungent odor made her cough.

Unable to scream and feeling lightheaded, she became disoriented, and like a curtain descending on a stage, darkness enveloped her vision. The last thing she remembered before drifting deeper into the void was her parents arguing, unaware of the peril that had fallen upon her.

Michelle had not noticed Sally Palmer standing behind an old maple tree, talking on her cell phone. "Once Piper hands off the Arnold girl to me, she will be in Miami on schedule," she told Luis. "I just hope there aren't any witnesses."

Chapter 22

Michelle was now shivering uncontrollably as she stared at the scary giant guard. Soon, it would be her turn to enter the room from which no one returned.

She squeezed her eyes shut, pressing her face once again into her thin hospital gown. She found herself once again trapped in her nightmare, her mind cruelly forcing her to recall anything that might provide a clue about where she had been taken. She didn't understand why she was in her current situation.

At some point during her voyage, she realized she was not going to be removed from her cage. She had finally received a thermal long-sleeve tee shirt with matching long johns, an oversized parka, and bib overalls. Her warm, thick socks provided welcome relief, as her toes had no feeling. She remembered the nurses talking to a man who seemed in charge; they were pointing at her. He nodded with a smile. At that moment, she knew she had been spared.

However, not all of the children were as fortunate. Some of them remained still as the nurses tossed clothing onto their quiet bodies. They were silent, a different kind of silence, distinct from that of someone who might be sleeping.

Michelle picked up a lot of profanity in different languages from all the various foster homes she had stayed in, and when the nurses spoke in Spanish, she realized their words weren't meant for young ears.

The silent children were carried out of the room, their heads bobbing loosely and their eyes rolled back in their sockets. She valued her new clothes and warm snowsuit jacket—simple emotional pleasures at that moment. She had to survive and attempted to forget about the children who were no longer in her cold metal room. She was alive for now, and that was all that mattered.

The nurses returned to give her and the remaining children a shot that made her feel lightheaded. The room filled with cages started to spin wildly, and then darkness enveloped her once more.

When the sedative wore off, Michelle was no longer in the cold, dark, swaying purple room of the ship. She found herself in a van speeding up a bumpy, serpentine road. The temperature continued to drop, and she noticed how her ears were reacting to the pressure of ascending to a higher altitude. She couldn't tell if she was shivering due to the cold or because she was terrified. Either way, she knew she was in serious trouble.

Trying to gather her emotions and compress them so she could think was proving difficult. Nonetheless, she had to regain control of herself. She had felt this cold before, and the pressure on her ears had been encountered many times. Her parents used to take her to the mountains every winter, where she would ski on the most challenging slopes with her father.

The van made a sharp turn, slamming her head against the metal wall. Fear swept over her petite body like a flood. She no longer felt brave as she watched the next child being escorted to the exam room.

The cold continued to intensify, and she found herself shivering more than she had inside her cage on the ship. Michelle's mind was now racing chaotically. She mentally drifted back to the van that kept climbing the mountain.

The van continued to race up the steep hill, and so did her panic. Michelle looked around the cold metal shell. Two guards sat on a metal bench, guns gripped tightly, chatting in a foreign language she did not recognize. They seemed indifferent to the other whimpering children.

Michelle kept telling herself to survive, struggling to brace herself each time her bruised body was tossed against the metal cargo container. She refused to show her fear, even though it felt ready to explode out of her.

She took a deep, shivering breath. The cold, bitter air burned her lungs. The other seven children riding with her, their faces numb with fear, looked just like her: lost and alone in a strange place.

Michelle had been jolted awake from her relentless nightmare as the mean woman called out the next child's number.

"Number sixteen," the heavy-set woman in her tight-fitting nurse's uniform yelled. Michelle stared at the large number pinned to her hospital gown: twenty-three. She still had the plastic arm bracelet bearing her name, age, sex, and two letters with a dollar amount next to them: S.P. $150,000.

She knew her nightmare was about to get even worse as she entered the exam room. Now she believed that something terrible was going to happen to her. She had heard from her parents and teachers many times what to do if a stranger wanted to talk to you: "Run away from strangers," but that advice was useless at that moment.

She was trapped. She felt weak and helpless in the cold, concrete hospital, with no way to escape.

Michelle was very street-smart for her age, thanks to all the foster homes she had lived in over the past three years. She had run away many times. Her mind tried to come up with a plan, but what could a frail little girl do in a land of ogres holding guns?

Her father had drilled different survival scenarios into her. She learned how to survive alone, whether on the streets of Manhattan or high on a snowy mountain. She looked around the waiting room and realized her current situation had not been anticipated. There has to be some way out of here, she silently screamed to herself. A loud cough from the large guard brought her back to her perilous situation in the waiting room.

Then she spotted a door and an opportunity. She didn't know where her courage had come from in that moment. Time was running out before her number was called. Her eyes darted around the dull room, lit by bright lights reflecting off the white walls. She squinted and slowly shifted her gaze from left to right, searching for an escape route.

The guard at the door looked like Bigfoot, his limbs wider than her body. Her heart sank as she realized she couldn't possibly overpower the giant in the room. She remembered the Ninja Turtles movie and wished she had superpowers at that moment.

Michelle slowly raised her hand, staying quiet and following the instructions she received when she first entered the room. The heavy-set woman, her cheerful face trembling like a Jell-O cube, scowled at Michelle's raised hand.

"Good little girl, you didn't speak without permission," she said with an evil grin and a strange, gruff accent. "What do you want?" she barked. "Be quick about it. I'm swamped," she admonished her.

In a whisper, Michelle's eyes, unable to face the mean witch, tried to control the tremor in her voice, but it failed. "I...I need to go to the bathroom," she told her, burying her head into her knees and hiding her tears with her hospital gown.

The woman moaned. "Let me see your number." She shrugged her shoulders in disgust. "Make it fast," she grumbled. She pointed to the other side of the room, where a symbol of a woman was displayed on a door.

Michelle jumped up, her legs stiff from sitting so long, and limped toward the restroom. She hadn't realized how weak she was until she strained to open the heavy metal door. Her heart sank as she noticed there was no lock on the door. *"I guess privacy isn't an option,"* she sarcastically told herself.

The bathroom was colder than the waiting room. Her already frozen body began to shake uncontrollably. Her heart thumped loudly, drowning out any noise from outside. *"Stay calm, you fool, you have to hear everything outside so that you won't get caught.*" Her scolding had worked, and she started to rein in her nerves.

As she looked around the small room, she noticed a heating vent near the floor, just the right size for her body. It was sealed with large screws. Her tiny fingers tried to turn the screws, but she couldn't loosen them. Frustrated, she knew she had to find another way out before they entered, looking for her. She was startled by a commotion in the waiting room. Her heart pounded so hard against her ribcage she thought it might burst. She pressed her ear to the door and listened.

"Were they upset with me for leaving the line?" she mumbled.

Then it became clear that another group of children had entered the room. The heavy-set woman started shouting for all the children to be quiet and fall in line. Maybe the woman would forget about her, she prayed.

"You're all out of order now," Michelle heard the mean woman shout. Then the room erupted into a cacophony of cries and screams. "Shut up," the mean woman said louder, which only worsened the situation. Michelle could tell that the heavyset woman had become flustered. Even her attempts to calm the children down with a soft, mellow voice only intensified the chaos.

Then another voice filled the room. It was a man's voice. "Everything will be…" he paused. "Just calm down and try to be quiet. I'm Dr. Kane, and nothing bad is going to happen to any of you."

Hearing the doctor's melodic voice and his name triggered another memory of her first day at the concrete hospital, the nickname she had given the place. She remembered Doctor Kane greeting them. He was a man of average height, with a stocky build and a long scar that twisted from his left ear to the corner of his mouth. When he smiled, the thick line on his face made him look monstrous. He assured them then, in a calm, tranquil tone, that everything was going to be all right. "What a liar," she whispered.

However, Michelle remembered his eyes darting nervously, like Sally Palmer's. She knew he was lying. She recalled the children in the van with whom she had arrived at the concrete hospital, who had not returned to the large dormitory where they all lived. One by one, they had been taken and replaced by new children. She was only nine, but she had the common sense to realize these strangers were not her friends. The last words she remembered Doctor Kane telling everyone were that they were in a new and better foster care facility. If they cooperated, they would be reunited with their families permanently. There was something about how he spoke that made Michelle know he should not be trusted.

In her panic, she looked up. Another mesh vent stared back at her. You have no other choice, her mind told her. Now jump up there to escape, she encouraged herself.

From what she could see by craning her neck, it had a simple lever and hinges. She had a slim chance, nonetheless.

All she had to do was climb up to the ceiling and get into it. Without considering the risk of injury or the danger she'd face if caught, she hopped onto the toilet seat and pulled herself up to the partition that separated the two stalls. She was grateful for her gymnastic lessons. They provided her with the agility and strength to pull herself up and balance on the narrow edge of the metal stall divider.

Her hands stretched out but couldn't reach the vent's lever. Disappointment drained her resolve. Then she tried again. With one hand on the wall for support and standing on her tiptoes, she strained her shoulders, reaching out for those last few inches. Her fingers extended as she struggled to grasp any part of the vent. As she worked, her feet wobbled in her thin cloth slippers, and she lost her balance, falling hard onto the tiled floor.

Michelle immediately covered her mouth with both hands, stifling her pain. She realized that this time she had better not cry; the punishment would be worse than what had happened that day in the park. She stood and moved her limbs, which all seemed to work naturally, except for the pain between her shoulder blades and the back of her head, where she had landed. She felt a small, painful lump growing on the back of her skull.

She paused for a second, listening to see if her thump had been heard. No footsteps approached the door. She exhaled slowly. Relief was brief when she heard number twenty being called. "Girl, you've got to get out of here right now!"

Without hesitation, she leaped onto the toilet seat and returned to the spot where she had initially started. "This time don't mess up," she told herself.

She stood securely, curling her toes and gripping the partition tightly. Her small feet ached as she balanced all her weight on the thin edge of the stall wall. The pain shot up through her frozen legs.

Blocking out the pain, she stretched as if she were Elastigirl, the superhero she had once seen in a comic book. Extending her body and arms, she muttered a short prayer as her fingers crawled like a spider closer to the latch. "Please, God, let me make it," she whispered.

She kept one hand firmly against the wall, leaning closer to the latch. Her free hand was just a hand's width away from the lever.

Her hand started to climb up the wall toward the ceiling tiles. Panic overwhelmed her. She wobbled again, trying to steady herself, knowing she couldn't afford another fall.

As she brought her left hand closer to her right, she became stiff as a statue, yet still managed to move her right hand toward the lever.

Relief flooded her body as her hand grasped the vent, just an inch away. Struggling to keep her balance, she scooted toward the lever. A loud crash echoed against the bathroom door, startling her. She slipped, ending up straddling the partition, and a sharp pain shot through her. Her heart pounded. She focused on the bathroom door, holding her breath and using her hand to mask the cries she desperately wanted to release. She prayed the guard wouldn't force it open.

She contemplated abandoning her plan. When no one entered the room, she quickly jumped up, using the last bit of balance her bruised and tired body could muster, and grabbed onto the lever.

Without looking back, she lowered the metal screen and hoisted herself up into the dark, cold metal tunnel. She reached back and locked the screen. Quietly, she moved in the only direction available to her.

"Daddy, I hope you'd be proud of me, at least for trying," she told herself, wiping away the tears that had begun to cascade down her cheeks. *"Be strong and think smart,"* she repeated her father's words that he had drummed into her head on each of their camping trips.

Chapter 23

Doctor Kane sat nervously behind his large teak desk, files scattered haphazardly as he listened to the man who supplied him with his children.

"Aren't you overreacting?" Kane said, his lips pursed. "We've never been close to getting caught. This is a great business for both of us.

Piper scratched his nose and shook his head slowly. His long, light brown hair, which falls just short of his shoulders, ripples like ribbons in the wind, hiding his deformed ear.

"I'm the one who needs to end this relationship. There are plenty of other brokers who would love to serve your business. It's time for me to retire and spend more time with my family," Piper said coldly. He didn't enjoy having to explain himself to anyone, let alone the crazy doctor. "Within the next few months, I want our arrangement severed. Your remaining orders will be completed, nothing more, nothing less," he said, rubbing his palms back and forth, signaling he was done with the meeting.

Senator Jarvis placed his hand on Piper's arm and said, "You have to give us at least a full year to build our new contacts. I have numerous orders that need to be fulfilled for my factories. If you stop supplying, it will ruin my business."

Doctor Kane nodded in agreement. "I'm close to curing your disease and extending my life," he said cautiously to Piper. "Think about it. You might be able to enjoy your retirement like a normal person, off your psychotropic drugs that are killing you."

Piper surveyed Kane's office, his eyes carefully scanning the doctor's face. He could tell from his eyes that he wasn't going to give up. He paused—his cold gaze fixed on the doctor for a few seconds before he shot a scowl at Senator Jarvis. Both men looked noticeably uncomfortable. He then met Luis's gaze, weighing whether to put an end to it right there and then. "Kane, I've heard these same lies for almost ten years. I'm willing to take my chances with my drugs."

Kane was determined not to let Piper have the last word. "What if my serum works? You would start to forget about your past, like it never happened. Just that thought alone has to make it worth your while. Give us just one year, a few more special children, and you can ride off into the sunset and never hear from us again?"

Piper's cold, dark eyes were empty vessels. His body remained still. He was lost in thought, weighing the growing risks. Once again, he looked at Luis, looking for his opinion. All he got was a slow shake of the head.

"Three months. That's it. Don't make me end our relationship sooner. You know what I am capable of," Piper threatened, massaging his temples with his fingers. "Kane...Senator, you do understand?"

Doctor Kane spun around in his chair and grabbed a bottle of Scotch from his credenza, full of excitement. "Let's drink to our last few months together," he said, pouring each man a four-finger shot.

* * * * *

Two hours after Piper and Senator Jarvis left his hospital, Dr. Kane administered his daily injection. He needed it to steady his hands before he operated on the next toddler.

His stem cell research was close to a breakthrough. He strongly believed that his experiments on young patients would cure his cancer. He was confident that his research would also reverse aging and eliminate most major diseases.

Kane wanted to be the first to benefit from his new therapy. He knew time was running out for him. With Piper closing down shop, he needed to switch to plan B.

He walked quickly toward the next child, lost in thought. Inside the operating room, a ten-year-old boy lay strapped to a metal gurney, his eyes wide with fear. He seemed to relax when he saw the doctor, the kind doctor who talked to all the children about their imaginary illnesses and how he was going to help them. They were innocent and believed his lies.

Doctor Kane walked over to the boy. He held a clipboard, appearing concerned as he took some notes. He wore light green scrubs with his mask resting on his forehead, humming a tune only he understood.

"Today, my young friend," he looked at the arm bracelet, "Thomas Miller... this is interesting? We have the same first name. You are about to become part of groundbreaking research, a study so important that it will save many lives in the future. Think of yourself as a young hero. Your organs will be used to develop a special serum," he paused, noticing that the boy's eyes had closed from the anesthesia. "Oh well, you probably wouldn't have appreciated my little pep talk anyway."

He snapped on his latex gloves, mumbling to himself. He shrugged his shoulders, pulling his surgical mask over his nose and mouth, and began to excavate the boy's organs.

Doctor Kane was an artist, as he opened the boy's chest with two quick cuts, and then, with a stainless-steel chest spreader, he was able to expose most of the organs he needed. He had done this a thousand times, and within minutes, he had the parts he wanted. He left the operating room as fast as he had entered, leaving the nurses to handle the cleanup.

Outside the operating room waited two men smoking nervously, wearing janitorial overalls, and anxiously awaiting to dispose of the body in the crematorium. No matter how many times they fired up the ovens or how many times they carried a lifeless, mutilated little body to the ovens, it took all they had to hold back the bile and vomit that followed.

* * * * *

Doctor Kane sat in his office, holding a photo of his father surrounded by hundreds of his father's patients inside one of the many concentration camp laboratories established by the Nazis. There, Hitler hoped that one of his doctors would discover a serum for his eternal youth.

Doctor Hans Kane was among the hundreds of scientists from the Third Reich who traveled to various camps to conduct experiments, promising to advance science. Thomas Kane sincerely wished that his father were alive today to witness his work and the progress he was making. The doctor closed his eyes for a short catnap before the next operation.

Chapter 24

Special FBI Agent Meredith Crawford from the Violent Crimes/Major Offenders Squad was interviewing Sally Palmer regarding the disappearance of Michelle Arnold. The DCF Director was evasive with her answers.

Agent Crawford didn't believe a word Palmer was saying. She was assigned to Deputy Director Evans, who demanded answers about how Michelle Arnold could go missing within the newly formed federal foster care agency.

Agent Crawford, who was naturally impatient, wanted to slap Palmer and get her to tell the truth. However, as the rookie, she had to keep her temper in check, at least for now. At the same time, her partner, Special Agent Todd Ellenberg, interviewed the Federal DCF assistant director and the other foster care officers at the FBI's downtown San Diego field office.

"The Arnold girl's parents..." Palmer's face had turned beet red, disgust spewing from her mouth toward Crawford. "They're losers. I had to go all the way to New York to save that little girl. They're the culprits responsible for the girl's disappearance," the DCF Director said with uncontrolled fury. "They were seen arguing...," Palmer, the perfect drama queen, paused to take a quivering breath as her eyes grew moist. "I feel so guilty that I hadn't taken Michelle away from them permanently sooner."

Crawford's face has become crimson. "What does any of this have to do with her disappearance? She was in your custody and in one of your approved foster homes."

Palmer had gotten flustered and went off on a tangent. "They're drug addicts and drunks. I still believe the little girl had been physically abused." She sucked in a raspy breath, "They don't deserve to be parents," she said, swiping away a well-orchestrated solo tear that she caught perfectly with her long nail before it could cascade down her cheek. Palmer wasn't exactly lying about the abuse, just about who was responsible.

"You're still not answering my fucking questions," Agent Crawford cursed. "Where the hell is Michelle Arnold?"

"I had warned them many times. Here, it's in their file," Palmer said, tossing the thick manila folder with an arrogant smirk on her face at Crawford. "I never should have allowed them to see their kid unsupervised," she continued ranting.

Special Agent Crawford's eyes narrowed as she watched Palmer speak. DCF Director was a little too rehearsed. She knew that when the guilty exaggerate, they appear overly upset while remaining focused on their inflated accounts of due diligence. Nine times out of ten, it's more a cock-and-bull story than the truth. *"Just one hard slap,"* she thought silently. With her lips pursed she was ready to pounce and strangle the pompous bitch.

Agent Crawford could no longer hold back. She blurted out her feelings a little too negatively. By then, restraint had gone out the window. "I've interviewed the Arnolds three times since their daughter's disappearance. My takeaway from my time with them is that they are loving parents," Crawford affirmed. "There's something about your account of the Arnold case that smells like subjective bullshit. I'm not convinced they had anything to do with Michelle's disappearance twelve days ago. I don't understand why you're not having the NYPD detectives follow up on the witness?"

Palmer's face had lost its color. She crossed her arms. "How I handle my job is none of your business," she huffed. "The witness was a homeless drunk," she claimed, defiance etched on her face.

Agent Crawford had become enraged. "Miss Palmer, our investigation is all about your agency, and we'll keep tearing into all of your missing children's files until we find the proof we're looking for."

Palmer continued defending herself. "After questioning the homeless man, he was way too drunk in my opinion about what he saw," she shot back, turning her nose up at the ceiling tiles. "I cannot afford to make subjective decisions when it comes to my children. Just the facts, and the facts reek of abuse."

"Yeah, right. I want to question that witness and convince myself that he's unreliable. There've been too many children under your watch turning up missing lately, Miss Palmer," Crawford said, waving her index finger at Palmer. "Something just doesn't smell right. I'll figure it out. My daddy used to say, "You know if there's manure by your feet, the donkey is close by." Agent Crawford smiled while scratching her cheek with her middle finger. "I know a jackass when I see it."

Agent Ellenberg had entered the interview room and positioned himself between his partner and Sally Palmer, gripping his partner's arm tightly while flaring his nostrils in anger.

"Crawford, go get some coffee," he said coldly. "You've been at this too long. We all have. Take a break."

"It's bullshit and you know it. This whole thing stinks," Meredith told her partner as she stormed out of the office.

Palmer had beads of sweat forming on her brow. She resembled a chilled glass of water on a hot summer day. She was breathing heavily and struggled to speak.

"I've never been so insulted…I want her off this case, or I'll be talking to Director Jenkins. You hear me?" she shouted. "The Arnolds are guilty as sin, and they will pay for what they have done to their adorable little girl."

Ellensburg shot back. "You only have circumstantial evidence," she cut him off.

"I don't need more evidence," she told him. "I have so many parents stealing their children and making them disappear, it would make your head spin. Have you spoken to any of Arnold's friends or family? Maybe the girl's being hidden there?"

Agent Ellenburg was losing it with Palmer and her lies. "That was one of the first things I did when she was first reported missing. The San Diego police department has already placed Michelle's case at the bottom of all the recent missing foster children files."

"Like I told you, my department and the police department are so underfunded that Michelle's file does not have a detective handling her case."

"My primary concern is locating Michelle. I require your full cooperation," Agent Ellenburg demanded. "I want access to all the case files of every missing child under your care. I've been doing this for many years, and I can tell when parents are the culprits. In my opinion, the Arnolds are either great actors or they had nothing to do with Michelle's disappearance. We're still talking to more of the neighbors near the foster home you had placed Michelle for any clues that might have been overlooked." The Agent's frustration with the case is starting to show.

Todd Ellenberg tried to remain calm and composed. His tone carried an accusatory edge that he could no longer suppress. "You're in charge of every DCF agency around the country. Tell me it's not just a coincidence that since you became director, more and more children under your watch are turning up missing."

He watched as Palmer's face turned ashen, and he knew he had touched a nerve. Before she could reply, he rattled off some unsettling statistics.

"New York, just last month, could not account for fifty-five newly placed foster kids. Florida misplaced eighty-two. Washington D.C. one hundred forty-three," he said, his face flushed with fury. "Shall I continue?" He raised his hand to stop Palmer from responding. "It was a rhetorical question, Ms. Palmer. In one year, 1.8 million children across the country who are placed in foster care have gone missing," Ellenberg had become livid. "Would you say the Federal Foster Care Program you're in charge of is doing a good job?"

His sarcastic question seemed to take the wind out of her sails. Palmer's face had turned beet red from the reprimand.

"You bastard. I'm doing the best I can with the resources given to me," she scowled. "I've been doing this for over fifteen years. How long have you been on these cases?"

Agent Ellenburg gave her a wink. "You're somehow involved with these kidnappings, and I'll find the evidence to put you away in Federal Prison for life."

Palmer had become belligerent. "Don't put your foot in your mouth before you have all the facts. When parents believe they will never see their child again, they generally do the most hideous things, even murder. It's the same story across the country. Abusive parents are abducting children, and with every social services agency being understaffed, they cannot keep track of every case," Palmer contended. "The NYPD and DCF are proceeding with or without your approval to arrest the Arnolds. The crime took place in New York, and the perpetrators will be put on trial there. I'll be talking to FBI Director Jenkins about your disgusting attitude." She stood up abruptly, causing her metal chair to crash backwards.

* * * * *

"I'm telling you, Palmer is a real piece of work," Agent Crawford said, frustrated as she pounded her palm with her fist. "I could hear her crap in the outer office. I want to find that witness. I'm not so sure the detectives are telling us the whole truth. Palmer seems to have a long reach in areas where she shouldn't be involved."

Agent Ellenberg placed his hand on his partner's shoulder. "You're a real bulldog. Maybe I should get you a studded dog collar and a short leather leash?" he grinned.

Meredith returned his grin. "That's the first kinky thing you've said to me all day. What about some whips and chains?" she laughed. "What about the bitch? We have to do something before more children go missing."

"I think you're right," Ellenburg agreed. "I'll bet she knows perfectly well what happened to the Arnold girl. We missed our twenty-four-hour window for finding her, and I'm afraid we're now looking for a dead little girl. I've scheduled an appointment for us to interview Doctor Harding, a specialist who works in California. The girl's New York DCF psychologist has been reported missing, which is a troubling coincidence. Doctor Harding has the case file now."

Agent Crawford slapped her palm against the elevator wall. "I'll bet my rookie career that Palmer is high on the food chain in the Pied Piper organization or one of his brokers who supply him with children."

"If you can prove that I'll recommend you for a promotion," Todd smirked. "Now, calm down and listen. I'm not sure why the girl's file is with a California doctor. All I know is that Michelle's New York psychologist brought him in a few months ago for a second opinion. It's sketchy, but it appears that Dr. Williams disobeyed Palmer's orders when he called in Dr. Harding, and now he's missing. I did a little digging, and Harding and Palmer have been at each other's throats for a long time ever since Ashley Seymour went missing after a suspicious car accident that killed one of our most decorated agents, Jack Seymour."

Agent Crawford was reviewing Harding's file, looking confused. "It says here that Harding is Special Agent Edward Seymour's adoptive father. Should we tell him we're going to interview his father?"

"We'll tell him once we're done. We don't need another agent homing in on our case," Ellenberg said, lost in thought.

Meredith raised her eyebrows. "It's your call. Now, tell me why Palmer would object to a second opinion?" asked Crawford.

It seems Palmer and Harding dislike each other. Harding's a crusader. Nearly twenty years ago, he worked closely with Agent Seymour's father. The grudge between Palmer and the doctor has a long history," Ellenburg admitted.

"I'm surprised Harding's still alive," Meredith said mockingly.

"All I know is that his notes in the Arnold file contradict Palmer's opinion of Michelle's parents."

"I'd like to nail that bitch's ass to the wall," Meredith told him. "Let's get the fuck out of here. I have a bad feeling about all of this. I hope I'm wrong."

Chapter 25

The aluminum air ducts had become unbearably cold. Michelle could not control her shivering and feared that the sound her trembling body was making would alert her abductors. She had no watch or sense of distance, but she estimated she had been traveling for at least an hour. It felt as long as her favorite TV show, Smallville. She scolded herself for getting distracted while she was escaping. She wished Superboy would come and save her.

As she crawled like a caterpillar, she froze when she heard voices. She held her breath and curled into a tiny ball, arms hugging her thin legs to her chest. Once the voices disappeared, she resumed her crawl.

Slithering like a snake for another fifty yards, she heard loud arguing through a small ventilation grate. She recognized one of the voices as belonging to Doctor Kane, but the other two were unfamiliar.

She carefully positioned her eyes against the small wings of the vent opening and noticed a familiar face. It was the distinguished man, in a dark blue suit, from the first ship she was imprisoned on. The man spoke in English with a foreign accent. She tried to understand what they were saying, but it was difficult as she tried to control her shaking.

Doctor Kane had addressed the man in the suit as Piper, which seemed like a strange name for a man. Michelle kept staring as the men argued. The doctor called the other distinguished-looking man "Senator." He had blonde hair and the bluest eyes she had ever seen. He appeared old to her, with his midsection spilling over his belt.

Michelle heard the man, Piper, speaking angrily to Doctor Kane. From the expressions on the doctor and the man called "Senator," she could tell that Piper scared them.

Michelle focused on the man called Piper and what he was saying. *"Everything will end in three months, maybe less, unless you two piss me off. No mistakes...no extensions. Our business will end on my schedule,"* Piper demanded, waving his index finger at both men.

The entire room fell silent at Piper's words. When the phone rang on Kane's desk, it broke the tension in the room. Kane shrugged and answered his phone, annoyed. "Yes?" he barked. "Palmer, why the fuck are you calling me now? What? That's bullshit," he yelled back into the mouthpiece.

Michelle gasped, her cold hand covering her mouth. *"What does Ms. Palmer have to do with Doctor Kane?"* she thought.

She noticed that Piper had leaned forward and taken the phone from the doctor, pushing back the hair that covered a deformed ear. He put the phone on speaker. "Palmer, you've got Kane pissing in his pants. What did you tell him?"

Palmer stammered, trying to speak. "The FBI has unleashed two aggressive agents on me. Senator Jarvis was supposed to help, but they're now interviewing Doctor Harding about Michelle Arnold. If she's not dead now, she should be. I'm scared that messing with the FBI wasn't such a good idea," she said nervously.

Michelle was shocked by what she was hearing from Ms. Palmer. The anger on the distinguished man's face frightened her.

Piper held the phone away from his mouth, uninterested in Palmer's paranoia. "Get a fucking grip. Cover your ass. Kill those FBI Agents and let Deputy Director Evans know I did it," he demanded. "Now get some balls and leave me alone," he paused, taking in a deep breath. "Don't force me to deal with you, too," he said menacingly.

Michelle could hear Sally breathing heavily. Her voice sounded as if she had sand in her mouth. "My house is in order. I just…"

Piper interrupted him again. "There, then, you have nothing to worry about. I have good news for you. I've told Kane and Senator Jarvis that my business relationship with all of you will end in three months, if not sooner. You should have my final order ready within the next week. Then you'll be back to doing your foster care shell game." He tossed the phone back to Kane and leaned back in his chair.

Michelle took one last look at the three men, doing her best to imprint their faces in her exhausted mind. She knew she needed to escape and started slithering again. *"The FBI is looking for me?"* she thought. *"Maybe Uncle Elliot is on my trail,"* she muttered in a low whisper.

Michelle could not stop thinking of her uncle and the FBI coming to rescue her. She was excited. *"Uncle Elliot will show me a photo disarray. I think that's what he calls it. He'll be so proud of me. Now, get a grip, girl; you're still stuck in a cold duct."*

Her confidence quickly vanished as she realized she still had to escape from her cement prison on her own. Crawling slowly, she began imprinting the three men into her tired brain.

Doctor Kane would be easy. The Senator would also be easy. He was missing a pinky finger. The man called Piper had a deformed left ear hidden beneath his long hair. It looked like someone had snipped the top of his ear with scissors. Without hesitation, she quickened her pace.

The direction she was heading seemed to get colder and colder. She was beginning to feel sleepy. Her hands and feet felt very numb. She imagined herself being frozen and dying in intense pain. "Stay awake, you ninny, or you'll die."

Any normal nine-year-old would have given up, but not Michelle. She was a bulldog. Her mother once told her father how she wouldn't give up on anything she did at that moment; her mother's words now seemed a million light-years away.

She was feeling drowsy as her mind wandered to warm memories of the life she shared with her parents. She rubbed her hands together and then massaged her exposed feet to get her cold blood flowing.

She knew she could not fall asleep. She knew the consequences all too well: instant death. Michelle sucked in a deep breath; the cold air made her lungs ache and her throat burn. She wanted to disappear, to transport herself back to the warm, safe arms of her parents, but that was just a wish. Her instincts took over. She began to recite the "Lord's Prayer" like her father told her to do when she felt lost and abandoned.

"You might be alone at times and scared, but you can call on GOD to help you find a way to survive whatever bad things are happening to you," he said while cradling her in his arms. She covered her mouth with her hand, stifling a cry for her mother.

At that moment, God had given her strength, and she continued her perilous crawl toward an unknown destination. Michelle cried silently as she glided through the dark metal tunnel; crying silently was something she had learned during her time in unloving foster homes.

Then she saw it, a faint light. Or was it the bright light she had heard people with near-death experiences describe? Her exhausted mind kept tormenting every thought she had.

She pressed on, hoping she was nearing the end of the air duct. If not, she knew her remaining energy would be depleted, and her heroic escape would ultimately end in tragedy.

She was forcing herself to be strong and survive. She kept making frequent stops, blowing her warm breath, the only heat remaining inside her frail body, onto her hands and doing the same for her feet.

She remembered her father saying that this would only work for a short time. Once her body temperature dropped, the rest of her would gradually become stiff, and she would start to feel sleepy. If that were to happen, he had told her, she would die like a frozen Popsicle.

She crawled faster and faster like a frightened caterpillar, her father's words swirling in her mind. Finally, after being in the dark for what felt like an eternity, she had reached the end of her cold tunnel.

She could see rays of light streaming from what appeared to be another grate in the air duct. She hoped it was similar to the one in the bathroom. If not, she would be trapped, lost in a tomb where her parents or Uncle Elliott would never be able to find her.

At that moment, she wished her childish imagination would leave her alone and let her be the brave adult she wanted to be. Unfortunately, her wishes went unfulfilled, as fear and panic overwhelmed her body and mind, destroying what little resolve she had left.

Michelle had finally reached the end of the air duct and the grating dead end, a pun she did not find funny. Uncertain whether the wicked nurse dressed in white had realized she was missing. She cautiously peeked through the grill, hoping it would be safe to exit her private tunnel that had started an eternity ago.

Chapter 26

Michelle sat at the edge of the grate, shivering and unable to control her small body any longer. She grabbed the handle and was about to open the grill when she heard two men talking. She froze, trying to stifle the noise her cold body made.

The two men looked up, their eyes searching the room. One of them got up and began inspecting the ceiling, pulling out his flashlight and panning the area around the vent grate.

Michelle saw the beam coming closer and tried to back away from the opening, hoping the men wouldn't hear her. It was hard because her arms felt numb and her body wouldn't move as she wanted. She closed her eyes and prayed as the bright light shined through the slats, slicing the beam like it had gone through a deli meat slicer.

She heard the other man call his partner to come over and check things out. He spoke in a language she recognized from the van.

"Hans, do you see something up there? Look, right by the opening to the air vent."

She watched his partner get up from the table, reluctant to leave the large bowl of hot, steaming soup and the hefty loaf of bread he had been enjoying. She held her breath. She knew it was over. Her heroic escape was finished. She fought to hold back her tears.

The stocky, muscular man wearing a guard uniform looked up, his face agitated. "You're imagining things," he said as he squinted, trying to focus.

He was startled when the emergency alarm went off, a piercing, undulating whine filling the room and echoing inside the metal tunnel. He pushed his partner aside, grabbed his Uzi and parka, and ran out into the hallway. He called out to Fritz, who was still holding his flashlight at the grill. "Stop your foolishness and let's get going. It's probably a rat looking for food."

Fritz reluctantly followed orders, craning his neck and keeping his eyes fixed on the grill as he ran out the door. "That must have been the biggest rat I've seen so far," he shouted at Hans as they jogged to their command station.

Michelle let out a deep sigh and quickly opened the grate. It swung down with a loud crash. Struggling with her aching, frozen hands and arms, she dangled helplessly, trying her best to hold onto the edge of the air duct. She only had three feet to jump. Usually, such a task would have been easy for her, but when she landed, her numb feet and legs hit the cement floor hard, sending a jolt of pain through her brittle, cold feet. They felt as if they had shattered. The sharp pain radiated through her body as her unsteady, stiff form struck the concrete floor, unable to bend to absorb the impact. A thousand needle pricks shot through her feet and legs.

Michelle had entered a kind of dressing room for skiers. Much to her surprise, there was a heater and enough ski clothing and skis to outfit at least twenty large men. After warming up her hands and feet, she finished off the guard's lunch and felt energy gradually flowing through her body.

The undulating siren had stopped, which only meant they were coming to get her. She nervously scanned the room for ski clothing that would fit her. She stood four feet five inches tall—tall for her age, but way too short for the clothing she was searching through.

As she continued searching for a suitable solution, the last ski outfit turned out to be her best option. It was a woman's outfit. She slipped on some long johns to help insulate her body from the cold.

Even though the clothing was too big, she made the best of the situation. She layered her tired, bruised body with three different types of clothing: a thermal top and bottom, a nylon T-shirt, a thick, itchy sweater, large ski bib overalls, and a white hooded parka. It had been days since she had felt that warm.

Her next obstacle was the woman's ski boots. They were too big for her, and she knew that wearing oversized boots would make skiing very difficult.

She found a cardboard box filled with thick socks. She put three pairs on her feet. Then, she stuffed more socks into the toe of her boots. It took four pairs to make her feel somewhat secure on her feet, allowing her to maneuver her skis.

Michelle grabbed the smallest pair of skis and the shortest poles she could find. She found a red backpack filled with survival gear. Struggling to lift the heavy backpack, she almost fell backward.

She pretended it was as heavy as her school backpack, lifting it onto one shoulder and slipping her padded arm through the other strap.

First, she considered not taking it. She knew that would be foolish. She understood she might not reach safety before nightfall. The backpack had to come with her. Her father's words echoed loudly in her mind: "BE PREPARED!".

She discovered a large automatic rifle with a thick shoulder strap. Her father had taught her to shoot while skiing, but it was with a lightweight Remington 22. This rifle was much larger and heavier. She found extra magazines of ammunition and packed them into her backpack.

"Be prepared, be prepared," she said aloud, trying to motivate herself to move forward and stay brave.

She hobbled toward a double door that led outside. She looked more like a child dressed up pretending to be an adult, playing a make-believe game. But this was no game.

The ski parka and bib she wore wouldn't seal properly, exposing her to the cold mountain air the moment she stepped outside. Cold would be her biggest problem, but what was the alternative? She argued with herself.

Her small body had started to sweat as she dragged her weak legs, struggling with the weight she was carrying. Before pushing against the two double doors leading outside, she braced herself. She took a deep, brave breath and then pushed the door with all her might.

Michelle knew this wasn't make-believe and pushed down on the bar that opened the door. She had heard about it enough times from her father and mother that she might only be nine, but she acted like she was thirty.

At that moment, she wished she were older; she really wished she could be back in Riverside Park playing.

It took less than a second for the alarms to screech again, and a series of red blinking lights started flashing all around her. The hair on the back of her neck stood up, frozen like porcupine needles. Her heart raced uncontrollably. The loud pounding in her chest was drowned out by the piercing, undulating noise that had alerted everyone she was outside.

There was no turning back. Michelle dropped her skis and snapped each boot into the bindings. She struggled to push herself down the slope. She needed momentum and gravity to get her safely to the bottom, if there was any. She was too heavy to glide on her skis and was slowly sinking into the soft snow. "Lift your legs and walk," she shouted to herself. "You've made it this far, don't give up now." Her pep talk must have worked, as her tired, weak legs pushed her forward.

She had no idea where she was or where she was headed, except downward. The cold, icy air ripped through her ski gear, finding every opening to seep in and chill her small body. Her clothing stretched as if someone had inflated a plastic doll.

She pulled down her woolen ski mask, which was way too big for her small head. Despite this, it did its job and kept her face warm. It wouldn't stay in one place and shifted, covering her eyes.

It didn't matter as sirens blared in her ears. She thrust her poles into the snow, grunting as she tried to build momentum. She struggled desperately to get away from the building. She scanned the area, and her heart sank. A dense forest of trees had her cornered. She knew she had escaped one dangerous situation and was now heading into another.

The beginning of her ski run was nothing like the ones her father had taken her on. She kept glancing around, adjusting her loose ski mask. There it was, only a hundred yards away. A narrow trail into the woods. She prayed it would lead her down the mountain.

After just a few minutes, exhaustion and the freezing cold took over her. Her legs stiffened again, and her thin arms throbbed from the icy air. She looked over her shoulder. She had only traveled ten yards. She pressed her poles into the snow, pushing harder, and finally started to glide.

Her momentum picked up when she heard gunshots. Bullets hit the snow beside her. Her adrenaline surged. Her arms moved like tiny pistons, up and down, her poles pounding into the snow. She could now see the trail, her escape route. She prayed it would lead her to safety.

It was nearly impossible for her to maneuver her skis with her oversized boots. She thought tight, form-fitting ski boots would have been better and told herself, "Beggars can't be choosers."

She was out of options as she rushed down the hillside like a bullet, moving in quick bursts while venturing deeper into the woods. Michelle pushed through the first cluster of trees, each branch trying to grab at her. Another gunshot shattered a branch, sending a large clump of snow crashing onto her head. She tried to duck down but couldn't, as her thighs were already burning, causing her pain she had never felt before.

Everything she wore made it difficult to stay balanced and find her center of gravity, which she desperately needed to outrun her pursuers. She had started moving at an uncontrollable speed, faster than she had ever skied before with her father. Although she was confident in her skiing skills, the steep slopes and the slalom course of trees she faced put her in an unfamiliar situation. She hoped her thin thighs would stay strong and not give out from the fatigue she was already experiencing.

Her mind drifted back to the time she had been skiing with her father in the Tahoe area of Nevada, when they accidentally found themselves on a diamond slope that scared her to death.

"Michelle, let's pretend this is an emergency. We both need to stay alert and aware of our surroundings," her father told her.

At that moment, she could tell her father was scared and trying to hide it from her. "Michelle, sweetie, we can do this together if we keep our wits about us," her father said. "As the slope gets steeper, your fear might make you panic and lean forward, but don't do that. When you feel the gravity of the hill pulling you forward, sit back as far as you can, putting all your weight on the back of your skis.

She remembered her fall that day and how painful it had been. However, with her father's encouragement, she was back up and confidently moving down the steep slope, even though there were no trees in her way that day.

She tried to build that confidence in her mind as more trees whizzed past her. She had taken a watch from the security room and realized she had only been outside for ten minutes. "I'll never make it at this rate. I'll fall down and never get up, frozen like an ice cube," she scolded herself. Struggling to move between the trees, the rocky terrain had become a tough obstacle course even for the most experienced skier.

Without hesitating, she pressed on. The freezing air stiffened her limbs, and the loose-fitting ski mask slipped down, covering her eyes and blinding her. Now in a frantic panic, she struggled with impaired sight and felt the soft branches of the trees scrape against her parka. Each branch felt like a thousand hands reaching out to catch her, to hold her until the patrol caught up.

She shook her head to adjust the loose ski mask, but it barely helped. Now she could see out of only one eye as her speed continued to increase. A branch almost knocked her off her skis, but she squatted down and stayed balanced.

Her speed kept increasing, and she was starting to lose control. Her exhausted, cold body struggled to hold on. As the ski mask covered her eyes, she hit a large rock sticking out of the soft, powdery snow. She felt her right ski catch as it hit the obstacle hard, spinning her around like a top.

She fell hard, tumbling down the slope like a rag doll, her body sliding uncontrollably before suddenly stopping and slamming into a tree. Her skis snapped off as intended and bounced further down the slope, far from where she lay bruised and gasping for breath.

Michelle started crying, her tears freezing on her cheeks, just like the rest of her body. "I'll never do this," she sobbed. Then she heard the voices. The woods acted as an echo chamber. She could hear the guards coming down the slope, their angry shouts growing louder and louder. She looked up at the well-defined trail she had left in her wake on the freshly packed snow. Fudge, I've led them to me.

She realized then that if she wanted to win and survive, she had to get up, find her skis, and race down the hill like a cannonball. The wind had started to pick up, making the chill even worse. As she struggled to grab her skis, she knew she only had about an hour before nightfall.

She scanned the area and saw a small cave about a hundred yards to her right. To her, it felt like miles. Her body was stiff, her mind wanted to sleep, and the voices of the guards were getting closer.

She slid down the hill and grabbed her skis, which now felt incredibly heavy. Then she noticed a cliff to her left. She had seen a similar scene in a movie once. She wasn't sure how much time or energy she had left before the security teams would find her, but she had to try; she wanted to survive.

She put her skis back on and skied toward the edge. She could barely use her tired legs to stop her exhausted body, but she managed to do so, sliding onto her side and stopping just before she fell to her death.

Michelle peered over the edge. The drop seemed endless. Using her skis, she began knocking off the snow that was lightly packed on the edge, hoping the guards would believe she had gone over.

She took off her skis and started walking along a snowless path. To her left, she noticed what looked like another cave. She glanced over her shoulder, feeling relieved that she hadn't left any footprints.

It was a small yet sufficient cave. Michelle felt happy that her luck was still with her. Her temporary shelter seemed deep enough to shield her from the strong winds that had started to blow. The afternoon sun had fallen behind the mountain, casting shadows over the forest.

She collected some fallen pine branches and built a door to cover the cave's opening. She pulled a solar blanket from her backpack and wrapped it around her cold, exhausted body. It amazed her how something so thin could warm her so quickly.

Her ears perked up when she heard men shouting in a foreign language. She prayed she had tricked them as she ate a bar of dehydrated food she found inside the backpack and washed it down with a bottle of icy water. She knew she had to hydrate, one of the many lessons her father had drilled into her during their survival training.

* * * * *

As the sirens kept pulsating across the mountain-top hospital, Dr. Thomas Kane had been shouting at his staff for nearly fifteen minutes. His face was flushed, and his eyes burned with intensity. He was striking the woman who had let Michelle go to the bathroom unattended.

"You idiot," he yelled as he punched her face. "How could you let a nine-year-old escape?" He looked at the rest of his security team. "She needs to be stopped before she reaches the town, or we're all going to suffer for our sins. I don't want her alive. Bring her back dead, and we'll feed her to the dogs." Kane watched as his security guards scrambled out the door and back to the ski room.

Fritz looked at Hans, his face twisted with disgust. "She was in the air duct. I was right. I want first crack at her." They sprinted and were the first to reach the security room.

They were almost dressed when the rest of the patrol entered. Without a word, they were out the door, their Uzis strapped to their backs.

An hour later, Kane listened as his men confirmed the girl had skied off the edge of the mountain and was dead.

"Did you find a body?" he asked skeptically. "Find the girl's body and I'll feel a lot better."

Fritz was the first to speak. "Sir, with all the bears and wolves out there, she might already be inside their stomachs." Fritz knew Kane was not buying his lazy excuse. "We'll leave first thing in the morning with the helicopter and search for her body."

"Just don't fuck up. I don't want you back here until you have something," Kane frantically said. "I don't want to have to punish any of you for this screw-up."

* * * * *

Dr. Kane knew he had to call Piper and explain how a nine-year-old girl could have escaped from his fortress. "Sir, we have a problem. Michelle Arnold has escaped."

"How the hell could a small nine-year-old girl escape?" Piper shouted.

"One of my nurses allowed the girl to go to the toilet unattended. She was small enough to climb up in the air duct that led to our security room. From there, she took skis, a survival backpack, and a woman's warm ski clothing," Kane nervously told him.

"I'm not interested in the fucking details," Piper cursed. "You'd better find Michelle Arnold. I remember her. She knows what I look like. I cannot afford to be exposed before I retire. After that, it won't matter," he scowled.

"You need to make sure she dies on your mountain, or you'll die in her place," he threatened.

Kane dialed Sally Palmer, blaming her for his troubles. She had hung up, shaken from the tongue-lashing Doctor Kane had given her. She looked at her brother-in-law, Earl Mathews, with a confused expression on her face. "The Arnold girl has escaped from Kane's laboratory. We've got a problem," she said. "Her parents have to have an accident."

Chapter 27

A loud siren jolted Agent Seymour awake, pulling him out of the nightmare that had haunted him for seventeen years. Now, he was caught in another frightening dream. He could feel the breathing tube inside his mouth. He blinked rapidly, trying to focus and orient himself. Doctors and nurses watched closely as machines hummed and beeped around his battered body.

Then everything flooded back in a terrifying rush. The semi-truck, his partner's face, the bullets tearing through his body, and the Pied Piper calling out to him. It was now swirling chaotically inside his mind. He was devastated with guilt that clenched his heart over his partner's death.

He tried to speak, but the respirator tube made him gag. Deputy Director Robert Evans stepped between the doctors and nurses. He tried to smile, but the pain of the past few days was etched on his face. Seeing his agent helpless on the hospital bed was more than he could bear. He was reliving the death of Eddie's father, Jack Seymour, once again.

"You're one lucky son of a bitch," he said, his voice cracking. "Jamison didn't make it," he told him.

Seymour nodded.

One of the doctors moved Evans aside and checked his patient's oxygen levels. He reviewed the latest blood workup. "We can remove the tube now. He's been breathing on his own long enough."

A pretty nurse with bright red hair and a New York accent spoke next. "Mr. Cummings, when I count to three, I want you to cough as hard as you can. That's when I will pull the tube out," she told him. "It will hurt. Your body hasn't fully healed from the gunshot wounds." Before Seymour would signal her to wait, she started counting.

"Ready. One... two... three." Before he could cough, she was yanking on the tube. He felt like he was being turned inside out.

Uncontrollable gagging continued as Agent Seymour struggled to catch his breath. His throat felt raw, as if a blowtorch had been inserted into his windpipe. He tried to speak, but all that came out was a raspy, gurgling mixture of profanity. It took only seconds before his body stopped heaving.

In a strained whisper, he spoke, his eyes looking for Evans. "How long have I been here?"

"Thirteen days," Evans shrugged. "The doctors had given you up for dead. I knew you would have a say in the matter. You never listened to anyone before, and I didn't think you'd start even in your condition."

He looked at Evans, puzzled. "Mister Cummings?" Eddie struggled to say.

Evan shook his head. He put his finger to his lips, signaling his agent to stop talking. He looked around at the nurses and the doctor and asked them to leave the room.

"You're here under a different name. I wasn't sure who I could trust. The Pied Piper is now murdering FBI agents without a care in the world. I think it's best if he believes you're dead for the time being," Evans informed him.

"Do you have any idea who our mole could be?" Eddie asked.

"Not at this time. I have my suspicions."

"Who's on top of your list?"

"I'd rather not say at this time. Someone at the FBI leaked your position to the Pied Piper," Evans responded. "Shit, he knew exactly what our plans were that night."

Eddie was deep in thought. "I need to get out of here. If we have a spy then I am not safe here," Eddie demanded. "I need to let my father know I am okay."

Evans shook his head. "I haven't told your father yet. It's better this way if everyone believes your dead. I'll be putting you in a safe house no one at the Bureau knows about. I'm not going to let another Seymour die at this monster's hands. I need you alive if we're going to arrest that asshole."

Seymour eyes grew wide as the ambush flashed in his head. He bit his lip hard while drawing blood. "I'll bet my life that it was the Pied Piper. I heard him. I'll never forget that voice," Eddie told Evans. "He taunted me right before he tried to kill me. He said my sister Ashley's alive."

Evans couldn't hide his shock. "His arrogance will bring him down. He's nuts if he thinks he's better than us. I've got to get the President on board. We need to use every resource we have to get this motherfucker."

Eddie's frustration grew at Evan's words. "We're stretched so thin. The FBI's only priority is the President's war on terrorism. We don't have the manpower or resources to look for him. I hate to say this, but he knows it and is laughing at us."

Evans sucked in a deep breath. "You may be right. First, I need you to get well. We're running out of time. I believe more than ever that the Pied Piper is closing down his trafficking business. We may only have a few months, if that, to find him or he'll be long gone, becoming another cold case for the FBI to file away."

"I need to get out of here. I won't let that bastard win again."

"You can't leave the hospital. Not until the doctors clear you. Once I get the okay, I'll have you in my safe house convalescing. I'm gathering a few agents I trust. The rules don't seem to apply here. Your father tried to warn me many years ago that sometimes following the rules doesn't work well with the bad guys. I now realize this a few years too late," Evans confessed.

"Harding said what?" Seymour asked, his face expressing confusion.

"No. Your biological father, Jack. If you're on board with my plan, we'll become the judge, jury, and executioner. No more rules or politics. This guy is a dead man walking," Evans said, his face flushed with rage.

Eddie seemed puzzled. "You'll risk your career or possibly federal prison to kill the Pied Piper? I, too, want to see him dead and lying at my feet, but not if it means being locked up."

"I want this guy as much as you do. Blanchard and his partner, Elliot Burns, are on board and will be part of our team. You know Ted? You'll like Elliott. The Pied Piper also took Burns' niece a week ago."

Chapter 28

Austrian Forest

Michelle Arnold didn't get much restful sleep. The sounds of nocturnal creatures roaming the woods in search of food kept her on edge, afraid to sleep, her rifle tightly clenched in her hands. When she finally dozed off, she dreamed about her home and her parents.

Her dream was disturbing; the memory seemed too real. She was sitting in her living room, listening to Sally Palmer speaking harshly to her parents.

"Until you can prove to me that both of you are clean and sober, adhering to the court order, Michelle is going to stay in foster care. I want her packed and ready to go by 5:00 P.M. tomorrow. Mess this up and you'll never get your daughter back," Palmer scolded.

Now, huddled inside her cave, she was convinced that Sally Palmer was linked to the rest of the evil men who were after her. Michelle's body started to shake inside the damp, cold cave. She was not actually cold. It was the memories of being dragged from her bed and thrown into a dirty, roach-infested room. Palmer said it was her new home for a while.

The sound of a twig snapping woke her from her dream, alerting her that she was in danger of being caught or attacked by a bear. Michelle tried to wipe the tears from her eyes. She was crying quietly, trying to stay calm and not be scared. But she was only ten years old and was starting to lose control.

Michelle's tough shell was cracking. She was losing hope of ever reaching the bottom of the mountain. She tormented herself with wild images of how Dr. Kane controlled the entire mountain, even the imaginary town she hoped to find. However, the thought of getting home to her parents kept her from giving in to her fears. She stood, stretching her stiff limbs and bumping her head on the jagged ceiling of the cave. She was determined to survive another day. Taking a cold morning breath cleared her mind. She had a mission, and nothing was going to stop her, she hoped.

She forced herself to gather all her trash and fold her blanket neatly, returning everything she had taken out last night into her backpack. A loud noise echoed through the forest as she peeked out of her shelter. It was a large black helicopter with a man standing on its landing rail. He was strapped to the outside of the hull, using binoculars to scan the area near the cliff.

"Oh, poop," she said, terrified. "If they now have a helicopter, they'll be able to see me skiing down the mountain." She began to sob uncontrollably. The brave little girl who escaped yesterday had transformed back into a frightened little ten-year-old girl.

Then, as if God had answered her prayers, the helicopter descended the side of the cliff where she had faked her death. She quickly slipped into her boots and pushed them back into the bindings on her skis. Her toes and shins still ached from the bruising they suffered yesterday from her oversized ski boots.

The air felt much warmer than yesterday. The wind had turned into a gentle breeze. Small icicles covered the pine trees, having formed overnight in the damp conditions. It was still very cold, but the sun's rays filtering through the trees provided some warmth. She knew that out in the open, the sun reflecting off the snow would help warm her body, aiding her escape.

She remembered from her father's survival training that a mountain's weather can change suddenly. She knew she had to move quickly if she wanted a chance to get down the mountain safely. This was her last hope. She prayed her white parka and white bib overalls would blend with the snow, providing enough camouflage to avoid detection. Then, she looked at her red backpack. "I'm going to be a little red dot traversing down the mountain," she whined.

She thought about leaving the backpack behind, but that seemed silly. "Be prepared," she scolded herself. Her small body didn't feel as exhausted as the day before, but she could still sense the pain from the bruises she got during her escape. She was able to handle the skis more easily and chose a spot at the bottom of the hill to aim for. "Go for a target," she told herself.

She pushed off, racing down the hill with the sun on her face. She knew she was going east. She burst into a clearing from the forest, amazed at the bright blue sky that spread out before her. It was the most beautiful sight she had ever seen.

Her amazement was overshadowed by the horrible glare that blinded her eyes. She had forgotten to get goggles. She looked at her watch. It was eight minutes past seven. She was happily traversing down the slope toward the bottom, optimistic that she would find help.

* * * * *

Fritz had the helicopter circle the area where he believed Michelle's body would logically be, but there was nothing rational about his little girl, he thought.

There was a clearing inside the small canyon. He ordered the helicopter to descend. He had five of his best men with him, and they began their search. There was no sign of her body. Could she have survived the fall? He shook his head. That's impossible. It's a thousand-foot drop.

He pressed his fingers to his temples, pressing hard, hoping a reasonable answer would come. "Let's search the woods, no more than a five-hundred-foot radius from the point where she allegedly went off this damn mountain," he shouted, his face twisted with anger. He was furious that a child could be so elusive. He wiped the spittle from his lips as he barked out his orders.

After another hour of trying to locate the girl's body, the search ended. They had no evidence to give Dr. Kane.

Hans looked at his partner. "Maybe she fooled us and was up on top this whole time, hiding. She seems to know how to ski. Someone may have taught her how to survive in the wilderness, too?"

Fritz grunted. He was pissed. "Let's head back to the top and search the area."

Fritz and Hans had brought their skis. They were part of the Austrian Olympic ski team in ninety-six. They both knew no child could out ski them. They quickly located the cave Michelle used for shelter and found her tracks and discarded rations.

"Smart girl," Fritz said with a hint of admiration.

It wasn't easy to estimate how much of a lead she had on them, but Han realized she was heading toward the town of Turin. "Let's assume she has at least an hour lead on us. If she's that good a skier, she should be about fifty-five minutes from the bottom."

Fritz signaled the helicopter to lift off. "She is only ten fucking years old. She's going to need to rest."

Hans, accompanied by another guard, both armed with sniper rifles, headed down the slope following the trail Michelle's skis left behind.

Chapter 29

Michelle had been out in the open, easily crossing the mountain and steadily heading toward a small town she had spotted twenty minutes earlier. The sun's glare reflected into her exposed eyes, gradually blinding her vision.

She tried to head east again, but the mountain had too many trails except the one she needed, which was straight down the steep slope. After skiing for another fifteen minutes, she saw what looked like ski lifts. She hoped the ski patrol was there to help her.

Michelle knew this was her last-ditch effort to get rescued. It all felt like make-believe to her tired body as she glided through the soft, deep, white powder. Her thighs started cramping. Her shins were raw from the constant rubbing against the loose boots.

She wanted to rest. She needed to, but something inside her told her to keep going at all costs. She paused for a second, holding her breath as she listened to the distant putt, putt, putt that kept growing louder. "The helicopter," she cried out.

She grabbed her backpack's binoculars and scanned the white hillside. Her eyes ached, but she could see two tiny objects following her trail coming into view. They grew larger and moved at a remarkable speed.

"They're coming," she stammered, her voice dry and raspy. She still had some distance to go before reaching the safety of the upper ski lodge.

She took one last look at the quickly approaching skiers and needed to lighten her load, or they would overtake her.

She dropped her backpack and pushed her poles into the soft snow, arching her back and turning 180 degrees. She tucked her poles under her armpits, leaned forward, and stayed as low as possible. She sped down the slope like a bullet toward safety.

She was like a human missile as the cold wind hit her face, feeling like sharp pins. She pushed herself to her maximum limits. The vibration on her skis was making it difficult to keep her balance. Her thin little thighs kept aching, ready to cramp up. Her shoulders were stiff from all the pumping.

Her ankles hurt, and she could hardly put any pressure on her shins. They were badly bruised from hitting the hard, loose-fitting lining of her boots. Every movement caused sharp pain to shoot up her legs.

She used what little energy she had left and pushed through the agonizing soreness that radiated through her body. She began singing songs in her head to distract herself from the overwhelming fear she was feeling. Then she heard a sound she had hoped she would never hear again. The helicopter was bearing down on her and was almost upon her when it made a sharp turn, kicking up the snow around her and creating a blinding snowstorm.

As the chopper moved away, the storm calmed, and she was able to get her bearings and continue toward the ski lift chairs and the skier's hut that now felt within her reach. She tucked her poles under her arms and bent her knees with her back parallel to her skis. She was heading down the hill, her skis close together, almost as if they were part of her body.

This was the fastest she had ever skied before. She hoped she wouldn't tumble, hit an object, or break a leg. Worse, she was afraid a ski might get caught in the snow, and she'd lose it. Her heart pounded so loudly it drowned out the chopper above her.

The helicopter followed her, and the men on board were amazed at how well a ten-year-old could ski. They were very impressed and began to cheer her on.

The pilot radioed Fritz and told him she was nearly at the top ski lodge. "The only way to stop her was to shoot her now, or it would be too late," the pilot told him.

Fritz had wanted to be the one to get the kill. Disappointed, he gave the order. "Kill the little bitch and bring the body up to me immediately."

The pilot turned to the men, still excited from watching the spectacular skier. His words sent a shiver down their spines.

"Shoot her now," he shouted. "She must not make it to the ski lodge!" he ordered.

Only one man had the courage to lift his rifle while the others watched. He adjusted his scope and aimed at Michelle, trying to get the tiny white object in his crosshairs as a gust of wind rocked the helicopter.

The chopper wasn't very steady, but he adjusted and pulled the trigger. The first bullet hit the snow just in front of his target. He shouted to the pilot to keep it steady.

He slowly squeezed off another shot and watched his young prey fall, rolling a few yards like a large snowball. He fired two more rounds into her tiny body as she lay still, watching the snow around her turn red.

The chopper landed fifty yards from the body on the sparse, bare ground of the snow-covered mountain. Two men jumped out, sinking deep into the soft, powdery snow. They heard at least two dogs barking, then saw, about 300 meters below them, three ski patrol search-and-rescue teams on snowmobiles. Their red vests with white crosses kept getting closer.

The two men panicked and crawled out of the deep snow back onto the helicopter. "What should we do?" the pilot said into his microphone. "Fritz, are you reading me?"

He and Hans looked confused. "Lift off and take a picture of her dead body. I'll deal with Kane with what we have."

* * * * *

The rescue teams hurried to what they thought was a small bear shot by poachers. To their shock and grief, it was a young girl with three gunshot wounds. One of the team members removed his glove and checked for a pulse.

"Get a Medi-Vac helicopter up here STAT. We have a young girl, about ten years old, her vitals are weak, and she's losing a lot of blood." One of the men had started to bury Michelle in the snow.

"What are you doing?" shouted an alarmed voice.

We need to keep her body temperature low. It will slow down the bleeding and her heart. It's her only chance to survive.

Michelle's eyes fluttered open. Before she blacked out, she whispered to one of the men, "Top…mountain…bad man…hurting many children."

Then she fell silent. Her pulse weakened, and the rescue team leader knew she wouldn't survive unless they got her to the hospital right away.

* * * * *

Fritz and the guard who shot the girl stood at attention in front of Doctor Kane's desk. The crazed doctor was examining pictures of Michelle in a fetal position, surrounded by crimson snow.

"I'm not happy. I wanted her body back here. Did she still have on her hospital gown?" the doctor barked.

Fritz looked puzzled by the question and shrugged. "I'll make inquiries in town tomorrow. Can we tell them that she was mentally disturbed and ran away? The mayor is your friend and supports the work you're doing with all these troubled children."

Kane's eyes were wide with rage. "I need her body. She's got Piper's wristband. It contains too much information that could expose all of us. If she's alive and able to talk… well, I'm not going to think about that. Just find her and bring her body back to me."

Dr. Kane had a few men on his payroll in the village. They worked within the local police department. If the girl had survived by some miracle, they would finish what his men could not.

Chapter 30

Deputy Director Robert Evans had been leading the Violent Crimes/Major Offenders Squad, also known as the Child Missing Persons Department, in Norfolk, Virginia, for the past ten years. He used to love his job. He was under great pressure from President Webster to solve the nationwide series of abductions. Witnessing the brutality the Pied Piper was inflicting on his agents, he was seriously contemplating early retirement. He thought that perhaps if he stepped away, the Pied Piper might stop targeting his agents.

Instead of being able to protect these children, it had become a political pawn in the West Wing and Congress as everyone prepared for the upcoming Presidential election. Terrorism was the top priority on President Webster's agenda, especially since he seemed to be doing a great job fighting it—at least from the media's perspective—and that was all that mattered to him and his poll numbers.

President Webster's staff put up firewalls that would damage his popularity. Each failure by the FBI had started to weaken the president's approval ratings.

Evans needed a private talk with the President. He believed Webster was a fair and moral man. If he knew the truth about how Senator Jarvis and his political appointee, Sally Palmer, had manipulated the Federal Foster Care agency, heads would roll.

Evan's boss, Director Jenkins, sometimes seemed supportive of his task force. But when it truly mattered, Jenkins would step back and allow Senator Jarvis and Sally Palmer to have their way.

A handful of influential elected officials were supporting the Pied Piper while he was killing American citizens and FBI agents. Evans believed the leaks were coming from inside the FBI. He didn't want to believe his boss's loose lips were leaking information that was getting his agents killed.

His agents were chasing their tails, always coming up late, while children and the kidnappers would vanish into thin air. Amber Alerts, cooperation with local authorities, and even working with Interpol all proved useless.

Evans suspected that the Pied Piper had hundreds of government employees and elected officials embedded within the current administration. During all the years he had been chasing the lunatic, he had no clues to his true identity.

Evan's desk was cluttered with case files of missing children. The papers were scattered in all directions, mirroring his chaotic mind. It was case number fifty-six, involving FBI Agent Elliot Burns' niece, Michelle Arnold, that had him more upset than usual.

Evans knew Michelle's parents. They weren't perfect; in fact, he had known about their flaws, but he believed they had turned their lives around. There was no way they could be capable of what Sally Palmer had accused them of doing. What was happening under Palmer's watch—thousands of missing foster children—had skyrocketed.

Evans didn't believe it was the system. Deep down, he knew that Palmer President Webster, whom he trusted, was somehow trafficking these children. He just didn't have the proof he needed to arrest her.

He wondered if Agent Seymour truly heard the Pied Piper call out to him and boast that his sister Ashley was still alive. Then, Palmer's involvement with Eddie during his childhood and Michelle Arnold's abduction started to seem more than just a coincidence. He needed proof, and the two kidnapped girls who could provide it were missing.

He asked his administrative assistant, Alice Dickerson, to gather all documents related to the Seymour car accident and Ashley Seymour's abduction. He needed to refresh his memory. He had an itch that needed scratching.

Evans kept wondering if Sally Palmer was a criminal or just a careless bureaucrat. She was Teflon-coated from head to toe, and she had the president's ear.

Evans had burned his share of bridges recently, sending one of his agents undercover to find the Pied Piper and his human trafficking brokers. It had cost that agent his life twelve days ago. Now, another good agent was dead. One was seriously injured, and there was a deadly threat from the Pied Piper: more would die if he didn't back down.

Over seventeen years ago, he and Blanchard received their first threat after Jack Seymour's death. After many years of silence, the threats had resurfaced, bringing more serious consequences.

He pushed back his chair and walked around his desk, straining to pick up the papers from Michelle Arnold's file. He held her picture, staring, unable to hold back his tears as he thought about the pain Elliot Burns must be feeling.

The adorable girl with pigtails, freckles on her cheeks and nose, and the biggest smile made his stomach tighten. Just then, a headache in the middle of his forehead exploded, as if he'd been hit by a baseball.

What made things worse was that Burns was the girl's godfather and uncle. Evans pushed back his chair and stood, stretching his arms above his head. He noticed his reflection in the mirror above the credenza behind his desk. He was forty-eight but looked seventy. The black circles around his eyes and the etched lines of sadness on his face made him seem like a stranger to himself. He stood there frozen, unable to summon the energy to move.

He was pulled out of his brooding thoughts. His phone snapped him back to reality. "Evans," he shouted sharply, his voice raspy and irritated.

"It's Agent Ellenberg, sir. We need to meet ASAP! It's about the Arnold girl—" Evans abruptly cut him off.

Another call had come through. Alice's loud voice over the intercom startled him. She seemed excited as she told him the call was from Austria. "Ellenberg, you'll need to hold. I have a long-distance call I need to take. Let me have your number and I'll call you as soon as I'm done." He scribbled the agent's cell number and then pressed line two.

"Deputy Director Evans here," he said anxiously.

"Deputy Director Evans, I'm Inspector Klaus Shultz, Commander of the Austrian Secret Police. I received your fax a few days ago regarding your Amber Alert for a ten-year-old girl, Michelle Arnold. I was initially hesitant to call, recalling how uncooperative your country had been with our government a few years back," Shultz said seriously.

Evans suddenly cut him off. "What's this all about?" he asked, holding his breath as he looked at Michelle's picture.

Inspector Shultz kept his formal monotone. "I believe we found Michelle Arnold."

Evans sat still in his chair, unsure of what to say. He inhaled deeply, hoping that what he was about to hear would be good news. "At this point, I'll take any news you have that could help this case."

Klaus cleared his throat and began to speak. "We found a young girl who might match one of your BOLOs. This poor child had been shot three times on one of our ski slopes. The strange thing was that she wore an adult ski outfit with an Advanced Biotech logo on the back of her parka. Another oddity was that the young girl had a plastic, bar-coded identification bracelet on her wrist and was wearing a hospital gown with the abbreviation: ABL."

Before Klaus could say another word, Evans suddenly asked, "Is she alive?"

"Yes," he said somberly. "But, I am sorry to say, barely. Her gunshot wounds were extensive," he confessed. "She had one bullet in her thigh, and then another in her head and one in her neck, just missing her spinal cord. She was hypothermic from all the blood she had lost.

Evans' hands began to shake. "What's her prognosis?

"She's a very strong girl, a real fighter. Her last words before she went into her coma were hard to understand," Klaus told him. "One of the rescuers thought she had said she had come from a cement fortress and that children were being hurt there.

"A cement fortress? Are you familiar with what's on top of your mountain?" Evans probed.

"Yes, I am. What the young girls said made no sense. Dr. Kane, the owner of Advanced Biotech, is widely respected. His company has been helping many children with mental illnesses."

Evans' tone had escalated. "Have you gone up to the lab and searched the place?" Evans demanded. He immediately wondered if more of his unsolved cases were about to be solved.

Klaus didn't seem too upset by Evans' attitude. "I have a warrant. I called you as a courtesy. I thought you'd want to be part of the search, yes? My country says no, but I don't care. I am, as you Americans say, sticking my neck out."

Evans' tone seemed to simmer, his voice calmer. "I appreciate your cooperation. I can be there tomorrow. Would it be possible for you to send me a DNA sample for our labs? We have an extensive database on thousands of missing children, and I was hoping I could be sure it's Michelle Arnold."

"My team analyzed her DNA. What is your facsimile number? I can send it now.

"Klaus, thank you for your help. This is the best lead we've had. Could you please make sure she's well protected? If she escaped from her

Steve Jaffe

kidnappers and they were the ones who shot her, they might be trying to find her to ensure she's dead," Evans recommended.

"My finest officers guard her hospital room. I will tell the ski patrol that she did not survive. No one will get past my men," the inspector said confidently. "This I promise you," he added sternly. "We are professionals here in Austria," he replied; his formal, controlled tone sounded a bit defensive and ended the call.

As Evans opened his office door, he heard the fax machine printing. He hurried over and saw the DNA report on the little girl. He buzzed his secretary, Alice Dickerson, to get the report to forensics. He told her he was leaving town for a few days and that he'd call her to share his schedule. Then he noticed the note to call agent Ellenberg and tucked the paper into his shirt pocket. He planned to call him once he arrived at the airport.

Evans looked at Alice with cold, menacing eyes. "I'm flying to Austria tonight. As far as anyone is concerned, I'm taking a few personal days. No one...I mean, no one can know where I'm going." He knew Alice was a pit bull when it came to protecting him from unwanted intruders. There was no one he could trust now, not even his boss, Director Jenkins.

"Yes, Robert," she replied professionally and took the papers.

Evans was out the door before she could say goodbye. He understood Alice's moods better than anyone else. Their close working relationship was more like a long, tense marriage, and he knew she was pissed at him for not talking to her about what was going on.

He turned and faced her. "Alice, stop pouting. The less you know, the better. I need you to call this number," he said, tossing a piece of paper with Agent Ellenberg's phone number onto her desk. This agent has information about the Arnold case. See if you can get him to overnight whatever he has to you. I'll let you know the fax number where I'll be. Tell him I'll speak to him when I return.

"You use me for all your dirty work," she said with sad puppy eyes. "I should at least know what you're up to. It would make it easier to cover your ass, which by the way I am quite good at," she said with a sweet smile.

Chapter 31

Agent Ellenburg couldn't hide his disappointment. "I can't just send what I have. It's sensitive and for his eyes only. It's regarding Agent Burns' niece. When's he due back?" he asked.

Alice had dealt with all kinds of pushy agents over the past fifteen years. Agent Ellenberg sounded like a complete pushover. She had the confidence of a Master Sergeant. She knew how the game was played at the Bureau and how to make an agent tremble when she spoke. This one was just too easy to read.

"Are you telling me that you are refusing an order from Deputy Director Evans?" She threatened. "I did not read into his request that there was any room to negotiate."

Ellenberg stammered, trying to reply. "I…I…I'm not arguing with you or Evans. It's the chain of custody situation. It's evidence, and I'm following what I think is the right thing to do here. Please read into it what you want. Just tell Deputy Director Evans I will be available to meet him when he returns."

"You've got balls, young man, I'll hand you that. I'll convey your objections to him the moment he calls in. Good luck," she said, ending the call abruptly.

* * * * *

An agent whose desk was in earshot of Alice's desk. He had been eavesdropping on Alice's phone call, and he couldn't believe what he had just heard. He knew he had to convey this information to Senator Jarvis immediately. What the hell has the Arnold case got to do with Austria? What does Ellenburg have that's so secretive?"

"Yes, Senator, I heard him say Michelle Arnold and that he was going to Austria. Also, Agent Ellenburg has some evidence that pertains to Agent Burns' niece."

"You've done well. This will help me show the president how messed up the FBI has become." Before the agent could reply, Jarvis hung up the phone.

* * * * *

Ten hours later, Evans sat emotionless at the hospital in Bern. His exhaustion had worsened over the past ten hours.

He leaked to the press that Michelle Arnold had died when, in reality, she was still alive and in a coma. DNA confirmed she was his agent's niece. Her parents agreed to his plan, understanding that her safety was the top priority while she fought to stay alive in a foreign country.

Holding tightly in his hands was a directive from his boss, Director Peter Jenkins. It made no sense, and he thought about pretending he had never received it. However, he had enough problems to deal with at the moment.

He unfolded the fax once more and read Jenkins' words: "Do not disturb or enter Advanced Biotech Laboratories. You are off this case. It is now in the hands of the new director of the Federal Office to Combat Trafficking in Persons, Nancy Rutman. The Austrian government has agreed to cooperate with her only."

Evans couldn't believe how quickly Jenkins had found him. He knew Alice hadn't told anyone. It had to have been the Austrian government.

Evans knew it would take weeks, maybe even months, before anyone searched for Doctor Kane's hospital. Any evidence, including missing children, would be gone.

It did not matter. He had one of the Pied Piper's victims, and she was alive. His first mistake, and he was going to make him pay for it.

Now, all he wanted to do was get Michelle home to her parents, then fight with Jenkins over how he was handling the Pied Piper kidnapping ring.

* * * * *

Later that evening, another painful phone call pierced his ears. The phone call had been from Special Agent Elliott Burns. He was crying, totally out of control.

"Young man, get a grip. You're an FBI agent. Curb your emotions and tell me what's wrong," Evans said sternly.

Burns' breaths were loud and rapid. "My brother and sister-in-law were sideswiped in their car last night, heading down to our field office in Manhattan. They're dead. First my niece, and now the only family I had left," he sobbed. "What the fuck's going on?"

Evans was speechless, standing outside Michelle's hospital room. "Were there any witnesses?"

All I could gather from the police report was that a large dark-colored pickup truck deliberately rammed into their car, sending their sedan careening off the Henry Hudson Parkway. Their car then went off a bridge and burst into flames upon impact.

"Shit." Evans cursed. "There has to be a connection to this and Michelle's kidnapping. The original kidnappers must know of her escape and have been ordered to eliminate any links to them?"

Burns sighed. "It's all fucked."

"At this point, you're right," Evans replied. He put the phone down, his head falling into his waiting, cupped hands.

Evans knew there were no coincidences with criminals, only dots that needed connecting. His head would not stop pounding. There were too many possibilities, too influential people within the loop.

Director Jenkins was the first person who came to mind. Then he remembered how nervous Agent Ellenberg had been when talking to him about what he had gotten from Doctor Harding, Agent Seymour's stepdad.

He grabbed a phone near the nurse's station and dialed Alice.

Evans sounded agitated when his staff assistant picked up the phone. "Alice, did you get hold of Agent Ellenburg?"

"Something's wrong. I can hear it in your voice," she said.

"Too much to talk about over the phone," he replied. "Is Agent Ellenberg sending the package he has for me?"

Alice hesitated, unsure how to approach her boss. She knew him too well and didn't want to shatter her eardrum when she told him the agent disobeyed his orders.

"He has it and feels it shouldn't leave his custody due to its sensitive nature. He's waiting to meet with you when you return," Alice told him. "You need to tell me what's happening. Jenkins knew exactly where you were an hour after you left. What is going on?" she asked.

"It's the Arnold girl. She was found shot on an Austrian ski slope," Evan replied. "Her parents were murdered a few hours ago, and the place where we believe she had been held captive…Jenkins has ordered me to back off. Whoever is controlling this kidnapping ring is very well-connected and willing to do anything to cover their tracks," Evans told her. "They're burning their bridges. We're running out of time."

"Slow down," Alice interrupted. "You're going to blow a gasket."

He was about to chew her out for talking to him that way when he saw Inspector Frankel walking toward him. He did not look happy. He cut off Alice and ended the call.

Before Evan could ask his question, the inspector spoke in a low, raspy tone. "Dr. Kane's entire laboratory has been destroyed".

Evan's eyes widened, his face turning white as he realized what was happening. "That's bullshit!" he said, his hands shaking. "Doctor Kane has some big balls on him."

Inspector Frankel put his arm around Evans's shoulder. "Be assured that this won't stop our investigation," he said curtly. "If Kane panicked, he might have called the original broker that took Michelle... they might be covering up any links to them." He handed Evans Michelle's ID bracelet, a broad smile on his face. "Maybe the FBI can figure out what the barcode has on it? I'll check Doctor Kane's phone records."

Then, Evans informed the inspector about Michelle's parents.

Frankel nodded slowly, his eyes tightly shut as he spoke. "That poor little girl," he said.

"Do you know yet what happened up there?"

Frankel became emotional. "The explosion flattened the entire hilltop. Except for the billowing smoke, the mountain looks as if a meteor hit it. My men have told me everything had been leveled, and most of what once were buildings is now dust and rubble."

Evans leaned back in his chair. He craned his neck, letting out a loud pop that echoed inside his head. Nervously, he massaged his temples with his fingertips, struggling to find the words.

Inspector Frankel had a distant look. "We received a press release from an Advanced Biotech spokesman. They say it was a gas leak. Doctor Kane is devastated over the death of all the children and his work."

"That's a load of crap!" Evans said, rolling his eyes. "I'll bet all the records of the children were conveniently destroyed."

"Yes," Frankel replied, taking a seat next to Evans. "Damn, this does smell rotten." He gently patted Evans' back before speaking. "Whoever these people are, they must have a lot of friends in high places. We need to be careful. No one seems to be safe, if you know what I mean," the inspector whispered. "I would like to be part of your investigation."

"Am I hearing you correctly? You want to help? Evan asked.

"When children are involved...well, I've got two daughters and if this had happened to one of them...I don't know what I'd do. Yes, I want to help, but my way. I've suspected for some time that many men around me would sell their children for a few dollars. How I operate within my government might seem slow, but that's the only way it will work here without raising any eyebrows."

Evans was starting to like the inspector. "I can't believe a man like Kane would destroy everything. I have a friend at the NSA. He'll help me even though I'm technically off the case. It's a long shot, but maybe one of our satellites picked up something before the explosion?"

Chapter 32

Miguel Guzman wasn't surprised by what he saw hours earlier. The explosion had rocked his helicopter as it flew around Doctor Kane's fortress of horror. The last cargo van managed to get down the west side of the mountain. He knew Doctor Frankenstein would be back at his second lab, hidden somewhere remote in Burgundy, France.

The French government ignored what Dr. Kane was doing as long as he kept supporting the French economy with his money. They had enough trouble managing their large Muslim population and didn't want additional distractions.

"Luis, our plans need to be moved up. We can't wait any longer," Piper confessed. He had just a few more items to finish, and then he could finally disappear into his cave. He was lost in thought, more melancholy than usual.

Luis forced a smile, lost in thought about the prophecy. Was this the first sign I was told to watch out for? Could it be the young Seymour girl? "A year might be too long to wait, my brother. Piper, let me dispose of this girl." Then he considered the young girl's brother. Is he really dead? He was pondering the prophecy that a fortune teller had told him about. Was he the young boy from Piper's past who would destroy him?

Luis was superstitious. Not finding Seymour's body did not sit easily with him. Etched in his mind was the prediction. Someone else might see the old fortune teller's warnings as vague, confusing, and nonspecific, but

Luis was a believer, and now with the signs staring him in the face, that's all that mattered. Three of the signs were coming true. He had to protect his friend before they all suffered. He loved his friend and understood that the things he did, the horrible way of life he was born into, were not his fault. He was ill and had no choices.

Piper turned his head and shook it slowly. "No. Let Kane and his team handle their mess. We need to start separating our business from all of this. That includes Doctor Kane, Sally Palmer, and Senator Jarvis. It should be done as quickly as possible. We can't afford to be careless, and yes, I really cannot wait a year. I feel our good luck is running out, along with my patience."

"I'll ask you again. What about Ashley Seymour?"

Piper ignored the question. "Isabella wants to be a mother since I can't get her pregnant," He replied, exposing a deep sadness on his face.

Luis's face knotted as he felt his friend's pain. "Adopt?"

"The doctors say my medication has affected my sperm count... she's a good woman and deserves better," he paused. "She's agreed to adopt. Palmer is arranging it with one of her Miami DCF contacts. It will be a blessing for me, as one of my other problems needs to be punished. Blanchard is next and will suffer while my wife gets what she deserves." He wore an eerie smile.

Luis understood what Piper meant. "Another FBI agent?"

Piper nodded.

"What about Palmer? The Senator? Kane?" Luis asked.

"I need time to sort out the order of things," Piper told him.

Luis complained, "We're exposing ourselves too often."

Piper raised his hand to stop Luis from speaking and closed his eyes. He had just taken his cocktail of drugs, and it was beginning to take effect. "Tomorrow I'll give you all the details. What I've come up with is a good plan. My best. But now I need some rest," he said wearily.

Sleep was what he needed. In eleven hours, he would be addressing a group of people he hoped still saw him as a philanthropist. Piper was worried as it was becoming increasingly difficult for him to switch from the sociopath he made his living from to the man millions of people admired for the good he was doing worldwide.

He was being honored for his charity work and for his hospital ship, which traveled the world to help the sick, especially children in impoverished countries. It had been nearly twenty years since it served as the perfect cover for his child trafficking activities. While he appeared to be a selfless man saving lives, he was also destroying them under the guise of being the new Mother Teresa.

Over the last few years, the small amount of reason he could gather made him believe that once he stopped the evil and his uncontrollable urges, he would be normal. God would forgive him eventually if he only used his hospital ship for good. Helping millions of children around the world would wipe out the thousands he had led to slaughter. The Pied Piper would once again be Miguel Guzman, a hero.

As he drifted off to sleep, a smile appeared on his face. Everything was going to be all right very soon.

* * * * *

Doctor Kane sat behind his desk, overlooking the rolling green pastures at his chateau in the French countryside. His mind was racing. It was the timetable he had been given; it would take him two, maybe three months to get this lab up and running. Piper was being unreasonable. He also understood his new reality. He knew no one had ever ended a relationship with Piper's group and lived to talk about it.

Kane was on the phone with his Russian broker, Ivan. He knew it was time to strengthen new business relationships.

The Russian Mafia was the top choice. Aside from Piper, they had the best distribution channels for smuggling young girls. While they preferred older teenagers and young women, they were becoming more open to his world of infant organs.

"Ivan, Dr. Kane here. It's been way too long since we've talked," he said jovially.

"Ah, Doctor Kane. You only call for reason, not social, huh?" the Russian said, struggling with his English.

Kane smiled. He appreciated that Ivan was all business. "It's refreshing to talk to a man who only focuses on making money. I have a problem that requires your immediate attention. If you handle it quickly, it could mean billions for you and your team."

"I always interested in the American dollar," he said, laughing. "When shall we meet?"

"Say…two days. I'll call you with the time and location."

Chapter 33

Doctor Harding stood, unanimated. His legs felt like Jell-O, the energy draining from his body. He had become disoriented, his mind exploding with horrible thoughts. He re-read the words he had copied from a notepad at Sally Palmer's office prior to their meeting.

The information was convincing. He questioned his motives. Was it his hatred for this woman that fueled his suspicions? He was a psychiatrist, a rational man who relied on objectivity — well, most of the time.

The note he had read, though brief, could only mean one thing: missing foster children. He thought about the missing children from the past, especially Ashley Seymour. However, his heart told him that the past mattered less than what he believed Palmer might be doing right now.

He wanted to run this by his son, Eddie, but Eddie's phone went unanswered. He tried reaching agents Ellenberg and Crawford but was equally unsuccessful.

Harding recognized that he was becoming a threat to Palmer. She had slandered him as an alarmist, accusing him of jealousy over her achievements. "He's trying to undermine my authority and tarnish the outstanding results owed to President Webster and his heroic vision for the abused children throughout our country," she stated before a congressional committee.

Harding had been warned many times and threatened that if he did not stay away from Sally Palmer, his boss would be forced to fire him. He no longer cared about his job. It had become ugly, draining his spirit and his courage to fight for the children he promised to help. His patients kept disappearing. He had become demoralized with the entire foster care system. He felt powerless and knew it.

Palmer and her staff, consisting of her family, had become the Gestapo of Child Services, snatching infants, toddlers, and young children, mostly in the middle of the night, with presidential approval.

These were the forgotten children. The young who did not have parents who wanted them or foster parents who did not care about their welfare.

They were invisible. If they went missing, it wasn't reported. These missing children never appeared in the media. Foster care kids had become the easiest targets for people like Sally Palmer and especially the Pied Piper and his organization.

Sally Palmer had the authority to act without any court orders. She didn't need to justify her actions or prove that any children she labelled at risk shouldn't become part of her secret agency. She had presidential backing, along with support from Senator Jarvis and his committee. Once a child entered her system, they vanished from sight. It had become the perfect operation.

The Senate Committee on Children, Youth, and Families in Washington, D.C., engaged in its usual political posturing about the missing children Harding had brought to their attention. Hearings after hearings would pass without any resolution to the issue. The doctor's complaints, while acknowledged, were never taken seriously. He was like the Don Quixote of Social Services, fighting unstoppable windmills. Until now, he only had speculation and conjecture. He second-guessed himself as he re-read his note once more.

He looked at the stacks of manila folders piled on his desk. He knew they would never be cleared. What could one man do? He'd complain about too many cases and not enough time, but no one listened. No one listened to anything he had to say anymore, even his adoptive son, Special Agent Edward Seymour, ignored him.

He had grown to hate the system he worked under, despised Sally Palmer, and was ashamed of becoming helpless within a system that punished him every day he came to work.

He looked again long and hard at the note. The decision was made. If his suspicions were right, the biggest scandal in California's child services history was about to come to light. Influential people would be dragged down, careers destroyed, and reputations ruined. He re-examined the folded note he had copied from Palmer's office.

Children need to be exchanged at Pier 54, San Diego Harbor, 11:00 P.M. Thursday, August 12th
P.P.

He just needed to speak with someone at the FBI about the note.

His mind drifted back to the meeting earlier that day with Sally Palmer. He was engaging in idle chitchat with her secretary, who was also her sister, Lisa Matthews.

She seemed pleasant in a sweet way but was overly nervous as she spoke. She had been interested in his son and asked to see a picture of him. All Harding had was a picture of Edward when he was twelve.

Doctor Harding failed to tell her he was an FBI agent. After a few minutes of examining the photo, she became emotional, rushed out of the office, and left him with a confused look, crying.

Embarrassed that he might have said something wrong, he glanced down at her desk. That's when he saw the note.

At first, it didn't make any sense to him. He noticed that Lisa, while taking the message, must have been doodling. She had drawn a circle of dollar signs around the message. Then a light bulb went off in his head. He jotted down everything he read.

The note troubled him deeply. He felt the color drain from his face. He was frozen, lost in thought. The clicking of women's high heels on the marble floor in the corridor made him jump, his heart pounding. He hurried back to the armchair where he had been sitting moments earlier. He folded the copy of Lisa's note and slipped it into his jacket pocket. He was surprised to see Sally Palmer enter her sister's office, her expression angry.

"How long have you been waiting here, alone?" she asked nervously, her demeanor cold. She was scanning the outer and inner office for her sister, clearly upset.

He offered her a relaxed smile. "Not long. Your secretary was entertaining me. She just went to the restroom."

Sally was lost in thought, biting her lower lip. She signaled for him to follow her into her office. "Let's get started with this meeting. I have to be out of here in fifteen minutes."

The meeting ended up being more of a harsh reprimand. Palmer delivered her scolding like a machine gun, tearing through her target. When Harding tried to reply, she cut him off sharply.

"I know you've kept complaining about me and my program. I don't appreciate what you've been accusing me of," she said sternly, waving her finger at him. She was unable to keep her composure. Her hatred for him exploded on her face.

Harding appeared unaffected by her emotional outburst. I don't appreciate not being allowed to follow up on my patients. I must be able to review how they're adjusting.

"Not this same shit again," Palmer cursed. "You know the new rules. You haven't been given that level of clearance, and it doesn't look like it will happen anytime soon. Your complaints are so noted, again," she said in a frustrated huff. She had other, more urgent issues and didn't need to be distracted by Harding right now. "Nothing ever will be done about your complaints while I'm in charge," she told him.

179

Her behavior seemed strangely odd. She was growling like a rabid dog, with her teeth exposed, and it looked as if her incisors had grown, ready to tear him apart. She appeared more troubled than usual. The verbal assault he was experiencing, he sensed, was coming from something beyond her anger toward him.

She waved a hand dismissively at him. "This meeting is over, and I suggest you just do your job, or you might find yourself out of one. Just one phone call from me to your boss and you're done."

Her irrational behavior he had seen before and knew that any further arguing would be pointless. He stood suddenly, lost in thought. She's hiding something. Maybe the note does mean something?

Sally saw him pause briefly at her door before turning away. He looked lost in thought. "Do you have something to say?" Palmer asked uninterestedly.

Harding shrugged and smiled as his hand touched the folded piece of paper in his jacket pocket. "Something's going on," he said with a feral grin. "You have the same expression the day I got Edward Seymour out of your system. I believe what you're involved with has nothing to do with your federal foster care program." Before she could reply, he was out the door.

Palmer wheezed a deep breath, her nerves frayed. "Lisa, get the fuck in here," she shouted, rattling the wall hangings in her office.

Lisa Mathews stood in front of her sister's desk, her hands waving like fans attempting to dry her nails. "Hey, big sister. You're about to explode. What's up, sweetie?"

Sally could not control her frustration. "Is it so hard to ask you to be professional?" she sighed.

"How the hell did you know I was doing my nails?" Lisa replied, embarrassed. "I don't like you always chewing me out," she pouted.

"Why did you leave Dr. Harding alone?" Sally asked. She realized her sister did not know how to conduct herself professionally. Her eyes rolled up inside her head, realizing Dr. Harding had seen something on Lisa's desk. "Call Earl," Palmer ordered.

Lisa kept waving her wet nails, blowing on them, a look of disinterest on her face. "I'll call hubby and get him down here pronto." She stood at attention and saluted her sister, then stiffly turned and marched back to her desk.

Chapter 34

Sitting in his office, trembling, Harding's thoughts spiraled out of control. Paranoia was consuming his body. He tried to calm his nerves by taking deep breaths as his eyes darted around, feeling the mistrust settle in.

Who was he kidding? He knew he couldn't relax in his current state. Still, he had to do something, or he would chicken out. If that happened, he'd never forgive himself if the note proved to be accurate.

He carefully considered who to call and concluded that his longtime FBI friend, Special Agent Ted Blanchard, was his only choice. When the phone rang, he recognized his friend's voice immediately.

"Ted, it's Philip." At first, he thought Blanchard didn't recognize his voice, so he

Called out, "Philip Harding," his tone agitated.

"I know who you are. I'm just surprised to hear from you after all these years," Harding cut him off.

"I have something important to tell you," he said in a whisper. "I know the location..." he sucked in a deep breath. "where there will be an illegal exchange of children. I believe Sally Palmer is involved. You know her. She's the woman who runs the new federal foster care program. Same one involved with Jack Seymour's son Edward." His voice started to tremble. "Maybe it involves the Pied Piper... the note I read had the abbreviation PP on it."

"Calm down," Blanchard said, his tone skeptical. "Can't you first say hello? How's it going? How's your love life? Would that be so difficult?"

His friend's overly friendly attitude did not sit well with Harding. He wanted to be taken seriously. "Yeah, yeah. Hello. How are you? How's it going? I don't care about your love life. Blah, blah, blah, blah. Satisfied? Can you get serious?" Harding demanded. "I believe I have a lead on the Pied Piper."

Blanchard sighed loudly. "Okay. What's so important that you can't be civil?"

"I know the location where missing foster children will be sold to the Pied Piper," Harding told him.

"And, you know this how?" Blanchard responded suspiciously.

"I just do. It has to do with Sally Palmer. I found a note with the location and time for an exchange of children. Note referenced a man with the initials PP, which could only mean the Pied Piper. I rewrote a note on Palmer's receptionist's desk. You do believe me?" Harding begged.

Blanchard hesitated, allowing too much silence to transpire.

"Are you hearing me?" Harding raised his voice.

"I'm thinking. Where and when is this exchange going to take place?"

"Tomorrow night, eleven o'clock, Pier 56, San Diego Harbor," he answered, trying to catch his breath.

Blanchard didn't know what to say. Deputy Director Evans' orders were very clear. *"Under no circumstances, go after any leads that have the Pied Piper written on them unless you have my approval and adequate backup."*

Ted sighed loudly. Evans' orders still echoed in his mind. "I'll contact the local field office and see what they want to do. I hope you didn't misinterpret what you read. Our department has had enough fuckups from wrong tips about the Pied Piper. He's now murdering agents. We can't afford to screw up again."

"Just do what you can," Harding begged. "How could it hurt to observe? If nothing transpires, then who will ever know?"

Blanchard started to believe the doctor and wanted to help. "I'll take my partner with me and observe," he told him. "I just don't want to be made a fool of."

"But what if I am right?" he asked.

Harding hurled the crumpled note into his trash can. He snapped his cell phone shut. "He's not going to help," he muttered. He pressed one on his speed dialer. "Eddie, please pick up."

Chapter 35

9:00 P.M. Hotel Del, Coronado Island, San Diego, California

Loyal cheering supporters filled the banquet hall for Miguel Guzman, the man of the hour. Dignitaries from around the world, especially from developing countries, attended to honor the man who, through his charity and love for children, had saved countless sick and homeless babies worldwide with his free medical care.

The large hall off the main lobby at the Hotel Del Coronado featured a hundred round tables of ten, set beneath the turn-of-the-century tongue-and-groove wooden domed ceiling that has hosted presidents, prime ministers, and even dictators who were allies of the United States.

Two thousand eyes, wide with excitement and all smiling for the man they paid thousands of dollars to hear speak, sat anxiously awaiting the man some say should receive a Nobel Prize. He stood behind the oak podium, gazing over the heads of his supporters, lost deep in thought, and then, without a word, sat down.

On each side of the raised stage, long tables were covered with red, white, and blue tablecloths for the representatives from the U.N., the United States, and the generous Miguel Guzman and his Ship of Hope.

Doctor Harding was the only person in the banquet hall who did not want to be there. Palmer had ordered him to attend, and her orders left no room for negotiation. He disgustingly dusted off his tuxedo and dragged himself to the charity event he had no desire to attend, especially not with Sally Palmer and possibly the other criminals who were destroying families and innocent children.

Philip Harding took his seat, his mind drifting to his earlier conversation with Special Agent Blanchard. Images of the children being offloaded on a pier that same evening a few miles across the harbor from the Hotel Del tore at his heart.

Ted will do the right thing, he tried to convince himself. He snapped back to the present when a deep, raspy voice boomed over the PA system.

The Vice President of the United States, a stocky man with salt-and-pepper hair and wearing Ben Franklin reading glasses, had begun addressing the audience. His accolades for Mr. Guzman kept being interrupted by applause and standing ovations.

Harding had never met Guzman in person. Like millions of others, he admired the selfless work Guzman did for innocent children around the world.

Bending toward the microphone and yelling over the cheers, the vice president continued his introduction. "No one in the history of the world has taken on a noble act of charity like Miguel Guzman has in our lifetime, with his Ship of Hope, fully funded by Guzman Enterprises. Through his selflessness, Miguel Guzman has brought a high level of medical care to countless countries that could not provide for their poor and starving."

The Vice President turned his head toward Guzman, giving him a supportive wink. His hand kept trembling from his MS, but it didn't matter. He ignored his condition and continued with his speech. "Miguel Guzman, with selfless hardship, has revived the institution of charity with his money and compassionate heart. By serving those in need without the bureaucratic red tape most governments create, Miguel Guzman, unlike any government...including my United States," the vice-president said sadly, "has, with greater flexibility and discipline, accomplished so much. I know I can speak for everyone here in saying how deeply indebted we are to his generosity. Tonight, for his wonderful work..." he paused... "work that this country wants to see continue, I want to present Mr. Guzman with a ten-million-dollar check."

Everyone immediately stood up, cheering with hoots and whistles. The vice president's voice could not break through the excited crowd. He tried to wave his hands to quiet the room, then gave up and joined in the loud applause.

When the room finally quieted down, Vice-President Jack Fitzgerald continued his speech, this time turning his weak body toward the guest of honor. "I speak for President Webster that it is our government's commitment to help support the wonderful work that you and your staff of doctors and nurses are doing." Fitzgerald turned and faced the audience, a broad smile on his face. "I now ask each of you to dig deep into your pockets tonight and help the needy children of our world."

Miguel couldn't believe what he heard. He quickly jotted down the amount on a cocktail napkin, folded it, and slipped it into his jacket pocket, smiling broadly.

Guzman stood and slowly approached the vice president. He placed his hand on his chest, tapping it gently to signal that the vice president had touched his heart. Miguel appeared very humble, which was his intent.

The hug he gave the vice-president seemed forced, a little stiff. Guzman hated being touched or touching others. Nevertheless, it went unnoticed.

Then he turned to the audience. The cacophony of noises hurt his head. The room seemed to take on a demonic wind. He looked at the table he had just left, and the dignitaries were all smiling back at him. They had taken on a bestial glow. Was his medication wearing off? He prayed he could hold out.

He could almost read their minds, sensing their lying thoughts about him. Then he turned his head to look at the cheering crowd, a smile cracking on his face as he realized he had made himself the perfect hero that adults and children around the world loved and wanted to emulate.

He let his wild thoughts fade away. He accepted the gift with the humility and grace of the great man the world believed he was. Guzman was a showman, something he had been taught by his father—more accurately, beaten into him. If it weren't for his mother sending him to the United States in his youth to learn their ways, he might never have been able to accomplish any of this. He played perfectly to the cameras, constantly hugging the vice president, always ensuring his face was pointed at the flashing strobe lights.

He watched Vice-President Fitzgerald struggle with his MS, trying to make his way to his chair. Guzman hurried over to help. A few sighs echoed through the banquet hall from the women dressed in evening gowns. Miguel was once again the brave hero. He was untouchable and could do nothing wrong.

When he returned to the lectern, he first bowed his head to gather his thoughts. Then he slowly looked up, nodding a few times, which only caused the audience to cheer again. They were under his spell. He knew it and loved it. Then, with just a hand gesture, the audience fell silent, anxiously waiting for him to speak.

"I am honored," he said softly. He paused, pinching the bridge of his nose to dramatize his feelings. "And at the same time, humbled by this wonderful gesture from the people of the United States." His Spanish accent was barely noticeable. "As I've said before, I do not expect help and will continue to provide for all children who need medical care..."

He kept his speech brief. After thirty minutes of recapping his worldwide accomplishments and plans for the rest of the year, he gracefully concluded his address.

Miguel Guzman waved to the audience. "I want to thank everyone on the committee who put together this wonderful event. Unfortunately, I must leave early. Please excuse my rudeness. I normally don't eat and run, especially after receiving such a generous gift." He held the check high above his head. "I must go now to prepare the necessary documents so my ship can leave San Diego," he told the audience. "My crew needs some last-minute instructions before I fly home. Again, thank you all for your support." Miguel waved to a standing ovation.

He quickly left the stage and headed toward the side door of the banquet hall. He was immediately surrounded by five armed FBI agents. Miguel whispered to his security chief, Luis, as he was led through the kitchen. "I'm getting too good at this. It's a little scary how easy it is to gather money nowadays."

Luis nodded, handing Guzman a piece of paper. "We might have a problem this evening." He watched Miguel's face lose its color.

"Palmer screwed up again?" Miguel said with a disgusted look on his face. He did not expect an answer.

Chapter 36

Deputy Director Evans had just returned from Austria. Before he could unpack, Director Jenkins assigned him to the Guzman detail. It was not his usual duty. His boss was asserting his authority, while Nancy Rutman, the new Director of The Federal Office to Combat Trafficking in Children, was trying to figure out her new responsibilities.

He didn't know any of the men in his detail. He wanted his team, but Jenkins was angry and refused to listen to his Deputy Director. His men were now ready to escort Guzman to the pier where his ship was waiting.

He had just finished reviewing the satellite report from two hours before Doctor Kane's laboratory exploded. Five large vans snaked down the mountain, along with four flatbed trucks carrying some cargo hidden under a tarp.

Evans noticed Dr. Kane sitting with Senator Jarvis and Sally Palmer in the ballroom. "Bullshit, it was a fucking gas leak," he mumbled. He closed his file as Miguel Guzman approached. He gave Dr. Kane a hard stare. "Could the bastard doctor be the Pied Piper?" He refocused his attention on Guzman.

"Wonderful presentation, sir," said Evans stiffly. When their eyes met, even though he had never met the man personally, there was something familiar about him. He shrugged it off. He had seen Guzman's picture in the newspaper and on TV numerous times. His jet lag was playing tricks on him. His mind was elsewhere. His thoughts drifted to Michelle Arnold.

She had not taken the death of her parents well. On top of that, someone at the FBI had leaked the story about Michelle's incredible escape from her kidnappers, and that she survived.

Evans was furious with Director Jenkins, eager to find out who leaked the story that put Michelle's life in danger again. Once the young girl returned from Austria, Palmer took her back into her care. She was being difficult about transferring the custody to her uncle, Special Agent Elliot Burns.

The question of what the best home for the traumatized girl was had fallen on deaf ears. Sally Palmer could not be reasoned with. She cited a laundry list of reasons why her uncle would not be fit to care for such a fragile child.

Using her power and influence over President Webster, Palmer placed the Arnold girl, as she so eloquently referred to her, in a temporary foster home until the custodial arrangements could be sorted out.

Evan's thoughts spun like a wild tornado as his eyes fixed on Doctor Kane. Seeing Palmer and Senator Jarvis talking to the doctor as if they were close friends only deepened his suspicions. He wanted to believe it was just a coincidence, but he didn't buy into coincidences.

He watched Guzman wave to the three of them. Even that gesture from the well-known man seemed familiar to Evans. He tried to remember anything, but nothing came to mind. "Evans, you're letting your imagination run away," he scolded himself. He glanced at his watch. It was 9:15 P.M.

The Deputy Director almost slapped himself when he realized that Guzman's selfless desire to help children had placed him in many circles of influence, and he didn't believe Palmer, Jarvis, and Kane were crusaders committed to stopping the worldwide trafficking of children. Another happenstance he could not pursue without unequivocal, damning evidence.

Evans tried to push his crazy thoughts out of his head, telling himself it didn't mean anything. However, his mind wouldn't stop thinking about

Doctor Kane. How does that bastard Kane have the nerve to show up here only days after blowing up his lab?

Evans shook his head in disgust. He was brought back to his task at hand when Mr. Guzman touched his shoulder.

"Thank you. I didn't get your name?" Guzman asked, extending his hand. He knew who the Deputy Director was but wanted to look into his eyes to sense if the FBI agent recognized him. He remembered Evans that rainy day, twenty years ago, when he captured his cousin. He wanted to bait him but thought better of it. He will feel more pain soon enough.

Evans' eyes blinked a few times, trying to regain his focus. "Assistant Director Robert Evans, sir. We're ready to go when you are."

Evans saw Guzman glance back at his friends one more time, gesturing with his hand to call them over.

With somber expressions, they all nodded. They kept their pace and returned to their intense conversation with Sally Palmer.

Evans's feelings for Michelle made him somewhat paranoid. He was again considering Guzman, Kane, Jarvis, and Palmer as suspects. He knew it would be nearly impossible to get support from Jenkins or anyone in the administration to investigate these highly respected individuals, especially Miguel Guzman. And now, with the president giving him a ten-million-dollar check, it would be infeasible to accuse Miguel Guzman of anything without solid evidence.

"When I figure this all out," he told himself. *"If it is any of those bastards, they'll get what they deserve."* He turned and headed for the garage where Guzman's limo had been waiting.

Chapter 37

Two Days Earlier. Lake Atitlan, Guatemala, Central America.

Luis was a superstitious man who would visit a clairvoyant named Maria Ruiz before each mission. He always asked for her blessing. She lived among the indigenous people who inhabited twelve villages around Lake Atitlán in Guatemala, about an hour's helicopter ride from Piper's ranch. Tonight's mission didn't have Maria's approval.

Maria had always blessed their operations, which eased Luis's mind. It hadn't happened this time; however, he couldn't stop the wild thoughts filling his head about her prophecies involving Piper, which had started eighteen years ago.

Maria was in her forties when Luis first met her. However, the life she had lived and the way she survived made her look much older. Her skin was like leather, dark brown and hardened by the region's hot, humid temperatures. Her skin had become shiny, not from moisturizers, but from years of neglect. Her distinct facial tone was only matched by her colorful, hand-woven Indian clothing.

Her bright blue eyes were shadowed beneath a band of multicolored, one-inch-wide cotton ribbons wrapped around her head, with an eight-inch brim shading her face. By unwrapping the strips of her ribbons, she helped supplement her income by selling yards of these colorful, hand-woven bands to tourists.

193

Every time Luis entered her adobe clay shack, he remembered the old life he once had. His past mirrored hers, as they both had lived in a run-down one-room hut without electricity or running water. The smell from his youth would flood back whenever he saw her.

The village looked like a cesspool. Still water puddles were full of mosquitoes and horseflies—some as large as bats. The infestation thrived on feces and decaying trash. The orphaned dogs, searching for scraps to fill their thin, starving bodies, wandered the streets. Nevertheless, Luis never forgot that these people were his own and felt compassion for their struggle to survive.

When Maria spoke in her Indian dialect, Luis would try not to stare at the decayed teeth in her mouth. Some were twisted, and others were missing. "I see disaster in your future," she had predicted. She shook her head, her lips pursed, her eyes squeezed shut as sorrow spread across her face. She had never told Luis anything positive. Still, Luis had to reinterpret her prognostications to protect Piper.

She'd sway back and forth in her old wooden chair, low, eerie sounds slipping from her mouth as she chanted during their sessions. He was recalling her prediction for tonight's job.

"The man you call Piper will descend into an even darker side after your next business trip, causing death to everyone around him," Maria told him.

Luis became confused and bewildered. He tried to ask a question, but Maria had fallen even deeper into her trance. Her voice sounded eerie as she kept muttering.

"They will destroy all of you," she ranted in a vague tongue, as her body twisted and shook. She had drifted deeper and deeper into her spell. "Luis, stop your friend now from angering God again, or you will all be condemned to hell!" she shrieked, her body arching in her chair.

Luis tried again to speak, but she was now too distant and far away. A puzzled look creased his face. "I don't understand?" he whispered.

Maria had fallen quiet, lost in her strange world. Luis used that moment to think about his boss. Sometimes Maria would remain silent for five minutes, sometimes an hour. It never mattered. Luis had to wait. It was part of the process.

Luis was part of the process, the unbreakable bond that, if broken, would disrupt the vision. He needed to understand what might lie ahead for himself and his brothers.

Within an instant, Maria's voice turned loud and raspy. She snapped out of her spell, visibly upset. "Look out for a once young boy and a young girl. They will take control of your friend. You must kill them both before Piper's forty-fifth birthday, or death will come to you and the man you protect."

Before Luis could respond or ask her the questions he needed, she fell back into her trance. He sat there, bewildered. The shanty once again grew lively. Maria's body resumed its spasmodic movements. He caught a moment of clarity and seized it before she drifted away again.

"Maria, can we discuss the boy and the girl?" Luis cautiously asked, rubbing his hands and then massaging his beard nervously.

Her eyes were glassy. Her face remained ashen from where she had been. "The boy is now a man," her raspy voice echoed. "Be cautious of Piper's obsessive actions, which will turn on you and your brothers. The boy is connected to Piper's past when his father murdered his mother and killed himself. The girl had come from one of your brokers. A she-wolf. You will have only one opportunity to destroy them, or the prophecy will be fulfilled." She paused; her voice had become a whisper. "They have to be killed together, not separately. I will pray for you and your brothers."

"How will I know who to choose?" he asked nervously.

She lifted a clear glass containing a dark liquid. "It will happen during a time when what had seemed normal is no longer." Her eyes rolled back, revealing only her yellowish eyeballs. She rocked feverishly, then a loud shriek burst from her lips.

The drink, a mixture of local herbs, was what she relied on to help her body recover. It was Luis's cue that the session was over. He left his payment on her table. He was deeply shaken.

Luis craned his neck, glancing back at the strange woman as he parted the hanging beads that served as her door. He watched her fall silent and then nod off, her chin resting on her chest.

Chapter 38

Present Day: 11:00 P.M., Pier 54, San Diego, California

Luis pulled back the sleeve on his nylon jumpsuit, checking his watch. "He's late again," he grumbled. Out of all of Piper's men, he was the most superstitious. The signs and severe warnings had been popping up these past few days faster than he expected.

Luis Rodriguez knew it was unusual for Piper to be late, but he was, while his jittery crew waited anxiously in the cold, windy rain. They had bypassed protocol for this exchange. It was a small order, mainly for Doctor Kane.

What troubled Luis the most was Piper's obsession with punishing Deputy Director Evans and Special Agent Ted Blanchard. He had become reckless, sometimes even overconfident, with each act of retribution.

Luis protested whenever a change occurred. He was a creature of habit. He preferred everything to be in order, with all the "I's" dotted and the "T's" crossed. He believed his obsessive routines kept him and Piper safe.

He anxiously checked his automatic weapon while trying to stay dry. He remained silent, signaling his men and sentries with hand gestures to position themselves in the dark corners of the pier as the heavy rain hammered down on their location.

Earlier that evening, when Piper was told that Agent Blanchard and his partner would be at the drop without backup, he became ecstatic. "It's going to be too easy," he told Luis. "I need Blanchard alive for a while. Kill his partner. I have one last punishment he has to witness."

"Yes, it will be easy. We have ten of our best men. It will just be the two of them, and then we can leave," Luis said.

Piper hugged Luis. "Tonight, another FBI agent will die, and Deputy Director Evans will once again feel my wrath."

Luis trusted no one except Piper. He had seen how quickly men can turn on each other. He watched Piper's father betray his family and wondered if the same thing might happen to him and his brothers someday.

Luis received a tip from Senator Jarvis that two FBI agents would be at the pier that evening, observing. The Senator had proven his loyalty over many years, but Luis didn't trust the Senator as much as Piper did. The man was greedy and only motivated by money. He was a politician.

He knew Jarvis might be lying and that Dr. Kane was setting them up. The Senator, Kane, and Palmer all understood how Piper ended relationships. Now that Miguel had told them their business dealings were coming to an end, they were capable of anything. Tonight, Luis knew he needed to stay alert.

Luis loved Piper like a brother. He was aware of the signs of the prophecy. As Piper's forty-fifth birthday approached, he grew more nervous. Maria, the fortune-teller, had a premonition: *"A young girl and boy, once young, would destroy Piper and all that he loved."*

He believed that Agent Eddie Seymour had once been a young boy. What better person than someone with revenge in his heart to destroy Piper? It didn't help that his friend's arrogance in telling Seymour his sister was still alive was an arrogant mistake.

Luis was convinced that Michelle Arnold had to be the girl. No child had ever escaped from Dr. Kane, let alone Piper, and survived. This young girl was a miracle, he thought. Only a phenomenon like her could destroy everything he and Piper had built for themselves.

Piper had watched the boy's desperate attempts to find his sister for the past seventeen years. Telling him she was alive two weeks ago was a mistake. It only gave Seymour more reason to keep searching and to kill them all. Without finding a body, he wasn't convinced Eddie Seymour was dead.

If he were dead, it wouldn't matter, but there was no report that two FBI agents had died that night, only one. Luis believed the prophecy that was lingering, with only a few months left before Piper's forty-fifth birthday. He needed Sally Palmer to bring him, Michelle Arnold, while he looked for Eddie Seymour.

Luis, a short, stocky, bowlegged Guatemalan with black mutton-chop whiskers and a flushed face, still couldn't shake Maria's prophecy as the rain soaked his face. He stepped back under a small awning that barely covered the loading dock. Nervously, he checked for the fourth time to make sure the $500,000 for the drop was actually inside the metal briefcase.

The truck with the human cargo would arrive in half an hour. The ship of horrors, called the innocent children's floating home, had been prepared and was waiting to take all of them to safety at sea. It had been the perfect crime scene for the last eighteen years.

Even the new Lifeport kidney transporter and the Transmedics Organ Care System were on board, following Dr. Kane's instructions. Kane wanted to avoid risking any organ loss, since this was their final order.

"Just a little bit longer," Luis mumbled.

Luis couldn't stop the terrifying thoughts racing through his mind. The erratic shifts in Piper's personality had become more frequent. His friend had become distant and disconnected from his true self. The monster stayed longer, completely consumed—like Dr. Jekyll and Mr. Hyde—yet this evil force was overtaking what was left of Piper's sanity.

He knew that someday, his friend and boss wouldn't understand or even recognize the friendship and loyalty he'd been shown for all these years. Still, a mercy killing was out of the question. He had sworn long ago to give his life for Piper's, and that promise was what set him apart from other men.

Still, when the signs appeared—the frightening omens—he prayed he could act quickly, with deadly intent, to save his friend. He believed he could change the future by killing the albatross before Piper's birthday. The first part of his plan was underway. Sally Palmer had taken control of Michelle Arnold and placed her in one of the corrupt foster homes she managed, awaiting her orders from Piper.

As the heavy rain hammered down above him, the sound, like tiny pebbles, riveted the thin metal shelter. He checked his watch once more. With Piper's tardiness, he had time to reflect... reflect on better times.

Questioning whether his past was better was a paradox. He was once a poor street thug, and now he was a wealthy, respected criminal. The loyalty he owed Piper had no price, only his life as a sacrifice.

After Luis's mother died of cancer, Piper let Luis's brothers join them. His four brothers pledged their loyalty to Piper just as their brother had.

They all understood that what they agreed to do to the helpless children was horrific, but they stayed loyal. They had endured too much, and now someone else had to bear that burden.

Luis never questioned Piper's justification that the children they kidnapped were better off than what their future held for them in foster care. His mindless daydream was suddenly interrupted by the sound of the transport truck as it appeared from a passage between two warehouses.

It stopped, cutting its lights. Luis, using his flashlight, signaled with three quick beams.

The large moving van slowly made its way toward the drop-off point. Like a mother lion bringing her whining cubs their meal, the crying children's voices grew louder. Nothing was going to happen until Piper arrived.

The truck turned off its engine and waited for the final signal to go. Hearing the soft whimpering, the prophecy once again filled his mind.

Chapter 39

11:30 P.M, Pier-54, San Diego Harbor.

Agents Blanchard and Burns waited nervously near a cluster of loading docks and warehouses, both on edge for different reasons. The thunderous explosions that shook the FBI surveillance vehicle had faded, replaced by sheets of rain that kept them hidden in the darkness.

The smell of the thousands of crusty barnacles attached to the tar-covered logs supporting the pier overwhelmed Ted Blanchard's nostrils. He had a lot on his mind, but none of it compared to how he would explain to Deputy Director Evans his blatant disobedience of the order he had been given. He was counting on catching the Pied Piper in the act and finally closing the case that had haunted both of them for over twenty years.

The two FBI agents sat in silence—a cold, heavy silence between them. The only sounds inside their car were the relentless rain pounding the hood and roof of their rental. It took some persuading, but Burns reluctantly agreed to come along. Blanchard was stubborn, and once he fixated on something, nothing could stop him from doing what he wanted. Rules were for the other guy, not him, and tonight was no different.

Burns couldn't stop fidgeting. He doubted what they were about to do, especially since he knew exactly what Evans had told both of them about pursuing any Pied Piper lead on their own. He understood protocol and was beginning to regret not having backup in place.

"We've been here for two hours," said Burns, with a nervous edge in his voice.

"Soon," Blanchard whispered. "It will end tonight. I feel it in my gut. We'll be heroes."

"Yeah, right. A hero's someone who can keep his mouth shut when he's done something noble," Burns said. "If you're right about this, keeping your mouth shut would be a miracle. So, let's not get ahead of ourselves with this hero nonsense. I want to get this over with. I need to get back to dealing with Sally Palmer about this custody issue with my niece."

"After tonight, you'll have Michelle, I guarantee it," Blanchard said. "Have I ever been wrong?"

"Let me count the times," Burns said sarcastically. "Nevertheless, I do hope you're right. Michelle needs some stability in her life," Elliot told him. He didn't know how to broach what he was about to tell his partner. It seemed like the right time and place. He reached inside his coat pocket for an envelope. "I was going to tell you later, but now's as good a time as any to tell you..."

Blanchard wasn't paying attention. He was focused on the lights that appeared in the distance. Burns put the resignation letter he had planned to give to Deputy Director Evans back into his coat pocket, disappointed that his good news was on hold.

Blanchard had gotten way too excited. "This is what we've been waiting for?" he boasted, elbowing his partner in the ribs. "Maybe Harding was right, and this is Sally Palmer's operation."

Burns sighed. "I thought you said we'd see the Pied Piper tonight?"

Blanchard took a sip of his cold coffee, making loud slurping sounds before responding. "It's possible. Nothing's certain when it comes to that bastard. We get Palmer... maybe she'll get us the Pied Piper?"

"Do you really think we'll ever catch the bastard?" Burns asked.

Ted shrugged. "Evans feels that he's winding down his operations and will disappear soon."

Burns shook his head. "How does someone like him wind down? Psychopaths hunger for what they do, and this guy can't just turn it off that easily. Evans is dreaming that it might soon be over." Elliott was chewing on a sub when Blanchard belched; the foul odor from the cold, chilly dog he had been chewing made his partner gag.

Burns waved his hand to fan away the disgusting smell from his sandwich. He just sat there, shaking his head hopelessly. "You can't say you're in good shape eating that crap twenty-four seven? Have you ever eaten anything healthy, let alone exercised, since we became partners?" Burns snarled, poking his partner's midsection, his fingers disappearing into the mound of fat that lopped over Blanchard's belt.

Blanchard eyed Burns with a devilish grin, stroking his gun. "This is all I need to do my job," he said, swallowing hard.

"Your gun won't help if you have a heart attack or, worse, drop from exhaustion chasing someone," Burns teased.

However, tonight, Burns' mind was focused on his niece and the intense fight he was having with Palmer to gain legal custody. When he heard they might catch the bitch red-handed tonight, he couldn't pass up the opportunity. Arrest her, and all his problems would be solved.

Off in the distance, the activity had become lively. Men were shuffling around a large moving van. "This might be it?" Blanchard said nervously. "Tonight, we're going to rescue children. I can feel it," he said, running his fingers through his messy mop of brown curly hair.

He knew that Guatemala and Honduras had long been hotspots for child abductions. It had now crossed the border into the United States, enabling the Pied Piper to freely kidnap America's neglected foster children. Tonight, it will end.

Blanchard hated the Pied Piper, but he admired the character's ruthless, sociopathic skills. He was organized and methodical, always staying a few steps ahead of law enforcement. No matter where he struck around the world, he always disappeared with the children. The Pied Piper was nothing like his character in the children's fable. He was a murderer who deserved to die.

Blanchard wanted to catch him more than anything, but deep down, he knew nothing involving the Pied Piper ever came easily and tonight felt way too simple.

Blanchard hoped the Pied Piper would come. He remembered Deputy Director Evans' recent update on the psychopath: twenty-five hundred missing infants in the United States over eight years. All cases are still unresolved with no leads.

While the media in the United States kept the Pied Piper off the front page, the international press made him a major news story. He was portrayed as a ritualistic killer, a sick and twisted person without a conscience. Unfortunately, any journalist or editor who slandered his character, describing him as a monster, faced harsh backlash that affected their families.

The Pied Piper made it very clear that no one could tarnish the image he had crafted of his beloved, legendary hero. If his threats didn't get the response he wanted, he'd send messages to the media and law enforcement, threatening harsher punishments for the families of the children he abducted. When they refused, he'd start killing the parents of the kidnapped children, leaving his personalized notes on their brutally tortured bodies. Then, his vengeance would target the reporter and his boss, who had allowed the news story to air.

Burns shook Blanchard's shoulder. "A moving van has turned the corner," he said, waking him from his trance. "It's heading toward that loading dock," he pointed. The truck was slowly inching toward the far end of the shipping warehouses. "Someone's standing on the loading dock with a flashlight. You see the signal he just gave?" Elliott sighed nervously as the flashlight went dark, and the spot where the exchange was taking place was once again cloaked in darkness. He had a terrible feeling about what they were both about to do.

Blanchard didn't respond immediately. He blinked several times, trying to focus. "This is it. The kids must be in the cargo container," Ted said. He was beginning to get a pounding headache. His blood was rushing wildly through his body.

"You circle around the back," he told Elliott. "Make sure you get video of the money changing hands and the children," Ted ordered.

"I'm ready. Are you?"

Blanchard took a deep breath and nodded. "Yeah," he said with conviction. Then he slapped his partner's shoulder. "Remember, don't worry about the men delivering the children…we want the ones taking them. Be on your toes. I don't want to lose any children." He said, swallowing hard.

Elliott frowned. He was troubled by Ted's plan. "We shouldn't be doing this without backup. I have a bad feeling about this," Burns said nervously. "You said we'd call for backup if we saw something. You heard Evans. He'll cut us a new one. We need to call it in first and wait. If this is the Pied Piper, it could get us both killed."

Ted nodded. "Yeah, yeah. But not until I know for sure the kids are here. As soon as I see them and you've got the video proof, then I'll call it in. I promise."

He was a poor liar and noticed Elliott's exasperated expression as his eyes rolled back into his head.

"You can't be a cowboy tonight. I've got Michelle to worry about," Burns reminded his partner again.

Ted ignored him. He was the first to open his car door, then Elliott. The rain now poured fiercely, pounding hard into them.

"Shit," Elliott cursed as the wind-driven rain pushed him back inside the car. "Fuck, this isn't right," he said. He gave Ted a menacing look but left anyway.

Elliott darted to his right, running hard and trying to crouch without slipping on the oily asphalt. He had to navigate around the warehouse and take a position unnoticed.

Burns' bad feeling about what he was doing suddenly hit him. The elements put him at a disadvantage. Running into the wet, dark abyss on the pier, he realized it was reckless.

Ted moved carefully along the dock, staying close to it. His soaked clothes and extra seventy-five pounds made it difficult to move smoothly. He was a big target while trying to stay hidden in the darkness.

Blanchard heard the back of the truck open. He stopped and craned his neck. He heard the faint whimpering of children. Two men, whom he assumed were the buyers, looked into the truck and said in Spanish, "Perfecto." Another man, hidden in a dark corner of the dock, handed the truck driver a briefcase. He watched as the driver counted the tightly packed bills.

Blanchard saw the silhouette of another man; a faint light from the loading dock illuminated his colorful costume. His heart raced. He was now panicked. "It's him," he moaned.

His head began to throb intensely. He felt the veins pounding painfully on his temple as the rush of blood to his brain surged like a raging river. Then his heart stopped. He was like a deer caught in a car's headlights, noticing the man in the colorful costume looking through binoculars fixed on his position.

"Did he know I'd be here?" he wondered. That's when he realized he and Burns had been set up.

Blanchard tasted the bile in his throat. "We've been made," he muttered into his two-way. The pouring rain drowned out his voice. His legs felt like Jell-O when he realized that the costumed man was directly in Elliott's path.

A cold chill ran down his spine, and his hands started to shake as he realized he had sent his partner into a trap. He fumbled with his two-way radio, trying to warn his partner, but his sweaty, rain-soaked hands caused the transmitter to slip and fall onto the cement driveway, shattering into a million pieces.

"Fuck," he moaned. He clutched his gun tightly, trying to steady himself. He knew he had made a big mistake. He misjudged his abilities and underestimated the Pied Piper's power. He understood that if he didn't regain control quickly, Elliott would be dead within moments.

The men near the truck heard the faint sound of the transmitter fading away. They quickly turned around, scanning the area with their flashlights.

Without hesitation, they drew their guns. The bright beams of light reflected off Ted's eyes; he stood frozen, soaked to his core.

Ted fumbled to pick up what he dropped, but it wouldn't have mattered. The transmitter was broken. His eyes widened with fear as he realized that the only way to communicate with his partner, let alone call for backup, now lay useless in a puddle of rainwater. A sign of what was about to happen to his partner.

Before he could look up, the first shot struck him in the shoulder, knocking him to the ground. His gun flew from his hand, sliding across the asphalt and out of reach.

Had Elliott heard the shot? he prayed.

Blanchard hoped his partner was more capable than he was and had already drawn his gun. Then he heard the shots from the other end of the dock.

When Burns turned the corner, he indeed had his gun drawn in his right hand and the video camera in his left. He skidded to a halt, slipping wildly. He was face-to-face with Miguel Guzman, who was wearing a jester's costume and had a broad smile on his face. "Hello, Elliott. Did you think you'd capture me tonight or even save your niece for what I have in store for her?"

Burns' mouth was agape. But before he could react, he was met with an explosion of bullets that ripped a hole in his Mylar vest. The blast went right through his chest, shattering his spine. Burns dropped like a ragdoll, dead before his body hit the loading dock.

Piper shouted gleefully, "Roadkill," as he slapped his leg in triumph. "Now find Blanchard. I want him dead. Then we can get the fuck out of here," he frantically ordered.

Earl Mathews, Sally Palmer's brother-in-law, glanced at Miguel Guzman, who was dressed in a jester suit. "Can I go?" he asked nervously.

The Pied Piper's eyes resembled narrow slits, lost in thought. "Get the fuck out of here. I'll be talking to Palmer about this breach of security."

Earl ran as fast as he could, jumping over the twisted body of the dead FBI agent. He made it around the corner, grateful that his wife Lisa was still waiting for him.

His wife's face was pale. She knew something serious had just happened. She had never seen her husband so frightened.

"What happened? I heard shots," she ranted, pulling on his jacket sleeve.

"It was a trap. The FBI was here because of your screw-up the other day. You're a useless piece of shit. Let's get the fuck out of here," he bellowed. "We're all in trouble now."

* * * * *

Blanchard's shoulder was on fire; he had never been shot before. The pain was unbearable. He had seen other gunshot wounds on suspects before and knew the bullet had shattered bone.

He was trying to hide under the cover of night behind some trash bins. He hoped he could stay hidden until he passed out, but he was such an easy target, and with no backup coming, he knew it was pointless to try.

He heard two voices approaching, their flashlights sweeping the area near him. He hoped they wouldn't find him. He was unarmed and upset that he hadn't brought his backup revolver.

His clothing was just too tight to hide another weapon. After tonight, if I'm still alive... his thoughts drifted to Elliott... shit, what have I done?

Elliott, please stay safe. Echoes of his partner's words haunted him: We need backup! A kicked trash can startled him.

The voices grew louder. The pain from the gunshot radiated through his entire body. He was now breathing heavily, his heart pounding loudly. He bit down on his handkerchief to quiet the sounds echoing inside his head.

He lay there cold and wet, shivering uncontrollably, mostly from shock. At that moment, he wished they would find him… he didn't want to live anymore, knowing he had gotten his partner killed.

He trembled like a scared child.

A distant voice shouted, "Forget about him. We've got to go, now," Piper yelled. "We have to get the children out of here." Piper paused, taking a deep breath. "Agent Blanchard, if you're still alive… please convey my condolences to Deputy Director Evans. Tell him it's not over yet."

Luis looked at Piper, his eyes wide with disbelief. "You're taking too many risks lately. It's not smart to taunt Evans or let Blanchard hear your voice."

Piper pursed his lips. "I'm the Pied Piper," he whispered. "I'm untouchable," he bellowed, tilting his head so he could catch the cold rain.

The voice had sounded familiar to Blanchard, but amid the loud rain, his terrible pain, and the fear that overwhelmed him, his mind was now tricking him.

He almost recognized it but was still befuddled. It did not make sense to him. He huddled tightly in the darkness. He heard the van leaving. Blanchard continued to shake, knowing another group of children had been sent to their deaths, and he had failed.

The thunder had begun to quiet, and the rain had turned to a soft drizzle. Only to be replaced by a ship's horns in the harbor signaling they were ready to get underway.

"How am I going to explain this one?" he sobbed.

Blanchard staggered over to where his partner had gone, praying he was still alive. When he rounded the corner, he saw a body twisted in a pool of blood. He knew immediately that Burns was dead. His stomach clenched, and he threw up his burrito. He stumbled back to his car to call for help. He sat on the driver's side, speechless at this new turn of events.

Blanchard fought back his tears. The Pied Piper didn't deserve that satisfaction. At that moment, he had no willpower. He tried to regain some control, some sense of professionalism, but couldn't stop the surge of anger toward himself.

Chapter 40

Since his return from the child exchange at the warehouse, Piper had spiraled into uncontrollable rage. The only break he took was to shed his jester outfit. His fury was evident on his face, fueling his growing distress. The calm, composed Miguel Guzman was gone, replaced by a frightening version of his father, Frederick. If he had the family belt, he would have used it on Luis, who stood in the corner of his cabin watching his friend deal with his illness.

Fifteen minutes later, after taking a series of calming breaths and exhaling slowly with his lips pressed tight, taming the teapot boiling inside him. The transformation was incredible. Miguel Guzman had returned.

"Luck was with us tonight, thanks to the Senator. It could have turned out a lot worse," Miguel declared, his mood composed.

Luis nodded in agreement, but his face wore a somber expression. "Killing FBI agents… this punishing of Evans has you so consumed, it has to stop. Enough is enough. Our luck, if all of this is luck, will surely run out if you continue like this," he scolded.

Piper had returned, his eyes like small pools of lava, as he glared at Luis. He hated being criticized. "This was Palmer's fault. She must pay, and everyone associated with her."

Luis ignored his boss's last comment and was determined not to let Piper's obsession with Evans continue. "It's gone on long enough, this thing you have with Evans. You're putting all of us in jeopardy. Our plans for retirement will be six feet under the ground," he told him.

Piper's eyes widened in disbelief. He wasn't used to being spoken to that way, especially by Luis. "Don't ever question my methods again," he said menacingly. "I will play my game the way I want to, and you'll do as I say," he added with a finality that made Luis's face drain of color. "I want Palmer and her idiot brother-in-law, Earl, dead. Then find out who tipped off Blanchard and kill the bastard, too. We have a few more details to handle before I'm done with Evans... no, the FBI."

Luis pursed his lips, trying to find the right words that wouldn't upset Miguel. "Blanchard and Burns have been close to capturing you before. Maybe they just got lucky this time?" Luis implied.

Piper exhaled a puff of smoke from his cigar. "I'd be surprised if that were true. My mole inside Jenkins' office told me that Blanchard and the rest of his agents in this so-called task force were to back off from me. There was no way they could have known about our location except for the information we gave Palmer. Someone found out what I told Palmer."

Luis nodded nervously. "We have another problem. It's the Arnold girl, the one who escaped from Kane's lab. She knows too much."

Piper grinned upon hearing the words. "That bitch Palmer, in her panic, well, she stupidly murdered Arnold's parents. They were Burns' brother and sister-in-law."

Luis could see that Miguel was drifting back to the Pied Piper. "You've backed Evans into a corner. He can be, how do the Americans say, a loose cannon. You do remember, he was the one who helped capture your cousin Mario. He's a righteous son-of-a-bitch. If he decides to go after us on his own, well, we won't be able to control the situation like we have in the past."

Miguel closed his eyes, deep in thought, before he responded. "I hope I've pushed him over the edge. It will make the game even more enjoyable. Just don't worry about him. Senator Jarvis will have Jenkins controlling him. He's a loyal FBI agent and will never break the rules. It's what defines him. Anyway, time's running out for him, and all of this won't matter in a few more weeks. It's almost over, I promise," he said, running his fingers through his hair.

Luis understood Piper's anger toward Evans. He saw it every day in his deformed ear. He took a deep breath. There would be no more arguing. He knew it was pointless. Piper's indifferent attitude, the irrational game he had to play, would play itself out. He raised his hands, palms open in surrender.

"And Palmer, how should I handle her?"

Piper's mood abruptly changed. "You don't... no... no, not yet. Isabella needs her child. I need Palmer to handle everything. We have one last order to finish. Then we can cut all ties to us. Soon, Miguel Guzman will be the only remnant of the Pied Piper, as the world continues to idolize me," he boasted.

"I understand the child for Isabella. That's important. But the prophecy — the signs are here. I believe the Arnold Girl and Agent Seymour are the children Maria predicted would destroy all of us. Let me focus on them first, before your birthday. I'd feel much better if they were out of the way first."

Piper chuckled. "You and your stupid superstitions," he said sharply, unaware he had hurt Luis's feelings. "What do I need to do to get you to relax and focus on our business?"

Luis scratched his head, biting his lower lip before speaking. "I support everything you do, but this time I'm scared."

Piper nodded. "Maybe Senator Jarvis will have more information on Seymour. You can ask Palmer where she placed the Arnold girl and then handle it. If this will make you feel better, well, I give you, my friend, permission to do what you think is best. I want this stupid prophecy out of your mind and for you to focus on what lies ahead. Is that clear?" he said, hugging Luis tightly.

"Yes, sir," Luis replied with a broad smile on his face.

Luis was tired. He had to talk to his brothers and make plans.

He knew that hurting Blanchard the way Piper planned would only worsen the situation they seemed to be heading toward. There were plenty of beautiful children being prepared for the final selection, all perfect for Isabella to choose from. He thought about reminding Piper, but stopped himself. He realized this was part of his game. He shook his head. "The game again. When will it end?" he muttered to himself, cursing under his breath as he walked away.

Piper did not see Luis leave the room as he studied the ship's manifest of the live cargo he was shipping to Kane. A small grin began to form on his face. "So much money for these children," he whispered. "The doctor is such an animal." He closed the file and prepared to leave the ship. His medication had taken effect. He needed to be somewhere safe so he could sleep.

Chapter 41

Twenty-five miles off the coast of San Diego

An hour later, three decks below Piper's command room, two petite nurses with their hair pinned in buns under white nurse's hats led twelve children ages six through eleven to the preparation room.

The guards took the infants, all under two years old, to the holding cell hidden deep within the ship's hull. The older children, those over twelve, were thrown into four-by-six-foot steel cages with just a bucket and a blanket.

Back in the operating room, it had the unmistakable smell of a hospital—powerful disinfectant, bright white metal walls, and stainless-steel floors with four drains that collected waste and carried human remains to the ocean.

Neatly arranged next to the operating tables were surgical trays fully stocked for the upcoming procedures. The Lifeport Transport equipment was designated for the specific organs listed on the work orders. There were ninety-six orders that the doctors and nurses had to complete within an hour. These organs were not intended for other infants in need, but for Dr. Kane's sinister experiments.

When the children were finally brought in, they began screaming. They knew something was wrong. A chain reaction of loud cries filled the steel-enclosed butcher's room.

The children who could walk had started to break away from the nurses, knocking over a few of the surgical trays that were in their way. They could run, but they couldn't escape.

It was like a slaughterhouse, with squealing pigs all aware of what was about to happen to them. It was too much for the two nurses to handle, so they called for help.

It had taken no more than five minutes, and all the children were on the cold metal operating tables, arms and legs strapped, tranquilized, and ready for the doctors to do their jobs.

If the nurses felt any remorse for helping Piper, it didn't show on their faces. They held the light blue surgical gowns for the doctors to slip their sterile hands through. Then, the latex gloves were snapped on.

The doctors were emotionless. Music played in the background, just like in any typical operating room. But this wasn't a standard operating room; there was no recovery room for patients afterward.

When the metal hatch in the operating room opened, the screeching of the cutting tools echoed loudly throughout the ship. Luis and his brother were walking past the open metal door of the operating room, sickened with what they were hearing.

"Close the fucking door," Luis shouted above the noise. His brother Herman, without looking back, kicked it closed.

"I'll never get used to that sound or seeing the young children being slaughtered like animals," Luis complained. He offered his brother a cigar while he nervously puffed on his own. "I'm leaving now. We'll meet back in Belize in a week. I have a few loose ends I need to attend to in California."

* * * * *

Later that evening, after Miguel woke up from his deep sleep, Luis waited with his boss until he was alert and ready to listen to the briefing.

Luis spoke first. "My brothers seem happy, even relieved that it will soon be over."

217

Miguel had a strange look as he stared at his friend's eyes, looking for some sign of betrayal. Luis did not flinch. He'd been tested on many occasions before and knew it would happen again and again as Miguel's condition got worse.

"Do you remember the promise you made to me when we first met?" Miguel asked, his voice calm and controlled.

Luis had nodded, keeping his eyes glued on his friend. "Have I done something that has led you to doubt my loyalty?"

"Answer the question," he barked with a raised voice

"You have nothing to fear about my loyalty, or my brother's loyalty, to you," Luis replied with conviction.

Piper expelled a large plume of smoke. He fixed his penetrating gaze. "Good. I can't finish my work without any of you. You're my family. I need to trust all of you." He waved his hand dismissively at Luis.

When the hatch closed, he stared at the ocean from the large porthole on the starboard side of the ship. He thought he heard some hesitation in Luis's voice but shrugged it off. He always felt paranoid during his transition back to Miguel Guzman, which was becoming more difficult.

He sat in his leather captain's chair, drawing in deep, slow breaths and savoring the warm smoke filling his lungs. Point Loma was fading in the distance. They soon would be in international waters.

Miguel leaned forward, his forehead pressed against the cold, thick rectangle window, waiting like an excited child for a treat. What was about to come was not a pleasure for most.

Miguel was looking for the discarded body parts from the group of children that had been butchered. The remains, the food for the frenzied hungry sharks. This had become his entertainment while he began his heavy drinking.

Chapter 42

La Jolla, California. 5:30 A.M.

Blanchard had been in the ER at Scripps in La Jolla under tight security. With another FBI agent dead and another wounded, especially with the Pied Piper's mocking threat, Evans wasn't taking any chances.

Blanchard squeezed his eyes shut, fighting back the emotional pain in his heart, which at the moment had numbed the pain from the bullet that shattered his shoulder.

Deputy Director Evans had been ranting about his agent's botched secret surveillance, but Blanchard's own internal screaming was even more intense, drowning out the Deputy Director's loud verbal attack.

The fog inside Ted's mind started to lift. His eyes began to focus as he drowsily watched his friend, his boss, and first partner adjust his bow tie. Blanchard's ears popped, surprising him. The loud, icy, authoritative tone directed at him nearly made him sit upright on the gurney. If it weren't for the drugs and pain he was feeling, he would have jumped up to attention.

"I ordered you not to do anything regarding the Pied Piper without adequate backup. What the fuck were you thinking?" he scolded, pacing wildly around Blanchard's gurney. "I was two miles away, putting Miguel Guzman back on his ship. And you were playing Rambo with the elusive Pied Piper. You've really messed up this time. Did you think I was joking about not pursuing this psychopath without an army of agents?" Evans' face was beet red, matching the fire in his eyes.

"I'll take whatever punishment you want to give me," Blanchard said somberly. Maybe it's time I retired. I don't think I can do this job any longer.

Evans kicked the gurney, startling his agent. "Can you just shut up? I need to figure this out."

"How can I?" he sobbed. "I just killed my partner. I'm the one responsible. I misled Burns. He didn't understand what I wanted to do." He turned his head away from Evans, unable to look him in the eyes. "Do what you want with me. I really don't care." Noticeably in pain, with one arm in a sling, he wiped the tears streaming down his cheeks with his free hand.

"Stop feeling sorry for yourself. I've lost enough agents lately. We still need to bring down the Pied Piper. You've got two weeks to get your head screwed on straight," Evans said coolly. "Go somewhere. You have enough vacation time. Chill out and get your ass back to me ready to find the Pied Piper. I'm putting together a task force. I'm going after the bastard, and I need you."

Blanchard looked surprised. "Task force? I thought Director Jenkins pulled you off this case?"

Evans stared incredulously at his defeated friend. He took a deep breath and spoke softly. "No one knows about this unit," he leaned closer to Blanchard, "Not even Jenkins. I can't trust anyone except my team. There won't be a trial or jury—just the judge and executioner," he winked. "Are you in or out? No more following the rules. This guy's gotta die, and I want to be the one to do it."

Evans's words caught Blanchard off guard. "Who are you?" he asked, dumbfounded. "I've never heard you talk like that before."

I remember what you and Jack Seymour told me in Guatemala twenty years ago. It's time I grew up and became a better field agent. Are you with me?

"I'm in… I think," he replied sadly. "You know…I heard the children. They were crying," he said, swallowing hard. "It was the Pied Piper. He taunted me. Shit, he knew it was me. The bastard even wanted me to tell you he sends his regards. The strange thing was that I recognized the voice. I just can't, for the life of me, put a face to it."

"If you heard it again, would you recognize it?"

"Definitely."

Evans's eyes grew wide with excitement. "The Pied Piper's playing a dangerous game with us, and so far he's winning. He's made his first mistake by losing Michelle Arnold. Maybe a strong offense can turn into a good defense for all of us. He wants us to kill him. I just feel it. I'd like to grant him his wish." He stared off into the distance, thinking about Michelle Arnold now losing her only remaining relative. His heart pounded hard inside his chest. What else could she endure? he wondered, forcing his emotions back inside his iron heart.

"I really thought we had him. It should have been me lying there dead," Blanchard could see that Evan's mind was somewhere else. "Someone tipped him off. Have we swept our phones recently?" he asked, trying to get Evans' attention.

Evans was now thinking about Agent Seymour in the hospital recovering, and then about the dead faces of his three agents, all lost within two weeks.

Blanchard shook his friend's arm hard. "Have you heard a word I just said?"

Evans, like a parent ignoring a pesky child, raised his hand, signaling he needed another minute. "Just hold on. I'm thinking," he whispered.

"Don't do this to me," Blanchard shouted. Before he could speak, a voice boomed on a TV monitor near the nurse's station. It was familiar. He closed his eyes and immediately recognized it as the Pied Piper. "That's him," Blanchard screamed.

Evans snapped to attention. "What the fuck are you screaming about?"

"That voice. It's the Pied Piper. I'll never forget it." Blanchard leapt off the gurney, pulling his IV from his arm and stumbling through the curtains toward the sound of the TV. Evans followed right behind him.

Blanchard's mouth dropped open. He couldn't believe what he was seeing.

Evans frowned at his agent again, clearly skeptical. "And you're basing this on what, the fact that during a gunfight, pouring rain, and the emotions of being shot, the Pied Piper sounded like Miguel Guzman? Are you nuts? I was with this man while you and Burns were on the pier. It's impossible. Millions around the world love this man. Even our President loves him. He couldn't be the Pied Piper."

Blanchard kept staring at the masked face of the Pied Piper. He closed his eyes and listened closely. He was certain he was hearing Miguel Guzman's voice, whether Evans believed him or not. "It's him, I'd bet my life on it. He owns a hospital ship. He was near the pier at the time of the exchange. I'm right. I know I'm right," he said, his voice cracking.

"You must have hit your head after you were shot. Just because Guzman owns a ship and was in port last night doesn't make him the Pied Piper. Four ships left port last night. He'd be one hell of an actor to pull something like this off. The world's worst criminal, supported by hundreds of governments around the world, let alone protected by the most powerful country in the world..." Evans paused, mulling the scenario over in his mind.

Evans was deep in thought. The Pied Piper always seemed to be one or two steps ahead of the FBI. How can someone continually slip through law enforcement's nets so easily? Only if they're getting help from the inside. Not since the Bureau's founding has there been such a methodical attack on agents.

He led Blanchard back to his room, quietly keeping his thoughts to himself. He needed to think carefully about all of this, and it was starting to make more sense. If the Pied Piper is Miguel Guzman, then his problems are worse than he initially thought.

He needed to get the Arnold girl into a safe house, along with Seymour. Blanchard had to leave town while he assembled his team without the Director finding out. It would be like walking naked in front of the White House and not being noticed.

Knowing he couldn't go to the Director with his problem, he thought of the next best option: Attorney General Jerome Mulligan, a close friend.

The Attorney General had repeatedly expressed frustration about being limited by Jenkins and the president, unable to prioritize the Pied Piper case and the foster care scandal.

Evans took a deep breath before speaking. He could tell that Blanchard knew what was next.

Evans bit his lower lip, appearing uneasy about what he was about to say. "I'm sorry to have to do this to you. You know the drill. You're on paid administrative leave until this investigation into Burns' death is resolved one way or another. I'll need your badge and gun," Evans said, wanting to keep his agent away from the hot zone until he could figure things out.

Blanchard raised his hand, pointing toward a chair with his neatly folded, bloodstained clothing. His face revealed it all—he no longer cared about anything. "My badge and gun are in the plastic bag over in the corner. Take them and leave me alone."

He watched Evans leave, and once alone, was unable to hold back his sobs.

"I've killed my partner and those children, he shouted inwardly. Then the real guilt hit him. Burns was so happy that he was going to get custody of his niece, Michelle Arnold. *"Shit what have I done?*

* * * * *

223

Evans's mind felt numb from what Blanchard had told him. He sat in his car, feeling more confused and hopeless than ever. The hospital parking garage was cold and empty, just like he was feeling at that moment. He had so much to do and figure out. He knew his plan had to be perfect.

Three things had to happen first before he could activate his task force and put all their lives at risk, but he had no choice if he wanted to end the reign of terror of the Pied Piper. He made a few notes on a small pad and pulled out of the garage. Once he walked through the door he was about to open, it would lock him out of ever returning to the job he once believed in.

Chapter 43

Doctor Philip Harding dropped his coffee mug as "Good Morning America" was interrupted by a "Special News Alert." The reporter was discussing two FBI agents, one critically wounded and another shot and in serious condition from a failed FBI raid to catch the Pied Piper. He knew the reporter was referring to Blanchard and Burns.

His head throbbed from drinking too much champagne at last night's fundraiser. His persistent depression returned like an old friend, filling his thoughts with all the missing children and what he had told two FBI agents.

The shock from what he was seeing on TV numbed his headache and pushed him deeper into his pit of despair. Watching the camera focus on his friend being lifted onto a gurney and placed inside an ambulance, and the coroner's van hauling away the black bag of his partner, pushed him over the edge.

The reporter described Blanchard's injuries as critical. His guilt consumed him when he heard the reporter's description of what had happened.

The FBI failed once again in their attempt to catch the elusive Pied Piper. The agency seems powerless to apprehend this criminal. I was told by an anonymous source that these two agents chased the world's most notorious criminal, but they were poorly prepared and lacked sufficient backup.

"Is the Pied Piper smarter than the FBI?" the newscaster asked, wiping a tear from her cheek. *"It's still unknown how many children this country has lost. It seems the President is more focused on his re-election campaign than on stopping this evil man."*

Harding changed the channel only to see another special news bulletin. He sat there emotionlessly. "What have I done?" he moaned.

He dialed his friend and private investigator, Chip Turnbull. The PI had been hunting for Ashley Seymour for nearly sixteen years and had never told Eddie about it. Now, Harding wanted Turnbull to look into Sally Palmer.

"Chip, Doctor Harding here. Have you listened to the news this morning?"

"Yeah. Wasn't that your FBI friend who got shot?"

With a nervous quiver in his voice, he responded, "I'm responsible. I gave him a lead I found at Sally Palmer's office. I was convinced she was handing off a group of missing foster children to the Pied Piper the night before. It's my fault another person got killed because of my foolishness," he admitted.

Are you talking about Jack Seymour or what happened last night?

"Both", Dr. Harding replied.

Turnbull took his time to respond, choosing his words carefully. "You can't keep beating yourself up over what happened nearly eighteen years ago and last night. That was Jack's job back then, and yours now. Plus, it was a car accident that killed him, not Sally Palmer or the Pied Piper," he said.

"So, how do you explain the note the Pied Piper left at the scene after Ashley was kidnapped, and the fact that the person who hit them was her brother-in-law, Earl Mathews?" Dr. Harding replied. "This child trafficking cartel has one boss, the Pied Piper."

"I've been investigating these missing children for the last twenty years and trying to bring some closure to the grieving parents," Turnbull said. "What I've concluded is that Sally Palmer is connected to all the missing children nationwide and might be an active participant in the kidnappings. Everything I have is circumstantial. I'm not sure what you want me to do at this point?"

Doctor Harding sighed, his voice trembling. "Can you dig into Palmer's life, both personal and professional..." he paused, his breathing showing his hesitation about what he was asking of his friend. He didn't want to put him in harm's way like he did with Ted Blanchard and his partner. "I've looked into her background, but there are many gaps in her life, and investigating further could be risky," he cautioned his friend. "After last night, I'm convinced she's involved with the Pied Piper."

"That's very interesting. Her name came up when I first started searching for Ashley Seymour. Unfortunately, my leads hit too many abrupt dead ends.

"Just be careful...please," Harding begged.

"Careful is my middle name," Turnbull said cockily.

* * * * *

Agent Eddie Seymour's eyes were like dead pools as he stared at the TV monitor. He knew Agent Burns, not very well, but he considered him a fellow brother. He was now dead at the hands of the Pied Piper. Blanchard was another story. He had been his father's partner before he died.

Seymour felt completely helpless in his safe house. He wanted to call his adoptive father, opened his cell phone, and was about to press the send button. Then he snapped his phone shut and sank back into his hospital bed. He remembered that he was supposed to be dead. His thoughts flashed to Ashley and what the Pied Piper had shouted at him.

He felt guilty about being in an induced coma and missing his sister's eighteenth birthday and the chance to wish her a happy birthday for the first time since she was kidnapped.

He reflected on the mock funeral ceremony before he was shot and the birthday letters he had buried in the tiny coffin. He wanted to retrieve them to show Ashley when he found her. He leaned back against his pillow, his eyes closed, suppressing his pain, which transported him back to the accident, his parents' death, and Ashley's kidnapping.

He could still vividly see the ambulance with Ashley heading toward the freeway while the police car he was in drove him in the opposite direction. It was the first of many confusing events after the accident.

As if it were yesterday, he could still hear the police officers' worried voices whispering as they led him into the emergency room. He asked a nurse where his sister was. "Ashley Seymour," his high-pitched voice demanded. "Where is she? I have to see her now." The nurse typed something on her computer and shook her head slowly.

"Young man, are you sure she was brought here?" the nurse asked politely.

He looked at the grim faces of the police officers. They seemed just as confused as Eddie.

"Where's my sister?" he yelled, shoving one of the officers forcefully. Their confused looks told him something bad had happened.

He collapsed on the floor, crying for the first time since the accident. That night, Eddie slept in a strange home. It was the first of many foster homes he would stay in during the first eighteen months after the accident.

He continued, catching a glimpse of a distant world he had forgotten. One bright spot in his ordeal was Philip Harding, his father's closest friend, who had adopted him. The adoption had upset Sally Palmer; it was another confusing time he'd rather not think about right now. Right now, he had Ashley on his mind and finding her.

He looked at his cell phone again, wanting to call Philip. He knew Evans was right. He had to disappear for a while. The Pied Piper and Sally Palmer had to believe he was dead.

Chapter 44

Oscar Weidman, owner and editor-in-chief of the San Diego Union Press, couldn't control his temper. He kicked over a chair while his reporters stared, stunned and dumbfounded, as they listened to their editor chew them out.

"Again, the Union Press misses out on a front-page story. Not just a story, but possibly the biggest crime to hit San Diego in the last two centuries?" He shook his head, looking downcast. His eyes were laser beams aimed at his staff of writers. Sitting at the back of the room was his son, a silly grin on his face. He knew his father's bark was worse than his bite, but nonetheless, he had to act like he was scared.

Oscar Weidman's square chin clenched, and his face flushed. "We need to be stationed at the police department, FBI office, anywhere a story might develop. The public needs more information about the Pied Piper, not just the rumors circulating. Washington isn't taking this guy seriously. I want hard facts," he yelled, his voice raspy. "Dig deeper. Maybe one of you can find out why the president has his head so far up his ass?"

His facial muscles tightened as he surveyed the room. Through their nervous expressions, he knew they understood he would hold each of them responsible if a story didn't arrive on his desk soon.

"I want something from each of you on my desk by Monday. That's six days from now," he held up six fingers. "I want to know how this bastard got started. I want to see a trail. I want dots connected." He placed his fists on his desk as he stood, his nostrils flaring like a raging bull. "Now get the fuck out of here and do your goddamn jobs."

Oscar immediately picked up the phone and dialed Deputy Director Robert Evans at the FBI. A soft-spoken receptionist, with a monotone voice, answered with a boilerplate greeting she must have given to everyone who called.

Weidman demanded, "I'd like to speak to Deputy Director Evans, please."

"Who might I say is calling?" she asked, with that same robotic AI voice.

"This is Oscar Weidman, Editor in Chief at the Union Press in San Diego," he replied, tapping his fingers anxiously on his desk. "Be in Evans," he mouthed silently.

"I can patch you through to his cell phone now," she said. "This is just a temporary office for him when he's in the San Diego field office."

The phone appeared to die. It felt like an eternity before a raspy male voice broke the silence.

"This is Deputy Director Evans. What can I do for you, Mr. Weidman?" he said, not expecting an answer.

"We've never met," Oscar said. "I think it's time we do. I have a lot of questions about the two FBI agents who died in San Diego over the past week, and how it might be connected to the Pied Piper kidnappings. The public needs to know the progress you've made in catching him." The editor's tone had turned demanding, which he instantly regretted. He held his breath. Weidman heard the silence, his eyes closed, waiting for a reply. Are you still there?"

"I'm here. I'm not at liberty to say since this is an active investigation. What comes to mind is nothing," he sarcastically replied. Evans did not want to discuss any of it, knowing how Director Jenkins felt about speaking to the press. "We're doing everything we can to stop this maniac, but as you already know, we've had little luck. I've got another dead agent and one in critical condition that needs my attention. We'll have to talk some other time."

Oscar refused to give up. "Last night's botched job at Pier 56 was that the Pied Piper work?" he snarled, hoping to provoke a reaction from Evans. But what he received was unexpected.

"I don't know who the fuck you think you're talking to, but you don't know what the hell you're talking about." Evans was furious as he ended the call. "God damn it," he yelled, pounding his fist on his helpless steering wheel.

He pressed his speed dial for the Attorney General.

Jerome, we have a serious problem. I need a face-to-face with the President.

"What about Jenkins?" the Attorney General asked. "He should be in the loop, right?"

Evans exhaled wearily. "I believe the issue I want to discuss is something only the president should hear. Look, what I have is speculative, but my gut is telling me something isn't right with Jenkins and his connections to Sally Palmer and Miguel Guzman. Too many of my agents are dying needlessly. I believe I have a mole, and it's pointing at Jenkins."

"That's a serious accusation. If you're wrong, you know your career's over," Attorney General Mulligan said. "Let's have a face-to-face first, and you can explain what's spooking you. If you're right, you'll have your meeting with President Webster."

"Fine," Evans answered.

Chapter 45

International Waters, 100 miles off the coast of Baja California

Luis had never expressed his anger verbally before. His rage continuously erupted physically. He preferred using his fists rather than his words. His voice, like a barking dog, resonated inside the phone Sally Palmer had pressed hard against her ear.

"The operation last night was screwed up by someone in your organization, Palmer! Piper's furious. I'm furious. And you don't want both of us angry at you," Luis threatened. "I want a full report on the leak. Call me tomorrow. I don't want to hear any of your fucking whining, only the name of the person who screwed up," he cursed. He slammed his phone down before Palmer could respond.

Sally looked at Earl, then turned to her sister Lisa, who was admiring her long, red, enameled nails. Palmer wondered if Harding had actually found something on Lisa's desk that tipped off the FBI. She knew about Harding's friendship with Evans and Blanchard. Their connection came from Eddie Seymour's father, Jack.

Sally zeroed in on Lisa, their eyes locked. Her sister started squirming in her chair. Palmer's face puffed out like a blowfish, her nostrils flaring, and then her voice erupted in a tirade. She knew her sister well enough to call her out upfront.

Someone alerted the FBI about last night's exchange. Piper thinks it was us. That's absurd, right?

Lisa had become more fidgety. She was twirling her long blonde hair and breathing rapidly, with guilt etched on her face.

"We need to figure it out quickly, or we're all dead," Sally barked, her stare still fixed on her sister.

Palmer knew her sister was guilty when her neck erupted in red blotches. "Lisa, what'd you do?"

Lisa nervously attempted to light a cigarette but dropped the match on the carpet. Her hands shook uncontrollably as she tried to light another match.

Earl realized his wife's guilty behavior. He scowled, glancing at Sally. "Lisa, what the fuck did you do?" he snapped. His open hatred for his wife flared up. "What dumb thing did you do again?"

Lisa's body began to quiver, as if she were out on a cold night in a short-sleeved shirt. Her voice cracked as she tried to explain. "Doctor Harding," she whispered.

She turned her back on her husband, looking directly at her sister. Tears had begun to stream down her cheeks and nose. "Remember, he was at your office the other day...remember? He must have seen...on my notepad," she sniffled, "the message from Piper about the time and place where Earl was supposed to take the children. You know how I forget things. I just wrote it down so I would get it right. I was only doing what you wanted. I didn't want to mess up again."

Sally was growing increasingly frustrated. "Stop with your silly little girl emotions and tell me everything."

She finally broke down, sobbing uncontrollably. Her emotions were frayed. "I had to rush to the restroom that day. You know how I've been. My bladder...the bleeding...my emotions...I couldn't control myself. He was waiting to see you, and he must have looked at my desk while he was alone. I'm sorry. I'm so stupid." She was now rocking, her body bending at the waist, her hands cupping her face, as she continued to sob.

Sally had always had a soft spot for her sister's weaknesses. She tried to hold back the frustration and anger she was feeling at that moment. "It's clear to me, Dr. Harding tipped off the FBI. But Piper's getting blatantly sloppy murdering FBI agents," Palmer said. "Now he's looking for a scapegoat, and believe me, it won't be any of us."

Earl stood pacing wildly. "If Harding did this, he's got to die. You hate him anyway. Let me... it will be my pleasure to rip his heart out."

Sally's long fingernails ran through her hair as she was deep in thought. "He has been a pain in my ass for years. It might make Piper happy, killing Eddie Seymour's adoptive father." Her voice purred as she looked at her brother-in-law. "If we kill him now, it will look too suspicious. If we do this, then we need the crime scene to point to the Pied Piper."

Sally could tell Earl's wheels were turning, thinking about how he would murder Harding. His face twisted like someone constipated trying to relieve himself.

Sally looked at Earl. "Do you have something to say? You have that befuddled look. It makes me nervous. I don't want you doing something foolish."

He rubbed his cropped, bleached blonde hair with his large, strong hands and leaned back in his chair. His tight facial muscles flexed as he began to speak.

"I saw the Guzman last night. He looked like a crazed clown in his Pied Piper suit. He's a weird dude. You should have seen him. Without any emotions, he killed that FBI agent." Earl wiped the sweat off his forehead with his sleeve. "Are you sure we want to stay connected with him?" he asked. "He's a raving lunatic?"

Sally knew it was illogical for Guzman to reveal himself in front of Earl. Then it hit her. "We need to watch our backs."

She had always known Guzman was the Pied Piper but was too scared to say anything. His reckless behavior frightened her. She was surprised that the FBI hadn't figured it out a long time ago. She knew she had to stay sharp to survive.

"Earl, make Doctor Harding disappear and make it look like the Pied Piper did it. Then, we'll complete this last order. Think this time," she scolded.

Lisa was mumbling incoherently. "Lisa, shut the fuck up," Earl yelled.

Sally watched Earl tighten his fists, which looked like iron mallets.

* * * * *

After Earl and Lisa left Palmer's office arguing, Sally opened Michelle Arnold's file. With her uncle out of the picture and no living relatives to stand in her way, she knew she was back in control to carry out Piper's order to bring him the Arnold girl.

Chapter 46

Piper had received a disturbing phone call from his cousin at the FBI. What else could be going wrong? he thought.

Jorge chose his words carefully. "Oscar Weidman, the editor from the Union Press, just called and wants to interview me."

"Can he be trouble for us?" Piper asked. "Is this line secure?"

"You think I'm stupid?" Jorge accused his cousin. "I'm in my office. I know this man. He's a bloodhound. He's been calling everyone about you. His entire team of reporters is digging into your past. It won't take long for him to realize that Enrique Ramirez and Miguel Guzman are the same person. He'll clamp down on you hard and have you plastered across every newspaper around the world. He has more resources than the FBI and Interpol combined."

"What's his name again?" Piper's voice was smoldering.

Oscar Weidman. I heard Evans' secretary patch him through to the Deputy Director's cell, Jorge told him. "The editor is a very influential man, with friends in high places—places where you don't have your fingers. You cannot afford to have his eyes looking for you. If he discovers the connection between your mother and mine, I'm toast."

Piper replied, trying to stay calm, "I'll handle this," he promised. "No one will touch my mother's nephew. Your mother was very kind and loving to me during those years I stayed with you in California. Those were some difficult times for my family."

The agent heard the click of the phone, and a throbbing headache pierced through his skull. He looked over at Alice Dickerson, Evans' staff assistant, wondering if she suspected he was a spy. He pulled out his side drawer, glancing at his gun, debating whether to end it all, except that the glaring photo of his wife and two children smiling back at him tore at his heart. He needed the money he kept receiving for each FBI agent he gave up. It was too good to pass up. He had no choice but to help his Central American cousin. Instead, he reached for his half-empty bottle of scotch, twisted the cap, and took a long, slow sip.

* * * * *

Luis had been listening to Piper's conversation on the speaker. "You're not going to let this Weidman character live?" Luis protested.

"I want you to gather a few men and take care of my cousin, the Arnold girl, and Weidman. Make it all look like an accident. I don't want an investigation."

Luis nodded. "It will be done," he smiled half-heartedly. He knew that too much was happening too fast, and unless he could get ahead of all of it, their house of cards would soon come crashing down on them. There was a lot of killing to be done, but it was necessary for their survival.

* * * * *

Michelle Arnold was beginning to recover physically from her injuries. However, her emotions were in ruins. With her parents' deaths and now her uncle's murder, her tears had run dry. A protective shield had taken the place of her once warm, loving heart. For the first time in her life, she felt utterly alone.

The same survival instinct that pushed her to escape from Doctor Kane's laboratory would have to unify her heart and soul into one cold entity; if not, she knew she would never make it through her world of foster care.

Her biggest problem, she was about to realize, wasn't her new foster parents but Sally Palmer and the Pied Piper. Deputy Director Robert Evans, whom she trusted, didn't believe his promise that no more harm would come to her.

Michelle couldn't tell the good guys from the bad. She tried to close her eyes and drift off, hoping to dream of better places and happier memories. Unfortunately, Deputy Director Evans had questions for her that she wasn't eager to answer. She heard her name called.

She squeezed her eyes shut, her face turned toward the ceiling in her new foster home. She was reliving every moment since her abduction. It felt like a slideshow. First, her parents argued on a park bench, caught up in their blame game, unaware of the danger right in front of them. In an instant, she was grabbed and vanished without a trace. Then the image of the rocking ship and the animal cage she had been thrown into flickered in her mind, followed by the cold pain she felt crawling through the air ducts of Dr. Kane's cement prison. Next, peering through an air conditioner grate, she watched two other men—one with a sliced ear, called Piper by the other man, who was missing a pinky. The man in a jester's costume, without a mask, addressed the man as "Senator."

Michelle had promised herself she would never forget their faces. She squeezed her eyes shut tighter, imagining herself on the mountain, and finally, the terrible pain from the bullets tearing through her already battered body.

She repeatedly watched her slideshow, never wanting to forget, never wanting to lower her guard, and never wanting to feel helpless again. The voice inside her head became her only companion.

She slowly opened her eyes and smiled at the Deputy Director. Her soft voice trembled as she spoke. "I'm ready to answer your questions," she said nervously.

Chapter 47

Piper took off from his hospital ship in his company helicopter, heading to LAX, where his private jet was waiting to take him back to Belize. Before heading home, he had a meeting with Doctor Kane at the Marriott on Century Boulevard.

Piper had transformed into his public persona as Miguel Guzman. He wore denim jeans, a light blue polo, and sandals on his bare feet. He had taken his medication two hours earlier and was relaxing before his appointment with Dr. Kane. Afterwards, he looked forward to the five-hour flight home to his wife, Isabella.

Miguel smiled as he thought about his wife while unbuckling his seat belt. The roar of the helicopter's engines was beginning to fade. He hurried down the short ladder onto the tarmac.

He was relieved that the Pied Piper's manic personality had left his body. *"It will never be over,"* a voice inside his head mocked him. He started trembling. The voice was his father's. Hearing those words and remembering his painful youth, his face turned ashen.

He wanted to see his American cousin, the same one he visited in his youth. With his influence and Senator Javis' help, he managed to get his cousin into the FBI as the most unlikely mole. Unlike his cousin Mario, whom Evans murdered over twenty years ago, Jorge would stay safe. It was ironic that this cousin shared the same office with Deputy Director Evans.

Miguel was using him to eliminate all the agents close to the man responsible for his mother's and cousin's deaths. He shook his head to clear his mind. He had urgent business with Dr. Thomas Kane and needed to stay alert and sharp.

Guzman needed to ensure Dr. Kane understood that his last shipment of children would be the final one. He knew he couldn't underestimate the doctor's broad reach, which extended to some of the most ruthless men around the world. The doctor made it clear in Austria that he was not pleased with Miguel's decision.

Guzman didn't want to think about anything except getting Isabella, her little girl. He had been planning this day for a long time. The hatred and disdain he felt for FBI agent Ted Blanchard, the last person on his revenge list, would be expressed through a brutal act against his sister and her family. His sister had the perfect baby girl, who would bring happiness to Isabella. This final act would bring his murderous game to an end.

Blanchard's niece had dark hair, hazel eyes, and light skin, which made her resemble Isabella as her biological daughter. He had not pressured Isabella to lose her excessive weight after her miscarriage a few months earlier. She still looked pregnant, and it was the perfect ruse, timed just right.

Isabella refused to go to the peasant market after losing her baby. Remaining in seclusion at the ranch suited his plans perfectly. His plan was flawless, just like all the other charades he had been playing for the past twenty years.

Once Blanchard's niece was safely delivered to his wife, he would then, without worry, share their personal lives with the public and announce the birth of their daughter. His driver's soft words, "Mister Guzman, we've arrived at the hotel," snapped him back to the present.

Kane appeared distant as he greeted Guzman. The doctor tried to be cordial, but it was not one of his strong points. He lived in his own strange world, defying all reason and logic in his experiments. But today, he looked more troubled. He nodded toward a couch and told Miguel to sit.

Kane's smile was stiff, and his facial muscles twitched as he became unusually nervous. He tried to speak, his voice revealing his tension. "The organs from the last shipment were excellent," Kane acknowledged. "I know you want to end our business relationship, but can't we just go a little longer? I need more specimens. I can't afford to slow down right now."

Guzman wanted to lash out at Kane, but hesitated. He's crazier than I am, he told himself. "I can modify this last shipment and include, say, ten teenage girls, but that's the best I'm willing to do. How much are you thinking of paying for this modification?" he asked, turning on his laptop. He was instantly at a file labeled FBI family members. If Kane wants to breed, then I have the perfect girls for him.

The doctor's facial muscles relaxed after hearing Guzman's proposal. "That might just work. I'm getting very close to finding cures, especially for your illness. Wouldn't you rather be a healthy retired father than the one who raised you? You know that your disease is progressing faster than your father's. If you don't watch out, you'll turn on your family before your forty-fifth birthday."

Miguel again contained his fury. He disliked what Kane was saying and didn't want to believe he would become his father. His eyes narrowed into small slits. He could sense that the crazy doctor had something up his sleeve. His illness kept him paranoid all the time, but the look in Kane's eyes was genuine. It confirmed his suspicions. The good doctor was planning something, and it wasn't a retirement party for the Pied Piper.

Kane's voice had turned caustic. "You know I don't care what you do to Palmer and Senator Jarvis. I expect that after this last transaction, I won't have to look over my shoulder?"

"I want nothing to do with you or this ugly human trafficking business," Miguel told him. "I'll be riding off into the sunset and starting a new life."

Kane knew that the Pied Piper would never disappear. He understood that Guzman's illness would worsen. He was aware that his life would be in constant danger. "Understand, I have an insurance policy that will keep you away from me and my business," he said as he grabbed a large white envelope and threw it at Miguel. "I have many copies of these photos. It tells a powerful story of a modern-day monster whom the world would love to see humiliated and then executed," Kane said, taking a deep, emotionless breath.

"Are you threatening the Pied Piper?" Miguel asked. "You know, I don't like to be intimidated. You've seen what I am capable of."

I'm not threatening you. On the contrary, I'm just keeping my options open. If you can occasionally send me infant specimens, I am confident I'll find a cure for your disease before your forty-fifth birthday. I want you to be free of your disease so you can live the new life you desire," Kane told him.

Miguel bit his lower lip and nodded slowly. "I've been hearing this bullshit for too long. How close are you? Show me your results," he leaned back against the soft pillows on the couch. He crossed his legs and folded his hands in his lap.

Kane had become more nervous. He did not know how to respond. White, sticky saliva clung to the corners of his mouth as he spoke. "I'm insulted that you'd think my promises are, as you say, bullshit. Scientific results don't happen overnight. I get closer every day. I need to keep our arrangement going for just a little longer. You owe that much to me."

Miguel shook his head. His eyes revealed his answer. "You're like your father… one crazy fucking snake oil scientist. I owe you nothing. If anyone owes, it's you. Your updated order will be on its way. You'll need to find another supplier. I can give recommendations if you want. Plus, if you try to expose me, you'll go down with me. Don't you think I've kept incriminating files on you and your experiments?"

Kane stood, even more agitated. He paced the room, flapping his arms like an injured bird, struggling to take flight. "You can't do this to me," he screamed.

Guzman pursed his lips tightly as his eyes turned bright red. His body stiffened, ready to lunge at the frantic doctor. He took a deep breath and said, "We have what you'd call a stalemate. Your actions right now are why we won't do business again. You've become very careless lately. Letting Michelle Arnold escape has changed everything."

Kane came to a sudden stop, standing right in front of Guzman with a threatening posture. "Don't throw stones. We are cut from the same cloth and we'll both burn in hell when our time's up, which for you could be sooner than you think."

Miguel could no longer control his temper. Standing nose to nose, Guzman grabbed Kane by the neck and squeezed slowly. "If you're truly thinking of hurting me...well...that's a mistake," he said menacingly, tightening his grip. "Maybe we should end our relationship right now?"

Kane backed away, breaking Miguel's grip on his neck. The doctor's eyes widened, anger flashing across his face. He tried to hide his fear. He had turned pale, gagging as he tried to speak. "What do you think you've been doing all these years? You've become worse than your father. He never would have let someone like me become one of his clients," his tone was insulting. "You are what you are, and no amount of medication will ever change that. Your hands have butchered thousands of children, destroyed families, and hurt the innocent. How can you possibly be a good, loving father? Every time you hold your child, you'll think of your sins. Your madness will consume you. You'll become your father, repeating a cycle that has haunted you most of your life." He paused, expecting Miguel to grab him again.

Luis had been listening to this exchange and placed his hand on his pistol. "Miguel, we need to go, now!"

Miguel signaled Luis to stand down. "We'll go in a few minutes. I want to hear what Kane has to say."

Kane pressed on. "I don't mean to be so harsh; we are who we are. It's too late for us to change, ask for forgiveness, and start over. I want to finish my research and find a permanent cure for both our illnesses."

Miguel sank back onto the couch, breathless. He sat there, overwhelmed with anger toward the man who had dragged him into the sinister world of selling infant organs. He wondered if Kane was right about his condition. His face turned pale as he slowly absorbed the doctor's words.

"Maybe you're right," he shrugged, defeated. Nevertheless, this will be our last order. I'll take my chances without you. I want your promise that our arrangement will be finished after this delivery is completed.

Piper looked at Kane, rubbing his forehead in deep thought. "Do we have an understanding? My ship will keep doing its charity work around the world. I will not be a butcher shop for you anymore."

The persona, the Pied Piper, who had desecrated the young, surfaced as adrenaline surged through his veins. Even with the medication in his system, the anger he felt at that moment was bringing back the person he hated. He was out the door and headed to LAX, his mind spinning out of control. He realized he had to act fast, or his offensive strike would arrive too late.

Chapter 48

Michelle was confused and overly anxious. Evans had brought a court-appointed psychologist with him, which only heightened her apprehension toward strangers. She watched as a tripod was set up with a video camera to record what she would tell them.

Deputy Director Evan politely and non-threateningly asked Michelle to please share everything she remembered about her kidnapping and her heroic escape.

Michelle sat stiffly, her voice trembling, arms crossed tightly over her chest as she tried to remember what happened after her abduction, genuinely. She turned on her internal slideshow to see everything clearly.

"I remember my parents arguing. I was sitting on a swing, feeling sad. I saw a man in a clown costume walking toward me, playing a flute. Then, someone grabbed me from behind. I smelled something bad, and everything went dark. Next, I was in a cage on a rocking ship," she said, tears starting to stream down her face.

Evans interrupted the interview. "Michelle, I know this is very difficult for you. Any time you want to stop, say so," he told her. He saw her shake her head. "Good girl, you're being very brave. I promise you. I will find the people who took you and hurt your parents and uncle. I need as many details as possible about what these people looked like. I promise they will be punished. They will never hurt any child again," he said, unable to hold back his emotions.

Michelle took a deep breath. "I hope so. They're very mean. They hurt lots of children," she said, her voice quivering.

Gail Hart, the psychologist, gently patted Michelle's small, trembling hands. "Take your time, sweetheart. We're in no rush. I've found that if you close your eyes, it can help you remember better."

Michelle shook her head firmly. "I don't like closing my eyes anymore. I dream. They're not nice dreams anymore."

For the next two hours, Michelle tried to remember every detail, stopping several times to calm herself. Evans couldn't write fast enough in his notebook. What he was hearing was the most accurate information linking the Pied Piper to Sally Palmer, Senator Jarvis, and Doctor Thomas Kane. He was impressed with the vivid description of Senator Jarvis, right down to his missing pinky finger, and the other man in a clown costume with a partially missing ear. That last detail confirmed what he had suspected: that Miguel Guzman and the Pied Piper were the same person. Now he had a credible witness to obtain the search warrants he desperately needed.

When Michelle had nothing more to say, she fell silent. Evans ordered two FBI agents to escort her to a safe house. His next challenge was managing Sally Palmer and her federal court order, which listed her as Michelle's temporary legal guardian.

Out in the hallway, Palmer waited for him. She stormed toward him yelling and using vulgar language. Meanwhile, Michelle had already slipped out the back door of her foster home while Evans endured her harsh words. He wasn't about to put that little girl back in harm's way. She was his key witness.

He was now sure that Palmer was working with the Pied Piper and Senator Jarvis. He needed more time to set his trap. It wouldn't be easy to convince Director Jenkins or the President about Palmer and the Senator, especially with his upcoming re-election campaign.

Palmer was appointed by the president, and because he was close friends with Senator Jarvis, it could lead to a scandal that might endanger his presidency and re-election campaign.

Evans cut Palmer off. "You tell Director Jenkins anything you want, but there's no fucking way you're getting custody of Michelle Arnold, not until I clear up a few things about the department you are in charge of. Now, get your sorry, fat ass out of my way before I put my foot up it," Evans barked, a feral grin on his face.

Chapter 49

Livingston, Guatemala, Central America

Guzman took a deep, exhausted breath, pausing under the plane's hatch. The warm, humid air filled his lungs with the scent of the sweet bread his mother used to make when he was a child.

The bright yellow sun filtered through the fluffy white clouds as he looked at his ranch house. A hundred acres of lush pastures and jungles surrounded his compound along Livingston, Guatemala. It was just a short distance from the Belize Harbor where his Ship of Hope remained docked.

Every time he returned to the only home he had ever known and his beautiful wife, Isabella, a gentle sense of calm would wash over him. It was his childhood home, which he purchased under the name Miguel Guzman, giving him a sense of security while also stirring up the haunting memories the house held.

A smile spread across his face when he saw Isabella standing on the veranda, waving excitedly. The sun reflected off her black hair, highlighting her red streaks that floated like ribbons. He loved the Camelot life she had created for him. For some reason, he couldn't explain, Isabella today resembled his mother.

She was wearing a multicolored sundress made by local artisans. She kept waving her arms enthusiastically, her emotions always obvious, causing her cotton dress to sway and cling to every curve of her body.

Miguel wasn't expecting his wife to recover so quickly from her miscarriage and had hoped her forty pounds gained during pregnancy would still be there. He looked stunned to see how quickly Isabella had slimmed down. He smiled, knowing it probably didn't matter, but he had to reconsider how he would explain their new baby without raising suspicion.

As soon as his feet touched the soft dirt of the runway, Isabella started running toward him.

"Miguel, my love. I missed you so much," she joyfully wept. "I don't like that we're apart so much."

He gently pushed her back and, with his finger, wiped her tears away. "These are the tears of an angel," he said softly, tasting his finger. "I have good news, my love. I've found an agency with a little girl we can adopt. Her parents recently died." He was speaking in the past tense, even though he knew the tragedy had not happened yet.

"How sad," she responded.

"She needs a good home." He watched Isabella's face light up at the news. Her sweet smile melted his heart. He reached into his inside shirt pocket and pulled out a photo of the infant, handing it to his wife. "I think she looks a lot like you."

She held the photo as if it were a fragile piece of crystal. Her hands trembled. Isabella stared for the longest moment, expressionless. She seemed frozen in silence, then she looked up at her husband and smiled.

"She's beautiful. Are you sure we can have her? Where does she live? Is she in an orphanage? When can we have her?" she rambled excitedly.

"I'll know in a few days. She's in Florida. The agency is trying to bypass all the red tape. Way too much of it when an American child is placed with a foreign family. The United States has silly rules, but a good friend at the State Department's Office of Children's Issues is looking the other way in this matter."

"Are we breaking any laws?" she asked worriedly.

Miguel hugged his wife tightly, his eyes shut. He couldn't look at her and lie. "No. I would never break any laws. You know me." He always wondered if Isabella knew what he did for a living. He tried very hard to keep his horrible work separate from his family. He just prayed she would never find out the truth about the innocent lives he had ruined.

"I have a few contacts from my charity work, and the State Department wants to help us," he said, lightly kissing her on the lips. "I just need you to stay at the hacienda until I bring the baby home. I think it will be best for us to make it look like this girl is our biological child." He noticed the confusion on her face.

"I don't understand. I'm fine with people knowing our little girl is adopted," she said, cupping his face with her hands.

Miguel struggled to maintain his lie. He hadn't expected her to question his reasons for keeping the baby a secret. He gazed seductively into her eyes, his lips trembling, as he continued with his story. "This adoption, I promise you, is legal. However, it can't be made public. The authorities who bent the rules made me promise. It was part of the terms I had to agree to. You're familiar with American politics and everything involved with it. We need to follow their terms, or we won't be able to keep this beautiful child."

Isabella pursed her lips, lost in thought.

Miguel turned his face, unable to meet her eyes. "I had to make a choice," he paused, "your happiness came first, my love."

She pulled back, unable to speak at first. "I'll do whatever you think is best. I want this little girl." She leapt into his arms, her legs tightly wrapped around his waist as she kissed him passionately. She felt his physical excitement. She pulled him into the house toward their bedroom.

"You're the most wonderful kind man. I'm sorry I couldn't give you the son you wanted. I feel so ashamed," she said.

"Don't be. I love you, and if God won't let us have a child naturally, then He'll let us love this one who's all alone." Miguel didn't want to admit it to his wife, but he didn't want a boy. He wanted the Ramirez legacy to end with him.

They made love for two hours. But, before he fell into a deep sleep, he looked up at his wife and used both his hands to pull her head to his lips, kissing her.

He whispered, his voice loving, with a tired edge to it. "I love you so much."

Chapter 50

Evans rarely saw his job in a negative light. It was his career, a calling he swore an oath to uphold the FBI's principles and defend the Constitution. Until now, his job hadn't easily rattled him until the Pied Piper and all the young children being trafficked and murdered for their organs.

After hearing Michelle Arnold's recap and detailed description of what happened to her and the other children, he was determined to take down everyone involved in this heinous child trafficking cartel. He needed to forget about his oath to uphold the law and handle the situation himself. Unsure of how to begin telling the Attorney General what he suspected, he jumped right in without holding anything back. After just ten minutes, the Attorney General raised his hand, signaling him to stop talking.

Attorney General Jerome Mulligan shook his head in disbelief. "I've known Director Jenkins for over twenty-five years. He loves this country. He's one of the most loyal Americans."

Evans sighed. "The paper trail speaks for itself. I didn't want to believe it myself, but Jenkins has to be the one leaking information either to Senator Jarvis or Sally Palmer.

"Just because Senator Jarvis and Jenkins are fraternity brothers and talk to each other doesn't mean the evidence would hold up in court," Mulligan said. "It could be perfectly innocent—one friend helping another.

The Senator is head of the committee dealing with human trafficking. Logically, they'd talk openly. If what you're saying is true, then we're talking about treason."

Evans handed the Attorney General a list. These are the phone calls Jarvis made immediately after speaking to Jenkins on three occasions. The ones I've circled match all of my failed attempts to capture the Pied Piper.

"It still doesn't mean anything. Coincidences are just that," Mulligan said, frustrated.

Evans ran his fingers through his hair. "I find it very disturbing that after Jenkins and I discuss the Pied Piper case and what my next operation will be, he immediately calls Jarvis. Then Jarvis contacts a number either in Guatemala or on the Guzman Ship of Hope. Oh, by the way, explain your so-called coincidences that Guzman's ship has been in port when one of my agents gets murdered," he argued, throwing his hands in the air, surrendering to the Attorney General's unwillingness to help.

Mulligan, his face beet red, had finally lost his patience. "Are you implicating Miguel Guzman in your little conspiracy theory? Robert, you're too close to all of this. You need a serious vacation. You're starting to scare me. Next, you're going to claim little green men are abducting these children."

Damn it. I don't need a damn vacation. I need to catch the Pied Piper, and I need your help," he said loudly. "Jenkins and Jarvis, even Sally Palmer are involved, I'd bet my career on it.

"If we go to President Webster with this shit, you won't have a career anymore. I need more evidence," Mulligan noticed Evans' frustration.

Let's assume Michelle Arnold is correct. Also, let's suppose Dr. Kane, Senator Jarvis, and Sally Palmer are involved in the largest and most horrific human trafficking operation the modern world has ever seen. And if you are right that the most influential and beloved man in the world, Miguel Guzman, is the Pied Piper. What proof do you have besides the words of a ten-year-old girl who just woke up from a coma and is emotionally traumatized? I want to believe you, Robert, I truly do, but right now, your theory doesn't make sense to me. By the way, did you know Guzman visited the girl in the Austrian hospital when she was there, offering her support?

Evans was dumbfounded. "He did what?"

Mulligan tried to stay calm. "Guzman is like that. If he hears about a child in distress or needing medical help, he's there, Johnny-on-the-spot, trying to assist. She's probably remembering seeing him there, Robert."

Evans didn't want to accept it, but Mulligan was starting to make sense. He didn't have sufficient evidence to convince a judge to issue search warrants.

Palmer and Jarvis might be pawns for the Pied Piper. I just know they are working together to facilitate all these child abductions. If they aren't stopped soon—and I mean really soon—the Pied Piper will vanish. It will be checkmate, and then the game will be over.

Mulligan appeared perplexed. Evans was disappointed by the look of contempt on his friend's face. "I can't help you. And I definitely won't take this cock-and-bull story to the president. You're a good friend, Robert, and I usually trust you. What you have is a political nightmare for the President, especially with his re-election coming soon. You're too close and should back off for a while and take a breath."

"It's been politics all along that has endangered our foster care children. With Jarvis and Palmer running the show, nothing will ever change," Evans argued.

Mulligan looked at the Deputy Director, giving only a helpless shrug in response. "Get me definitive evidence that links all your characters to your little soap opera, and I'll arrest them myself," he said sarcastically. "Be careful. If you pursue this on your own without proper authority, not only will you piss off a lot of important people, but I'll also have to lock you up."

Evans stormed out of the Attorney General's office. "If I have to do this by myself, there won't be any judge or jury," he muttered.

Chapter 51

Senator Jarvis slammed his fist on his desk. One of the many flies he had on the walls at the DOJ had just informed him about the heated conversation Deputy Director Evan had with the Attorney General. The subject involved the Senator, Sally Palmer, and Miguel Guzman.

If that wasn't enough to push him over the edge, he was losing control of the Senators on his committee. The murder of Special Agent Elliott Burns by the Pied Piper had ignited a wildfire, and a major investigation was launched without his approval.

"Killing agent Burns was a big mistake. Everyone's calling for a full investigation. First, Michelle Arnold, his niece, then his brother and sister-in-law, and now this..." Jarvis paused, taking a deep breath. "I won't be able to do any damage control. Your actions are out of control," he accused Piper. "I don't know if I can stop the kind of investigation that's being demanded. My committee's talking about working with other countries, even the United Nations, to create stronger laws...shit...they're talking about investigating every sweatshop around the world. I'll be out of business. This will ruin me.

Piper's tone was calm. "The problem's being handled as we speak. Just have Jenkins contain things for a while longer. He's your friend and owes you for helping him get appointed as Director after Hollister died. Payback's a bitch," he said with a laugh.

"I'm not sure even the FBI Director can control this mess," Jarvis argued. "Deputy Director Evans suspects me and even Jenkins. He already suspects Kane and Palmer. The Arnold girl must have seen us together?"

"All he has are mere coincidences. Maybe the Pied Piper enjoys the game that's being played," he giggled. "The Arnold girl is being taken care of as we speak, and all Evans will have is the ranting of a disturbed little girl. So please relax and do your job."

Jarvis ignored Piper's nonchalant attitude. "Cancel my order. I'm going off the radar for a while. I need to distance myself from all of this," he complained.

Piper took a deep breath and slowly released a big sigh. "I cannot cancel your order. Your young slaves are being scooped up as we speak. You know the rules."

"But…" Piper's voice rang with frustration.

"Senator, no buts. I believe you should support your committee's plans. It will give me the time I need to step back from everyone's hair and tie up a few loose ends. By then, the Pied Piper will have disappeared, and you can return to your factories if you wish. You'll be back in business without any issues from all the new referrals I'll be sending your way. Now relax. You don't want me questioning your loyalty?" he threatened.

"Sure. Fine. Just be careful. You do know that Palmer doesn't have the Arnold girl. She's been placed in a safe house by Evans. Not even Jenkins knows where she is. What if she can really identify us? We were all there the day she escaped."

"Let me do my job, and you do yours. I'll have all of this taken care of very soon. Even the Arnold girl. Just keep your government off my back for a while longer. I've got to go. Say hello to Irene and give your two sons my love. Maybe we should get together real soon?" He heard Jarvis swallow hard. The senator's silence told him that his silent threat had made its point.

* * * * *

257

Miguel handed Luis a sheet of paper. "Luis, here are all the remaining orders. Kane wants more organs and some older girls for breeding. Jarvis needs additional workers. Call Palmer in San Diego, Brooks in South Africa, and Kim in Cambodia to fulfill these orders. I want them ready within thirty days."

A wide smile lit up Luis's face. Thirty days. That's good. He handed Miguel another list. It was for each of their brokers and the termination schedule.

Piper smiled. "Perfect. This should work out just fine. I need you to add Michelle Arnold to that list. Palmer lost her. Evans has her in a safe house somewhere near DC," Piper told him as he exhaled a large plume of cigar smoke. Find her. One of your moles must know where he'd take her. Find out and kill her. Once that's done, we'll dispose of Evans and Blanchard. Even Jenkins will go. Once we send President Webster the evidence showing that Palmer and Jarvis were working together and receiving help from his FBI Director, he'll bury it to keep his re-election bid alive. Trust me. It's the best plan I've come up with yet," Piper said, an eerie tranquility in his voice.

Chapter 52

Evan sat in his office at the Hoover building, listening to Agent Michaels, the forensic team leader, brief him on the crime scene where Elliot Burns was brutally murdered. He struggled to focus. So much information swirled in his mind, demanding heavy processing, as doubt gnawed at him. Michelle Arnold's hysterical outburst seemed convincing. He wasn't sure if the higher-ups would believe a traumatized ten-year-old.

All he had was circumstantial evidence. Was the scared little girl truly able to recall so many specific details about the men she saw at Doctor Kane's laboratory while being cross-examined by the defendant's attorneys? That was the million-dollar question he needed to prove.

He planned to video Michelle examining a photo array of twenty-four men and women, all exhibiting similar facial features. Among those photos would be Senator Jarvis, Dr. Kane, and Sally Palmer. It would serve as one of many tests to determine if Michelle's fragile emotional condition could withstand discussing her ordeal during a deposition and later in a courtroom. He deliberately excluded a photo of Miguel Guzman, whose face was recognized worldwide by millions. He knew that a skilled attorney would have rendered that part of her testimony inadmissible.

Agent Michaels noticed Evans wasn't paying attention and deliberately slammed his files on the desk. "Deputy Director Evans, have you heard anything I've been briefing you on?"

Evans nodded. "Yes, please continue."

Agent Michaels reluctantly pressed on. "The rain had washed the area clean, erasing any significant evidence or DNA," The agent told him. "However, after vacuuming Burns' clothing, we found hairs that weren't his. We haven't matched them yet. CODIS is a dead end. Hopefully, Interpol can assist, but I wouldn't hold my breath."

Evans pressed his lips tightly as he listened to the bleak briefing, falling into a frozen silence. He dismissed the forensic team and was alone in his office. He opened his briefcase and spread out a variety of files on his desk. All were pieces of the Pied Piper puzzle, and none of them connected until now. He knew he had to use Michelle as his main witness. He just wanted some solid evidence to support her story.

Everything about this case was moving at lightning speed, and he knew that if he could slow down and analyze everything, he'd find the correct answers. But slowing down was impossible because the Pied Piper was on a fast track to kill more FBI agents and taunting him with his horrific game.

Evans closed the Burns file and opened the discipline review file on Agent Blanchard. The director wanted Blanchard to be fired, while Senator Jarvis was demanding a Senate hearing, insisting that his committee question Blanchard.

He was glad that Blanchard agreed to take his long overdue vacation to visit his sister in Florida and meet his new niece. He hoped that his absence and being out of sight would help cool off the Director and Senator Jarvis.

Evans stood and looked out his office window. He watched Agent Blanchard get into his car in the parking lot. "Go and relax, my friend. Be with your sister and your new niece," he whispered.

The Deputy Director was heading to a Senate committee meeting on child abductions. He knew it was more of a witch hunt. They needed someone to blame, and Evans had become the target.

Sadly, no one was mentioning the Pied Piper in the equation. The FBI was on trial.

He recognized this as just another pointless political stunt by Senator Jarvis, designed to distract the media and the public from the Pied Piper. Evans was speaking aloud as if he were having a conversation with an invisible audience. He noticed Alice craning her neck to watch his ramblings, but he didn't care.

"Bullshit," he shouted as he continued arguing with himself.

His phone rang, breaking him out of his internal debate. "Evans here."

"Oscar Weidman, Union Press."

Evans sounded more at ease than during their first phone call. "What can I do for you today?"

I plan to attend the Senate Committee Hearings on Child Abductions, and I heard you'll be in the hot seat. I'd like to meet with you afterward to discuss how we can move forward. Our first conversation got off to a rough start, and I want to apologize. I may have been too insensitive after you lost one of your agents. I sincerely apologize for my lack of empathy.

Evans needed as many allies as possible, and the press could be a valuable resource. "I'd like that. I have something to show you. We'll have dinner. How about Del Mar at 791 Warf St S.W., around six-thirty? Just tell the taxi driver the restaurant's name. It's easy to find. Does that time work for you?"

Weidman was excited about Evan's complete turnaround. "I'm looking forward to it. I have some interesting information I think you'd want to see also."

Chapter 53

Deputy Director Evans strode confidently into the Senate committee chambers. He tried to keep his emotions in check, but seeing the pompous Senator Jarvis knocked the wind out of him.

The room, packed mostly with the media, had camera techs sitting in front of the Senators on the floor, ready to record his testimony. Today, he realized it was not going to be a friendly chat on Capitol Hill.

Heads turned as Evans entered with a confident smile. He didn't seem like a man under pressure. Despite his recent catastrophic failures that were broadcast on every media outlet, in every newspaper, and especially on President Webster's desk, the Deputy Director was not about to reveal the disgust and frustration he felt toward the "do nothing" committee led by criminal Senator Jarvis.

He was fighting to save his career, his team, and the agents who had died under his watch. That was all that mattered to him right now. Having to defend himself was stopping him from mourning his agents' deaths and focusing on forming his new task force behind Director Jenkins's back.

Evans noticed Oscar Weidman, a friendly face, sitting in an aisle seat to his right as he entered. Then, he quickly surveyed the room, using the method he had learned years ago, memorizing where all of his opponents were seated.

He paused briefly and whispered to Weidman, "I'm glad you could make it." Then he gave a polite, emotionless nod to Miguel Guzman, who sat beside Oscar.

Weidman had a stunned expression that matched Evans's. The editor noticed the cold look Evans shot at the distinguished man sitting next to him. He didn't have a clue that the Deputy Director suspected the man of being the Pied Piper.

What the fuck is he doing here? The Deputy Director thought.

The color drained from Miguel Guzman's face. He saw it in Evans' eyes, the way he was sizing him up. "*He knows*," he told himself.

The Deputy Director, with confident arrogance, winked at his nemesis, trying to suppress a feral grin that was threatening to break across his face. Evans continued toward his lonely seat and microphone. His mind raced uncontrollably as he felt Guzman's eyes burn into the back of his neck.

Evans missed the exchange of words between Weidman and Guzman. He adjusted his tie and took his place in front of the video cameras, carefully adjusting the table microphone. It was important for him to project confidence. He wanted to sit back in his chair, staying upright without leaning forward. He wanted the senators to strain to hear his answers so he could stay in control.

* * * * *

Before Evan entered the Senate chamber, Oscar Weidman introduced himself to Miguel Guzman. He was surprised that the philanthropist knew him.

Guzman leaned forward with his hand extended. "I'm Miguel Guzman," he said. "You must be Oscar Weidman from the San Diego Union Press?"

"Why yes," Oscar replied. "Have we met before?"

"No, we haven't. I thought since my face has been in your newspaper for over a year now, as Editor-in-Chief, you'd remember," Guzman goaded him, his stare sending chills down Oscar's spine.

Weidman blushed. "I didn't mean any disrespect," he responded.

"Don't worry. I don't enjoy being the celebrity everyone expects me to be. It can be overwhelming sometimes," Guzman admitted. "What brings you to Washington? Isn't there enough news in San Diego to keep you busy?" he teased.

"I'm here to see if I can get a story on that bastard, the Pied Piper. I'm trying to connect it to the recent murder of an FBI agent in San Diego a few days ago. It had to have been the Pied Piper," he said with conviction. "My staff is working on trying to figure out who the guy is."

Guzman tried to hide his hatred for Weidman, but it was slowly surfacing. He took a deep breath, attempting to keep the Pied Piper hidden inside before he spoke. "I read about it. How terrible," Guzman feigned sadness. "My, my, one more dead FBI agent and another shot. It was a miracle that Agent Blanchard survived in a drainage ditch," he told him. "I heard that the agent is on administrative leave."

Oscar hadn't heard about Blanchard's administrative leave, but given how his reporters gathered the news, anything was possible.

"I hadn't heard," replied Weidman, holding back his embarrassment.

Guzman struggled to keep his temper in check and maintain his humanitarian persona. However, he was pissed that he hadn't spent a few extra minutes to find Blanchard. The pain he had planned for the FBI agent was now swirling inside his head, and he was slowly slipping away and into the Pied Piper. He knew he had to retrieve it without arousing Weidman's suspicion. It was difficult, especially for a man who shifted between his two personalities as quickly as people brush their teeth.

Weidman paused for a long moment, gazing into Guzman's eyes. "Are you all right?"

"More or less," Guzman said in a soft whisper. "I get very upset when I think about what the Pied Piper has done to the children and those dedicated FBI agents. Unfortunately," he pointed at Evans, "it seems the FBI might have a scandal on their hands," he said, biting his lower lip. "They've lost more agents in the last month than they have in over five years."

Weidman was a handsome man. He was dressed professionally and seemed to be in good shape. His face was lean, with a square jaw and a small cleft that softened his features.

Miguel always admired a man who took pride in his appearance while also loving how they looked after one of Piper's beatings. He patted Oscar's shoulder, lost in thought, before speaking again. He was imagining the deceased editor's handsome features swollen and discolored from his untimely death that was yet to come. With the charm and grace of a diplomat, he continued speaking in a soft whisper.

Guzman sat up and turned to the committee. "I'm here to find out what this committee knows about the Pied Piper, too. You do know I've offered a five-million-dollar reward for anyone who has information that would lead to capturing or even putting to death such a despicable man. Maybe if you're not busy this evening, we could talk over a drink?"

Oscar was flattered to have a one-on-one with Guzman. It might help fill in the missing pieces to his story, he thought.

I've already made plans, but maybe a late-night drink at your hotel or mine?" he suggested.

Miguel nodded, content with the compromise. "I'm staying at the Grand on Pennsylvania. Let's say around eleven in the bar."

Chapter 54

The Senate committee, led by Senator Jarvis, appeared pleased that Evans took the time to speak with them. After being sworn in, the Deputy Director delivered his opening remarks. He was well-prepared and consistently covered the points he wanted to address.

After forty-five minutes, Senator Jarvis finally reached his limit and took charge of the meeting. His first question was harshly directed at Evans. His attitude toward the Deputy Director was well known throughout the Capitol.

"You might be fooling the other Senators today with your excuses, but I know better, Mr. Evans. Every single one of your agents over the last ten years—especially in the last few months—has bungled every attempt to find our missing children, whom the Pied Piper has kidnapped. There have been too many leaks from your agency—leaks that are causing too many international embarrassments for this country and the citizens I've sworn to protect while I'm in office." The senator went on for fifteen minutes, sometimes not even catching his breath, causing the veins on his neck and forehead to bulge.

Evans tried to hold his tongue but couldn't withstand the barrage he had received. "Senator, the Pied Piper is an instrument of barbarity. He's an animal—the lowest form," he paused and craned his neck, his eyes locking with Guzman's. *"Shit, that bastard is grinning at me."*

Evans sipped from his water glass, which was sweating like him, as he nervously shuffled his notes, trying to stay on track. He cleared his throat and looked up.

"The Pied Piper is in the United States and preying on our innocent children." Evans took a deep breath, swiping the beads of sweat that seemed glued on his cheeks.

Jarvis rolled his eyes in disbelief. "For all we know, the Pied Piper is just an urban legend, like the fable. The FBI... damn, even you have no concrete evidence that the recent abductions are the work of this mysterious crime ring. Am I right, Mr. Evans?" the senator argued.

The Deputy Director looked as if he were about to have a heart attack. His face turned bright red. He finally lost all control.

"An urban legend? A fable? Mysterious crime ring?" Are you that blind to what's been happening here and around the world?" Evans lashed out. What next shot out from his lips even surprised the Deputy Director.

"Senator Jarvis... are you fucking nuts?" Evans snapped. "We have three dead FBI agents," he inhaled sharply. "I misspoke. We have four. Special Agent Elliott Burns died last night from injuries sustained while trying to catch that bastard you claim is just an urban legend. Why don't you tell all the mothers and fathers who've read the sarcastic notes left behind by your 'FUCKING URBAN LEGEND' that he doesn't exist!" At that moment, Evans wished he had his revolver. Jarvis needed one right between the eyes.

He saw the fury building on the senator's face but kept speaking. "Unless your committee gets off their fat assess and tells President Webster that the Pied Piper is real, a scandal of the largest proportions, bigger than Watergate and 9/11 combined, will destroy a lot of career politicians...even you, senator." He stood waving his finger at the senator.

Jarvis was furious at Evans for showing such disrespect to him and the committee. "You're out of line. I won't be intimidated by threats. This committee has a direct line to the president, and I can speak for the rest of the senators here that we have found no evidence that the Pied Piper has entered our country or even exists." The senator looked left and right for support, but none came. It didn't matter; he kept yelling at the Deputy Director.

Javis continued shouting. "Director Jenkins has informed me that what we have here and around the world is a bunch of copycat kidnappers using similar patterns." The senator leaned back in his high-back chair, arms folded behind his neck, looking directly at Evans, a big smirk on his face, feeling like he had won that argument.

The Deputy Director, his face pale, attempted to respond, but Jarvis was not finished.

"You have to admit, even your department can't find a similar M.O. for any of the recent abductions.

Evans rested his fists on the table in front of him. "I won't honor your lies. Try speaking that way to all the mothers and fathers who have lost their children to the Pied Piper. Currently, the FBI and our own State Department are working together to connect the dots. The Pied Piper has become sloppy lately, and we are getting closer to finding him. We will apprehend this man and everyone connected to him very soon. We have a witness who can identify the Pied Piper, as well as some of the people who are currently helping him." The Deputy Director knew he had said too much. "*You idiot*," he scolded himself.

Evans noticed that his last comments had hit the senator hard. *Ah, the shit seems to be sticking to the bastard.* He nodded, his lips pursed, returning the smirk.

Again, he would not allow the senator to interrupt him. He raised his hand like a traffic cop stopping oncoming cars. "We have children disappearing every day around the world and in this country. Somewhere, they are either dead, their organs sold like used car parts, or, for the "fortunate" ones, they become someone's slave labor or sex worker in foreign countries. It's even possible some rich foreign families have adopted them," Evans didn't take a breath and continued his machine-gun assault toward Jarvis.

Senator Jarvis was banging his gavel and screaming at Evans. All he received was a single finger salute.

Evan ignored the Senator. "We have a problem, but it seems this committee wants to keep its head in the sand, hoping the problem will go away. I promise you this: I will find this subhuman, and everyone associated with him. When that happens, I will personally put the needle in the arm of the Pied Piper and whoever has been working with him."

Before Jarvis could reply, Evans stood, turned abruptly, and with long strides marched toward the exit.

Guzman wore a feral grin as he applauded Evans' emotional outburst. He threw a haughty kiss in his direction.

The Deputy Director paused for a fraction of a second, but reason outweighed the action he wanted to take.

Senator Jarvis was still angrily banging his gavel and shouting at Evans to sit down. The only response he got was another single finger salute as the Deputy Director stormed out the door.

Oscar Weidman looked dazed, frantically scribbling down everything he just heard. The editor excused himself and hurried after Evans.

Luis sat in the back corner of the room, watching everything carefully. He pressed his two-way radio to his ear and told his men to follow Weidman.

Outside in the lobby, most of the media covering Washington news tried to intercept the Deputy Director. He pushed through the microphones, cameras, and questions, then jumped into a waiting elevator before Weidman could catch him.

The hallway was filled with conversations about what had just happened, but when Guzman came out, people hurried to question him. He appeared cooperative as they surrounded him. A circle of flashing cameras and probing microphones formed the barrier they had created.

"Mr. Guzman," a female reporter yelled a question as she pushed her way as close as she could, her microphone brushing against Miguel's lips. "What is your take on what happened inside the hearing?"

Guzman, the showman he was, began circling slowly, giving every camera a good shot of himself before speaking. "I thought the committee chairman was quite antagonistic toward the Deputy Director. He came in voluntarily and treated him like a criminal. I believe Deputy Director Evans's remarks were important. I feel there is some truth to his accusations. I have not hidden how appalled I am by the number of children missing worldwide, and nothing is being done to stop the epidemic. It's a plague of massive proportions. The facts are clear: it takes only seconds for a parent to lose a child. As you all know, I am very active in tracking down the Pied Piper crime ring and have offered a five-million-dollar reward for any information leading to the capture of this terrible man. In fact, after hearing Deputy Director Evans, I am increasing the reward to twenty million dollars, which will be held in escrow at my bank for anyone who can bring this horrible man to justice." Miguel loved the game he was playing, especially how all the reporters' faces showed they were swallowing his nonsense.

Miguel flashed a big smile at the reporters and cameras, then pushed through the crowd surrounding him. "That's all I have time to say right now. I'm late for another appointment."

Suddenly, the circle broke apart, and the reporters hurried to their spots in the hallway. Like eager children, they used their cell phones to call their editors.

Chapter 55

Later that evening, Luis met Guzman at the Del Mar restaurant at the Warf. He had been informed by one of his FBI spies that Evans had agreed to a dinner with Weidman at the same restaurant where he and Piper were meeting. He reserved a table twenty-five feet from Evans and was hidden behind a tall fern. A miniature parabolic receiver was positioned under Guzman's napkin, with his earplug snugly inserted.

When Weidman arrived thirty minutes late, he saw that Evans had been drinking heavily. The Deputy Director's cheeks were blotchy, his nose was red, and his eyes were bloodshot.

The newspaperman was unsure how to dress for the East Coast weather. He must have been expecting a storm, as he wore a long tan trench coat, gripped a black umbrella in his left hand, and pulled a black fedora tight on his head. He looked more like he was headed for a secret meeting between two spies. He must have listened to a D.C. weather report, which, unbeknownst to him, was unreliable. Weather patterns in the nation's capital are like politicians; they shift quickly with little, if any, impact.

Weidman looked embarrassed seeing Evans in blue jeans, a tan button-down Oxford shirt, penny loafers, and Ben Franklin spectacles perched on the tip of his nose. He was reading a stack of papers laid out in front of him.

Weidman cleared his throat, extended his hand, and apologized again for his tardiness. He was unsure how to start the conversation and said the first thing that came to mind. "That was some speech you made today. You could have heard a pin drop in that room."

Evans kept his head down as if he were studying how the tablecloth was ironed. In a soft, sentimental tone, he replied, "Our government's filled with the most corrupt, inept, and evil human beings. Jarvis is the worst. This off the record? Right?" When Weidman nodded, Evans continued his aggressive rant.

I've been investigating the Senator for years until Director Jenkins, his fraternity brother, told me to back off. I've suspected he's connected to overseas sweatshops. I can't get through all the layers protecting him," Evans admitted.

"That's interesting. If your hunch is correct, it could explain why he's been stonewalling efforts to involve our country in curbing that form of slavery," Weidman replied.

Evans shrugged. "Well, it's just a hunch. What frustrates me the most is that whenever I get close to the Pied Piper, the political wheels here in Washington throw so many monkey wrenches into my investigation that nothing gets accomplished."

"What have you done to break through these roadblocks?" Weidman asked.

"I've complained many times about who might be involved in these kidnappings," Evan responded, slurring his words. "But would anyone listen? No. I got my best friend suspended, and three of my best agents have been killed." He looked up, his eyes red and glassy. "I'm sorry to burden you with all of this."

Oscar patted his arm and offered a reassuring smile. "Inside the chamber, you said four agents?"

"Right, four," he nodded. He forgot that Agent Seymour was listed as dead for his own protection.

The editor hadn't reached his current position by not being able to read people. His gut was telling him that Evans wasn't telling him the whole truth. He felt it instinctively. "You can trust me. Newspaper folks are known for protecting their sources."

Evans attempted a smile, but all he could muster was a faint smile. "Some things you can't know."

"You might not remember; it might have been before your time, but I lost a daughter fifteen years ago to the Pied Piper. I know how difficult it is to investigate this crime ring," Weidman confessed.

"Really?" Evans looked up, surprised. "I'm sorry for your loss," he said sincerely.

"I'd rather not talk about now. I wanted to let you know that we share a common interest and can work together. I can get the truth out to the American public easier than you can," Weidman said, biting his lower lip, trying to contain his emotions.

Before Evans could say another word, Weidman continued talking. "Did you know that Cervantes had said, *'The pen is the tongue of the mind'?* Why not let my paper be the vehicle you need to expose the scandal you believe is brewing in Washington?"

Evans shook his head. "I can't risk another life to the Pied Piper. We all know how he feels about newspapers and reporters. You've already lost a daughter; why put anyone else in your family at risk?"

"Let me worry about the risks. My little girl would have turned twenty-one in a couple of months. Part of my life died that day. I report the news and won't be intimidated by any political bullies or a threat from the Pied Piper."

Evans glared at Weidman. Had he found the perfect ally to push the Pied Piper to the surface? "Maybe we can work together? I'm putting a plan into motion, and your services could prove very useful."

Weidman smiled, pleased that Evans trusted him. "I have some interesting information that might help your investigation. I'd feel more comfortable discussing it somewhere quieter."

Evan nodded in agreement. "I've had one too many drinks tonight to be able to talk about the Pied Piper. Let's have a nice dinner, and tomorrow we can meet at my office to see what you have that could fill in some of the holes in our investigation."

Oscar became animated, rubbing his hands together. "I had assigned every reporter at my paper to find any strange coincidences after the Pied Piper had struck. I know you don't want to discuss any of this now, but I brought something you might find interesting." Weidman looked past Evans's head and paused. He saw two official-looking people walking briskly toward their table. He wanted to tell Evans about the organ-transporting equipment recently purchased by Miguel Guzman, Senator Jarvis, and Sally Palmer. It would be one thing to donate one or two machines, but over fifty didn't make sense. He hoped Evans had some answers.

Evans was about to speak when a man and woman flashed their FBI badges, interrupting him. "Agents Crawford and Ellenberg, sir, we haven't met. We've been trying to see you since we interviewed Dr. Harding. We're on a special assignment from the Office of Children's Issues. We're investigating our federal foster care program. I called you a few days ago, before…" his voice cracked. "Before Burns and Seymour were murdered. I know this is not the time, nor the place, but I do have to talk to you about the California abductions."

The Deputy Director was furious. When he drank too much, his patience vanished. "You've waited this long to bring this to my attention?" he barked, his voice loudly echoing inside Guzman's eardrum.

Agent Ellenberg did not flinch. "I tried to speak to you almost two weeks ago. It was the day you went out of the country to get the Arnold girl. You cut me off and passed me on to your secretary."

"Administrative Assistant," Evans corrected.

Agent Ellenberg could not contain his frustration. "I've left you at least ten messages, which you have not returned." Todd was getting a little hot around the collar.

Crawford interrupted. "Sir, if you have a problem here, it's with your secretary—I mean, administrative assistant. She's taken all of our messages. However, arguing right now isn't productive. We can either talk to you now or set up an appointment at your office tomorrow," Agent Crawford insisted.

Evans looked at Weidman with an apologetic expression. "Oscar, I'll meet you at your hotel tomorrow morning for breakfast. We can pick up where we left off."

Weidman's face reflected his disappointment. He extended his hand to the Deputy Director and then left the restaurant.

Evans did not notice the short, stocky Hispanic man follow the editor out of the restaurant.

"Well, sit down and tell me everything you know about the California abductions." He sounded skeptical. "I'm all ears," he said, pulling at his earlobes and then signaling the waiter for another drink.

Agent Ellenberg spent the next thirty minutes telling Evans about Doctor Harding's logbook and how the doctor believed that Sally Palmer might be the central figure feeding the Pied Piper the foster children under her care.

"She could be the Pied Piper," the agent implied, biting his lip.

Agent Crawford interrupted. "I believe that it was Doctor Harding who tipped off Blanchard about the exchange at Pier 54 in San Diego. They have a history that goes back nearly twenty years. The doctor was also a close friend of Agent Seymour's parents and adopted Edward Seymour. There are too many coincidences that connect Palmer and the Pied Piper."

Evans rubbed his face, deep in thought. "Anything else?"

Yesterday, an infant just weeks old was kidnapped in Florida after her parents were involved in a devastating head-on crash. The newborn was the niece of Agent Blanchard.

The color drained from Evans' face. He was reliving the exact accident that had befallen Agent Seymour and his sister, Ashley, twenty years ago. "Why hadn't I heard about this? Why wasn't Agent Blanchard notified?

"It never made the news. I was notified by a nurse in the ICU ward about the accident," Crawford told Evans. "Another coincidence is that Sally Palmer oversaw the caseworker who handled that DCF case."

"Shit," Evan cursed. "Everywhere I turn, Sally Palmer is smack dab in the middle of murder, the kidnappings, and missing infants."

It's clear Palmer is protecting this crime ring. By the time law enforcement is notified, it's already too late. In fact, most cases lack a photo of the child. My instincts tell me this woman's hands are as dirty as can be. If we don't act now, many more innocent children will go missing.

Evan sat upright, reading Harding's notes. I'll share some additional evidence we have for now, just the three of us. "Can I rely on your discretion?"

Both agents nodded. "You can trust us. We want to put down the Pied Piper like a rabid dog," Crawford said.

A big smile spread across Evans' face. "Michelle Arnold, during her escape from Dr. Kane's ice fortress, had seen and heard the Pied Piper, Senator Jarvis, and Dr. Kane. Dr. Harding's logbook might be the evidence to help us get some warrants," he told them. "I'm taking photos of all three men when I'm back in California for Michelle to look at, especially the one I believe is the Pied Piper. With Harding's book, we might finally be able to connect the dots. Be at my office tomorrow morning at six thirty sharp. No, let's make it eleven. I'm meeting Wieman for breakfast."

* * * * *

Miguel tried to stifle his laughter by covering his mouth with his hand, realizing how unaware Evans was of how close he was to blowing up his entire operation. "They are so close and don't even know it," he muttered.

Guzman watched Evans stand and stagger, stumbling forward as he tried to extend his hand to say goodbye to the two agents. He pressed the receiver to his ear, determined to catch every word.

"I'm going to call your supervisor," Evans said. "Beginning tomorrow, both of you will work for me. You'll meet the other members of my team in a few days."

"A team," Guzman muttered. "More agents to kill, how delightful," he grinned.

Miguel followed Evans outside, wanting to kill him then and there, but he knew that would be too easy. He didn't want it to be easy; he wanted Evans to suffer a little more.

Chapter 56

Weidman had just finished his shower when he heard a loud knock at the hotel door. He checked his watch. It was 2:30 a.m. "Who would be knocking this late?" he grumbled. He put on a plush hotel terrycloth robe and called out, "Who's there?" he demanded, clearly disturbed.

The banging persisted until he stepped closer and peeked through the security hole in the door. Three men, each flashing an FBI badge, waved their identification. As he opened the door, it swung open and knocked him to the ground. He looked up and faced three guns aimed at his face.

Luis swung his revolver, hitting Weidman in the face. Then Herman kicked the defenseless man in the ribs.

Weidman was gasping for air, unable to breathe. Struggling to speak, he managed to spit out the only words that came to his mind: "Please stop!"

The two attackers did as he told them. "Get dressed," Luis ordered. He pointed to the chair where Weidman had folded his pants and shirt. "Do it now before my brother continues with your beating."

Oscar was taking too long, and Herman grew impatient. Without warning, he slammed his pistol against Weidman's head. Weidman went down hard, blood pooling on the carpet.

Luis kicked the editor's legs to straighten them and pulled Weidman's suit pants up to his waist, tightening the belt. Then he put on his shoes. "Where's your logbook?" he demanded.

Weidman forced a strained smile and, in a low, guttural voice, replied, "It's Dr. Harding's logbook. I have not seen it. All I know is that Deputy Director Evans either has it or knows where it is."

Luis combed his fingers through his hair, realizing they were about to murder the wrong man. He was deep in thought before making his decision.

He and Herman grabbed Weidman by his armpits and pulled him into the hallway toward the stairwell. The editor tried to scream, but before any sound could come out, Luis had put duct tape over his mouth.

A few minutes later, Oscar was shoved into a white panel van, his head hitting the exposed metal and ripping a large gash on his face. He was now bleeding heavily and completely disoriented.

While Luis drove, Herman kept beating Weidman just for his own amusement. Before the editor passed out, Luis tilted his head and spoke to him in a calm voice.

"The Pied Piper doesn't like that you are working with Deputy Director Evans. You should have stayed in California and stayed out of it. No one can catch the Pied Piper," he boasted. **"Evans will know that he caused your death. It's nothing personal; it's just part of the Pied Piper's game he's playing with the Deputy Director."**

Weidman's eyes widened with fear, and he started to cry. Not because he was about to die, but because of the pain it would bring to his son and grandchildren. He closed his eyes tightly before the baseball bat struck his skull. It took two brutal hits, and he was dead.

Herman carried the lifeless body like a sack of potatoes and dropped it under a tree on the Capitol Mall near where other homeless men slept. He pinned a note from the Pied Piper to the dead man's chest. It was addressed to Deputy Director Evans from the Pied Piper.

* * * * *

Piper and Luis sat at Dulles waiting for their plane to refuel. They were heading to Miami to pick up Isabella's new daughter before Agent Blanchard arrived.

Luis's phone started vibrating. He picked it up and read the message. "Sir, the plane is ready," he told Guzman as he finished his last beer.

Luis grabbed Miguel's arm and pointed to the news playing on the sports bar's TV. The volume was low, but Luis recognized the location where the reporter was speaking, at the Capitol Mall, and knew they were discussing Weidman.

"They found Oscar Weidman's body," Luis said happily. Miguel just smiled.

As if they had just scored a touchdown, they both banged chests softly and marched out of the hangar to their plane.

"My game is almost over," Miguel stated. "Just a few more house cleaning items to attend to and then, Agent Evans. It's been a long journey, and my revenge is complete, Momma."

Chapter 57

Evans woke up to the loud alarm blaring. He quickly slammed his hand down to turn it off. He grasped his head tightly, and the TV turned on a few seconds after the alarm. He switched on the morning news.

He got up to rinse the foul, cottony smell from his mouth. He paused halfway through brushing—his mouth hanging open, causing foamy toothpaste to drip down his chin. Washington, D.C., had one of the highest murder rates in the country. Still, the murder the reporter discussed made Evan throw up. She was talking about Oscar Weidman.

"Fuck," he cursed, wiping the wet vomit and toothpaste from his chin. "It must have happened after our meeting." His thoughts raced backward, trying to piece together what could have happened.

The reporter continued her report without emotion. "The police are calling this a murder by the Pied Piper. The man was propped up against a tree on the Capitol Mall. He was brutally beaten with a note pinned to his chest. The note was addressed to Deputy Director Robert Evans:

My dear friend, Deputy Director Evans:
Please understand that trying to find me is pointless. Do not bring more people into your investigation, or they will face the same fate. You were warned before, and now the deaths of your FBI Agents and Oscar Weidman are on your hands. This is your final notice, or more people you care about will die.
Yours truly,
The Pied Piper

The reporter continued, "Oscar Weidman had been in Washington on business for his newspaper, the San Diego Union Press. His son had no comment at this time. This is Stacy Truman from KNXT Channel Four News."

Evan's mind raced with images of Miguel Guzman sitting next to Weidman at the hearing. His heart thumped as he thought about his agents. He grabbed his cell. "Alice, get me Agents Crawford and Ellenberg."

"Okay, boss," she replied.

"I mean now," he barked. I'll wait. Patch them in as soon as you find them."

"What's up? You sound terrible," Alice asked.

"I'm not in the mood for your nosiness. Just do as I say," he ordered.

Alice was back on the phone. They're on a plane heading to San Diego and should land in two hours. They left you a message saying they couldn't meet with you this morning because they had to place Doctor Harding in protective custody after receiving a tip that the doctor's life was in danger. Their phones are turned off.

Evans started to question whether it was worth trying to bring the Pied Piper to justice, risking more lives. "What have I done this time?" he slammed his fist into his bedroom wall. The hairs on his back bristled. He knew everything was moving too fast, like the Pied Piper was tying up loose ends before retiring. He had to act immediately or risk losing more agents. He didn't know which way to go or what to do next.

With death raining down hard on Evans from every direction, he sat on the edge of his bed, his head in his hands. He was startled when his phone rang. It was the Director's administrative assistant.

"Director Jenkins wanted me to relay this message to you," she said. "You need to release Michelle Arnold into Sally Palmer's custody immediately."

"What the fuck," he cursed and ended the call.

An hour later, Evans stormed into FBI Director Jenkins' office and lost his temper. He verbally attacked his boss. "Have you lost your fucking mind ordering me to release Michelle Arnold to Sally Palmer?" he shouted. "It was foster care and Palmer who instigated this mess in the first place. Have you ever counted all the children who have disappeared under her watch? I have a witness who ties Palmer to Dr. Kane, Senator Jarvis, and Miguel Guzman, AKA the Pied Piper. We've lost too many agents, and now Oscar Weidman. Aren't you a little worried that FBI agents are dead at the hands of this lunatic, and that Sally Palmer is somehow connected?"

The Director had a blank stare. "You've been saying this for quite a while now. It's just a sad coincidence. Weidman was mugged. It happens all the time in the mall. He shouldn't have been walking that late at night anyway."

Would a mugger leave a note signed by the Pied Piper? Did you know they found blood inside his hotel room?

Jenkins looked stunned. "I wasn't told that. That throws a whole different light on what happened."

Evans took a cleansing breath before speaking. "You think? Is it a coincidence that after I met with Weidman last night, and after he had told me he had proof about the missing children conspiracy, as well as who the principal people involved were, he turns up dead hours later? Another coincidence?"

Jenkins' face went pale. "You need to let the local police handle this. It's not an FBI matter," he ordered.

"I'm going back to the Del Mar restaurant and look at their security cameras," he responded. "I'll bet my career, Miguel Guzman was at the restaurant last night."

It was as if Jenkins wasn't listening. He began to speak incoherently. "And, as for the missing foster children, if not for Palmer's love and care, they would most likely be dead at the hands of their parents," he asserted.

"I just can't...I don't want to believe your conspiracy theories. She is an American Patriot. Now, are you going to release this little girl to Palmer?"

Evans just shook his head in frustration. "Hell no. I'm going to keep Michelle safe and hidden from everyone, including you, until she can testify."

Director Jenkins kept his poker face, but Evans's outburst was too much for him to bear. "I'm not interested in what you want right now. After your unprofessional conduct yesterday... shit... the insulting behavior you showed to Senator Jarvis, I'm going to place you on administrative leave. I order you to turn over all of your files on the Arnold case and have them on my desk by the end of today."

Evans looked at the Director, impressed that he had finally mustered some courage. He questioned why he was so blind to the link between Senator Jarvis and Sally Palmer and the child abductions. "You're playing into the hands of your so-called friends and risking the lives of our Agents and foster care children?"

"Senator Jarvis has been one of my biggest supporters and closest friends for many years. It's unfathomable he could be doing what you're saying," the Director said, his temper barely contained.

Evans bit his lower lip before responding. "Michelle Arnold can identify Miguel Guzman as the Pied Piper," he said cautiously. "She's also able to link Palmer, Senator Jenkins, and Miguel Guzman together in Dr. Kane's ice fortress. Your benefactor was wearing his jester costume with no mask."

The color drained from Jenkins's face. "How credible would a traumatized ten-year-old girl be in a deposition or on the stand?" Jenkins asked.

"Very credible. Can you explain how the Pied Piper knows our every move? You have a mole or moles inside the FBI giving the Pied Piper a heads-up on our investigation," Evans told him, waving his finger at Jenkins.

"This conspiracy theory of yours doesn't make sense," said Jenkins. "You and I are the only people who were privy to all the stakeouts. You can't believe I'm your mole? I didn't know what Blanchard and his partner were doing; even you didn't know what Blanchard was doing the other night," Jenkins said defensively.

For the first time, Evans realized that Jenkins might not be his mole, but simply a naive bureaucrat who cannot see the forest for the trees. If not him, then who?

"Please, for God's sakes, explain to me how the Pied Piper knows exactly when and where our agents are?" Evans asked.

Jenkins was lost in thought. "The only person who was always within earshot of my office was Agent Joe Estrada. He's been with the bureau for over 5 years, is a distinguished officer, and is well-respected by everyone. He was recommended to the bureau by Senator Jarvis and Miguel Guzman. In fact, he's the one who told me about your trip to Austria."

"You think that's another coincidence? I know this guy," said Evans, his eyes narrowing into small slits. "He's the geek who has his face plastered to a computer screen all day long. He's always given me the creeps. Always staring and lurking around. Have you run a background check on him?" Evan asked. "How is he connected to Miguel Guzman?"

Jenkins took a deep breath before responding. "Five years ago, Senator Jarvis asked me to push him through the academy as a favor," he told Evans. He looked like he had the wind knocked out of him. "Shit, he's the cousin of Miguel Guzman." "What a fool I've been. He's been in constant contact with Senator Jarvis quite a bit these past few months."

Evans pursed his lips, resisting his anger. "I hope you now see that there are no coincidences. I need to question this guy. He's got to understand what's happening. He must know the Pied Piper's next move."

Jenkins' voice cracked. President Webster is going to lose it when he hears about Palmer and Jarvis and is reminded that he approved Agent

Estrada's appointment. If Miguel Guzman is the Pied Piper, it will ruin his re-election bid. I don't want to be the one to tell him.

Evans scowled. "I don't think the President needs to know right now. We need to feed Estrada false information and set a trap to catch everyone in the act."

Evans was lost in thought. "Am I still suspended? If not, let's set our trap and see what happens.'

"Go do what you do best and find the Pied Piper and the proof I need to lock up Senator Jarvis and Sally Palmer," Jenkins ordered. "This Miguel Guzman situation is very delicate and needs kid gloves."

Chapter 58

Evans made sure he spoke loudly as he told Jenkins where Michelle Arnold was being held. If Estrada was the mole, he should call Senator Jarvis to set his trap in motion. Who the Senator relayed the information to would give Evans the evidence he needed to arrest Guzman.

Evans glanced at Agent Estrada. He was busy typing on his computer while talking on his cell phone. "Good, it's working," he whispered to Jenkins, giving a thumbs-up.

The tape recorder clicked on as Estrada made his call. It was, in fact, to Senator Jarvis. He and the Director listened:

Senator, I know where the Arnold girl is. I overheard Evans talking to Director Jenkins. The safe house where she's hiding is at 23568 Abbey Street in Thousand Oaks. There might be two locations. The one Evans gave the Director could be a false flag.

"Excellent. I'll relay this to Palmer and Guzman," Senator Jenkins replied. "Watch your back. Call me if you hear anything else."

"It's getting crazy around here. I want to get out before Jenkins puts two and two together and realizes I am a spy for Guzman. I have a bad feeling," Estrada confessed.

"Trust me. Nobody knows whether you even exist or have any connection to all of this. So, stop worrying." Jarvis abruptly ended the call without saying goodbye.

After hanging up the phone, the Senator called Palmer and instructed her to send some of her men to pick up Michelle Arnold. He then called Miguel Guzman.

Evans couldn't believe his luck. Things were progressing faster than he had expected. He glanced at Jenkins' shocked expression. "Are you now going to tell the President about this?"

"Let's let this play out before so I can give the President the proof he'll need to lock up these traitors," Jenkins nervously told Evans.

* * * * *

Evans, after leaving Director Jenkins' office, was on the phone with the two agents watching Michelle. He alerted them to proceed with Plan B and move her to the other safe house. "Our only priority is to keep the girl safe. Is that clear?" he said to Agent Ellenberg.

"We're monitoring Palmer's phone," Ellenburg told Evans. "I'll let you know when they are on their way."

"The moment you have Michelle in the other location, call me," Evans said.

Everything was moving too fast, which made Evans nervous. It was going way too smoothly, just like all his other operations involving the Pied Piper, except they never went according to plan.

* * * * *

Palmer had just received an encrypted message from Senator Jarvis. She was overjoyed. "We know the Arnold girls' location. Two agents are acting like a married couple," she told her brother-in-law, Earl. "We have orders to capture her unharmed and kill the two FBI agents."

Earl was rubbing his hands together, a feral grin on his face. "I'll kill the male agent, but I want to spend some quality time with the FBI bitch before I kill her in front of Michelle. Then I'll give the little bitch what she deserves."

Palmer shook her head. "We won't have time for your sadistic games. We need to be in and out within minutes and head back to San Diego. Piper was precise. He wants the Arnold girl alive. He has other plans for her."

"Are you counting on us having any resistance from the two agents?" Earl asked.

"No. They don't know we're coming. President Webster gave me the authority to have the Arnold girl released to me. We're leaving in thirty minutes. Bring your gun."

Chapter 59

Michelle Arnold had bonded with her female FBI Agent, Leslie Armstrong, and had opened up more. Her smile had returned as the agent treated her like family.

Agent Armstrong easily used her motherly charm, having two young daughters, ages eight and eleven. She brought some stuffed animals with her, hoping to let Michelle be a ten-year-old for a little while, without having to fight to survive every waking minute.

Every night, after a warm home-cooked meal, Michelle and the two FBI agents sat at the kitchen table, enjoying freshly baked double chocolate chip cookies with steaming hot chocolate topped with miniature marshmallows.

Michelle had become more communicative and was finally starting to trust adults again. FBI Agent Leslie Armstrong had taken a liking to Michelle and was considering, after this ordeal was over, adopting her. She would be a perfect fit for her two girls. The FBI Agent didn't want her to go back into foster care.

One evening, while her partner, Max Trumble, was doing his rounds outside, she decided to share her feelings. "Michelle, I know you've had an emotionally difficult year. I talked with my husband and two daughters, and we were all wondering if you'd like to join our family."

Michelle had begun to cry while listening to Agent Armstrong's loving words. "Can you make this happen?" she asked. "I like you very much and want to be part of your family."

They hugged, cried, and laughed.

That night, Michelle slept soundly with a big smile on her face. "Good-bye, Sally Palmer," she sang repeatedly. It was her new lullaby.

Agent Trumble was watching his computer screen when he saw that Sally Palmer had left San Diego and was on her way to their location. He quickly notified Evans. "Barring any traffic delays, I'd estimate their arrival around 10:30 P.M..

"I'm near your location with a team of agents," Evans told Trumble.

* * * * *

Earl Mathews and Sally Palmer arrived at 23568 Abbey Street in Thousand Oaks at 11 P.M. They noticed a tall, husky man walking around the property.

"Earl, don't do anything crazy that might put the Arnold girl in danger," she reminded him.

Earl had a puzzled expression. "I can still kill the two FBI agents?" Then he turned off the headlights and coasted to a stop four houses away from the safe house.

Sally turned his head and planted a wet kiss on his lips. "That was our deal. Make it quick and clean. No loose ends that would tie us both to what we were about to do."

"Are we still going to spend the night in Thousand Oaks? I get so horny before a kill," Earl said, cupping her supple breast.

Earl jumped out of his pickup truck and ran toward the FBI agent. His gun was aimed right at him as he approached. Before Earl could pull the trigger, the street lit up from the spotlights on the two safe houses.

Earl was like a deer caught in the bright lights and started to panic. He began to run again, heading toward the FBI Agent, when a barrage of bullets penetrated his torso. He fell on the street like a wet dishrag.

Sally Palmer sat frozen in the pickup truck, shocked at what had just happened to Earl. She needed to think fast, or she would become the next casualty.

Palmer got out of the pickup truck with her hands high over her head, waving the Presidential papers she had. Her brain was on overdrive. "I'm Sally Palmer and have papers signed by President Webster to release Michelle Arnold to me immediately."

Deputy Director Evans threw her to the ground and pressed her face onto the wet grass. He yanked her hands back and cuffed her. "Your days of freedom are over," he whispered in her ear. Two other agents lifted Sally.

"It's you, Deputy Director Evans, who will be put in jail for not identifying yourself before murdering my brother-in-law. He saw a strange man walking around the property where I believed you were holding Michelle Arnold. He was only trying to protect her. I am here on official government business on behalf of President Webster," she said. "Now uncuff me," she demanded.

Evans was interrupted by the paramedic attending to Earl Mathews. "Sir, this guy was wearing a Kevlar vest and only had the wind knocked out of him. He'll be alright," she said.

Sally Palmer laughed. "You can't do anything right. Now, hand over the Arnold girl, or I will talk to Director Jenkins about having you fired."

Evans was at a loss for words. Palmer must have Teflon on her back. "I am not done with you or your foster care agency. You'll not be getting Michelle anytime soon," he told her. "The next time she'll see you in Federal Court when she implicates you and Senator Jenkins as conspirators in your child trafficking cartel. She'll also be able to identify Miguel Guzman as the Pied Piper. Now get your fat ass out of my sight before I do something I might regret."

Agent Armstrong had been in Michelle's room, reading her a story when the shoot happened. Since the agents had suppressors on their guns, neither of them heard a thing.

A few minutes later, Michelle drifted to sleep in her new mother's arms. Agent Armstrong left her bedroom after receiving the signal that the threat was over.

* * * * *

Palmer sat on the edge of her hotel bed, trembling as her cell phone rang. It was Senator Jarvis following up. She suddenly shouted into the mouthpiece, interrupting the senator, "I just got handcuffed by Evans, and his agents shot Earl Mathews. You sent us into a trap, you bastard," she accused him. "They know about our entire operation."

Jarvis replied in a calm tone. "What proof do they have?" he asked.

"Michelle Arnold. During her escape, she saw you, me, and Miguel in Dr. Kane's office at his mountain-top laboratory. We're all in trouble."

"They don't have any evidence against me. I've been friends with Dr. Kane and Miguel Guzman for years. It's just a coincidence that we were there together," he told her.

"What about Guzman wearing his jester's costume without a mask. How are you going to explain that?"

"It's a simple and logical answer. Miguel, with all the wonderful things he does for children, dressed up as a clown to entertain the seriously ill children Dr. Kane is trying to save," Jenkins admitted. "You were there hoping to find some foster children for some needy families in the United States."

Sally wasn't buying his laissez-faire attitude. She ended the call and smiled as Earl came out of the bathroom naked.

Chapter 60

Miami Beach, Florida

While Deputy Director Evans was dealing with Sally Palmer, Special Agent Ted Blanchard arrived at Miami International Airport. He was eager for his thirty-day break, far from the memories of his fallen partner and the stress of the Pied Piper case. He was also excited to meet his new niece.

Blanchard tried to clear his mind as he walked quickly toward the baggage claim. He kept telling himself he was in Miami to relax, catch up on his sister's life, and get to know his niece for the first time.

Waiting at the gate was his sister, Mary, holding their three-week-old niece, Megan. His brother-in-law, Michael, gave him a big, burly hug, nearly lifting his two-hundred-and-fifty-pound frame off the ground.

"Put on a little weight, Teddy?" Michael teased.

Ted shot him a sharp look, especially because he was called Teddy. Only his mother had that right, and he almost decked his brother-in-law, who knew better. His smile vanished when Michael thoughtlessly mentioned his weight.

Mary instantly saw her brother react to her husband's words and punched him hard in the shoulder, making him recoil.

"Michael, I've told you before to think before you speak. You've upset Ted with your rude words." Her scowl could have melted an iceberg.

Michael, his face flushed, tried to apologize. "I was just kidding. I'm sorry." He shrugged, unaware of what he had done.

Ted looked at both of them, his smile returning. "He didn't say anything wrong. I just had a flashback to when Elliott died. It's been very hard for me to cope with all of it." He stretched out his big arms. "Now, hand me my niece and let me start getting introduced."

Mary still didn't like what her husband said and punched him hard in the shoulder again, "You jerk," she ranted as Ted carried Megan toward baggage claim.

Ted was glad he listened to Evans. Spending time with his sister and getting to know his niece already felt like the right medicine he needed. A new, warm feeling had come over him. He had never enjoyed children before; they made him nervous.

However, as he held his niece, her soft cheek pressed against his, the familiar scent of a young baby eased any apprehension he might have felt. She was instantly drawn to him, as if she knew he was family. He thought he should try practicing being an uncle. Being an FBI agent at that time didn't make much sense.

Megan Marie Morgan was his niece's name, a sweet choice for a girl. He had been told that the reason his sister chose a name starting with M for her daughter seemed silly, but his sister had always been silly and carefree.

His sister, Mary Marilyn Morgan, and her husband, Michael Marion Morgan, had many little quirks that brought them together as a family, and their names seemed to be one of their most notable oddities.

Ted found it bizarre, but who was he to judge? His track record with women didn't make him an expert on relationships, let alone marriage and family.

Mary was his only relative, and he didn't care how they named their children or managed their lives. They were happy, and that was all that mattered to him. At that moment, his depression evaporated.

That night, he had experienced his first home-cooked meal in years. Not since he broke off with Teresa Harper, the social worker at Carlsbad High School, his only true love.

I'm going to enjoy this life for a while, he thought as he watched his sister breastfeed Megan. Seeing his younger sister so mature and motherly made it hard for him to hold back tears of joy.

Once dinner was over and Megan was finished with her bath, his niece was finally ready for bed. Mary now had time to relax and catch up with the brother she was proud of and admired.

They spent the next four hours talking about their childhood, their memories of their mom and dad, and most of all, their lives.

His sister was five years younger, but in many ways much wiser. She had grown into a beautiful woman, wife, and mother. She seemed to have time to exercise as he watched her slender, fit body. Her short, pixie-style red hair was a new look for her, and it looked great, complementing her angular face. The wonderful weather in Miami had given her a perfect golden tan, highlighting her bright blue eyes.

Ted had almost forgotten how she had always been his cheerleader growing up and through some rough patches in his career at the Bureau. He loved her smile, especially the way it wrinkled her nose and furrowed her brow. Her five-foot-three-inch frame, combined with her natural confidence, made her seem six feet tall.

Ted's sad puppy eyes had become moist before he spoke. "I'm very proud of the life you've built for yourself. Mom and Dad would have been very happy to see how you've blossomed into a beautiful woman and mother, especially with such a wonderful family." He was breathing heavily, his sadness surfacing.

Mary patted his hand. "There's someone out there for you if you open your eyes and heart."

He shrugged. "I'd like to see life through different eyes. Eyes that see only joy and trust," his voice cracked as the painful words slipped out of his mouth. "But…" he sucked in a trembling breath. "I've seen so much cruelty, so many terrible things human beings can do to each other, and I just don't know if I could make a relationship work."

Mary tilted her head the way she always did when they were younger. "How come you've never settled down? At least give it a try. Wasn't there a woman, a Terry something?"

"Teresa. Teresa Harper," Ted replied, a painful sadness crossing his face.

"What happened? She sounded so nice. You sounded… well, back then… genuinely happy. It was a side of you I hadn't heard since you joined the FBI."

"Stupidity mainly," he said, adjusting his tight shirt that had been constricting his overweight body. "Teresa and I, for a time, loved being with each other. I did love her very much and still do. But…" he nervously ran his fingers through his hair. "I guess not enough and let my career interfere with my romantic desires. She wouldn't leave California, and well, a long-distance relationship was out of the question for her."

Mary gently patted his hand as he poured out his years of heartbreak over losing Teresa. She turned her body, crossing her legs, so she faced him as she listened. She smiled and looked directly into his moist eyes.

"Have you seen or talked to her lately? Maybe she could help you find some happiness now. You're not getting any younger, and retirement will be here sooner than you think.

"Maybe one day I'll have the courage to apologize. I left before she gave me her answer about marrying me. So, I just left and moved to D.C."

"Now that doesn't sound so smart. Why'd you do that?"

"Maybe I was afraid to hear her answer. Afraid of rejection. It was easier to act like a slob and disappear, I guess?" Ted had begun yawning.

Mary got the message that he wanted to stop because he appeared uncomfortable with all the questions. "Can we finish this another time? I'm beat," he said, leaning over and kissing her cheek.

She wrapped him in a big hug and kissed him back. "No matter what you do, I'm so happy you're here. Please stay as long as you like. You know I love you very much, and I want Megan to learn to love her uncle. Breakfast will be ready when you get up."

* * * * *

It had been two days, and Ted was surprised by how relaxed and friendly his niece had become toward him. He was amazed at how much Megan resembled her mother at that age. The change in atmosphere washed over him instantly, and he soon forgot about the FBI and the Pied Piper.

Mary put him on a low-calorie diet and exercise plan. She told him the only way to lose weight was to eat less, eat healthily, and exercise more. He had quickly lost five pounds, mostly water weight.

Ted let his pain be distracted by Megan's playfulness. He told Mary he wanted to help around the house, and his sister decided that long walks with Megan would be a win-win for both of them.

After eating breakfast and thinking about Mary's perfect life, he drifted back to the time he believed he was in love. He wondered if it was too late, as Mary had said.

He was forty-eight, alone, drifting back to a distant past. He was with Teresa Harper again. Back then, Dr. Philip Harding, a close friend of Jack Seymour, tried to play matchmaker by introducing him to Teresa Harper. She was a dedicated social worker who worked long, grueling hours, just as he did. They made a perfect pair whenever they were together.

Teresa managed Doctor Harding's home for abused children and women in Escondido, California, and counseled high school students at Carlsbad High. Ted instantly became infatuated with her, and she seemed to respond to his loving advances. They fell in love one night in each other's arms after making love. What was great sex had become something more—something they had never experienced.

They both felt confused about how serious their relationship was. Both experienced a loss of control, as if one of them would have to make a decision that could disrupt their career plans. This started to put strain on their time together. Neither wanted to give up their careers, and eventually Ted left, returning to Washington for a new assignment.

Megan, in her car seat on the kitchen table, quickly grabbed his finger, bringing him back to the present. He had forgotten she was beside him, cooing for his attention.

"Do you want to go for a walk?" he fussed back. She had started bouncing, rocking wildly. He loved her giggles. He lifted the car seat that snapped on her stroller and headed outside for their morning stroll on the boardwalk.

Chapter 61

Luis looked at Piper and grinned. "Blanchard looks like he's heading toward the beach again. Everything's in place when he makes his turn onto the boardwalk. That's when we make our move."

Guzman watched Blanchard's sister and brother-in-law wave goodbye to their daughter. They both turned hand-in-hand and headed back inside their single-story cottage. Piper wished her brother could watch him brutally murder his family, but not all of his revenge plans go as intended. Such an innocent couple with so much life ahead of them. It would have been the perfect scenario he wanted before he murdered the FBI agent.

"Luis, this murder needs your personal touch. Blanchard needs to be retching when he sees their bodies. Here's the note for my dear friend. I'll meet you back at the pier by three," Piper told him.

Piper wished he could see Blanchard's face, but just knowing the second-to-last act in his cruel game would finally be carried out on Evans' friend. He remained focused on his top priority. Snatching his niece.

He drifted back twenty years. It was a time he'd rather forget, and this second-to-last payback he planned would allow him to retire as a satisfied father and husband. Today, he wanted Evans and Blanchard to suffer for their interference during his initial snatch-and-grab of the two schoolgirls and the death of his cousin. He touched his mutilated ear, a lasting reminder of the beating his father had given him for his failure. He had been patiently waiting for his final revenge to settle the score with Evans and Blanchard.

"Agent Blanchard, you will very soon find out how errors in judgment can finally come back to haunt you," Piper muttered.

Luis watched his boss drive off toward the beach. He had gotten into another car where his two brothers had been waiting. As loyal as his men were, they did not like how their boss was deviating from their standard protocols.

* * * * *

Uncle Ted, the name his sister had given him and which he now loved, had been making silly faces at Megan as he pushed her stroller toward the boardwalk. The sun was intense, and he had started to sweat from Florida's sticky humidity.

He walked slowly, watching all the people out with their kids on this warm day. He knew he looked like a beached whale in his oversized Bermuda shorts and extra-large tropical shirt that hung over his uncomfortable belly of fat restrained by his belt. Although he had lost just five pounds, he still felt embarrassed by how he looked.

"You need to have patience. A beautiful sculpture is not created overnight. Progressive, progressive, progressive," Mary preached to him.

As he made his turn onto the boardwalk, he was distracted by his niece and her constant need for attention. An overprotective uncle had replaced the serious FBI agent. At that moment, his world centered on his niece, not the looming danger nearby.

He was not paying attention to his surroundings. He felt secure among the children and parents who surrounded him. He wanted to believe that, at least for now, this world was beautiful and safe.

On the boardwalk, it looked like a parade of carriages had started. Strollers of various sizes, shapes, and colors moved in a chaotic procession. Some mothers had twins, and he smiled when a stroller with three seats went by him.

"Triplets, how the hell can they do it?" he smirked. He passed a large U-Haul van, unaware of what its occupants were doing.

* * * * *

Deputy Director Evans arrived in Miami with a team of five FBI Agents. He received a tip that Miguel Guzman had been seen in Miami. Since Agent Blanchard was on a 30-day leave, Evans wanted to check things out to ensure his agent and his family were safe.

Evans' first stop was at Blanchard's sister's house, hoping to see Ted. As they approached the residence, they saw a black van idling in the driveway.

The hairs on Evans' neck stood up. He drew his gun and told his men in the second Suburban to get ready for trouble. "I think the Pied Piper is trying to snatch Blanchard's niece."

The two vehicles slammed on their brakes, skidding to a stop behind the van. As Evans exited the Suburban, he heard screams and shouting coming from inside the house. He ordered two of his men to secure the driver in the van and the other agents to split up, one to enter from the back door and the other to follow him.

As the Deputy Director was about to kick in the front door, he heard three shots ring out near the van. He looked back and saw one of his agents lying face down on the road, while the other agent was shooting at the driver.

Luis heard the gunfire and hurried toward the back door, searching for an escape route. He told his brother to kill Blanchard's sister and brother-in-law, and anyone who came through the front door.

"Herman, we can't let the FBI win. Do what you do best and take them all out," Luis ordered.

* * * * *

Piper pulled up on a looped thick strap and, with a hard tug, made the cargo cab's back door open like a curtain.

He handed a stroller to a pretty Latina woman with a life-sized reborn baby doll inside. He pointed out Blanchard and gave her his orders in Spanish.

She rushed to catch up to her target.

Piper put on his mask and found a spot on the boardwalk to entertain all the mothers and their children. He watched the Latina woman carefully as she approached the crowd of strollers, all gathered at the end of the promenade.

He could tell she was nervous. This was her first assignment. She was one of his nurses who only cared for the children when they were on the ship and in the operating room. He knew she would do well. She had a cold heart.

As the strolling parents reached a bottleneck on the boardwalk, the nurse accidentally bumped her carriage into the back of Ted's ankles. He cried out.

The nervous woman placed her hand over her mouth, her eyes wide with worry. "I'm so sorry," her cool, gentle hand touched his arm as she apologized. "I'm so clumsy. Are you okay?" she said sweetly with a slight Spanish accent.

Ted turned immediately. He was angry at first, but once he saw her pretty face, his mood softened. "I'm ok. Is your baby ok?"

A worried expression broke across her face. "Yes…yes, she probably thought I was playing with her." Panic engulfed her as Blanchard leaned his head into her carriage.

"She's adorable?" he remarked, straightening up. "How old is she?"

The woman wasn't ready for a conversation. She blushed. She's three months old. She sleeps most of the day, which I like the best.

Blanchard didn't realize that her stroller and the baby clothes the newborn was wearing matched Megan's exactly. "Nice talking to you."

The woman felt relieved that he did not try to touch her baby. The nurse waited until Blanchard was fifty feet away before resuming her mission.

Ted heard a loud commotion at the end of the boardwalk. The entire promenade was filled with street performers entertaining their young audience. The clowns, mimes, balloon sculptors, and jugglers all moved around, competing for every parent's attention and, of course, a generous tip.

As Ted massaged his sore ankle, he noticed a unique street performer in a colorful suit, a flute player who played magnificently. His music was lively and captivating.

The jester danced in rhythm to the music he played. The crowd of parents and nannies, all focused on his act, bumped and shoved their strollers to get a better view so their children could see. Megan giggled as the jester approached and made silly faces at her.

The young woman Ted had been talking to had started dancing with the performer. Ted could only see his eyes. They were staring at him as he blew into his flute. A stare that was so penetrating and familiar, it sent a chill through his hot body.

Blanchard's new friend seemed overly sweet and jovial with the animated street jester. Ted had become distracted. He found her attractive, his heart pounding with lust, and he briefly turned his attention away from Megan. A hint of jealousy crept in as she appeared to enjoy the strange street performer. He casually removed his hand from the handle of the stroller and began applauding his new friend, who kept dancing in a whirlwind motion.

Blanchard didn't notice the canister in her hand. She was using a small aerosol can that looked like a perfume bottle to spray her body, but nothing was coming out. His surprise at her clumsiness once again was a little strange.

He missed the signs. The clues were right in front of him, but he let his emotions interfere.

She had the sprayer nozzle aimed at him. Without warning, a light mist floated onto his face, momentarily obscuring his vision. At first, he felt dizzy and disoriented. When his eyes started to burn, he immediately knew what was happening. His heart pounded rapidly, drowning out the surrounding sounds. He was blind. He was panicking. He could hear Megan crying. He grabbed for his gun but remembered it was locked up at his sister's house.

He tried to grab his niece's stroller, but his hand kept clutching air as he frantically searched for the handle of her carriage. Panic had overtaken him. His instincts told him that he and Megan were in danger. He rubbed his eyes hard, which helped clear his vision somewhat. He kept turning, spinning wildly, trying to steady himself and protect his niece. However, the crowd of strollers made it hard. "Megan!" he yelled. He pushed aside strollers like a blind man fighting his way out of a crowd. Too many were blocking his path, and he began to stumble.

The baby stroller congestion had become a scattered puzzle, with pieces drifting apart as if a strong wind had blown them off a large board. It had started to look like a shell game, with the rainbow of strollers moving around, creating a kaleidoscope of confusing, blurred colors.

Ted was overwhelmed with panic as he pushed through the crowd. Five strollers, all identical to Megan's, were parked ten feet away from him. When his vision cleared, the man in the colorful outfit with a flute was gone. The area around the promenade started to thin out, except for the other street performers. They had stopped their acts and looked at each other strangely. At that moment, Ted realized they had seen something. The remaining parents quickly found their children and hurried away, some running to get out of the area.

"Shit, why is everyone running?" Ted screamed, still rubbing his sore eyes. He remembered something he had said to Evans. It only takes a second of distraction, and a child could vanish. He was circling, bobbing up and down like a wooden pony on a carousel. He was now in a state of uncontrolled panic. He looked for the pretty woman, but she was gone. He did not want to believe what had just happened. "This is not happening," he screamed.

Then he saw the woman who had distracted him running alongside the performer in the jester costume, who was now pushing a stroller.

Terror surged through him. It was Megan's stroller. Bile rose in his throat at the sight of the van. He instantly understood what was happening. He watched the woman toss Megan's stroller inside. Megan was in her arms. The Jester waved his flute at him and, with his free hand, gave him a one-finger salute.

"Oh fuck," he screamed. "The Pied Piper."

He turned again to the park bench and saw Megan's stroller. He let out a long sigh, feeling relieved that the attempted kidnapping had failed.

As he grabbed the stroller, he peeked inside, a big smile on his face. It was instantly wiped out when he saw the life-size doll inside dressed in Megan's baby clothes. A note was pinned to the doll's chest. He let out a loud moan that drew the attention of the other street performers around him.

He held the note tightly and read the words:
Dear Agent Blanchard:

You made a big mistake two decades ago, and now it has come back to haunt you. Karma is a bitch. You and Evans should have died then. Now your family's gone, just like your partner, Elliott Burns.

Blanchard, now you'll know how I've felt for the last twenty years. Alone with no family!

It has been nice playing with you all these years, but our little game is almost over. I've got what I want now. Don't come looking for me? You'll never find the Pied Piper's cave.

Love The Pied Piper
P.S. Megan has gone to a better life.

He surveyed the area. He was breathing heavily, feeling lost, with no idea what had just happened. He fell to his knees on the cement walkway, shouting the Pied Piper's name.

He saw a patrol car approaching and ran into the street, causing the vehicle to brake suddenly without hitting him.

"Are you crazy?" the officer shouted at him.

"My niece was just kidnapped. I believe my sister and her husband are in danger." He flashed his FBI badge and gave them directions back to Mary's house. He had a sinking feeling he was too late.

He ordered one of the officers to stay behind and take statements from the other street performers and any witnesses who might have seen anything. With the other officer, they sped toward his sister's house with sirens blaring.

Chapter 62

Blanchard's heart was pounding so loudly that he couldn't hear the screaming mothers rushing away from where his niece was taken. Bile had already coated his throat as his mind imagined what the Pied Piper had done to his family. His thoughts replayed all the gruesome scenes he had seen of the parents of a kidnapped child.

The police car's siren and flashing lights couldn't drown out his pounding heart. As he neared the street where his sister Mary lived, he wondered how he could live with himself for exposing her to the Pied Piper's cruelty.

As the police car skidded to a stop, he saw flashing lights and an ambulance parked outside. One gurney was being wheeled out with a black body bag. He jumped out of the car and dropped to his knees, crying.

"What have I done?" he wailed.

He forced himself to get up and burst through his sister's front door, shouting Mary's name. Deputy Director Evans stopped him, his face grim.

With Blanchard's years of experience, he knew that death had its own special quiet and scent. The house was way too silent, and he knew the worst had happened.

He pushed off Evans and hurried up the stairs to Mary's bedroom. His eyes widened in horror at the gruesome scene. He collapsed to the floor, crying. His sister's and husband's throats had been slit, their faces badly beaten. Pinned to his sister's chest was the same note that was on the doll in Megan's carriage.

Blanchard ripped the note off her body, folded it, and tucked it into his pocket. He tried not to stare at his sister, but something drew him closer. What was once a beautiful young mother, slim and athletic, had become a bloated, blue-gray corpse. Her eyes were fixed open, terror still evident in them. Her husband bore worse bruises on his face and cuts on his hands, some of which were defensive wounds from trying to fend off the intruders. A brave attempt that had ended painfully.

Ted began to focus on the large pool of blood that covered the bed sheets. One body can cause a terrible mess, but two in the same spot was devastating. He turned away after covering their bodies with a clean bed sheet he found in the bedroom closet.

Unable to stop his hands from trembling, he returned to the living room and sat down on the couch. It was the same spot where he and Mary had talked last night, catching up on their lives. Tears started to stream down his cheeks, falling off his chin like a waterfall. For the first time in his life, he felt helpless both as a brother and as an FBI agent.

Evans sat down next to his friend to comfort him. "Ted, I'm so sorry. We arrived just a few minutes too late. I shot the murderer but couldn't save Mary," he told him.

"How did you even know to come down here?" Blanchard asked.

"A lot has happened since you left," Evans replied. "We discovered that Agent Jose Estrada was our mole. He's responsible for over two dozen murders of FBI agents and parents of kidnapped children. We prevented Sally Palmer and her brother-in-law from taking Michelle."

Blanchard looked puzzled. "What does any of this have to do with what happened today?"

I'm not sure. It seems like the Pied Piper is tying up loose ends in his little game he's been playing with us. That's why I hurried down here when I received a tip that Miguel Guzman was in Miami," Evans disclosed.

"I can't deal with it right now. I need time to think and find my niece," Blanchard told him.

"Your niece? Where is she?" Evans asked.

Gone. Today was a carefully planned trap. A Spanish woman, I assume, working with the Pied Piper, distracted me while a performer kept my attention. That was when she took Megan. She even had the exact stroller and dressed her fake baby in the same clothes Megan was wearing.

"Shit," Evans cursed. "I will alert the Coast Guard, Homeland Security, and all airports to be on the lookout for Miguel Guzman before he disappears."

"It's probably too late," Ted replied. "I'm putting in my retirement papers and going to find Pied Piper and put a bullet in the middle of his forehead."

After Evans left, Blanchard heard the officer call in the murder and issue a BOLO for Megan. Then the officer began questioning Ted. He gave them as many details as he could about the young woman at the promenade, the busy boardwalk, and the street performer dressed in a multicolored jester's suit. He also provided the license plate number of the van used by the street performer.

Blanchard could tell from the officer's eyes that he felt hopeless. Ted knew that the Pied Piper was being arrogant. That was his first mistake. He pulled the note from his pocket and reread it.

He wondered what he meant in the note. "What happened twenty years ago? And then it clicked. The Pied Piper is Enrique Ramirez, and everything was starting to make sense. The last twenty years had been a revenge vendetta by a sociopath.

He needed time to think and gather his wits. For the first time, he would take the law into his own hands. It was his way of getting even and hopefully finding his niece. He understood that if they were going to catch the Pied Piper, he would need to assemble a team of retired FBI and CIA friends. His brief vacation was over, and retirement was about to begin.

Chapter 63

The morning after his sister's death and Megan's kidnapping felt surreal. Why was the Pied Piper so arrogant? The sarcastic note he left gave a clue, but Blanchard couldn't understand its meaning. All he knew was that this legendary children's character had taken revenge on him and the other FBI agents for something he and Evans had done twenty years ago. What frightened him most was the postscript: The game is over.

He popped three aspirins to ease his pounding head as he tried to remember something from twenty years ago. He kept muttering to himself, "What had upset this man, who has been masquerading as the fable hero, the Pied Piper? Nothing made sense to him.

He hadn't slept well in his hotel room. He kept having dreams about the abduction and losing his niece. He decided to visit the crime scene to look for more clues. He wondered if Evans had identified the man they killed. He made a mental note to call his friend.

Later that morning, when he entered his sister's house, the smell of death still lingered in the air. He had seen too many murder scenes in his career and was used to the horrible odor. But his sister's death smell made him dizzy. The images in his mind kept replaying, sometimes slowing down so he could see exactly what had happened on the boardwalk.

His FBI training taught him to notice things that seemed out of place. Unfortunately, he had left his FBI hat at home when he went on his well-deserved vacation. He kept noticing the pretty woman, all the baby strollers, and the man in the colorful costume playing a flute. He wasn't paying attention to Megan but instead watching the excited children and their joyful mothers. It was the woman who accidentally knocked his ankle that caught his attention. As he watched her dance to the jester's musical flute, he removed his hand from Megan's stroller for less than a minute.

He remembered her quickly pulling something out from beneath her dress. It happened so fast he couldn't react. She aimed a canister at him and released a mist that burned his eyes, leaving him disoriented. He tried to grab Megan's stroller, but his hand came up empty. He spun around, panic taking over, and frantically searched for the stroller.

A few minutes later, when his eyesight came back, he saw Megan's stroller exactly where he had left it. Relieved, he bent down to pick up his niece, but she wasn't moving and looked different. As he held her in his arms, he realized he was cradling a life-sized baby doll dressed in Megan's exact outfit.

Everything happened in less than sixty seconds. He remembered spinning around, searching for the mysterious woman while rubbing his burning eyes. He saw her toss a stroller into the back of a black van. The man in the multi-colored costume waved back at him with a single finger salute.

Damn, that was the Pied Piper," he acknowledged. He chastised himself, knowing he should have noticed the unusual surroundings, the jester's costume, but he didn't. He allowed himself to become distracted by a pretty woman, which led to his niece being taken. *"I'll never forgive myself,"* he mumbled.

He had a clear image of the woman who sprayed him, making it easier for the Miami Beach police sketch artist to create an accurate likeness. He re-read the last line on the note from the Pied Piper.

Blanchard, now you'll know how I've felt
for the last twenty years. Alone with no family!
Megan has gone to a better life.

Love The Pied Piper

Yesterday, he did his best to describe the man in the colorful costume, but he could only remember his piercing eyes, bushy eyebrows, and a flattened nose that looked like it had been broken several times. He recalled the jester had a deformed ear. All Blanchard knew was that he would never forget the man's eyes. The light blue color was distinctive and reminded him of someone he'd seen before.

Sitting in his car, he read the morning news article about the murders, the abduction by the Pied Piper, and next to it, the sketch of the woman who took Megan. It was a perfect rendering.

At his sister's house, he showed his badge to a Miami police officer and ducked under the yellow tape around the house. He was relieved that Evans had called in the FBI forensic team before the local authorities could mess up the evidence.

"I'm Special Agent Blanchard. Who's in charge?" he asked sharply.

The agent indicated toward his sister's bedroom. "See Agent Alexander. He's the tall one with white hair."

Ted slowly entered the room where his sister and brother-in-law had been brutally murdered. The bloodstained sheets were still there. The forensic agents were systematically searching for evidence.

Ted introduced himself with a pale face. He tried not to look at the blood, but he couldn't help it. "Agent Alexander? Special Agent Ted Blanchard from D.C. Find anything?"

"Nothing substantial. It appears that whoever did this was consumed by rage. The only fingerprints we found were your sister's and your brother-in-law's. We also found yours around the house, along with an infant's, which I assume was Megan's. They must have used gloves. A few hairs on the bodies will be sent to the lab. Under your brother-in-law's fingernails was skin, which we'll send to all of our databases here and in INTERPOL to try to find a match," Agent Alexander told him. "Your brother-in-law put up a brave fight, but these guys were... well... very sadistic."

Agent Alexander watched Ted turn away and walk out of the room, holding his mouth. He caught up with him in the bathroom.

"Sorry. I guess seeing all of this again... I couldn't control myself," Ted said, wiping his chin with his handkerchief.

"I know how hard you've been working to find the Pied Piper. Have you figured out why he's making it so personal?" Agent Alexander asked. "I've read all the notes he's left behind for you and Deputy Director Evans."

That's what I've been trying to figure out all morning. I don't know why us.

"Maybe you need a fresh set of eyes to help you see the clues. I want to help," Alexander offered.

Ted looked at him, his eyes moist with sadness. "I've been taken off this case. That's why I was down here. I was taking some needed vacation time after my partner was murdered," he admitted, "And now this. I'm too close to this case."

"I've been assigned your sister's case. I can work with you. I can keep you updated. Maybe use some of your input to help solve this crime," Alexander replied. "It might help me to know what cases or where you were at twenty years ago."

Agent Blanchard, for the first time since entering the house, felt relieved. He was scratching his head, deep in thought. "Let me search some of my old case files, and I'll get back to you," he acknowledged.

"Whatever you can do, I'd appreciate it." He didn't want to tell the agent he was retiring.

"Agent Blanchard, could you be at my office at noon on Monday? I should have the DNA results back from the hair and skin samples. Then we can see what pops up," Alexander said, extending his hand. "Also, if you have a timeline of what you were doing twenty years ago, it would be helpful."

"That will work out just fine," he replied. "Call me Ted if we're going to be working with each other.

Chapter 64

While Guzman waited for his head of security to arrive, he was reading the Miami Herald. "How the fuck could Luis and his brothers screw up such a perfectly laid-out plan?" he slurred his words as he sipped his vodka and orange juice. "Now another of Luis' family is dead at the hands of Evans."

Fifteen minutes later, Luis stood before Piper, unable to smile. He looked as if he hadn't slept. He was unshaven, still wearing the blood-stained shirt he had on yesterday. "I'm not in the mood for your scolding," he told him.

"Have you seen the paper this morning?" he shouted, holding up the picture of Estella Ruiz.

"No, I haven't, sir. You know I don't like to read the news," he smirked at the question. "You do understand I am mourning the killing of my brother," Luis sarcastically reminded his boss.

Guzman didn't seem moved by what Luis had said. "Don't be a smart ass. Your brother's death is the price we pay in our business."

"I want to know how Evans knew we'd be in Miami. That bastard must die a painful death at my hands and my hands alone," Luis demanded.

"In due time. Now look at this rendering of Estella Ruiz. If she's captured, Evans could link her to the ship and me." Guzman looked at Luis with an icy stare. Without a word, Luis knew what had to be done.

"I'll take care of it first later today on the ship. She'll be fish food for the hungry sharks," Luis assured him. "When can I kill Evans?"

Miguel had never been this angry with Luis and wanted to let him know how upset he was. "Not yet. I need a little more time to implement my final solution for everyone connected to us. Now, no more screw-ups. You and your brothers were sloppy yesterday, and it cost us your brother."

Luis was still mourning the loss of his brother and imagining brutal revenge against Blanchard and Evans. He cleared his mind and changed the subject. "Sir, good news. We received a FedEx package containing the official birth certificate for your daughter, issued by the Government of Belize. The girl's name has been legally changed to Anna Marie Guzman, and her hair has been dyed Auburn. Everything should go smoothly, and no one will ever know that the infant is not your biological daughter."

Guzman's facial muscles finally relaxed. "That's terrific news. What about the Arnold girl?"

"I spoke with Palmer yesterday. Getting custody of the Arnold girl is still a problem," Luis told him. "After Director Jenkins arrested your cousin, Jose Estrada, for treason, Palmer's up to her eyeballs defending herself. She's being investigated for all the child abductions under her watch. Her sister's husband, Earl Mathews, is also linked to these child abductions and murders of two FBI agents."

"What could they possibly have on Palmer?" Miguel asked.

Doctor Harding, Agent Eddie Seymour's adoptive father, was the person who notified Blanchard about the exchange at Pier 54. The doctor has been gathering evidence against Palmer, Jarvis, and Doctor Kane for the last twenty years. He kept a diary with the names and dates of the families the three of them have either been ruined or murdered.

Miguel was hyperventilating, trying to process what he had been told. "Now leave. I need to get dressed. Sally Palmer is flying to Miami to meet with me," he told him. "I'll be tying up some loose ends. I need to erase any connection I have to Palmer."

317

Piper set down his coffee cup, crossed his arms behind his head, and revealed his perfectly white teeth. "I need to move up my departure and get Anna Marie Guzman to Isabella."

"I'll be at the ranch in a couple of days while I attend to clean up the mess I had created," Luis told Miguel.

* * * * *

Luis had arrived at the Guzman hospital ship, which was docked at the Miami cruise line terminal. He got there just before it was about to set sail. He saw Estella Ruiz walking quickly up the gangway. He waited until she was inside her cabin before he confronted her.

He knocked on her door. "Estella, it's Luis. I need to talk to you."

Estella opened the door with a big smile on her face. "Señor Luis, we did well on the promenade. The little girl wasn't hurt," she boasted. Her smile quickly faded into fear when she saw the large knife in Luis's hand. She knew their meeting wasn't going to end well for her. She was a beautiful woman with street smarts, trying to find a way out of her desperate situation.

Luis was a man of few words when solving problems. "Yes, you did well. Piper was pleased with your performance and that you kept the baby safe. But we have a problem. FBI Agent Blanchard saw enough of your face to have a sketch artist draw a perfect likeness of you." He waved the newspaper article in her face. "We are concerned that if you get captured, you'd expose Señor Guzman and ruin everything he has planned for his family."

Estella started crying. "I would never hurt Señor Guzman. I promise," she begged. "I love my job. How can I convince you of my loyalty?"

Luis shrugged. "You'll have to show me."

Estella understood his response and began to undress. Within seconds, she was naked, revealing her perfectly shaped breasts and slender figure. She stepped back and fell onto her bed, gesturing for Luis to join her.

They made love for the next two hours. When they were finished, Luis slit her throat. He got dressed and went in search of his security team.

"When you reach international waters, dump this piece of trash and feed her to the sharks," Luis instructed. He left the ship for his long flight back to the ranch in Belize.

Chapter 65

Livingston, Guatemala

Piper had time on his five-hour flight home to review the carefully executed actions he had meticulously planned to ensure his own safety, his new child's, and Luis's. But something about this abduction had gone horribly wrong, triggering his paranoia.

Miguel couldn't stop thinking about the arrogant note he left behind. His cocky message might have pushed Evans and Blanchard to their breaking points. He respected the Deputy Director's belief that his last clue would bring Enrique Ramirez and that cold, rainy night in Guatemala out in the open.

Looking out the window of his plane, he believed the bright Guatemalan sun was shining again for Miguel Guzman. His happiest days came when the skies were clear, and the storm clouds had vanished. These moments made life seem perfect to him. He thought he was now done playing the Pied Piper and ready to enjoy his new daughter and become the father he never had, but he needed to tie up some loose ends.

He shook his head and cracked his knuckles, trying to dismiss the terrible thoughts swirling in his mind. All that mattered at the moment was getting home safely with his new child and the security of his ranch. A new life awaited him and Isabella if he could avoid any more mistakes.

He kept telling himself he was officially retired. The Pied Piper was gone for good. Unfortunately, his retirement wasn't really over; two more men had to die to keep Anna Marie Guzman safe.

The flight from Miami to his private airstrip on his ranch, which had a perimeter security system that matched any American military installation, was tense. Despite that, he couldn't stop worrying about his illness and the violence it caused. Could he keep it under control? He wasn't sure. He wanted more than anything to be with Isabella and their new daughter so that he could be a loving husband and father.

He wanted to prove to himself that he wouldn't become like his father and break the Ramirez legacy. His biggest concern was that the blackouts he was having were happening more often. He hadn't told Luis or Isabella. He didn't want to show any weakness, not even to his wife or best friend. If they found out, they would see him in a different light.

He heard the jet engines shut down and the side hatch open. He took Anna Marie from the nurse he had brought onboard. He held his daughter close to his chest, wrapped in a father's embrace, and kissed her gently on the cheek. She was still sedated.

Holding his baby had awakened something he hadn't felt since his mother was alive. As he stood at the open hatch, he looked toward the ranch house before starting to walk the two hundred fifty yards to his wife.

Isabella anxiously waited on the veranda, her hands near her lips, pressed together like a prayer. He lifted Anna Marie above his head, a proud smile on his face.

Isabella's hands fluttered wildly before she brought them back to her lips as her emotions overwhelmed her. She darted toward the plane and her daughter.

Miguel realized at that moment that the sacrifice Blanchard's sister had made for him and the risk he had taken had been worthwhile. He had promised that after his mother was murdered by his deranged father, he would never let his wife experience the same pain his mother had endured.

Miguel felt Isabella's emotions pour through him. The human side of him had come back. The feelings he had long given up as a young boy surged inside his cold heart. These new emotions felt good, but also oddly unsettling.

He had sworn to Isabella that he would always take his medications to free his mind and soul from the horrible person he had been as the Pied Piper. As he watched how overjoyed his wife had become, clutching Anna Marie, he thought about the last chores Luis had to complete before all of this was over. Palmer was the top priority.

Sally Palmer, he thought, deserved a thank you, but she wouldn't be getting one. She was about to learn how ungrateful the Pied Piper truly was. She and the others had to be disposed of quickly, along with Dr. Kane, since the final shipment of children was canceled. Luis and his men agreed to handle the final unpleasant details, letting Miguel enjoy the warmth of his new family.

While Isabella hurried into the house with her daughter, Miguel pulled the hacienda's foreman aside. He reminded him to make sure he and the entire ranch staff kept the miscarriage quiet. He was told to spread the word that the Guzmans had given birth to a beautiful baby girl three months earlier and that the family wanted some privacy with their new child before the celebrations began.

Miguel draped his arm around Angel Gonzales's shoulder as they strolled slowly toward the horse barn. A gentle, cool breeze brushed against their backs. "Repeat to me exactly what you've done and what you've said to everyone," he said, with a calming, relaxed tone.

"Señor Guzman, I did exactly what you asked. After you called with your happy news, the mayor, the priest at your church, and all the merchants in town were informed of Isabella's baby girl three months ago. You'll see inside the hacienda all the gifts everyone has started to send, showing their excitement for your new daughter. It was hard to keep Father Alvarez away; he was worried that you were waiting too long to baptize the baby. You should call him and set up the ceremony right away," Angel advised.

Miguel could tell how nervous the foreman had become. "You've done well. I'm proud," he told him, his tone reflecting concern. "Is there anything else I should know? You seem nervous."

Angel became animated as he stepped away from his boss. "No…no, Señor Guzman. I did as you asked. Nobody suspects anything other than what I told them. I just wanted to do everything as you wished, and I am relieved you are happy."

* * * * *

Later that afternoon, in his study, he reflected on the past week and how close he had come to being exposed and captured. He also thought about the Arnold girl.

Miguel understood how crucial the next few weeks would be. Everything needed to be done flawlessly and without errors. Luis' orders were absolute. The young girl, along with Evans and Blanchard, had to be eliminated.

The final solution had started while they were in Miami with Estella Ruiz. His most difficult task was Sally Palmer and Earl Mathews. He wasn't sure how they would react when they discovered Guzman wasn't there. Then, the most challenging murder of Evans and Blanchard would be his last housekeeping task. He needed to find out where both of them were and where Michelle Arnold was.

Miguel was confident that Luis and his men would not fail. He would have gone to help, but Isabella needed him. Anna Marie needed him. He was now a father. The Pied Piper was dead, and that life was gone.

One thing that troubled him the most was how to eliminate Senator Jarvis and Doctor Thomas Kane. He respected their skills and sharpness. They had survived, like him, under the toughest conditions.

The temperature rapidly changed, blowing a humid wind through the large open shutter doors in his study. He looked toward the grazing area where his young colts played with their mothers. His mind drifted, imagining Agent Blanchard's bloodied sister, her terrified face, and grin. He wished he could see what Luis was doing on his behalf.

Chapter 66

Deputy Director Robert Evans hadn't had time to process everything that had happened in the past few days. He was furious that the FBI mole was Special Agent Jose Estrada.

Evans always believed that the bureau was beyond reproach. That all the men and women who swore an oath to the United States to defend the country from both foreign and domestic threats were true patriots.

Agent Estrada's treacherous actions caused the unnecessary deaths of many good FBI agents, the disappearance of thousands of young children, and the brutal murders of those children's parents. Later that day, he planned to visit the Federal Penitentiary in Hazelton, West Virginia, to interrogate the traitor and obtain the proof needed to arrest Miguel Guzman, Sally Palmer, and Senator Jarvis.

He started sorting through a large pile of files that dated back twenty years and included all open Pied Piper cases. After two hours, he was caught off guard by a loud bang on his office door. He looked up, surprised to see Special Agent Eddie Seymour standing in front of him.

"When did you get released from the hospital?" Evans asked.

"A week ago, I kept up with everything the Pied Piper has been doing. You know I've never stopped searching for my sister. I think I've found the location of my sister, Ashley," he told him. "You'll not believe who has had her all these years."

"Are you going to tell me?" Evans asked.

"For all the years I've been an agent, it didn't make sense that my sister could vanish so quickly the day of the accident that killed my parents. I've always believed her abduction was part of a major cover-up by some very powerful people in the government," Agent Seymour explained.

Evans took a deep breath before answering. "Back then, we didn't have many answers or assistance from the Department of Justice. They were only focused on finding the Pied Piper and thousands of American foster children who went missing. Your sister was just one missing child out of a thousand. So, she slipped through the cracks."

Eddie didn't like the answer Evans gave him. To him, Ashley was his only priority. "If you and Blanchard had looked a little closer, the clues and answers were right in front of you the whole time. Why didn't you investigate who authorized the road closure and who Earl Mathews was?"

"We were so devastated by your father's and mother's brutal deaths that we devoted all our effort and manpower to tracking down the Pied Piper's cartel, hoping to find Ashley. The Director assigned your sister's case to a rookie FBI agent at that time.

Eddie bit his lower lip. "It's going to shock you when I tell you the agent's name," he teased. "It was FBI Agent Jose Estrada, the traitor you locked up in Hazelten. He's the cousin of Miguel Guzman."

Evans' color drained from his face. "Are you shitting me? Where is Ashley now?"

"I believe Sally Palmer gave Ashley to her sister, who had a miscarriage on the day Ashley was born," Eddie said.

"That's not possible," Evans replied. "If you're right, then Palmer is responsible for your parents' murder."

I was surprised back then that you didn't put two and two together and realize Earl Mathews was married to Palmer's sister Lisa."

Evans stood up. "We need to get a warrant and visit the Mathews immediately."

Eddie waved the warrant above his head. "I'm well ahead of you. I want Blanchard to come with me and confront Lisa Mathews," he requested.

"First, we need to go interrogate Estrada and get him to sign a confession naming everyone involved with the Pied Pipers Cartel and Palmer's child trafficking ring," Evans explained. "We need to do everything by the book. Also, we shouldn't alert the Mathews just yet that we know Ashley Seymour has been living with them for over seventeen years."

Eddie was shaking his head. "The only thing Lisa and Earl Mathews need is my kind of justice. They have to pay a heavy price for what they've done."

"Have you talked to Blanchard lately? The last I heard, he was retiring and pursuing the Pied Piper on his own," Evans told him.

I spoke with him this morning, and he's on board with what I want to do to settle everything and bring Ashley back to me.

"I have a few loose ends that need tightening. Let's meet tonight in George Town at Martin's Tavern and map out our next moves," Evans suggested.

* * * * *

Evans' main priority was Michelle Arnold. His entire case depended on this young girl's ability to tell her story. If she couldn't testify, justice wouldn't be served for the thousands of missing children and their parents who had been murdered by the Pied Piper, Sally Palmer, and Senator Jarvis.

Evans knew he had to seal the leaks inside the FBI to keep Michelle safe at the off-the-books safe house. He trusted no one except the agents on his team.

She was in Canoga Park, California, with Janet and Arthur Franklin. They were two retired FBI agents who had worked with Evans earlier in his career. They also disapproved of what was happening to the innocent foster children under Sally Palmer's supervision and eagerly offered to help keep Michelle safe.

Evans realized that everything was moving too fast now. It felt like the Pied Piper and Sally Palmer were slipping through his fingers once again. President Webster and Congress kept blocking him. No one wanted to bring up the corruption inside her agency. It was always the wrong time—either before the midterms or too close to another president's re-election bid.

This time, it didn't matter to him. He had Michelle's positive identification of the three traitors at Dr. Kane's laboratory. He needed more, and Agent Estrada was the only other person who could dismantle the Pied Piper's Child Trafficking ring if he could have his death sentence reduced to life in prison in exchange for his testimony.

Before he left to meet Seymour and Blanchard, his phone rang. It was Director Jenkins. "No, I can't meet now. I have a meeting with Blanchard and Seymour before they go to Hazelton to interrogate Agent Estrada."

"That can wait," Jenkins said. "That won't be necessary. Agent Estrada was found dead in his cell an hour ago. He hung himself with a bedsheet," the Director told him. "I need to know where you're hiding, Michelle Arnold," he demanded. "Sally Palmer has been causing a big stink with President Webster and the Attorney General. She's threatening to go to the press to tell them that the FBI has one of her foster children hidden from her."

"Let her huff and puff. We've discussed this before. Sally Palmer is connected to the Pied Piper and only wants to get her hands on Michelle to make her disappear permanently," Evans argued. "I won't let that happen. I'm very close to having all the proof I need to show that Miguel Guzman, Palmer, and Senator Jarvis are responsible for the missing children and the deaths of our agents."

"You need to hand over all of your evidence for my review," Jenkins ordered. "You're walking on thin ice. President Webster can't afford any scandals to come out right now."

"That won't happen until Palmer and Senator Jarvis are behind bars," Evans objected. "Now more than ever, with the death of Agent Estrada, Michelle needs to stay hidden."

"One other bit of information, Sally Palmer knows where your secret location is and where you're keeping the Arnold girl. She's heading out there as we speak."

Evans ended the call abruptly and rushed out of his office. In the elevator, he called Agents Armstrong and Trumble. "We have a problem. Palmer knows where I've hidden Michelle. I need you and Trumble to get there yesterday. If you need to stop her physically, you have my permission." "I'll send Agents Crawford and Ellenberg as your backup," he said.

"We're on the way. We should be there in two hours," Agent Armstrong responded.

"Proceed with extreme caution. I'll also alert the local authorities that a possible child abduction is about to take place and that they should not let anyone inside the house who's not an FBI agent. He looked at his watch. It was 3:00 p.m. on the West Coast. He prayed that he was not too late.

Chapter 67

Earl Mathews was dressed in a black jumpsuit, wearing a woolen ski mask with cutouts for his eyes and nose. He carried a Glock equipped with a silencer. He carefully jimmied open the back patio door, moving slowly while hugging the hallway wall.

He was tiptoeing toward Janet and Arthur Franklin's bedroom. He noticed they were sound asleep, buried under their covers. He felt an adrenaline rush when he killed someone. Murder was his aphrodisiac. He was as hard as a rock, as his brutal personality turned him into a monster.

Two nightlights lit up the dark bedroom. He could make out the shapes of the Franklins' bodies enough to get a clear kill shot. He took four steps from the door, positioning himself at the foot of their bed. Without any emotion, he fired six shots into their bodies.

Next, he had to seize Michelle. He crept toward Michelle's room, tempted to shoot her, but Sally's orders echoed loudly in his mind. She was clear. She needed the girl alive for Piper.

He entered Michelle's room, his heart pounding so loudly it drowned out his thoughts. He pointed the gun at her head and aimed. *Bang, bang, you're dead, you little bitch,* he mocked. He checked his watch and realized he had taken too long.

Before he could grab the girl, he heard distant sirens wailing and panicked. Then he received a text from Sally telling him to abort and return to his truck.

As he rushed toward the back door, the Franklins stepped in front of him, guns aimed. "Drop your weapon and get on your knees," Arthur commanded.

As Karen tried to secure Earl with zip ties, he suddenly stood up and hit her chin with his head, making her drop her weapon and lose her balance.

Earl, with cat-like speed, grabbed her gun and shot two bullets into Arthur's chest. He quickly grabbed his Beretta and ran to the truck just as Michelle entered the kitchen. He looked back and shouted, "I'll be back soon to get you," threatening.

As he bolted off their back porch, the whole neighborhood came alive. Lights from dark porches began to brighten the street. Dogs were howling, and Earl kept cursing as he jumped into the driver's seat. He saw two police cars heading straight toward him. He quickly did a U-turn and sped out of the once-quiet neighborhood toward the interstate.

"What the fuck happened in there? You were taking too long," Sally reprimanded him.

"I shot the Franklins while they were sleeping, I thought. They must have known we were coming and fooled me with pillows under their blankets. They were waiting for me at the back door. They pointed their weapons at me and tried to zip tie my hands. But I was too smart for them and knocked out the Franklin woman and shot her husband dead center in the chest," Earl boasted. "The Arnold girl saw me, but I'm sure she didn't recognize me with my mask on."

"You stupid moron. Did you say anything to Michelle?"

"I just told her I'll be back."

"You're a fool. She knows your voice and can identify you," Sally scolded.

Earl Mathews knew he had escaped a near-fatal disaster. He drove as fast as possible toward the freeway and headed south toward San Diego.

"Well, Sally, at least the Franklins are out of the way," he laughed.

* * * * *

Michelle Arnold was sitting on her front steps when the police arrived. "What happened?" she asked. "I thought no one knew where I was," she asked Karen Franklin.

Karen Franklin held Michelle in her arms and responded, "Deputy Director Evans called us after you fell asleep and warned us that Sally Palmer was heading our way from San Diego. We pretended to be asleep when Earl Mathews broke in," she explained.

Michelle looked at Arthur Franklin, confused. "I saw you get shot and fall to the floor."

Arthur squeezed her tiny hand. "I was shot, but I was wearing my old bulletproof vest. When you get shot, it feels like you were hit by a speeding bus. The multiple bullets knocked me out."

Karen kissed Michelle's forehead. "We promised Evans that we'd protect you, and this was the best idea we could come up with. We weren't going to let Earl Mathews or Sally Palmer take you. We'd have shot them first," Leslie admitted. "We've grown very fond of you. You're a remarkable little girl."

The police arrived first, followed five minutes later by Agents Armstrong and Trumble. Arthur provided the police with a detailed description of the truck and of Earl and Sally Palmer.

Michelle's life had once again been disrupted. Her trauma and suffering from the past weeks had resurfaced. She ran back into the house, unwilling to talk to the police. Earl's deep, raspy voice was etched in her mind. Her life flashed before her eyes as her fragile body trembled on her bed. She was once again lost somewhere deep inside her mind.

Agent Armstrong entered Michelle's room without knocking. She sat at the foot of the bed and touched her foot. "I'm here to take you somewhere safe," Leslie told her in a calm voice. "This time I'm going to watch over you and keep you safe, I promise."

Michelle frowned. "But I like it here. The Franklins have been treating me like I am their daughter," she objected.

"The Franklins are great people. They like you very much, but they are no longer FBI agents. We are responsible for your well-being," Agent Armstrong explained. "Didn't you like the time we spent together? I know I did."

Michelle pouted. "I did like being with you. I'm very scared and don't feel safe any longer," she confessed.

Agent Armstrong gently touched Michelle's cheek. "Let's stick to our current plan, and once all of this is over, and the Pied Piper is locked up with Sally Palmer, you can choose where you want to live for the rest of your life."

Michelle offered a smile and nodded. "I understand."

After packing up her small collection of belongings, they drove away from the Franklins' house. She took a final glance back and saw the police cordoning off their house with yellow tape, just as the media arrived. Things were starting to look a lot like Manhattan to her again.

She spent that night on a cot at the FBI field office in San Diego, unable to sleep as she waited to see what horrible situation awaited her next.

* * * * *

The next morning, after eating a warm breakfast, Michelle was taken to an interrogation room. She was asked a thousand questions by the two FBI agents who had driven her away from Franklin's house.

After about thirty minutes of answering questions, Michelle identified the three people she saw at Dr. Kane's laboratory during her escape. She confirmed that Sally Palmer, Senator Jenkins, and Miguel Guzman — who was wearing his costume without a mask — were all talking and plotting to find her and bring her to the top medical facility. The metal door swung open, startling everyone. Michelle's eyes widened with disbelief when

Sally Palmer entered the room. The wicked witch was acting overly concerned and worried about her.

Palmer immediately went to Michelle to hold her, but Michelle twisted her shoulder and pushed her chair away from the woman she hated the most.

"I'm taking over here. She's been through enough. Can't you see she's in shock? I have the authority as her court-appointed guardian," Palmer demanded, waving a court order in the agent's face.

Armstrong shook her head. She didn't believe what Palmer was saying. "I have my orders from Deputy Director Evans to hold Michelle until he arrives."

Palmer interrupted her mid-sentence. "I have the approval of Director Jenkins and a signed release from President Webster. A President and an FBI Director, I believe, overrules your Deputy Director orders," she grinned proudly.

Agent Armstrong looked at her partner, dumbfounded. "What just happened here?"

Agent Trumble shrugged. "I don't know. Maybe Jenkins spoke to Evans?" he said tentatively.

"This Palmer woman seems to be in the middle of a lot of bad stuff," Armstrong said. "I'm not letting her take Michelle. I'll wait for Evans to get here and tell me what to do, even if it costs me my job."

Sally Palmer began protesting when Agent Armstrong pulled Michelle away from the wicked witch. "Don't force me to cuff you," Armstrong threatened.

"You'll be losing your job over this," Palmer shouted.

Just then, Evans walked into the room. Following close behind were two federal marshals. "Palmer, you are under arrest for the trafficking of minors across state lines and the murder of my friend and fellow FBI Agent Jack Seymour," Evans told her with a big smile on his face. "We know you kidnapped Ashley Seymour and gave her to your sister. She's being reunited with her brother as we speak."

Palmer protested. "You have no proof I did any of the things you're claiming. I want my lawyer here. I'm not saying another word."

Chapter 68

The Deputy Director's reckless act of arresting the well-connected Sally Palmer wouldn't be his last. For the first time, he had eyewitness testimony to present to the Attorney General and a Grand Jury.

The Deputy Director's team of agents had become the "F" troop. For the first time in his career, he was close to capturing the Pied Piper, but doing so with President Webster's upcoming re-election bid could put him right on the chopping block.

The information Michelle had provided was vague at best. Still, now that Palmer was linked to her first kidnapping and the little girl identified Sally's brother-in-law as the man who tried to kill the Franklins, he had leverage to get the information he needed. When the LAPD CSI team found Earl's blood on the bushes outside Franklin's house, they had enough evidence to arrest him.

Next, Evans needed to obtain search warrants to board Guzman's Ship of Hope and thoroughly search every part of the vessel for DNA evidence and the cages Michelle had mentioned. Additionally, she had described Doctor Kane's laboratory perfectly. He had notified Interpol to see if they could persuade the French government to arrest Dr. Kane and dismantle his entire laboratory.

Inside an interrogation room at the FBI's field office, Michelle was shown a different set of photos. Once again, she tapped her tiny index finger on each picture. She stayed brave and strong, wanting to help catch

336

these evil people. Despite her courage, she was clearly frightened as she recognized everyone in the photos.

"That's... that's the... man with the cut ear," Michelle whispered, her finger tapping wildly on Guzman's face. Then, she focused on the senator. "That's the other man. He was angry and very loud. He said some very bad words to Doctor Kane. That's Sally Palmer. She's in charge of all the children. She's a mean witch."

The two agents looked at each other and then at Evans, their eyebrows raised in surprise. The Deputy Director realized he had to lure Guzman out into the open, but how? That's when the perfect idea came to him. He called Director Jenkins and, after getting his approval, reached out to Attorney General Mulligan. His plan was risky; he only had one shot at the man known as the Pied Piper, and everything had to be perfectly timed and synchronized, or it would fail.

* * * * *

Three hours later, Evans sat in an interrogation room at the San Diego downtown federal detention center. Across from him were Sally Palmer and her attorney. A sarcastic grin spread across his face as he saw what her first night in a jail cell had done to the once polished Federal DCF Secretary.

When Evans sat down across from Palmer, she folded her arms tightly across her chest—her face twisted with contempt. Her eyes burned like molten lava.

"How was your first night in lockup?" Evans smirked.

Palmer flipped Evans off. "You'll pay dearly for what you've done," she threatened.

Evans laughed. "After I get through with you, all your supporters will be running for cover. We have an arrest warrant out for your brother-in-law, Earl Mathews. We found his blood on a bush outside the Franklins' house. The very spot where he broke in."

What Evans had told her made her sick. She was furious with Earl. *"You're an idiot. How could you mess up so badly?"* she told herself. She wanted to grab a gun and blow a hole in his brain.

Palmer glanced at her attorney. "Why aren't you saying anything?" she asked, a puzzled look on her face.

Her head was spinning now. She didn't know what the Arnold girl had told the FBI. Had she seen Earl? Did the little brat remember her abduction from Riverside Park when Piper handed her off to her? Did she remember the ship, even Doctor Kane's laboratory? All she could think of was how her brother-in-law screwed up her entire life.

Not following orders was something Earl excelled at, except this time her house of cards had fallen. Her mind drifted back nearly eighteen years to the day when her sister's husband killed Jack and Betty Seymour, the first and only time he helped the Pied Piper. Her heart pounded as she realized they might find Ashley Seymour and gather more proof linking her to that kidnapping and murder.

Her face turned ashen. In California, she knew kidnapping with mitigating circumstances was a capital offense, punishable by death. Bile coated her throat as she sat across from Evans, trying to find a way to protect herself.

Evans was losing patience with Sally's silence. "It's over," he said calmly. "You'll be charged with conspiracy in a kidnapping and murder scheme, and all of the foster kids you made disappear. It's a capital crime in California. You'll get the needle," he said callously.

"You're basing all of this on the word of an emotionally disturbed ten-year-old," Palmer shot back. "Let's see how she'll hold up in court."

Evans knew she was partly right, but he was willing to risk a jury. "You have something I want. Here's the deal. I want the Pied Piper, which I believe is Miguel Guzman. If you cooperate, the Attorney General has promised me he'll remove the death penalty, and you can spend the rest of your life in federal prison. A gift, if you ask me. You have thirty seconds to decide. One way or another, I will get Guzman... you can make it easier for me if you cooperate now."

She didn't flinch. "What do you think I can give you?" she said arrogantly.

"We know now that you've been working with the Pied Piper, Doctor Kane, and Senator Jarvis. The clock's ticking, so don't waste my time." He craned his head, double-checking that the video camera was running.

Palmer looked directly into Evans's eyes and smiled. Any nervousness she had earlier displayed was gone. "If I speak, I want a better deal than life in prison, or you can go to hell. Whatever the Arnold girl tells you, it doesn't matter. She's ten years old, and I'm a well-respected government official with the President's ear."

Evans remained calm. He waved his hand at the large one-way mirror, signaling the Attorney General to come in. "You'll have the deal I just outlined only if we can nail Guzman, Dr. Kane, and Senator Jarvis with something that will stick. If not, you, your sister, and brother-in-law will be indicted for kidnapping and murder," he said, his face knotted with disgust. He knew he had made his point as the color drained from her face.

* * * * *

Sally Palmer was confessing and providing Evans and the Attorney General with enough evidence to arrest and convict everyone. She stayed calm and composed during the entire video recording, but what she shared would be the strongest testimony the FBI had against the Pied Piper's child trafficking cartel and the crazy Dr. Kane.

While the interrogation was in progress, Evans was gathering his unofficial team.

Agents Ellenberg and Crawford, along with Agents Armstrong and Trumble, had Michelle Arnold secluded in a mountain cabin in Lake Arrowhead. Special Agent Seymour waited for clearance to arrest Earl Mathews and his wife, Lisa, hoping his sister would be there for their long-awaited reunion.

The last person he wanted on his team was his Special Agent Ted Blanchard. He had been a loose cannon ever since his sister was murdered. For now, he needed to hide his team and his suspicions from Director Jenkins and President Webster. They wouldn't approve anything until after the upcoming presidential election. By then, it might be too late.

Chapter 69

Blanchard had been staring at his gun for the past two hours. His depression still gnaws at him. He failed his sister and couldn't protect his niece, Megan, from a world where no one ever comes back.

His hotel room off the beach in Miami was dark; the drapes hadn't been opened in days, and the 'do not disturb' sign was on the door. The empty bourbon bottles scattered around the room were the only signs that some life still remained in him.

He still wore the same clothes when he took Megan to the boardwalk, but now they were wrinkled, reeked of booze and vomit. His face was pale, emphasizing the dark circles around his bloodshot eyes. He was barely able to stand, clutching a loaded gun in his hand.

He fondled his gun as he had many times before, massaging the barrel with his sweaty hands. He couldn't stop thinking about his niece and the smug look the Pied Piper gave him as he handed Megan over to a woman dressed in a nurse's uniform.

He held the Polaroid his brother-in-law had taken of him, with Megan on his lap and his sister sitting on the grass in their backyard. For the first time the photo was taken, he felt happy. He knew then he would finally be able to heal. Now, the only thing he thought about was not living.

He rolled the magic bullet between his fingers, the one he kept in his pocket for that one special occasion when life seemed hopeless. The booze had failed to drive the crazy thoughts away. The decision was made. He stopped rolling the bullet and, slowly, with his hand shaking, slipped it into the chamber of his gun.

His body trembled from the alcohol, but he knew that at such close range, with the gun pressed inside his mouth, he couldn't miss his target. He took a deep breath, gagging from the stench of two days trapped inside his hotel room coffin. He knew it was the foul smell of death waiting for him.

He felt the cold steel slide past his warm lips. He cocked the hammer and, with his sweaty index finger, gently placed it on the trigger.

"Mary, I'm so sorry, baby sister. Forgive me for what I let happen to Megan," he sobbed, as the barrel of the gun slipped deeper into his mouth. "I won't be seeing you in heaven. I'm going where losers like me go." He felt his finger stiffen as it pressed against the trigger.

There was a sudden, loud pounding on the door. It startled him so much that the gun almost went off. He started to cry, realizing that if he didn't pull the trigger now, he never would. The banging grew louder, and a man's voice began shouting.

"Ted!" the voice outside in the hallway screamed. The banging grew louder. It was Evans. "Ted...open up...I have news about Megan." The memory of losing his niece flooded back into his mind, triggering a wave of hopelessness and sadness.

The gunshot stunned the Deputy Director. Evan's heart raced as he panicked, worried he had lost another agent. He quickly stepped back and kicked open the door with his foot.

His agent slumped on the couch, chin on his chest, unmoving. A gun was in his hand, smoke rising from the barrel. His hand hung limply, still. Then Blanchard started crying as their eyes met.

"Are you fucking crazy?" Evans shouted. "I thought you told Seymour you'd go with him to find his sister and arrest Earl Mathews and his wife. Get a fucking grip on yourself. I have news about your niece. We are very close to closing the Pied Piper case and arresting everyone involved."

Blanchard's eyes were red and moist. His mind was spinning out of control, and he didn't acknowledge what Evan had said. "Megan? You have information about my niece?"

"Get your ass in the shower, put on some clean clothes," Evans ordered. "Meet me downstairs in the hotel's restaurant so I can get some food into you. I have an FBI agent from Miami's regional field office who told me he had information about the Pied Piper."

Twenty minutes later, Blanchard collapsed into the booth where Evans and an FBI agent were in a heated discussion. Blanchard was clean-shaven and neatly dressed, yet still looked terrible.

While Blanchard shoveled his breakfast into his mouth and gulped down his hot coffee, he listened to what FBI Agent Alexander had discovered. He watched the agent nervously fumble with a stack of papers in front of him.

"I've got good news and bad news," Special Agent Alexander said. When he saw Blanchard's face turn beet red, he realized how thoughtless his jest sounded. "I'm so sorry. I should carry a shoehorn with me. My foot gets stuck in my mouth way too often."

Blanchard brushed off his apology with a half-smile. "Just tell me what you've got on my niece."

"We have DNA from the hair found inside the stroller left by the Latina woman at the boardwalk."

"If this is the good news, what's the bad?" asked Blanchard, his face expressionless.

Agent Alexander took a deep breath, trying to be as cautious as possible. "We know that the man involved in your partner's murder was also connected to Megan's abduction. I had agent Elliott Burns' file sent to me. CODIS hasn't matched anyone yet, so I forwarded the DNA results to Interpol and expect to hear back within a day or so. We're completely out of suspects."

"You've got nada, but you're sure who it might be," Evans scowled.

Alexander was searching for the papers that contained that information. "Oh, I almost forgot. The woman you identified who sprayed your eyes—her body parts were scooped up by a commercial fishing vessel early this morning. She had been executed, not before she was raped. We're trying to match the semen we found in our system. The coroner hopes the saltwater hadn't degraded the DNA. The medical examiner estimated the time of death as a day after her face was plastered in the newspapers."

Blanchard was close to frustration. "Tell me your good news about my niece," he demanded.

Agent Alexander sifted through his papers. "Your kidnapper... I mean, the Pied Piper seems to be cutting his losses. The woman who took your niece was a Guatemalan refugee, here illegally."

Blanchard looked at Evans, and his exasperation was about to explode. "Alexander, you said there was information about Megan. Get to the fucking point."

Alexander fidgeted in his seat. His hand massaged his scalp as he tried to tell them what he knew. "It seems that a TSA agent at the Miami/Dade International Airport had seen a young baby fitting Megan's age description. This is where everything comes to a dead end. The airport security cameras caught her being handed off to a woman dressed as a nurse and four private security guards, not airport personnel..." he paused. "I'm checking it out. They had this baby cocooned inside a tight circle as they left for an area designated for Miami's rich and famous...you know the ones who want to stay out of the paparazzi's way. All I was told was that the infant was flown out on a private jet. I've reviewed the tapes a dozen times, and we can't get a clear look at any of their faces or an ID on the plane."

"What about the flight manifests of all the planes departing that day?" Blanchard coughed out. "Have you checked them?"

Agent Alexander interjected. "I checked every flight plan for every private plane that left Miami that day. There is nothing that shows a little girl fitting Megan's description on any of those planes," Alexander rubbed his day-old beard, giving the impression he had more to say. Blanchard would not allow him to continue.

"That's bullshit, and you know it. We have an open kidnapping case, and you're telling me that a child who matches my niece's description got lost at the airport and was then taken out of Miami on a private plane to nowhere?" Blanchard questioned.

Evans kept his eyes fixed on Agent Alexander, studying his face for any sign of deception. He seemed too cooperative given the situation. "Is there something you're not telling us?" the Deputy Director asked, struggling to keep his temper in check.

Alexander swallowed hard. "This could all be a bad coincidence," the FBI agent said. The little girl on the surveillance camera doesn't seem scared or upset with the people she's with. It might be something very innocent… like grandparents sending their grandchild back to the child's parents.

That's a load of crap. She must have been sedated. You've said it yourself that this little girl did not get on any planes. Do you have a list of all the private planes that were at the airport that day?" Evan's tone had turned abrasive. "Was Miguel Guzman's plane there?"

Alexander's face drained of color. "No, I was refused access to those records," he said sadly. "The FAA and Homeland Security won't cooperate. It's a matter of privacy. If I screwed up…," he apologized. "I feel so bad about this."

Blanchard turned to Evans. "Stop feeling sorry for yourself, Agent Alexander. Evans, you need to call Director Jenkins and get us those damn manifests for every private jet that flew in and out of Miami a week before the kidnapping and three days after. I want to know their exact destinations," he demanded. "Maybe the scent on my niece is still warm?"

Alexander's phone rang, breaking the tension at the table. "Yes. Are you sure? Thanks, that will help," he said happily.

Evans looked at Agent Alexander, his eyes narrowing into little slits. "Was that phone call something that can help this case?" the Deputy Director asked.

Agent Alexander finally had a smile on his face. "I'm not sure if this means anything, but Miguel Guzman was seen in the main area of the airport. He usually has his driver take him directly to his jet. He was near the spot where we believe Megan was handed off to the nurse."

Blanchard leaned back in his chair, a burst of excitement across his face. "Miguel Guzman. How very interesting. The Pied Piper's first screw-up."

"There could be any number of reasons for him to be at the terminal before boarding his plane," Alexander interrupted. "One other thing. I discovered that at Miami's DCF office, one of the supervisors helped push through a birth certificate for a little girl approximately Megan's age, size, and complexion, days before the kidnapping. However, that infant had red hair. It could have been dyed. It seems that Sally Palmer and Senator Jarvis were somehow involved with the Guatemalan government, acting as advocates for an undisclosed foreign family."

"Why would a Senator and the Director of DCF need to be involved? Couldn't the Guatemalan Embassy handle this matter?" Evan questioned.

"That's all that I was told," Alexander replied.

Blanchard demanded, "We need to talk to the DCF supervisor who handled this."

Alexander swallowed hard. "She's missing. She has not reported to work in two days," he confessed.

Evans' mind raced. "You didn't think this was important to tell us ten minutes ago?"

Now, Michelle Arnold's recorded identification of Senator Jarvis from a photo array, as well as Miguel Guzman and Sally Palmer, began to flash before Evans, marking the end of years of confusing clues. Images of his first trip to Guatemala, twenty years ago, to take down the Ramirez Cartel, exploded inside his mind.

Evans needed Guzman's DNA more than ever. The more evidence he obtained, the easier it would be to lock this man up forever.

"Can you get the shipping manifests for all the ships that were in Miami harbor during the same period?" Evans asked Agent Alexander. "Here's my cell number. Call me as soon as you know."

Blanchard stood and grabbed Evans' arm. "We've got to go. We have a lot to talk about."

In the hotel lobby, Ted stopped Evans. "You know, I don't believe in coincidences. Read this fucking note the bastard left me."

"It's the same fucking clue on the note he left me," Evans acknowledged. I was an arrogant rookie back then. We were in Guatemala… shit, you saved my life."

Blanchard had a blank look on his face. "What does that have to do with my niece?"

"Remember that young man who escaped that day. He was Frederick Ramirez's son. I thought the whole Ramirez family died that day, but maybe not all of them."

Blanchard slapped his forehead. "Frederick's son Enrique could have disappeared right after his father killed his mother and himself," he said. "Enrique Ramirez's mother's maiden name was Guzman. I never thought of that until now."

Evan's face lit up. "I know, I know," he nodded. "There are no such things as coincidences. The Pied Piper is having us suffer the way he did when his father killed his mother."

"Do you believe he took Megan to be his daughter?" Blanchard asked.

"It's possible. Guzman doesn't have any children," Evan replied.

Chapter 70

Five hours after Miguel returned to his ranch, his phone rang while he was playing on his office rug with his new daughter. "Jarvis, why are you calling me now?"

Senator Jarvis swallowed hard. "The Arnold girl has identified all of us. And, before you killed your cousin Jose Estada, he gave a recorded deposition naming all of us for the child abductions we were involved in, and he told them you were the Pied Piper."

Miguel snapped his fingers, signaling the nurse to take his daughter away and to close his office door. "I don't want to be interrupted by anyone, even my wife," he told the nurse.

Guzman was on the phone, demanding to speak with President Webster. He was put on hold for fifteen minutes, which only made him angrier.

When President Webster responded, Guzman was furious. "I just heard that your FBI and Attorney General have an arrest warrant out for me. Is that true?"

Webster remained calm before he responded. "I've seen the evidence and listened to two recorded depositions that name you as the Pied Piper. The deposition also named Senator Jarvis and Sally Palmer, describing in full detail their involvement in the kidnapping of thousands of foster children over the last twenty years."

"That's bullshit. After all I've done for your upcoming presidential re-election and your country, you're going to use me as a scapegoat for all your missing children," Miguel shouted. "I've been trying to help your FBI find all the guilty people in this horrible child trafficking business. I was close to exposing three of the main characters."

"Are you denying that you weren't seen at Dr. Kane's mountaintop laboratory during the time of Michelle Arnold's escape?"

"I was there in an investigative role. What the Arnold girl saw was me telling Dr. Kane, Sally Palmer, and Senator Jarvis that I knew what they had been doing," Guzman told the President.

"But Michelle Arnold saw you in a colorful costume?" Webster told him. "She also heard all of you talking about finding her and bringing her back to the hospital and Dr. Kane."

That part was true, but she didn't hear all of my conversation. I told Dr. Kane that once he finds Michelle, he shouldn't hurt her. I was going to take her back to her mother.

"What about the colorful costume you were wearing?" Webster questioned.

Guzman sucked in a deep breath before responding. He was searching for a believable answer. "I was there to entertain the sick children," he told him. "I help children and would never intentionally harm them."

Webster had listened to Michelle Arnold's deposition. The young girl was very convincing, which only made his decision more difficult. "If what you say is true, then please come back to the United States and defend yourself. I will tell the Attorney General to rescind the arrest warrant if you agree to turn yourself in voluntarily."

"If I agree to do this, I don't want the press notified or for this to be a photo op to boost your chances of re-election. I'm only coming back to prove to you and the Attorney General that I am not the Pied Piper," Guzman stated. "No handcuff!"

"When can I expect you?" the President asked.

Give me three days. I have some important business that requires my immediate attention first.

* * * * *

Miguel took Luis into his office to explain what was going on. "Luis, we have a serious problem that could expose all of us," he told him. "I won't let this happen. Isabella would be devastated. Could you please do one last job for me? It will be very risky, but I have no other option."

Luis looked closely at Miguel, watching for any signs of his illness showing. "What do you need me to do?"

"President Webster asked me to come to Washington to clear up all the rumors about me and my connection to the Pied Piper and all the missing foster children. I told him I'd be there in three days," Miguel told him.

Luis was shaking his head. "That's a crazy idea. It's a trap, and I disapprove."

"You have three days to make this all disappear," Miguel told him. "If you can eliminate Michelle Arnold and destroy the recorded depositions that the Attorney General has, the case against me will be dismissed and will never see a courtroom."

"I can kill Michelle Arnold, Robert Evans, and Ted Blanchard, but how can I get inside the Attorney General's office or find out where they might be holding these tapes?" Luis asked.

Miguel handed Luis a folded piece of paper. "Contact this person and tell him what you need. He's another mole I have inside the Attorney General's office. Getting him to cooperate might require some persuasion. Kidnap his wife and two children and show him the photos. Then, warn him that if he doesn't cooperate, they will die. Don't kill Evans and Blanchard. I want them to live with the pain I've caused and watch me ride off into the sunset a free man."

"I'll need to take a dozen of my men to get this all done. I'll need your plane to fly to Washington, D.C.

"All the necessary phone calls with Homeland Security and TSA have been made. Be on the plane in one hour," Miguel ordered.

* * * * *

That evening, Miguel, after dinner, sat down with his wife in front of their roaring fireplace. "Isabella, I need to go see President Webster about an important matter. I will be leaving in three days and should be back within the following week," he told her. "Then, all of my business holdings will be either sold or dissolved so we can grow old with our daughter."

Chapter 71

Evan stayed silent as he examined the DNA results. His team anxiously waited for him to speak. A smile spread across his face when he saw what Interpol's lab had discovered.

The hairs found at the murder scene and inside Megan's stroller belonged to Miguel Guzman. It was part of the evidence he needed. Now, the trap had to be set.

The man he thought was the Pied Piper was one of the world's most respected individuals. His entire case involved some compelling and well-respected people, supported by President Webster, especially at a time when a political scandal could ruin his chances in his re-election bid.

He had been told that the FBI was non-political and strictly adhered to the Constitution. He wasn't going to let politics interfere with his goal of bringing Blanchard's niece, Megan, home safely, returning Ashley Seymour to her brother, and arresting Guzman, Jarvis, and Palmer.

He knew he had to handle this carefully. He needed to arrest Guzman on American soil. Doctor Kane was a different case, as he was hiding in France, knowing that the French government wouldn't have an extradition treaty with the United States. That's why he turned everything he handed over to Interpol.

He needed to set a trap but didn't have everything in place yet, and time was running out. Sally Palmer had been released from jail after posting a $1 million bond. Senator Jarvis was missing and believed to be in hiding.

Evans placed his file on a worn pine table. He and his team were all inside a small mountain cabin near Langley.

The Deputy Director inherited the rundown shack from his uncle. This was the third place Michelle had visited, as the shell game kept shifting to protect her. This location was the safest he had, and no one knew about it.

Agents Seymour, Trumble, and Crawford were talking, while Blanchard, Armstrong, and Ellenberg sat quietly, their heads tilted toward the arched-beamed ceiling. They were bored and eager for the meeting to begin.

Okay, team..." Evans took a nervous breath. "We now have DNA evidence that confirms that Miguel Guzman is the Pied Piper." He knew he had his agent's attention as they all straightened, backs stiff, their eyes wide with anticipation.

"Hey, boss," Agent Seymour shouted. "Why don't we just kill the motherfucker and be done with it?" He was holding the worn note the Pied Piper had left him nearly twenty years ago. "Do you really believe President Webster will allow us to arrest him and put him on trial before the election?"

That would be too easy. He's in Belize under their protection. We need to lure him out, but this time to play in our sandbox. Everything about the other suspects is just circumstantial. We have no solid proof linking any of them directly to the Pied Piper, except for the testimony from Michelle Arnold and Sally Palmer. We could lock Palmer away for life and maybe Jarvis, but I want Guzman, and I want him badly.

Blanchard threw his hands up in frustration. "Yeah, yeah, let's cut the crap. We're talking about a group of smart people who've managed to stay under the radar for nearly twenty years. That's a long time to stay hidden. If we're going to take down Guzman, I mean Enrique Ramirez, we have to be as ruthless as he is. We need to be like them. We have to get dirty and follow our own version of street justice for this mission. If we're fully convinced about this, then all three of them must die. If we don't do this, our justice system will screw it up, and none of them will ever see a courtroom."

Evans grinned. "I like it. We challenge his ego. Destroy his so-called philanthropic persona, and he'll lose it as he has before. He's one cocky son-of-a-bitch, I'll give him that. He believes he's untouchable... shit, they all think they're untouchable, but they're in for a big surprise. We need bait..." he said just as his cellphone rang.

It was President Webster. "Everyone, be quiet. The President is calling."

"Deputy Director Evans, President Webster here. I've been told you asked the Attorney General to issue an arrest warrant for Miguel Guzman. We have rescinded that. He's coming to us in three days to defend himself. He says everything he's accused of, especially being the Pied Piper, is false," the President told him. "I want you and your team to stand down until we hear what Mr. Guzman has to say in three days.

"Mr. President, I have new evidence that incriminates Miguel Guzman as the Pied Piper," Evans argued.

"You can present that to the Attorney General in three days when Miguel Guzman is here." The call ended as Evans's jaw dropped to his chest.

Evans glanced at his team. "We have a problem."

Chapter 72

Miguel Guzman read his email from one of his allies, a staff assistant to the acting chairman. He was furious. The Senate Committee, with Jarvis missing, had called an emergency, closed-door session. Another troubling point in the email was that Sally Palmer had been out of contact since her release from prison.

His mole had no idea where the Arnold girl was being held. Something was off, and his paranoia was in full swing. It was when his mole, Malcolm Davis, in the Attorney General's office, called him and gave him some more bad news that he realized he had to leave his ranch one last time to tie up some loose ends in the United States.

Guzman had learned to survive his entire life. He had a good sense of danger, and something didn't feel right. He needed to reconsider his current plan. He could smell the vultures overhead, ready to pick at his decaying carcass. He knew his luck would someday run out, but he hadn't expected it to happen after he finally had the family he always wanted.

What needed to be done now could only be handled by him and Luis. As before, he felt threatened and was ready to face his problems in the only way he knew. He looked at his wife's photo on his desk, holding his new daughter in her arms. Both of them looked back at him, their eyes full of trust.

"All these years, you trusted me. Am I still your hero? The Pied Piper has one last job, and then he will vanish," he mumbled, catching a tear before it fell. He picked up the phone. He had to warn Luis.

* * * * *

"That's right. Do this before you go to the United States. Use the plane and take your men. I want it done in this order: Schmidt in Argentina, Brooks in South Africa, Faed in Somalia, the Russian Ivan, and Kim in Cambodia. All my clients need to be terminated with extreme prejudice to send a message. Then I need you to meet me in Washington, D.C. Can you do it?" he asked anxiously.

Luis detected the nervousness in Miguel's voice. "You sound troubled. Tell me."

"I believe your prophecy is coming true. Too many unexplained things are starting to happen in the United States. I'll feel safer if we…

"What about the Arnold girl? he asked.

"I'll be dealing with that on my own now."

* * * * *

High in the Austrian Alps, Dr. Kane and Ivan Rosinov were meeting. "Your little mice are buying your chicanery," the Russian told Kane. "What would you like me to do next?"

There was a long silence. "Do nothing at this time. Let the FBI do their jobs. They might do my dirty work for me," he laughed. "Remain my little fly on their walls."

* * * * *

Two days later, Miguel had been playing with his daughter for the last hour before he flew to Washington. It had been one of the happiest times of his life. His illness seemed to fade away when he was around the new addition to his family. He was relieved by how loving and gentle he could be as a father, joyful that he had not turned out like his father.

He looked at Anne Marie and then Isabella. He couldn't imagine killing them. He wasn't like his father. He tried to convince himself. Nevertheless, those thoughts spun around inside his mind.

As they tumbled on the front lawn, Isabella approached them; the sadness on her face said everything. Miguel looked up, noticing she was holding his private cell phone.

"I guess this means you'll be leaving us now." She picked up Anne Marie and stormed back toward the house, slamming the screen door behind her. He could hear her soft cries.

Guzman yelled into the phone. "Luis? Something's wrong, right?" A cold chill ran up his spine. His friend masked problems very well, especially those that triggered Miguel's uncontrolled rage.

"Miguel, you know how careful I am when I kill. Before Ali Hadad in Somalia died, he begged like a screaming pig for me to spare him. I guess he knew that Allah was not going to be too pleased with the life he had led."

"Please get to the point, my friend. You tend to be melodramatic."

Luis chuckled at the description of himself. "It's the only way I can find peace in what I do. Well…Ali wanted to bargain with some information he thought would save his life, so I let him live for a few extra minutes."

Miguel expelled a frustrated sigh.

"I know, I know, I'm getting to the point," Luis explained. "Kane has hired a Russian named Ivan Rosinov. The crazy doctor has a contract out on your life, which includes all of us, Isabella and Anne Marie."

Miguel's heart began pounding, unable to believe Kane had the nerve to put a hit out on him and his family. "What do you know about this Russian?"

"He's a low-life gangster. An independent. No affiliation to the Russian Mafia, as far as I know."

"So, he's harmless?" barked Guzman.

357

"I wouldn't say that. He's a master at staying invisible. If he doesn't kill you, he's already planted enough evidence to convict you. Either way, he gets paid for the deed," Luis told him.

"Evidence," Miguel sounded puzzled.

"One of our other friends at the FBI says that something's stirring with Evans and Jenkins. They believe they have your DNA and hair, which places you at Blanchard's sister's house on the day of the murder, and they also found your hair in the discarded stroller."

Miguel could no longer control his temper. He had been walking slowly back toward the house when he lost it. "That's fucking impossible. I never set foot inside the house. My body hair had been shaved, and my head was covered. You believe it's the Russian?"

Luis tried to hide his panic, but Maria Ruiz's words and her prophecy kept flashing inside his mind. "We need to think everything through. I don't think you should leave for the United States right now and leave Isabella and Anne Marie without proper protection."

"When can you be back at the ranch?" Miguel asked.

"I have one last job to complete. I can be back late tomorrow." Miguel hadn't noticed Isabella standing by his open office door.

"What was Luis talking about that happened in Miami?" Isabella demanded, her face knotted with sadness. "I feel you did something horrible."

The hair on his neck bristled. His world started to fall apart. "I'm not leaving at this time. It's not safe for all of us."

He needed one last lie, one more convincing act for his wife. Then his past would be behind him forever. "It's just some minor business that needs to be sorted out so we can have the life we've planned for so long, my love. Nothing bad can happen to me. I'm still your hero, right?"

She nodded, unable to stop her trembling lower lip. Are you going to answer my question?"

"I will, but not now until a few things are straightened out."

"Let's take a walk for a bit. Leave Anne Marie with the nanny," Isabella suggested.

They had been walking hand in hand for the past hour. The ranch had never felt more peaceful. The vibrant jungle had come alive as they approached. The trees were filled with various Trogons, and Isabella's favorite, the golden-green and scarlet Quetzal, Guatemala's national bird, had begun singing with its high-pitched voice.

Isabella had rescued many birds that were nearing extinction, giving them a safe refuge from poachers who sold them worldwide. She never understood how people could be so cruel to the innocent birds she loved deeply.

"We've done well," Isabella said, squeezing Miguel's hand. "Protecting the helpless, even if they are just birds to the uneducated. I am proud of how you've worked to save them, just like you've done all these years for the children around the world."

Miguel looked away, unable to meet his wife's innocent eyes. He couldn't imagine what she'd think of him if she knew what he really did.

The dirt trail ended at the edge of the trees. When they looked back toward the house, the elevation was high enough to see the aqua-blue Caribbean waters behind the hacienda. A gentle breeze had started to make the tall, wild grass sway in a slow, hypnotic motion, as if God had lifted the ground like a bedsheet, slowly moving it up and down in a smooth rhythm.

Miguel stopped to face his wife. "I'm not worthy of having someone like you in my life. God has blessed me," *I hope for a bit longer,* "with a true goddess."

They walked the rest of the way home with his arm around her shoulders and her arm around his waist. A foreboding chill ran through him as Luis's words filled his thoughts.

Chapter 73

The next morning, Miguel went to Belize City for a press conference. His main goal is to maintain his image as a philanthropist and to introduce a groundbreaking new sanctuary—a combined home and school for underprivileged children.

He reached out to Belizean and Guatemalan news outlets in hopes of broadcasting this extraordinary act to distract attention from his upcoming visit with President Webster. He desperately sought support from his beloved Central American homeland, a country where he had invested millions.

As he stepped onto the stage, Miguel faced the eager crowd and cameras. Unscripted, he felt oddly confident. A forced, yet practiced, smile brightened his face as he spoke to the audience.

His gaze was focused directly on the cameras. "My friends in Belize and Guatemala, as well as around the world, my past philanthropy has made a difference," he declared, his voice thick with emotion. "My global humanitarian efforts—rescuing countless children from desperate situations—are well known," he continued, deliberately ignoring a journalist's question. His boldness, however, was a strategic move to garner significant support.

Addressing a crowd of reporters in the scorching tropical heat, Miguel Guzman announced ambitious plans to ease the suffering of impoverished children in Guatemala and Belize. He glanced at the female reporter who kept trying to get his attention. He looked away and continued his speech.

"Countless vulnerable youngsters," he declared, his voice resonating with conviction, "lack not only the fundamental necessities of life— nutritious sustenance and loving homes–but also the educational opportunities essential for their future prosperity and the economic advancement of their nations."

He paused, taking a refreshing sip of water as condensation formed on the glass. "Therefore," he proclaimed, his gaze sweeping across the assembled journalists, "I am proud to announce the upcoming construction of the Isabella Guzman Sanctuary, a comprehensive facility that includes a residential complex and a K-12 school, offering complete and entirely free care and education to all deserving children."

The persistent reporter finally interrupted Guzman. Brook Simon of the Miami Herald, her voice piercing the expectant silence, leveled a serious accusation: "Mr. Guzman, allegations are circulating in both Miami and Washington that the Attorney General of the United States has issued an arrest warrant for you. Could you address these troubling claims? And what are you being accused of?"

Guzman dabbed his sweaty forehead with a linen handkerchief. His response was quick and decisive: "I am traveling to Washington, D.C. to meet with President Webster and the Attorney General to promptly and clearly refute these baseless accusations. I am confident that my complete innocence will be quickly proven." With that, he suddenly left the stage, the sound of unanswered questions ringing behind him.

* * * * *

While watching her husband on TV, she noticed Miguel's deceptive mannerisms. Isabella suddenly stood up. She saw a Miami newspaper on his desk with a chilling headline.

The article described a brutal murder and kidnapping of an infant. The timing aligned with Anne Marie's arrival in their lives. The description of the missing baby struck Isabella with a terrifying familiarity. The photo of the child, Megan Marie Morgan, closely resembled her daughter, Anne Marie. A trembling hand rose to her mouth, suppressing a sob.

Isabella was determined to confront her husband when he returned, but the idea scared her. The fear of uncovering a terrible truth and provoking his anger froze her in place. Holding Anne Marie close, she carefully gazed into the baby's innocent eyes. "My darling," she whispered, her voice thick with emotion, "nothing can ever change that you are my daughter."

Her cellphone vibrated, breaking the tense silence. It was a text from Miguel. The urge to ignore it battled with a sense of obligation. She steadied herself and replied, "My dearest, I just heard your speech. It was incredibly generous. I feel truly unworthy of such an honor—to have my name associated with such a significant complex."

Miguel stopped texting and called her. "Your value is immeasurable. I want this to be your lasting testament, long after I'm gone."

Please, don't speak so gloomily," she scolded.

"My inherited affliction, the Ramirez curse, is a constant shadow," Miguel confessed. "Should its presence intensify, I'll go away to shield you and our daughter from its reach. That reporter's insensitive inquiry following the address has forced me to fly to Washington to clear my name."

"The thought of you leaving us right now is unbearable," she told him. "Will we be safe while you're gone?"

"Luis has fortified our ranch and the surrounding property with over twenty-five men who have sworn to protect you and Anne Marie to their death," he assured her.

"How long will you be gone?"

With any luck, not too long."

"Miguel, please, be safe," she implored, her voice trembling.

As the call ended, Isabella hurried out of her husband's study, her heart pounding like a drum against her ribs as she searched for her daughter. The nanny was handing her a bottle of warm breast milk from a local nursing mother. She gently took Anne Marie in her arms and made her way to the veranda.

"My darling girl, a magnificent future awaits you," Isabella whispered, her emotions overwhelming her. Tears streamed down her face, blurring her vision as she moved toward the veranda. She sank onto a wicker couch, the soft yellow floral pattern starkly contrasting with the turmoil inside. She muttered a silent prayer as she looked at her daughter, "Miguel, what have you done to our family?"

* * * * *

As his aircraft took off, heading to meet President Webster and the Attorney General, Miguel felt the familiar weight of his deception. He had carefully crafted a facade for Isabella, a story of humanitarian work and selfless care that was very different from the harsh reality of the Pied Piper. Her trust in the good he claimed to do for children worldwide now carried the cruel irony of his lies. This meticulously built persona, this life he envisioned for his family, was falling apart.

He tilted his head back, reviewing his plan to eliminate all his enemies. He just needed a quick distraction before reaching Regan International Airport. Then, he would be able to clear his name.

In his hand was a photograph of Isabella and Anne Marie, their trusting gazes fixed upon him, piercing his carefully constructed armor. Their eyes saw a hero, but he knew himself to be a monstrous villain, a depraved predator. He squeezed his eyes shut, seeking respite before the landing at Limberg Field in San Diego. "Another charade," he whispered, stroking the silken fabric of his jester's costume, a fitting disguise for his final wicked game.

Chapter 74

Deputy Director Evans was meeting with his team at the FBI's regional headquarters in downtown San Diego. He briefed everyone about the trap he and Director Jenkins had set to arrest Miguel Guzman. The meeting was interrupted when his cell phone rang. It was FBI Director Jenkins.

"Director, what can I do for you this morning?" he answered curtly. "I was just briefing my team on our plan."

Jenkins's voice, tense with urgency, cut through the air: "The plan has changed. Guzman altered his flight from his original itinerary to land at Reagan National. He's now headed to Lindbergh Field in San Diego and should arrive there around 11 A.M today."

Evans' mind was racing. "That's two hours from now. Why am I just hearing about this so late? When did all of this happen?"

"The change happened mid-flight," Jenkins told him. "Do you think he was tipped off about what we had planned for him?"

It's plausible," Evans responded, his tone filled with chilling certainty. "He must still have informants within the FBI, maybe even the White House. I'd bet my career that Guzman is in panic mode and planning to eliminate his perceived enemies in California. Over the last week, four child traffickers around the globe have been savagely killed.

Jenkins agreed. "I need to inform the President about Guzman's change of plans."

"No," Evans said sharply. "If there are more informants, updating President Webster could accidentally alert Guzman."

"I can't hold back this information. You'll have twenty-four hours," Jenkins said. "Then I notify President Webster. Arrest Guzman with handcuffs if you can. If he resists, well, you know what to do."

Evans finished the call and returned to his meeting with the team. "Our plans have changed," Evans told his agents. Guzman is not going to Washington. He's landing at Lindbergh Field in two hours. If my gut is right, he's going there to tie up some loose ends."

"You mean kill all the witnesses?" Seymour confirmed.

Evans nodded. "Exactly. Without our witnesses, Guzman could go free. I can't let that happen. First, we must move Michelle Arnold right away and get her to another safe house. Ellenburg and Crawford, you need to relieve Armstrong and Trumble."

The two agents stood up and exited his office. He looked at Blanchard and Seymour, noticing they seemed confused. "What's bothering you two?" Evans asked.

Blanchard spoke up first. "I want the first shot at Guzman. After what he did to my sister and niece, he can't go unpunished."

"I understand your frustration, but first, we need to protect the few witnesses we have. I don't like saying this, but we must protect Sally Palmer."

Eddie Seymour stood up and began pacing around the office. "What about Earl Mathews and his wife? What about my sister Ashley? I need to confirm that their daughter Simone is my sister," he said. "She and the Mathews might be one of the loose ends Guzman needs to eliminate."

"The best way to protect everyone is to put a tail on Guzman after he lands. We follow him and maybe Earl Mathews and catch them in the act," Evans said.

* * * * *

After the meeting, with his office empty, Evans tried to process everything that had happened. He struggled to adjust to the last-minute changes. He needed time to plan, but this time he didn't actually have that luxury. He couldn't believe Guzman had irrationally changed his plans. Now, all he had to do was stay focused on him.

The Deputy Director had limited options and knew he had to act quickly and decisively, or the Pied Piper would be lost forever. He only had one chance to make everything work.

Evans's small team of FBI agents, along with five forensic specialists who agreed to work with him, had been carrying out their assigned duties. He also had a group from the State Department and Interpol ready to act. Everyone wanted the Pied Piper dead, along with all the brokers who supported him.

Evans made a promise to himself. He was determined to find Blanchard's niece and Seymour's sister and reveal that Miguel Guzman was the Pied Piper. He now had the full resources of the State Department, which allowed him to conduct a worldwide investigation. Blanchard and Seymour had become partners. He hoped they could support each other in handling the loss of their partners. He needed their minds to stay sharp, or everything would fall apart.

Evans had one shot to cast his net and capture Senator Jarvis and Doctor Kane. There was no room for mistakes. Unknowingly, other forces beyond his control were assembling against him and his team.

Chapter 75

Ted Blanchard's fragile emotional stability, which he thought couldn't get any worse, until Eddie Seymour became his partner. The young agent had a bad attitude and a reputation for being a renegade, unlike his father. He didn't want to see another Seymour's death on his watch. He complained to Evans but was unwilling to change the dynamics of his ragtag team of agents.

For the Deputy Director, the pairing couldn't have been more perfect. He needed Blanchard's mind focused on his hatred for the Pied Piper and on finding his niece. Seymour was exactly the right person to keep his blood boiling as he searched for his sister.

Blanchard had blinders on and kept his sense of justice tied to them. He was not about to let anyone throw off his obsession with revenge, a hunger of biblical proportions he was determined to satisfy. He knew that Megan's life depended on him finding her quickly before she got lost in the child trafficking world.

Blanchard was set to meet Seymour at Lindbergh International Airport in an hour. He kept rehearsing what he would say and how their investigation would unfold. His phone rang, interrupting his train of thought.

"Hey Ted, sorry to hear about your partner. I feel so responsible," Doctor Harding said somberly.

"It was a strong lead. You were right. I just messed up and got my partner killed," Blanchard admitted.

Harding's breathing was heavy as he spoke. "What's with your boss, Jenkins? He won't let me see my son's body. I'm at my wits' end. Can you pull some strings?"

Blanchard had forgotten that Harding didn't know his son was alive. He swallowed hard. He hated lying to a friend, especially one who had been there for him many times when he needed someone to talk to about his troubles. Keeping Seymour dead was

Evans' idea to keep him safe.

"Let's just say that you'll be seeing him soon enough. That's all I can tell you for now."

Harding had always kept his emotions in check; however, this time, his despondent demeanor erupted. "That's bullshit. He's dead, right? You're my friend...tell me the truth," he pleaded.

"I'm not at liberty to say. You'll have to accept that answer for now," he said sternly. He needed to change the subject quickly before he said something he'd regret. His voice cracked as he spoke.

"You heard that the Pied Piper murdered my sister Mary and her husband Michael. My niece Megan...well...she's gone also...taken by the bastard," he said, choking up. "So that's how well my life's been going." An air of sarcasm filled the phone line.

Harding apologized, saying, "I'm so sorry to have called you at this time."

Ted interrupted. "You called me, so tell me what's on your mind. I get the feeling you weren't just calling about Eddie."

You're right. Long ago, I hired a private investigator to find Ashley Seymour. I felt I had to do it, even though it seemed pointless, but I did it for Jack and Eddie," Harding told him.

"Maybe it isn't as hopeless as you might believe. Things here are moving quickly, and we might be close to catching the Pied Piper and finding Ashley."

Harding sighed. "Really? With everything going on lately, I had my PI tail Sally Palmer. He has dates, times, and locations of meetings, as well as photos of the people she has met. I gave a lot of my files to agents Ellenberg and Crawford. But…there's more. I have photos of Palmer with Senator Jarvis, Director Jenkins, and Miguel Guzman. Can we meet and go over what I've got?" Harding pleaded.

Blanchard exhaled a frustrated breath. "Can you fax it to me? I can't see you right now. I need to be somewhere in less than an hour."

Harding sighed. "I'll try. Oh, one more thing, my private investigator is checking out a hunch that might lead to finding Eddie's sister."

Blanchard cursed. "If you've got information about your son's sister, you need to give it to me right away. Your PI could jeopardize our investigation, even endanger her life if whoever has her finds out they're being watched."

Harding's tone turned icy. "He's very good at what he does. I'll have him call you, and the two of you can see who can spit the furthest. The FBI hasn't done such a good job lately," Harding replied sarcastically. He heard Blanchard moan. "Ted…shit…I'm sorry. I'm just too stressed out lately with not being able to bury my son. Forgive me for my rudeness."

"It's okay. I probably deserved it. Just give me your PI's name so I don't hang up on him when he calls," Blanchard wrote down Chip Turnbull's phone number. "I'll keep you posted on this... I promise. Sit tight and think positively about your son. He's in a better place now. There's always a light at the end of the tunnel," he said, then hung up.

Harding stared at his phone, trying to understand what Blanchard had just muttered. "Better place? Light at the end of the tunnel?" he scratched his head, more confused than before he called.

* * * * *

Blanchard's mind raced with Harding's words. It was overwhelming for him to process. If he told Seymour, Dr. Harding's PI, that he knew something about his sister, Seymour would be relentless, squeezing every bit of information he could.

Blanchard knew he had to find Megan first before she vanished into the Pied Piper's deadly world. His decision was final.

Blanchard dialed Skip Turnbull. "I'm Special Agent Ted Blanchard. You don't know me, but I am a friend of Doctor Phillip Harding. He said you have information on Ashley Seymour?" There was a long silence.

"Oh yes. I read about you in the Tribune. Sorry for your loss," he said emotionlessly. His tone was standoffish.

"Harding said you have information about Ashley Seymour?"

Turnbull waved to his secretary to close his door. "I'm not sure it's anything. Dr. Harding hired me to find the Seymour infant girl after the tragic accident that took her parents' lives. Ashley's disappearance has long baffled me," he explained.

Blanchard cut him off. "It was a kidnapping by the Pied Piper, not a disappearance," Blanchard barked.

Sorry, yeah, kidnapped. Well... it seems that a Sally Palmer... you know her?

"Yes."

"She's a piece of work, that woman. She has a set of balls on her that would make any man proud."

"Turnbull...cut to the chase. I don't have all day,"

Blanchard scolded.

The PI was getting testy. "Look, you called me. I'll tell my story the way I want to...so don't rush me." There was a long silence, then he continued. "On or about the time Ashley Seymour was kidnapped!" he emphasized the word with a hint of sarcasm. "Palmer's sister had mysteriously appeared with a new baby daughter matching the description of the Seymour girl."

Blanchard could not hide his excitement. He suspected that the Mathews had Ashley, but this confirmed it. "Was she pregnant? It could explain why she had a baby."

Turnbull whistled. "That's where this gets interesting. Lisa Mathews, who is married to a scary-looking guy, had a miscarriage a few months earlier at Scripps Hospital in Encinitas, the same day Ashley was born. It would be impossible for her to have had another baby that quickly unless she had a miracle child. I know God works in mysterious ways, but this is not His usual way. She's no Virgin Mary."

Blanchard's attitude had cooled off. "Can you dig a little deeper and get me some photos of the girl? Even DNA would help."

"I'll get back to you in a couple of days," Turnbull sounded excited. "Thanks for trusting me on this," he said.

The PI didn't realize that Blanchard had his reasons, and they didn't involve Seymour. "Sure. Just be careful and don't get made."

Chip let out a deep sigh. "When I'm on a case, I focus on the job I'm hired to do. I look for what the client wants from me, not paying too much attention to other details that at the time seemed irrelevant to my investigation. I'm no superhero trying to save the world. Just doing my job to pay the bills," he told him.

Blanchard silently moaned and hung up the phone. He checked his watch; he had twenty minutes before meeting Seymour. With Turnbull working for him, any guilt about focusing solely on Megan had faded. He figured he could kill two birds with one stone.

Chapter 76

Earl Mathews was backing out of his driveway in La Costa Canyon when a light green taxi pulled up to the curb. His eyes widened as he saw Sally step out.

He slammed on his brakes, skidding onto the lawn that lined the long, winding driveway. "Where the fuck have you been since being released?" he angrily asked.

Sally had no time for explanations and headed straight into her sister's house, with Earl trotting close behind. When Lisa saw her sister, she didn't seem surprised.

"Did you take a little vacation?" Lisa smirked. "Piper's been looking for you. He needs you and Earl to be at the US Grant Hotel no later than 5 p.m. tomorrow."

Sally had a puzzled look on her face. "Let me see the message. Did he have any other instructions or what this meeting was about?"

Lisa was rummaging through her large straw beach bag, which she used as a purse, searching for the second email he had sent. "All I remember is that he's pissed that you've been out of touch. He wants the location of the Arnold girl, or there'll be hell to pay."

Palmer turned pale. "I don't have her or know where the Feds are hiding her."

Lisa couldn't stop rambling. She had more to tell her sister, but Sally raised her hand, signaling her to be quiet.

Sally hated betraying her sister and Earl, but she had an agreement with Deputy Director Evans that she needed to uphold. "Earl and I will go to the US Grant Hotel and find out what Piper wants from us. You stay here and keep an eye on Simone."

"Why don't we all move to another state or country and start over?" Lisa asked.

"That's a stupid question. Piper's reach is everywhere," Sally scolded her sister. "We all would be dead for betraying him."

Earl grabbed Lisa's hair and hit the back of her head. In a low whisper, he scolded her. "You ass. You're so fucking stupid. I should kill Piper and our problems will be over."

Lisa held back her tears as she rubbed the back of her head. A small lump had begun to swell from the impact of Earl's skull ring, which he had bought at Disneyland's Pirates of the Caribbean ride. "I'm not as stupid as you, you big fuckup," she said, sticking her tongue out at him.

Sally was already putting her plan in motion. If Evan's trap worked, she would be free of the Pied Piper. "Earl, you need to first dispose of Dr. Harding before our meeting. I'll meet you at the hotel by 5 P.M."

Earl had a confused look. "Where should I kill this motherfucker?" he asked happily. "How would you like me to do it?"

First, we have to make Piper believe we're all headed to the US Grant Hotel. He can't suspect anything's wrong. If he does, we die.

Lisa was nodding excitedly. "I suggested to Earl that we should find a girl of the same age and stature and pass her off as Michelle Arnold."

Sally groaned as she shook her head. "That won't do. Piper knows exactly what the girl looks like. He's too smart to fall for a lamebrain idea like that," Sally admonished her sister. She was hoping Evans was listening.

"Would he be foolish enough to use Michelle as bait?" She hoped so, or her plan to save her neck would not work.

Outside by Earl's pickup, Sally whispered in his ear, her moist lips touching his earlobe as her hand caressed his already hard erection. "You need to kill Dr. Harding in his office. If he leaves, it would be next to impossible to do the job on the highway. You can't afford another fatal crash with your pickup," she said, gently kissing his cheek.

"Perfect," he whispered.

Ensure Doctor Harding is confirmed dead before our meeting. Take a photo as proof of his death. Here's a typewritten note with the Pied Pipers flair. Pin the note on Harding's chest and arrive at the US Grant Hotel by 5 P.M. tomorrow.

* * * * *

Two hours later, Earl waited outside Harding's office in the parking lot. He didn't have a plan; instead, he kept fantasizing about being in bed with Sally after they met with Piper.

Fantasizing about being with Sally caused him to lose track of time as he watched Dr. Harding get into his car. "Oh, shit. Sally is going to kill me for letting him get on the road."

Dr. Harding was heading toward Rancho Santa Fe Road. He then turned left onto Camino de Los Conches, heading toward La Costa Canyon High School. He was late for his appointment with Simone Mathews. He was oblivious to the large pick-up truck that had parked two rows away.

Chapter 77

Simone Mathews, daughter of Lisa and Earl Mathews, sat nervously in a small room next to the nurse's office at her school. It was just another unremarkable room, like all the others at La Costa Valley High School.

The room featured a couch likely from a garage sale, a coffee table that looked like it had been used for arts and crafts in a busy household, and an armchair probably meant for the doctor. It was the newest piece of furniture from the Relax the Back store. The walls seemed freshly painted a light, pale pink; the fresh paint smell still lingered in the small room.

The walls had been decorated with Success Posters to boost motivation and inspiration. The framing looked inexpensive, which Simone guessed came from Posters R Us, a store at the Carlsbad Mall.

The room made her feel very uneasy, especially having to wait alone for the school counselor. She twirled her hair, a cute habit she had when she felt awkward.

Teresa Harper, the Principal and close friend of FBI Agent Ted Blanchard, was asked by Dr. Harding to join a special program for high school seniors. All she knew was that a psychiatrist aimed to understand how seniors were preparing emotionally for college.

It was five minutes past four, and Dr. Harding was late. Just five minutes, but in her nervous state, Simone felt like it was an eternity. She didn't know if he would ask her to read inkblots, lie on her back on the couch, force her to reveal her most intimate secrets, or even use some form of mind control or hypnosis to make her confess her deepest, darkest secrets.

Get a grip, girl; you're not a criminal, she told herself.

* * * * *

Principal Teresa Harper was pleased to see Dr. Harding jogging toward her. "You're late," she scolded, tapping her finger on her watch face.

"Had some pressing business that needed to be handled," he responded. "I'm a doctor and allowed fifteen minutes of leeway," he replied with a silly grin.

Principal Harper updated him. "Agent Blanchard filled me in on the Simone situation. I hope you're right. She's a very impressionable young woman, and this little ruse could cause her emotional trauma." She handed him the FBI file on the young girl.

* * * * *

There was a light knock at the door, which Simone found strange. It's not my office. Do I say, 'Enter'? she asked herself. "It's open," she shouted. She was startled to see a handsome older man holding a clipboard. He was unsmiling as he walked in.

"Hi, I'm Doctor Philip Harding. I'm the school's psychiatrist, and you must be Simone Mathews?" he said with a smile as he extended his hand to her.

Simone furrowed her brow before responding. "That's me. I've been that person my whole life. Yes, sir, that's me," she nervously chattered.

Doctor Harding tried to hold back a giggle that was about to burst from his mouth at Simone's silliness. "There's nothing to be uneasy about. All we're going to do today is talk and get to know each other. We'll save what you're here for when we meet next time. How's that?"

Philip glanced at the baby picture of Ashley Seymour, FBI Agent Edward Seymour, and their mother, Betty Seymour. He immediately saw the resemblance. He also had two photos, one of Lisa Mathews and the other of Earl Mathews. *"No way these two people are her parents,"* he told herself.

Chip Turnbull, his PI, had briefed Dr. Harding on Palmer, Lisa Mathews, and her daughter. It was too much of a coincidence that Sally Palmer's sister had given birth on the same day Ashley was born.

Simone was bouncing in her chair, overly animated. "That will be great. I'm a nervous wreck. I've never spoken to a therapist before. This doesn't feel very cool."

"We'll go as far as you like and discuss anything you want. Maybe something's been bothering you about leaving high school. I'm in no rush," he said, his voice remaining soft and comforting.

Instantly, Simone began to relax. She felt a connection. Her voice had become gentle and calming. "Well, I've been having these strange dreams for some time. I'm not sure if it has anything to do with going off to college, but it's my nickel, right? Maybe I can jump into this and see where I go with it?"

Doctor Harding nodded as he jotted down what she was describing. He kept his eyes fixed on Simone. "I have an extra bottle of water. Would you like one?"

"Sure. Thanks," she said, her tone jovial. "Well, I've been having these nightmares where I'm in a car accident. Every night, it ends the same way," she said, blushing as the words slipped out. "In my dreams, I hear a young boy's voice yelling as I'm being taken away. Then, I wake up," Simone described.

Harding started writing in his notepad. He looked up, his bifocals perched on the tip of his nose. "Dreams sometimes bring to the surface bad situations or traumas that have been suppressed. Native Americans believe that dreams reveal truths that daylight cannot show. Do you remember anything else before your dream woke you up?"

"I'm not sure if it's part of my dream or just another dream," Simone told her. "There's a man in a clown costume carrying me away."

Harding kept jotting down what she was saying. Was she remembering the day she was taken? He knew that a three-month-old baby couldn't have such visions. *"It's strange she's recalling the exact details of the accident,"* he told himself. He was eager to learn more. "It could be that something that happened to you a long time ago got buried deep inside your subconscious, and now that you're older, it's trying to surface."

Simone looked confused by Dr. Harding's words. "I checked out a book on repressed memories from the library, but all it said was that the youngest child documented clinically was age two. In my dreams, I'm an infant."

Harding seemed interested by her comments. "That surprises me also, but as I have learned, I don't dismiss a problem based on what you read in medical journals. Psychology, by today's standards, is still in its early stages, especially regarding the brain and its functions."

They continued talking for the next hour about her life, her parents, school, and boys. They both agreed to discuss her dream at tomorrow's session.

"You're my last interview for today. I'll be back tomorrow to finish our talk. If you think of more things about the accident, write them down," he suggested. "I'll walk you out to your car. You do drive to school, don't you?" he asked.

"For two years now," she said proudly. "It's a blast. No more being carted around by my parents. The freedom's great," she giggled.

"You're going to be eighteen, right?"

"My parents have promised a big party. Eighteen is an important age. I'll be able to vote," she snickered.

Dr. Harding swallowed hard, almost gagging on what he was about to say. "Your parents seemed to have raised you well."

"Yeah, they're all right. For older folks, that is. My father's not the brightest person." She smiled as she bolted toward her car.

* * * * *

378

Across the parking lot, Earl Mathews raised his binoculars. What he saw made him frantic. "Damn, that's Dr. Harding, Eddie Seymour's father. Why is he talking with Simone? Does he suspect who she really is?" he stuttered, slamming his large fist against the steering wheel. He thought of calling Sally but remembered she had told him not to call her while the FBI was listening. Earl wanted to follow Harding and finish his assignment but decided to talk to Lisa about what had happened at school that day.

Chapter 78

Later that evening, Simone and her girlfriends were doing their homework at the Dove Avenue Library in La Costa.

They weren't exactly working. Today was more than just homework; it was a serious talk about a boy. A special boy. Steve Graham was going to be there, and rumors said he was planning to ask Simone to the prom. The girl's giggling had grown louder.

A matronly-looking librarian, dressed in her long, flowered dress, walked cautiously over to the loud girls with a disapproving look. She pressed her finger to her lips, scowling. Her large, black-rimmed glasses hanging on a chain against her ample bosom bounced with each heavy step.

Simone nervously looked at the librarian's hair. She figured it had been a tough day for her, as her usually neat hair in a bun was starting to come undone. The three young women fell silent, their eyes fixed on the anxious librarian.

Simone blushed because she didn't want to get kicked out of the library before Steve arrived.

"Girls, if you don't settle down and show me that you're here to work or look for a book to check out, I'll have to ask you to leave," the librarian said in a stern whisper.

Simone turned red and politely apologized. She walked over to one of the library's computers to look up books and articles.

She pretended to look busy until her potential prom date arrived.

Sitting at the computer made her start thinking about her conversation with Doctor Harding and her dream. She decided to look up some news about Carlsbad from about eighteen years ago. She had begun tapping the keyboard quickly, trying to look busy for the librarian.

Simone was determined to investigate her nightmares. She entered the keywords "auto accident," 1993, "fatalities," and "Carlsbad, CA." She pressed the Enter key and waited for the search engine to display a list. Within 10 seconds, 5 accidents that met her criteria appeared on the screen. Two were in Encinitas, one in Oceanside, three in Vista, and one in Carlsbad. The article was dated August 14, 1993.

Her heart stopped beating. Her mouth dropped open at what she read. The accident happened three months after she was born. Her palms had become clammy. On the screen was a picture of an infant and a separate photo of a young boy, with a smoldering car in the background.

The article reported that Jack and Betty Seymour had died that day. The Pied Piper had kidnapped the infant, and her brother was taken to the hospital for observation before being placed with Sally Palmer by social services. Her eyes widened as she saw her aunt talking to the police at the accident scene.

Then she enlarged the infant's image. The baby girl looked exactly like she did at that age. Her heart was now pounding hard against her ribcage. The young boy was identified as Edward Seymour. The infant's name was Ashley Seymour. The article went on to discuss the kidnapping and the Pied Piper.

Simone's head was spinning. She felt lightheaded and struggled to think clearly. She printed the article and then looked for other stories about the two children.

She searched for Edward Seymour on Google. After thirty minutes, she found fifteen different articles about him. The first article was dated October 11, 1993. She read it slowly, her voice a soft whisper. As she pronounced each word, a cold chill began to spread through her body.

Young Edward Seymour, after running away from his fifth foster home, was found safe. His foster parents had been murdered. Sally Palmer from Child Welfare said Eddie had never recovered emotionally from his parents' death and his sister's abduction by the Pied Piper. Now, with his foster parents murdered, she believed he needed special care that the foster system couldn't provide. He was being transferred to Sacramento and placed in a juvenile home for emotionally troubled boys. "Wow!" she blurted out, causing the librarian to look in her direction. She continued reading and discovered that Dr. Harding had adopted the young boy.

The other articles she found were about Special Agent Edward Seymour of the FBI. The most recent article stated that he had been killed in action just weeks ago.

Simone, dazed and dismayed, didn't know who to talk to about her feelings. She wondered what happened to her young sister, Ashley. She kept searching but found no other articles related to either of them.

She was back inside her nightmare, analyzing it. Her body had started to shiver. She remembered the stories her Aunt Sally had shared about her birth. How could her aunt have been involved with the young boy and the baby who looked like her? Was this just a coincidence?

Simone had to ask questions. She now wondered whether her dreams were truly real, nightmares, or just suppressed memories. Something about the article and the picture made her break out in a cold sweat. She felt like she had been there before. Something seemed familiar. She wondered how that could be since she would have been too young to remember that far back.

Simone darted off, clutching her pile of articles tightly. She found three more books that discussed repressed memories. She was so focused on her discovery that she didn't see Steve leaving the library, upset.

Simone looked for her friends, but they were nowhere to be found. She needed to talk to someone, but her friends wouldn't understand and would probably start stupid rumors that would follow her.

Her Aunt Sally might not like her probing, and surely her mother wouldn't either. Earl was completely out of the question. She looked at her appointment card for tomorrow with Doctor Harding. "Maybe that's a good place to start," she muttered.

When she got to her car, her friends were calling out to her, their hands waving excitedly.

"You're a dope. You missed Steve. He just left," Tiffany said, pointing her finger at the gold Mustang that was leaving the parking lot. "Jerk, where were you?"

"Oh, I just got caught up with some research project I had to finish for my history paper," she responded. She seemed distant and uninvolved in the problem her friends were focused on.

Janet punched her on the shoulder. "Steve was so upset. You might have lost a great opportunity."

"Ouch," Simone wailed. "That hurts," she said, rubbing her shoulder. "If he wants to meet me, he'll just have to try harder," she said, flinging her hair back from her face. "I've got to get home, so hop in, and I'll drive you two busybodies back to your cages."

Chapter 79

Luis arrived at San Diego Harbor on the Guzman Ship of Hope, a day before Miguel landed at Lindbergh International Airport. Everything was falling into place for the scheduled meeting at the US Grant Hotel.

Luis met his boss at the private airport hangar at San Diego International Airport. He immediately noticed a change in Miguel's behavior. "Boss, everything is going along as planned and should be over within forty-eight hours."

Miguel nodded silently, impatiently waiting for his situation with Sally Palmer and her foolish brother-in-law, Earl, to come to an end. He knew that what he was about to do carried some risks, but his life had always been full of unpredictable dangers. Being out in public was risky, but for his plan to succeed, he had no other choice.

Miguel stretched his arm high above his head as he walked down the plane's stairs. While looking at the clear blue sky, all the positive signs were visible: a cloudless sky with a large, warm, orange sun.

Luis could tell that his boss had reverted to the Pied Piper persona. It was apparent that Miguel was immersed in his darkness, trapped in a psychotic trance.

Miguel had revised his plan once more. He was confident that with perfect precision, it would bring everyone home safely and free from suspicion.

He wanted the Pied Piper dead and buried, while Miguel Guzman, the man everyone around the world loved and respected, thrived. The timing had to be perfect for any part of his plan to succeed. It all depended on his transformation back into Enrique Ramirez, the abused and battered child, for his final act of vengeance against Deputy Director Evans, Ted Blanchard, and all the people they cared about.

Luis spoke cautiously as he addressed Miguel in a wary tone. "This is no way for you to act on a day that should be a celebration. I bring you good news. Our business ties around the globe have been terminated permanently," he disclosed.

Miguel covered his eyes with his hands in the limousine. "The light hurts my eyes. Raise the sunshades on all the windows. I'm having horrible headaches."

Luis thought he understood but didn't want to speculate. "Is your illness returning?" he asked.

"I've been experiencing blackouts. The last one began on the plane, and after I woke up just before we landed," Miguel admitted, his voice a raspy whisper.

"You've had blackouts before. Is that all that happened?"

"I believe so," Miguel replied.

"Boss, please don't misinterpret. You need to stay sharp. We have one more job, and then it's all over," Luis reminded him. "The prophecy would have passed without harming any of us."

Miguel gave him an incredulous look. "I woke up holding a large butcher knife. It's happening... I know it," he said.

"We can get through this," Luis assured him. "You should go back on your medication and let my team and me handle our American problems. You should be with your daughter and wife."

Miguel shook his head. His mood turned hostile. "I'm on my fucking medication. Nothing is helping. The evil has consumed me. It's won."

"No, it hasn't," Luis argued. "You'll find another doctor and get stronger drugs. I won't let you become your father," he said sternly. "You should go back to the ranch. I'll make sure everything goes away."

Miguel shook his head. "No, I don't trust myself. I need to finish what I've started, or I'll never be normal. There's no other option. Stop arguing and tell me what to expect when we reach the US Grant Hotel."

Luis acknowledged, "Sally Palmer has confirmed she'll be there with her idiot brother-in-law."

Piper nodded approvingly. "What you've set up will work perfectly. While you were carrying out my orders, I made a few calls to our friends in Russia. They've located Kane's Russian assassin. He's gotten a room at the US Grant. Go there and bring him to the ship. I need him alive." His voice simmered with rage.

Luis looked confused. "How will I recognize him?"

"The hotel manager told me that there is only one Russian man at the hotel, and he's enjoying himself with all the beautiful women. He likes the company of whores before he starts a job.

* * * * *

While Miguel was on his plane, he called Senator Jarvis to notify him that the children would be exchanged at Pier 97, a small warehouse at the San Diego Harbor. He also said he wanted to give the senator a generous bonus for his years of service to the Pied Piper. The senator agreed to contact Doctor Kane and Sally Palmer.

* * * * *

Agents Blanchard and Seymour watched Guzman's plane taxi to the private hangar. Luis Rodriguez was waiting at the bottom of the hydraulic steps, which were being installed.

Blanchard elbowed Seymour in the ribs. "See that man? He worked for Frederick Ramirez. It was rumored he had died, but it looks like he's now working for Miguel Guzman, or should I say Enrique Ramirez."

"If Guzman was coming up to meet with President Webster, why would he need this man to tag along?" Seymour asked.

Since Guzman deviated from his original schedule, it suggests he's here to eliminate all witnesses who might testify against him, including Michelle Arnold.

"Our orders are to follow and not engage," Seymour reminded his partner.

Chapter 80

After Luis escorted Miguel to a waiting limo that would take him to the US Grant Hotel. After his boss drove away safely, he then needed to talk with his clairvoyant, Maria Ruez, via Skype.

Too many unsettling events were happening to Miguel at an increasingly rapid pace, and he needed to understand what his future held before finalizing the last exchange of children.

He sat in his car outside the air terminal hangar and made the video call. He had given Maria a laptop with internet access years ago, with the condition that she would always be available whenever he needed to talk to her. He needed reassurance from her that they would all be safe in the coming weeks.

Maria's health was rapidly declining. What kept her going was the hope that one day she would avenge her daughter's murder twenty years ago by Enrique Ramirez. A man, hiding his face from the laptop's camera, held her tightly by her thin arm, trying to keep her upright. She struggled to speak as she stared at her computer screen.

Her voice had grown older, raspier, and rougher. "The prophecy nears," she said without hesitation. She spoke with a confidence that seemed to flow from her. She appeared more animated than in earlier sessions. "Things have been happening that are not normal for you…yes?" she inquired.

Luis tried to keep his voice steady, but her questions unsettled him. "Normal? Nothing is ever normal in my line of work. In our ventures, not a day goes by that we don't have to adapt or handle a problem," he sidestepped the question.

"Have the girl and the boy, once young, appeared?" Maria asked. "You have to be honest with me, or I can't help you."

Luis swallowed hard before he spoke. "Yes, there's a young girl who's now a teenager. The boy, once young, I believe, has been eliminated." His tone lacked conviction.

"I hear doubt in your voice. I'm not seeing the young man dead, but alive. He's an FBI agent. I also see one other female, age ten, who will be the downfall of Miguel Guzman unless she's eliminated," Maria told him.

He told her about Michelle Arnold's escape. "The FBI is hiding this girl. I am unable to locate her," he said. "Does your vision show where she's being kept?"

Maria's eyes were black, empty pools staring through Luis. "First, tell me about the boy or the man you feel is part of the prophecy," she asked, her voice a low whisper.

He was an FBI agent named Edward Seymour. His father, Jack Seymour, was linked to your earlier visions.

She shook her head wildly, a weak laugh escaping as she rocked in her chair. "The Seymour boy is not your problem. It's someone close, a Judas within your organization. Find him before your boss's next birthday, or everyone around this man will perish."

"Tell me who he is. I don't have time for your silly word games," Luis growled.

Maria Ruiz, her eyes wide with contempt, scowled at Luis. "You've been coming to see me for many years. My words are not games or riddles. I see things others cannot. Enrique's illness is becoming uncontrollable, yes?"

Luis' heart began to race. "What else do you see?" His voice trembled.

In a trembling voice, she replied, "God will be watching you on your next journey," she foretold, slipping into her trance. Her voice had become rough and harsh. "Only redemption will cleanse the soul. All will be forgiven if you redeem yourself, Senior Luis," she said before sinking into a deeper trance.

Luis finished the video call and quickly transferred his usual payment to her bank account. Maria had scared him this time, and he regretted talking to her.

He was terrified, a feeling he had never known before. Her words were confusing, yet for some reason, he found himself trusting her. He verified that Miguel was in his suite at the US Grant Hotel. He couldn't stop thinking about the Judas Maria she had mentioned.

The valet at the US Grant parked his car. He then walked directly into the bar to find the Russian.

* * * * *

Maria's son, Jorge Ruiz, had been working for Guzman for over twenty years. His employer trusted him. He was given responsibility for overseeing the ranch when Miguel was far away, kidnapping young children.

After listening to his mother's prophecies, he knew it was time to carry out her revenge. "Is it time, Mama? It's been hard for me to wait so long," Jorge pleaded, his tone impatient. "Do you think it was wise to alert Luis that he has a spy at the Guzman ranch?"

"When they think they've discovered who their Judas is, it will be too late. Timing is so important. Remember, Enrique, I mean Miguel, killed your sister on his birthday, that stormy day in Santa Catarina," she sobbed. "I want my vengeance on his birthday. Have patience. You cannot act too soon. Your life depends on it. Humor your old mother for just a while longer." She grabbed her son's hand and brought it to her dry, caked lips.

Jorge kissed her forehead. "Señor Ramírez… I mean, Señor Guzman has records of every kidnapping going back to the time he took my sister.

We don't know for sure whether she died that day. She could have been sold to one of his brokers."

"I buried her that day when that bastard and his father tore my heart out. I know she's dead. I can feel it. I can't bear to hope anymore," she said, her eyes filling with tears as she spoke.

Jorge, his face twisted with anger, spoke. "Not all of Guzman's abductions ended in death. I will never lose hope. Not until I can verify his records. Hope is what keeps me working with that madman. But my patience is running thin. I can't wait much longer," he said, kneeling beside his mother, his head resting on her lap.

She stroked his tangled black hair, then brought his hand to her lips again, kissing him more passionately. "I know you're in pain for your sister. It will be just a few more days, and the prophecy I've planted in Luis's mind years ago will soon come true. You were just too young and vulnerable to fulfill my wishes back then. It's good that everyone at his hacienda trusts you. They will never suspect, and then it will be too late. Now go back before you're missed and questions are asked."

Jorge lifted his head and kissed his mother. The lines carved into her face were long and deep, and her eyes were constantly red from the tormented life she had been forced to endure. The revenge she had been planning for over twenty years would soon be her sweet victory.

Chapter 81

The US Grant Hotel buzzed with tourists and flight attendants from around the world. Luis had never stayed in a grand hotel like this before, even though he was now wealthy.

The description of the Russian that Piper had been given was accurate. Ivan Rosinov was exactly where he was supposed to be, in the bar, tucked away in a luxurious alcove with a velvet maroon curtain that the Russian had not fully closed.

Luis heard loud laughter, looked over, and saw him buying drinks for two beautiful Air France flight attendants. The air was filled with the noise of many different languages, sometimes quieting as the Russian's loud, drunken vulgarity grew louder.

Luis noticed that Ivan was drunk and laughing too boisterously. He had been drawing the attention of hotel guests who wanted to enjoy a quiet drink at the elegant bar.

Luis watched with amusement as a woman, swaddled by the Russian's free arm, politely broke free. She briskly walked, almost ran, away from Ivan. When the second woman ran out, Ivan was yelling profanities. He staggered over to the bar and ordered another drink.

Luis slid into the empty seat next to the Russian and immediately ordered a beer. He clumsily bumped Rosinov, lightly grazing the back of the Russian's neck with the palm of his hand, giving him a prick from his ring.

The Russian slapped his neck awkwardly. "Damn mosquitoes," he said, rubbing the area that had begun to swell into a red welt.

Luis watched as the sedative embedded in his ring took effect quickly. He snapped the gold-hinged flap shut again, then casually rotated the ring back to its normal position.

"My apologies, Señor. I can be so clumsy at times. Too many beautiful women to look at, he said, raising his eyebrows. "You know how it is? Never enough time to enjoy their company." He motioned to the bartender to bring his new friend another drink. His years on the streets and working for Guzman made him a master at distracting his prey with his smooth, likable demeanor.

"I'd like that," the Russian said, still rubbing the back of his neck. "I'm Ivan."

"Luis Rodriguez at your service," he said, extending his hand.

Ivan stared, his eyes fluttering, as he looked at his new friend. "You seem familiar. Have we met before?"

"I have one of those familiar Guatemalan faces. It's my Indian blood. We all look alike to you tourists," he laughed.

Rosinov could barely stay upright, wobbling on his barstool. The Russian's eyes were wide with fear, alert to the danger he faced. His pupils were dilated, and his face was twisted with terror. He reached for his holstered gun inside his oversized shirt, but Luis had already taken it when he sat down, slipping it into his waistband.

Luis leaned closer to Ivan. "It's time to get you somewhere safe so you can sleep this off," he whispered. He had the Russian's room key and settled his bar tab, charging it to what he hoped was Dr. Kane's credit card.

No one found it strange that Rosinov needed assistance to get back to his room. A few people in the bar watched the loud, obnoxious man being taken away, quietly applauding his departure; their lips silently mouthed a sincere 'thank you' to Luis.

* * * * *

393

Doctor Harding and Chip Turnbill headed directly to the hotel bar, just as two men leaving almost bumped into them. "That guy appears to have had way too many drinks," Harding chuckled.

"He seems to be high on something. He can hardly walk," Turnbull commented. "The man helping him looks familiar. I can't place where I've seen him before."

Harding and Turnbull shrugged and found a table inside the bar. "We're thirty minutes early for our meeting with Agent Blanchard. He won't believe what we've uncovered."

Luis looked back, confirming it was Dr. Harding he had passed. "What's he doing here?" he muttered. "I thought Earl Mathews was supposed to have handled him earlier today." He just shook his head, realizing who he was complaining about.

* * * * *

Inside Rosinov's hotel suite was his spiral notebook outlining Dr. Kane's plan to set up Miguel. Luis flipped through the pages, shocked by what Dr. Kane had plotted for his boss.

Luis immediately called Miguel. "You can't stay at the hotel. It's a trap set by Dr. Kane and Sally Palmer," he warned him. "I have the Russian, and I found a notebook the Russian had with all the details of what Dr. Kane has paid him to do."

"That little bastard," Guman swore as he threw a glass at the flat-screen TV. "When Palmer and Mathews are at the Hotel, bring them to me," he ordered.

"I think you should go to the ship now, and I'll meet you there. I'll bring Palmer and Mathews, along with the Russian. I have one other job I need to finish," Luis told him. He didn't want to tell Miguel that Dr. Harding was still alive.

"I don't like retreating, but I trust your judgment," Guzman agreed.

"Dr. Harding was with a man I did not recognize," Luis told Miguel. "I don't like coincidences, especially when the Gaslamp District has over a dozen hotels downtown."

"Do you think Deputy Director Evans set a trap for me?" Miguel asked.

Luis recommended, "My gut tells me it's not safe for you to be out in the open. Your ship can hide you until we sail home."

Luis forcefully pushed Ivan onto his suite's couch, holding him up so he could see what was about to happen. "You've aligned yourself with the wrong side," he told the dazed Russian.

Ivan was still paralyzed. He couldn't speak or move. Luis knew he could hear him. The sedative came from one of Isabella's jungle plants. It was a powerful weapon the Indians had used for centuries to paralyze their prey without killing them.

Luis held Rosinov's chin and looked into his cloudy eyes. "If you thought Doctor Kane was crazy, wait until you see what the man you came to murder has planned for you."

Chapter 82

Deputy Director Evans used an FBI helicopter to land on the rooftop helipad of the Century Plaza Hotel in Los Angeles. He requested a meeting with President Webster to bring him up to date on his team's progress. Time was critical for him, and he needed to attend this meeting.

Inside a small meeting room at the hotel, President Craig Webster and Attorney General Jerome Mulligan were on a campaign stop. They took time out of the President's campaign schedule to listen to Evans. They had only allocated thirty minutes, and that suited the Deputy Director just fine.

Evans had become nervous about speaking with President Webster and the Attorney General. He knew Miguel Guzman was the President's biggest supporter. He was unsure of the President's reaction after hearing his plans.

After shaking hands with President Webster and the Attorney General, Evans didn't waste any time telling them about his plan and the additional evidence he had gathered. "Getting rid of the Pied Piper might disrupt the human trafficking market."

"When can I see this new evidence you have?" the Attorney General asked.

Evans drew a deep breath before continuing. "Give me forty-eight hours, and I'll personally deliver the evidence to you," he responded. "Once the Pied Pipers network is eliminated, we still have thousands of human trafficking cartels destroying families. As long as Russia, China,

India, parts of Africa, and the worst offender, Guatemala, continue to ignore the problem of kidnapped children, the trafficking of the young will never stop."

"It's easier said than done," President Webster interrupted. "We can't even protect our children… how are we supposed to enforce protecting children thousands of miles away?"

Evans ran his fingers nervously through his hair. "I don't have all the answers, but we need to start revamping social services agencies across the country. Mr. President, you should consider disbanding your Federal Foster Care Agency and letting the states handle their own issues. They'll need federal funding to upgrade their systems, not a federal bureaucracy that only makes politicians look good. We can no longer afford to give the Sally Palmers of the world so much power. Create a plan for each state that meets your new standards. Then you'll gain the support you need for re-election."

"New standards?" the President asked.

Attorney General Mulligan interrupted. "I agree with Deputy Director Evans; we need to help every state move out of the Stone Age and into the computer era. They are understaffed and ill-equipped to handle their existing case files. Mr. President, you need to allocate federal funds so our country can properly care for our foster children."

Mulligan looked at President Webster and winked. "I'm sure your staff can come up with something to help your re-election bid. Don't you want to be the President who brought down the Pied Piper?" Webster nodded, deep in thought.

Evans sat on the edge of his seat, ready to continue. "If we set an example, maybe countries like India and Russia will crack down on their orphanages that are currently selling unwanted children for their organs. This has to be a worldwide effort, or it will not stop even after the Pied Piper is gone," he explained. "Once we capture this maniac, I would like you to establish an agency dedicated to monitoring and policing the human trafficking market around the world. The State Department is ineffective.

I'm talking about a Black Ops team that stays under the radar, working solely for you and future presidents. You have the power. It's the only way this will work."

President Webster looked at the Attorney General, rubbing his chin. "You okay with this?"

Mulligan nodded. "We have no choice, and it's within your authority to create your own private police force. Other Presidents have had their own secret police. You wouldn't be the first nor the last."

Evans watched anxiously as President Webster considered the problem. "You have your team in place?" he asked.

The Deputy Director nodded. "I have four agents on board and ready to serve the President."

"I will not commit right now, so you and your men can roam the globe. I don't want to lose control as I did with Sally Palmer. I'll see how you handle this assignment, then I'll make my final decision." He looked directly at Evans, his lips pursed, a look of worry directed at the Deputy Director. "Don't fuck this up. I want the Pied Piper and his group dead or alive, preferably the former." He paced, deep in thought. "Good luck," the President told Evans.

"Sir," Evans said. "We have one other problem. Doctor Thomas Kane might have American children at his new laboratory in France. He's as dangerous as the Pied Piper. I need to be able to go there with Interpol's help and stop him," the Deputy Director pleaded.

President Webster, with disbelief clearly on his face, barked, "Call the French authorities and have Kane picked up and extradited here for questioning."

Attorney General Mulligan swallowed hard before trying to respond. "The French government will not cooperate. I've tried. Even though they are among the many countries supporting the Hague Convention on the Civil Aspects of International Child Abductions, they will not subject one of their most distinguished doctors and research scientists to what they have coldly called the American Justice System's witch hunt."

The president interrupted. "That's total crap. Aren't they at least a little concerned about what happened in Austria? Kane shouldn't be someone they want to make a hero in their country."

Mulligan shook his head, showing a helpless expression. "They have not forgiven us for how we acted in Iraq without their approval," he said.

Deputy Director Evans, his face flushed with frustration, needed to refocus everyone on the task. He could see that the President and Attorney General had become emotional when objectivity was required.

Evans interrupted the President and the Attorney General. "I've spoken to some of my contacts at Interpol who are not loyal to the political football Doctor Kane has become. They want to end the Pied Piper ring just as much as we do, which for them includes Doctor Kane."

The District Attorney exhaled a deep sigh. "Good. I'm assuming we are monitoring Senator Jarvis and Palmer?"

"As we speak," he nodded. "The FBI is watching Guzman. There's a lot of activity among the four of them. The Pied Piper has called an emergency meeting in San Diego. I have my team in position at the US Grant Hotel. I sense something big is about to happen within the next thirty-six hours."

"You know I'm very nervous about accusing Miguel Guzman of being the Pied Piper," the president said timidly. "Is your evidence and witnesses solid?"

"All the evidence we have points to him. We have his DNA at the last crime scene. I know that for sure. It's a start. If my trap works, he'll show his hand."

President Webster leaned forward, his elbows on the conference table. "Your overconfidence is making me nervous. You've been confident before and look where that's gotten you. Four dead agents," the President said coldly. "I would look like an idiot if you're wrong and we damage a man the entire world loves."

"Michelle Arnold has identified Guzman at Kane's lab, and her description of the ship matches Guzman's ship of hope. Also, his ship has been in every port and harbor around the world during every kidnapping. His ship was in our harbors when my agents were killed," Evans said, showing his frustration. "She also picked Jarvis and Kane out of a photo array. Palmer has spilled her guts. She's helping us set the trap. This time, the Pied Piper will make his last exchange and be caught red-handed."

The President looked sternly at the two men. "I don't want these men in jail on circumstantial evidence mixed with too many unbelievable coincidences."

Robert Evans took a deep breath before responding. "I have been working on this case for nearly twenty years. I know what I'm up against," he said sadly. "The Pied Piper is severing all his ties with extreme prejudice. He's already killed twenty-four known child brokers around the world. I know we are running out of time. I promise you, I will get this done before we lose every link to this bastard."

President Webster raised his hand, signaling the Deputy Director to stop speaking. "Mr. Evans, may God be with you," he said.

Robert Evans nodded. "Thank you, sir. My team won't let you down."

Outside, Mulligan grabbed Evans' arm. "Why didn't you tell the President about your plan for the Arnold girl and agents Crawford and Ellenberg?"

"There are some things about this plan that are better left unsaid." A few minutes later, the Deputy Director was on his helicopter, heading back to San Diego and the US Grant Hotel.

Chapter 83

It was 11:45 A.M., and the bright sun cast orange shadows through the thick marine layer that engulfed the US Grant Hotel. Inside, four FBI agents, disguised as tourists, had their luggage carefully arranged to conceal their mission. They sat in a corner of the busy lobby, watching for Miguel Guzman, Sally Palmer, and Earl Mathews to appear.

Outside, Deputy Director Evans, his face showing the exhaustion of a long day, watched the hotel entrance with Agents Blanchard and Seymour. The tension inside their utility van was thick. Evans kept nervously checking his watch. "It's 12:25, and everyone is late," he commented, breaking the silence. The three of them were startled when a staticky voice blasted into their ears.

"No sign of Guzman, Palmer, or Mathews," Agent Ellenburg confirmed through the earpiece, his voice a low, urgent whisper.

"Did you check out the bar?" Evans asked.

"I did, and I discovered that Dr. Harding, who is testifying against Guzman, is sitting at the bar with his PI, Chip Turnbull," Ellenburg reported. "Was that part of your plan to use Dr. Harding as bait to draw out Guzman?"

"What the fuck," Evans barked. His face hid the internal chaos Harding had caused. His meticulously woven web of their sting operation, carefully constructed, now hit a brick wall. President Webster's words rang in his head.

Evans' mind raced. He needed a new plan. He had to find a way to salvage the situation and protect everyone involved. The seemingly harmless presence of Dr. Harding, Agent Seymour's father, and his PI, Chip Turnbull, in the hotel bar had just turned their carefully laid plan into a minefield.

The silence in the van that followed was heavy with unspoken possibilities. The risk of jeopardizing the operation was significant. Guzman, Palmer, and Mathews might escape. Even worse, Seymour's father, an innocent psychiatrist, could be put in immediate danger.

Agent Seymour's jaw clenched. "What the hell would my father be doing here?" he muttered, his voice thick with disbelief that bordered on panic. "He's right in the middle of our sting operation." The weight of family loyalty collided with the demands of duty, a silent struggle visible on his face. "Can I finally tell him I'm alive?"

Blanchard's face, already pale from the stress of the operation, turned an alarming crimson. "Oh, shit," he breathed, his words barely audible over the muffled sounds of the city. "I was supposed to meet with him. He had news about your sister, Ashley," he confessed, his voice filled with regret and guilt. "The meeting was set up before I knew about this operation. I forgot I was supposed to meet him here today." The simple statement carried the weight of a thousand unspoken regrets.

"I've got to get them out of the bar," Evans said. "Maybe we're early and might salvage this operation."

Evans approached, his movements like a predator in a dimly lit jungle. "Harding," he whispered, his voice low, barely louder than the muted chatter.

Dr. Harding looked up, his eyes widening slightly. "Evans. What…?"

"No time for pleasantries," Evans cut him off, his gaze sweeping the bar, assessing escape routes. He did not see Luis, Guzman's head of security, lurking in a dark corner. "You're in the middle of an FBI sting operation that might turn deadly."

Turnbull's face drained of color as his hand instinctively moved to the hidden bulge under his jacket. "How... how do you know?"

"Doesn't matter. We need to get you both out. Now." Evans glanced at his watch. He was still a few minutes ahead of schedule.

"But I have something important to tell Agent Blanchard," Harding stammered, his concern battling a sudden surge of fear.

"This can't wait," Evans said, his tone warning the doctor not to argue. "Your lives are in danger." He pointed toward the back of the bar. "Kitchen door. Stay close behind me," Evan ordered.

Harding, after a moment of stunned silence, nodded, a flicker of understanding in his eyes. Turnbull, still visibly shaken, followed suit. The escape was nerve-racking. Evans, leading the way, navigated the bar's back areas with practiced ease, his senses on high alert.

The clink of glasses being cleaned in the kitchen, the murmur of conversations between workers—each sound amplified in the tense atmosphere. He glanced over his shoulder, instinctively searching for any sign of pursuit, his hand never far from the small but deadly weapon hidden in his waistband.

This wasn't just about getting them out; it was about getting them out unnoticed. As they slipped through the kitchen's back door into the cool afternoon air, the surveillance van's engine hummed softly, promising safety. The driver, a silent figure cloaked in darkness, needed no introduction or explanation. He opened the sliding door and let Harding and Turnbull jump in.

Evans watched them disappear into the van, a deep weariness settling over him as he leaned against the cold brick wall. He had bought them some time. Still, how much time remained was uncertain. The real fight, he understood, lay ahead.

Inside the van, Dr. Harding came face to face with his son. Tears streamed down his cheeks. "I thought you were dead," he said, sobbing uncontrollably.

Agent Seymour, with pursed lips, tried to speak. "It was necessary to make everyone believe I was killed a few weeks ago. It was essential to our operation and the only way our trap could work so we could arrest Miguel Guzman, Sally Palmer, and her psycho brother-in-law."

Dr. Harding took a deep breath and pulled his son close. He kissed his cheek and then gave him a firm hug. "I found your sister. After searching for all these years, she's been living right under our noses in La Costa with Lisa and Earl Mathews."

Eddie Seymour thought his father was joking. "Don't play games with me. If I couldn't find her with all my resources, there is no way you or your PI could do it," he chastised his father.

"You know that I am the La Costa Canyon High School psychiatrist. A few weeks ago, at a parent conference, I observed Lisa Mathews and Earl Mathews with their daughter, Simone," Harding explained. "Sally Palmer is this young lady's aunt, which prompted me to conduct my own investigation."

"This doesn't prove Simone is my sister," Eddie argued.

It shouldn't be, but I discovered that Lisa Mathews had a miscarriage the day Ashley was born. How can this woman have another child with the exact birthdate as your sister's?

Eddie started to hyperventilate while listening to what his father was saying. "Why am I just hearing this now?"

"When I confirmed that Simone was Ashley, I thought you were dead. That's why I was going to meet with Ted today," he confessed.

"I need to go arrest the Mathews and pick up my sister," Eddie demanded.

Blanchard placed his hand on Eddie's arm. "Slow down. You can't go off half-cocked. You might endanger Ashley. If Palmer and her sister even suspect you know Simone is Ashley," he tried to reason with his partner. "Given Palmer's history and Earl Mathews's, they'd sooner put your sister with one of their human traffickers or even get rid of her in the middle of the ocean."

"Ted, I need to get to my office to gather all my evidence on Guzman and your sister," Harding demanded. "My testimony rests on this evidence."

Blanchard was unhappy about letting Harding leave custody, but he knew he had to be with his partner and confront Lisa Mathews. "Just go to your office. Then you and Turnbull meet us at the regional FBI building downtown."

* * * * *

Luis trailed the three men and watched Dr. Harding and his PI get into a large white van. He considered confronting Evans and shooting him, but he remembered that his boss had other plans for him.

He hid behind a large garbage bin as Evans walked back into the hotel. Fifteen minutes later, Dr. Harding and Chip Turnbull emerged from the van and walked over to the valet. Luis checked that he still had his ticket stub. "The Russian should be fast asleep for another four hours," he muttered. He needed to follow the doctor and complete the job Earl Mathews was supposed to do.

Chapter 84

It was eleven-thirty at night. Lisa Mathews, screaming into her cellphone, had woken Simone. Her mother had the speaker on, and her daughter could hear Earl shouting profanities at her mother. They had argued before, but nothing like this.

Simone slowly made her way to the top of the stairs. What she heard next didn't make any sense. Her mother's high-pitched voice pleaded with Earl. "We should get out of all of this and move away," Lisa begged. "We have enough money saved to start a new life for the three of us."

Simone heard Earl threaten to kill Lisa. He had threatened her before, but this time Simone was scared. She listened carefully. She had never heard her father that furious, at least not while she was home.

Earl's voice had gotten louder. "I have a fucking job to do. This will be our last. When I return with the children, we need to talk about your mood swings. I thought that when your sister gave you Simone, you'd be better and just leave me alone. But you're never satisfied. All you want is more children, which I don't want, especially with you. I never wanted Sally to give you that little bitch you call your daughter," he said, his temper now exploding out of control.

What Simone just heard puzzled her. "Aunt Sally gave me to Mom?" She could hear her mother crying, but Earl kept ranting.

"When I get back tomorrow, things around here are going to change, or we are all going to jail. Simone's not worth doing time for," he bellowed.

Maybe Sally can find you a new baby to keep you busy after we leave California.

Lisa began to cry loudly. "You don't know what you're saying. I'll die without my little girl. I don't want another baby."

Simone did not recognize her father's voice. He sounded like a deranged maniac. Now her mind flashed back to the article she had read at the library. She wasn't even sure Earl and Lisa were her parents anymore. From the top of the stairs, she saw Lisa rush out the front door. Her face was beet red.

Simone was in shock. What did Earl mean when he said Aunt Sally got me for my mother? Am I adopted? She ran back to her bed and locked the door. She buried her head in her pillow to muffle her deep sobs. When she finished crying, she unfolded the article she had picked up earlier from the library. Her heart ached as she realized that she *was* that little girl. *"Did Lisa and Earl have something to do with the Pied Piper?"*

She found Doctor Harding's card in her pocket and decided to call him. All she reached was his answering machine. She didn't want to stay in her house any longer. She needed answers. Was this just another of the twisted nightmares she would wake from soon? But something was wrong, and she needed someone to talk to.

With a small backpack, she snuck out of the house and drove her car aimlessly until she got to South Carlsbad Beach. Then she made a beeline to the jetty. It was her private place where she went when she needed a quiet place to think. It was one of the familiar places in her dreams.

She could not stop crying as she reread the article, looked at the ten-year-old boy, and at the photo of FBI Agent Eddie Seymour. Seeing his picture ignited more sobs as she read that the Pied Piper had murdered him a few weeks ago.

The full moon cast an eerie glow on the pounding waves, matching her throbbing heart. Simone's hand shook nervously as she dialed her aunt.

"Aunt Sally, can I come down to your house tonight? I need to talk. I know that Lisa and Earl are not my biological parents," she said, her voice cracking between sobs. "Is my real name Ashley Seymour? I found an article at the library…there was an accident…like the one in my dreams," she said, breathing heavily, not letting her aunt speak.

Sally could not believe what she was hearing. She was at a loss for words. She knew that Evans must have heard everything Simone told her. "I'm not sure I understand what you're talking about. Meet me at our private spot," she suggested. "Where are you now?"

"I'm at my secret spot. I had to get out of my house. Lisa and Earl frightened me," Simone confessed. "I'll be at our place later."

"Perfect. I'll bring a pizza and a chocolate milkshake. Comfort food when *US* girls need a little comfort when we're upset," she said, containing her anger. She knew Earl and Lisa had done something.

After a few deep, sobbing breaths, Simone had calmed down. "Aunt Sally, I feel my life has been a lie. I don't want to hear any more lies. I need to know who I really am."

"No lies, I promise. I'll answer all your questions." Sally slammed the phone down. "Damn, how could she know everything?" she muttered. "*I'm sure Earl's temper was out of control. I have to modify my plan,*" she told herself.

Inside her purse, she took out a small vial containing a liquid sedative. "*Simone, my dear, I'm very sorry, but you must go away. Dr. Kane could use a nice girl like you to breed a child for his experiments. You could fetch a nice sum of money.*"

She immediately sent an encrypted email to Piper that read:

I have a favor to ask. My niece might have compromised all of us. I am adding her to your order at no charge. Consider her a gift for Doctor Kane. She'll be sedated and ready when you pick up your final shipment. Everything on this end is going as planned.

Sally tried to calm herself. The tricky part now was moving Simone without getting caught.

* * * * *

Deputy Director Evans had listened to the conversation between Palmer and Simone Mathews. He snapped his fingers to get Blanchard and Seymour's attention. "We have a problem. Your sister has just discovered that she's Ashley Seymour. She's going to confront Palmer. She's heading to a special place she and Sally go to when they need to talk," Evans told them. "We need to intercept Ashley before she meets her aunt. We have two and a half hours to save your sister."

Eddie was livid. "We have just two hours to find my sister. I won't let her disappear this time."

"We need to figure out where her secret place is and stop her from leaving," Agent Blanchard proposed.

I've been going to this part of South Carlsbad Beach near the jetty. It's where my parents took us to watch the sunset and see a blue flash," Seymour told them. "It's just a hunch, but that's all I have."

"You two go find Ashley and get her to a safe location," Evans ordered. "I'll stay at the US Grant to see if Palmer and Earl Mathews show up."

Chapter 85

It was 2:30 in the afternoon when Eddie and Blanchard arrived at the jetty. "How should I approach her?" Seymour asked his partner.

"Don't act like an FBI agent. If she believes she's your sister, she's probably seen the news article about your death at the hands of the Pied Piper," Ted told him.

Eddie began scanning the area with his binoculars, searching for a seventeen-year-old girl who might be his sister. He wondered whether he should tell Simone Mathews that he was her brother or that he was an FBI agent who needed to talk to her about her parents.

He thought about the seventeen letters he had written to his sister on her birthdays. Should he tell her how their parents were murdered? He was sweating profusely. His nerves were beginning to overwhelm him. He was growing impatient because he still hadn't found his sister.

"What if she already left?" Eddie whined.

Ted grew frustrated with his partner. "Let me have those damn binoculars," he demanded, yanking them from Eddie's sweaty hands. Blanchard looked at the photo Dr. Harding had given him of Simone. Within a minute, he had spotted her at the far end of the jetty, her hands cupping her head. He handed the binoculars back to his partner.

Blanchard pointed to a spot on the jetty. "She's at eleven o'clock at the end of the jetty. See that young girl," he said, handing the binoculars back. He dropped the photo of Simone onto Eddie's lap.

Eddie stayed focused on the young girl. His heart kept pounding in his chest. "Shit, that's her. I'd recognize her anywhere," he said.

The two FBI agents couldn't wait any longer and headed toward the jetty. Navigating among the large rocks, they moved closer to Simone.

Eddie was the first to speak. "Simone Mathews, I'm FBI agent Eddie Seymour," he said, his voice cracking with nerves.

The young woman turned her head and looked up. "I'm Bethany, a friend of Simone's. You just missed her," the young woman replied. "She said she's going to meet up with her aunt Sally."

Eddie felt his knees buckle as he realized he had missed his sister. "Did she say where she was going to meet her aunt?"

"She didn't say. Simone was going home first to change her clothes."

Eddie suddenly turned and hurried back to their car. Blanchard tried to keep up, but he was overweight and out of shape. "Hey, Seymour, wait up," he said.

Eddie didn't give Blanchard a choice as he jumped into the driver's seat. He drove with his lights flashing and siren blaring. He headed south on Coast Highway toward La Costa Avenue. It took him fifteen minutes to reach the Mathews' house. The car skidded to a stop, blocking their driveway.

Eddie jumped out of the car and hurried to the front door. He rang the bell impatiently and then began pounding on the door. He heard shuffling inside; someone was coming.

The front door swung open. Standing there with a tiny white poodle in her arms was Lisa Mathews, her eyes wet and her lids raw. She looked as if she had been crying for a while. Eddie's stomach clenched as he struggled to speak.

"I'm Special Agent Edward Seymour," he said, emotionless, flashing his badge. "Is there something wrong?" he asked. He could smell alcohol and cigarette smoke on her.

Lisa tried to focus her eyes. "Do I know you?" she slurred. "You look familiar."

"No... we have never met before," he said, his voice cold. "I need to speak to your daughter," he demanded. He got chills just saying those words. The drunk he was talking to was not his sister's mother.

The question caused her to start sobbing again. She buried her face in her dog's fur, muffling her tears. "She ran away last night. I don't know where she is," she said, her tone becoming huffy.

Wild thoughts raced through his mind, wondering if he might be too late. "Has she run away before?"

"Never."

"Any idea why she'd run away? Do you know where she'd go?" Eddie asked in an alarmed tone.

Lisa shook her head quickly. "I have no idea. Are you here to help me look for her?"

"I want to help," he said sheepishly. "Can I come in?"

Lisa stepped aside and waved him in. They both sat on a gray couch in the living room. Eddie looked around and saw pictures of Ashley and the Mathews everywhere. Some were on the fireplace mantle, and others were on a baby grand piano. One large family portrait hung above the fireplace, with Sally Palmer sitting next to Ashley.

Earl Mathews' face once again stared back at him with the same chilling effect it had the day his parents died. This time, he recognized those eyes. It hit him hard in the gut. He was staring at the man who was driving the pickup that killed his parents. He felt his face flush with rage, his resolve evaporating.

"Where would Simone go if she were upset? A friend? Any special place she'd go to think? Would she go to a relative?" The last question caught her attention.

Maybe my sister Sally. She loves her Aunt Sally. I tried calling her this morning, but there was no answer. Lisa kept staring at Eddie's face. "I do know you. You're Doctor Harding's son. I saw a picture of you when you were younger, but you haven't changed much..." Then she held her breath. "What'd you say your name was?" she asked skeptically.

"Edward Seymour."

Lisa cupped her hand over her mouth and gasped. "You need to leave here immediately." She began to scream. "Leave... now."

Eddie could no longer contain his anger. "I know who Simone is. Her real name is Ashley Seymour... my sister, whom you kidnapped seventeen years ago after your husband killed my parents."

Blanchard interrupted his partner, spun the hysterical woman around, and said, "Lisa Mathews, you're under arrest for the kidnapping of Ashley Seymour and the murder of Jack and Betty Seymour. That's a good start for now. Put your hands behind your back," he ordered, pulling out his handcuffs from his back pocket.

Lisa's face was as white as a sheet, and she appeared lost in a trance. "I can't go anywhere looking like this. Let me put on something respectable," she whimpered.

Eddie led her upstairs to her bedroom, his gun ready to face Earl Mathews. The room was clear, and he let her go inside.

"You've got thirty seconds to put on something, or you'll be dressed the way you are," Eddie threatened.

"Turn your back. I'm a lady and very modest."

Eddie turned, his gun slipping to his side. Lisa kept talking about meaningless things. It didn't matter. His mind was on Ashley and whether she was safe. He never heard the rustling from inside the bedroom.

Lisa reached into her dresser drawer, searching for the forty-five Magnum Earl kept loaded. She slipped it into her purse and stepped out of the bedroom, dressed in a light pink spandex workout outfit with a matching sweatband.

At the top of the landing, Lisa clumsily moved behind Eddie, bumping into him. Before he could react, she shoved her shoulder hard into his back.

The force of her strength was too much for him to counter in time. He tried to catch himself on the railing, but his gun slipped, and he tumbled head over heels down the stairs. His gun went flying.

He was stunned to see Lisa, pointing a gun at him from the top of the stairs. "You should have died with your parents. I told the Pied Piper he should have killed you along with your parents. Even Sally wouldn't listen, as she shuffled you from foster home to foster home," she ranted, waving her gun in the air.

Eddie slowly reached for his ankle gun, hoping she wouldn't notice. He wondered where his partner had gone, but it didn't matter. He was in survival mode. He carefully grabbed his gun and gently grasped the handle. She kept spewing her nonsense as he prepared himself. Then he made eye contact with Blanchard, who was walking slowly from the living room with his gun drawn.

Seymour mouthed orders to his wide-eyed partner. He watched him head toward the dining room, which he hoped was connected to the kitchen and offered a good angle to cover his ass. He wanted Lisa Mathews alive and hoped she would not force them to kill her.

Lisa was still screaming at Seymour. "Earl's a fucking idiot. He's the one who killed your parents and is going to kill Doctor Harding. I just wanted a little girl of my own," she said, closing her eyes for a moment. When she opened them, Eddie was standing with his gun aimed at her.

"Drop your gun," Seymour yelled. "Don't make me shoot you," he tried to reason with her. She clung to her gun, lost in a trance. Then she did something unexpected. She started shooting. He fired three shots into her chest. He watched her twisted body tumble down the stairs.

"What have I done?" he moaned. "I'll never find Ashley now."

He called in the shooting and tried to find Evans. His sister was out there somewhere, he prayed, alive.

Chapter 86

Deputy Director Evans had received an alarming phone call from the SDPD. Agents Armstrong and Crawford were dead, and Michelle Arnold was missing. This time, two of his agents did not just die quickly. The brutality inflicted upon them sent a chilling message. Once again, there was a note attached to their torsos by two large hunting knives.

My dear, dear Deputy Director Evans:

I told you our little game was almost over. I always play to win at all costs. Agents Ellenberg and Crawford did not die without a fight. But you have had to pay the highest price for what you did thirty years ago.

I only regret that I won't be able to see you, Blanchard, and Jack Seymour's son suffer. Don't come looking for me. I promise that you and all of you will also die a slow, painful death.

You've been a valiant opponent since I had Jack Seymour killed, but you and Blanchard started our little game. I was punished severely for it. I will never forget it. The pain you caused me can never be equaled.

Life is a series of games. You win some, and you lose some. But for me, winning at all costs is all that matters. I am the Pied Piper, you know, so I hope you've appreciated the flair I've shown over the years.

I'm sorry we will never meet face-to-face. We might have been friends.
Yours truly,
The Pied Piper

Evans reread the note and realized he was reading the thoughts of a lunatic who was losing control. There was no telling what he would do now. He sensed he had a wounded animal that did not want to be captured.

The alarm bells went off in his head. Evans called Agent Blanchard. "Ted, is Dr. Harding in a secure location? The Pied Piper has murdered Agent Armstrong and Crawford, and taken Michelle Arnold," he told him.

Blanchard was furious after Evans read him the note. "That bastard's one fucking asshole. Justice tonight will prevail. It just won't be in a federal court, but in my court."

"Just be sure Dr. Harding is safe," Evans ordered. "We can't afford to lose him."

Blanchard swallowed hard. "He needed to go to his office to get the evidence we needed. His PI is with him," Blanchard confessed. Seymour and I will go to Harding's office and secure him and his evidence."

Agent Seymour didn't like what he was hearing. "What about my sister? I need to find her first," he demanded.

All that mattered to Evans now was keeping Harding safe and finding Michelle Arnold. Sally Palmer had the answers he needed, but now she was in the wind. "First, secure your father. We still have time to find Ashley."

Everything was falling apart. Evans needed the exchange's location. He called the Coast Guard, demanding the manifests of every ship that had entered port a week ago and which of those had plans to leave tonight. He was not going to allow the Pied Piper to win his twisted game. He had to brief the President tomorrow morning, and he didn't know how to sugarcoat this royal fuck up.

Evans sighed loudly. He felt defeated. Blanchard's words were just that, words. If they could not find the exact location of where Michelle Arnold was being kept, then, like every other time, the Pied Piper would vanish with his hostages.

"We need to regroup," he confessed to Blanchard. "We have one round to go, and it will take a knockout punch to win this fight. He looked at his watch, and it was almost 8 P.M."

"Twenty-four hours left, and we've gone backward," he told himself. He tried to control his emotions, but Michelle's trusting face was all he saw.

* * * * *

Miguel thanked Luis for the good news. "I have the Arnold girl," he told him.

"That's great," Luis said proudly. "Let's just kill her now and go home." His voice had a disturbing tone.

"It has to end with Evans, Blanchard, and Seymour watching the people they love die before their eyes. Then they can die, their bodies on top of Kane, Jarvis, and Palmer. I must end the game this way," he said coldly. "Or all these years of planning would be for nothing."

"I know," Luis nodded, frustrated. "Life is one big game. I want us to go out as champions. I've handled Dr. Harding and have all his evidence against you. We should know when to retire," he said fretfully. "The careers of Deputy Director Evan's, along with Ted Blanchard's and Eddie Seymour's, will soon be over."

Miguel ignored the comment. He patted Luis on the shoulder, trying to soothe his nervous friend. "Has the Russian cooperated and called Doctor Kane?"

Luis took a deep breath. "Yes. Kane should arrive at 2 A.M. He did not feel good about what Piper had planned; nevertheless, he was loyal and would do anything to get Miguel home to Isabella and Anne Marie for their new life together."

"Kane believes he's coming to witness your death, an egotistical, foolish mistake. Jarvis is scared shitless. He's being investigated for his ownership of a few dozen sweatshops worldwide and for how he came to have so many young children working for him. They have your initials on it," Luis briefed him. "I sent those files to the Attorney General?"

Piper smiled, nodding.

Luis continued. "And your dear partner, Sally Palmer, believes you're going to get her out of the country with a new identity. She told me she's bringing Dr. Kane a gift. It's her niece and Agent Seymour's sister. It looks like you're going to have a wonderful birthday, my friend," Luis said, rubbing his hands nervously.

Chapter 87

Agent Seymour's heart hammered against his ribs, a frantic drumbeat in the silence of the parking lot at his father's office. The stark white of the San Diego Police Department CSI van, parked incongruously outside his father's modest office building, was a harbinger of dread.

"What the fuck did we do, letting my father go alone?" he muttered, the words laced with raw, bitter self-recrimination.

Blanchard, his seasoned partner, nodded. The grim set of his partner's jaw confirmed Seymour's worst fears. Experience had taught him that the presence of CSI rarely heralded good news.

Blanchard opened the car door and got out. "Let's go inside and see what happened," he said, his voice low and devoid of its usual easy camaraderie.

The waiting room, usually a sterile space with beige walls and worn magazines, was now a scene of controlled chaos. Chip Turnbull, Harding's PI, lay sprawled on the floor, his body a grotesque display of bullet wounds.

The vibrant blood stained the pale carpet, a stark contrast to the crime scene tape's clinical white. Seymour and Blanchard, their badges flashing briefly in the harsh fluorescent light, were quickly fitted with booties and gloves.

The air was heavy with the metallic tang of blood and the acrid scent of gunpowder. They navigated carefully around the forensic technicians, their movements precise and measured, a stark counterpoint to the violence that had unfolded. In his father's office, the scene was even more brutal. Dr. Harding, Seymour's adoptive father, lay twisted amidst scattered papers and overturned furniture. The bullet holes pocked the walls like angry eyes, a testament to the ferocity of the attack.

Seymour knelt beside his father's body, the rage building within him, a molten core threatening to consume him. The carefully constructed composure he usually maintained crumbled, replaced by a grief so primeval it threatened to choke him.

"You never should have let my father go to his office without an escort," Seymour choked out, his voice thick with unshed tears. The words were directed at Blanchard but carried the weight of his own self-blame. His anger, a raw, potent force, threatened to overwhelm him.

Blanchard, his gaze fixed on the devastation around them, met Seymour's eyes. "I agree. I fucked up," he admitted, his voice tight with regret. "Based on the damage—the bullet trajectories and the way the room is saturated—we might have been outnumbered and part of the murder scene as well. This wasn't a hit on your father alone. This was… calculated assassination and another warning from the Pied Piper."

"What did my father have to deserve this brutal murder?" Seymour questioned. "We need to find my sister before she disappears again."

Chapter 88

Earl drove a large moving truck with the sedated children inside the cargo area. He had injected them with a potent sedative. He needed rest, but it would come once he had dropped off his cargo to the Pied Piper. He stopped at the final warehouse and waited for Sally to show up.

Inside the air-conditioned warehouse, Rita, a pretty young student nurse Sally had hired, was watching twelve infants. She was apparently frustrated when she saw Earl. "Where have you been?" she said in a huff as she gathered her things. "I'm going to be late for class and can't babysit these brats any longer."

Earl clenched his fists. "You're not going anywhere. Your job's not finished," he barked. "I need your pretty young ass to get all your children into the truck's cargo area. Make sure they stay quiet. I have a fucking headache and don't want any lip from you," he said, slapping her firm ass.

Her face knotted with a befuddled expression. Her head shook wildly. "Rear of the truck? No way, Jose," she said, arrogantly. "You told me Social Services would pick up these kids an hour ago. I'm out of here."

Earl's facial muscles tensed. His forehead veins bulged. Without warning, he slapped her across the face, knocking her down. Blood oozed from the corner of her mouth.

"What was that for?" she sobbed, holding her pink cheek, which had begun to swell. "What's going on here?" she said, drawing her knees to her chest and sobbing.

"I'm the only person you'll be seeing," he said, grabbing her long ponytail and lifting her off the cold cement floor. "Just do as you're told, and you won't get hurt. Do you understand?" Spittle was flying from Earl's mouth. "Now get the other children into the back of the truck and keep quiet. I don't want to hear your fucking whining voice anymore."

He loved seeing her fear. He was getting aroused. "Damn, not enough time," he mumbled.

"I won't go anywhere with you. That wasn't our deal," she argued, stammering for the right words. She watched Earl move toward her and raised her hands to protect her face.

"You'll do as I say," he said, his face beet red as he reached for her. He lifted her and tossed her like a sack of potatoes into the back of the truck. She hit her head hard against the metal floor, dazing her.

Earl leaped into the cargo area and jammed the barrel of his gun hard against her ribs. He whispered in her ear. "Just cooperate for a while longer, and I won't have to shoot you. It's only an hour and a half to where we're going. There's plenty of diapers and food for all of you, and if you need to relieve yourself, I left you a bucket," he grinned.

Earl had started handing her the sleeping infants from the warehouse without uttering another word. When he was finished, he lowered the cargo metal door, fastened the lock, and hopped behind the wheel.

Rita's aching jaw dropped four inches as she saw the seven cribs fastened against the cabin walls, infants no older than nine months fast asleep. There were four metal animal cages, each with two sleeping toddlers. She placed the infants she had cared for in the remaining empty cages. She cried silently. "What have I gotten myself into?"

Rita might have been nineteen, but she was not stupid. She had read about the foster children's abductions in California and realized she was in mortal danger. She guessed that once Earl had no more use for her services, she would be dead. She panned her enclosed space, hoping to find a weapon to aid her escape.

She reached for her cellphone. It was not in her back pocket. "Darn, it must have fallen out in the warehouse."

The truck had picked up speed, bouncing her around the cargo area. She cried out when the cargo truck made a sharp turn, and she banged against one of the metal cages, the sharp edge digging into her ribs. She sat down, her knees to her chest, trembling.

Earl called Sally on his cell. "Hey, it's me. Where the fuck are you?" he cussed. "Everything okay on your end?"

"Just peachy. You have an ETA for Solana Beach?"

"Should be there…", he glanced at his watch. "It's 9:30… let's say two hours tops if there's no traffic. I'm hungry and have to drop off the student nurse somewhere off Interstate 8. I'm not sure where yet."

Sally responded impatiently. "That's a stupid idea. Bring her back here, and we'll send her to Dr. Kane. I have Simone and will give her the Guzman. He can figure out what to do with her."

Earl always got horny when Sally scolded him. *"Maybe Rita needs to find out what a real man feels like before she's gone forever,"* he thought.

Palmer sighed. "Just don't mess with Rita. I don't need more problems right now…understand?"

"Whatever you say," Earl sighed.

Chapter 89

Seymour's anger was boiling over as he sat in the conference room at the FBI's regional office in downtown San Diego. He couldn't stop thinking about the error in judgment that had cost his father his life. He was now panic-stricken for his sister. He could not afford to let the Pied Piper win again and take his only remaining family from him. He listened to Evan's new plan, which, to him, felt like a Hail Mary. "Are you sure this is going to work?" Eddie asked.

"No, but it's all we've got right now. CIA Brian Patterson, the Director of the State Department's Office to Monitor and Combat Trafficking in Persons, has his team monitoring the encrypted emails from Guzman. We have Guzman's and Palmer's IP addresses. We don't have to know what they are saying, just when they are communicating and, hopefully, where the transfer of children will take place."

"Will we know where the exchange is taking place with enough time to stop it?" Blanchard asked. "What good will it do us if we can't interpret it quickly?"

"It's a long shot. The CIA has assured me that once they lock onto an encrypted email, they can pinpoint the last location it was sent from," Evans said, lacking conviction.

Seymour interrupted Evans. "You think the Pied Piper is that stupid? Palmer, yes, but he's got Michelle Arnold, maybe even my sister. He's in full control and might have us chasing our tails, like he has before."

Evans bit his lip and shrugged his shoulders. "It's all we have at our disposal right now."

"Maybe not," Blanchard blurted out. "We know the Pied Piper is out of control and making mistakes. We know Palmer sent Earl Mathews to pick up a load of children and take them to a designated drop-off location near a cargo ship. He has to bring them somewhere this evening. Maybe to a warehouse near the cargo ship."

"Earl Mathews, we know, is a fucking idiot," Seymour told them. "What if we get the coroner to bring Lisa Mathews's body to her house? We nail a note from the Pied Piper to her chest?" he suggested. "We know that Palmer ordered Earl to pick up his wife, and I bet that when he reads the note, he'll go half-cocked and lead us to the drop-off location."

The fax machine interrupted their arguing. Evans pulled off the three sheets. It was the San Diego Harbor Manifests he had requested earlier. "Before we all go off half-cocked, I've got a list of all the warehouses expecting a shipment of goods tonight and the ships scheduled to leave early morning."

Seymour and Blanchard grabbed a sheet and began scanning the list. "That's over fifty warehouses that are scheduled to have shipments delivered, and there are ten large ships, including Guzman's Ship of Hope, that have been cleared to depart between 1:30 A.M. and 3:30 A.M.," Blanchard said. "There is no way we can monitor that many places with the few agents we have."

Seymour found it first. "Guzman's 'Ship of Hope' entered port five days ago and was scheduled to embark at one-thirty in the morning tomorrow." Eddie's eyes were like tiny lasers boring in on the ship's name. "He's one bold mother fucker."

"He's playing his game," Evans said. He showed his agents the notes left on Agents Armstrong and Crawford. "I'll bet the obvious is not the obvious. He wants to hurt us more than we've been hurt before. I don't believe he'll use his ship. He's got to be planning on taking the children out some other way."

Seymour's face twisted. "We don't have the manpower to investigate so many possibilities. I still believe my idea about Lisa Mathews will work."

Evans had turned somber. "I like your idea. It's worth a try," he said. Blanchard knew his friend and could tell he was hiding something from them.

"Robert, is there something else you want to tell us?" Blanchard asked.

"Soon," Evans said. "Let's get Seymour's plan moving forward."

Blanchard was already calling the coroner. "Jack, Blanchard here. I need you to return Lisa Mathews to her house ASAP," he ordered.

"That's highly irregular," the coroner replied. "By whose authority?"

"Deputy Director Evans. We need to set a trap so we can rescue two dozen infants and Agent Seymour's sister."

"I can get her there within the hour," he replied.

"Try for thirty minutes. I'm running out of time for this to work."

Evans knew that what he was asking his team to do would most likely send them all to prison, but he needed to give them the choice to stop the Pied Piper. "I wasn't going to tell you guys that I spoke to President Webster an hour ago. He's called off our operation. Director Jenkins and the President's Chief of Staff convinced him it would be political suicide to accuse Guzman at this point. Did any of you listen to the news earlier today?"

"Are you joking? "We've been up to our eyeballs in problems, no time for the news," Blanchard sarcastically told his friend.

"Guzman turned over years of investigative files on the Pied Piper to the Attorney General. He's been investigating Dr. Kane, Senator Jarvis, and Sally Palmer for years. He released evidence that Enrique Ramirez did not die that night twenty years ago. The world now knows that Enrique Ramirez is the real Pied Piper."

"It just sounds too convenient. Why is he coming forward now with this shit?" Blanchard responded.

Evans sighed. "We have another problem. Guzman suggested that another ship might have been following his schedule and setting him up. Maybe we're barking up the wrong tree?"

"What are you saying?" Blanchard asked, his face full of rage. "If it's not Guzman, could it be the real Enrique Ramirez?"

Seymour frowned. "We need to go with what we know and pray we're right. What about our witness's testimony? They all pointed to Guzman as the Pied Piper," he reminded them. "Unless we can convince the local police to help, we're on our own. Three old Musketeers fighting their last battle." His melancholy tone infuriated Blanchard.

Maybe you've given up, but I haven't. The Pied Piper and Palmer have your sister. Now he has Michelle Arnold and my niece. If Enrique Ramerez or Guzman wants this to be his last game, let him bring it on.

Chapter 90

Sally nervously pecked out her email, which instantly converted to Piper's encrypted code. She knew his response would not be immediate; it was not like communicating via Google's instant messaging. She was waiting patiently for Earl at the Solana Beach motel. It was a quarter mile from her rental property, which she used to house the foster children before handing them off to the Pied Piper.

Palmer checked her gun for the hundredth time. She did not trust Guzman after listening to his bullshit press conference a few hours earlier with President Webster. "He won't be able to convince the world that Miguel Guzman is not the Pied Piper." She'd feel better when Earl arrived. He was experienced at killing. She had never fired a gun in her life.

Her laptop screen had started beeping. Guzman's email was transmitting.

* * * * *

Earl backed into the serpentine driveway at the Solana Beach house. He parked the truck by a slump stone utility building in the backyard. Sally's car was not there. He was relieved. He was too tired to face her.

He offloaded the cages first, carrying each one into the thousand-square-foot room that resembled a day-care nursery. He saw Simone handcuffed to a pipe next to a bed, her eyes wide with disgust as she saw him.

"Is that any way to look at your father?" Earl said, grinning.

"You're not my father," she screamed back at him, thrashing at her handcuffs. "Let me out of here."

Earl could not stop staring at Simone's torn blouse and the thick cleavage it exposed. He licked his lips slowly.

She immediately covered herself, her face crimson. "You're disgusting," she shouted.

"Not really. Since I'm not your real father, being your first wouldn't be that immoral," he laughed.

"I'd die first," she yelled.

"Don't wish for something you're not ready for, my little virgin."

When Earl finished unloading the truck, he began sedating the children again. He sat down across the room on a battered leather couch, staring at Simone.

"Simone," he tried to say, but she cut him off abruptly.

"My name is Ashley Seymour. If you're going to hurt me, maybe kill me, I want to know who I am and why my parents had to die. You owe this 'VIRGIN'," she emphasized the word, her eyes red with fire, "that much."

Earl seemed surprised by her boldness. It aroused him even more. He gave a rushed account of the Pied Piper, the favor Sally owed him, and the day his pickup truck killed her mother and father.

"But why would this Pied Piper want my parents dead?" she asked, her eyes moist.

"I haven't the foggiest," he shrugged. "Maybe you could ask him after you're dropped off in a few hours?"

"And Lisa...she knew about all of this?"

"Lisa is a crazy bitch. Always has been. But she believed she loved you. She, in her stupid way, believed you were her real child. But you already know how psychotic your mother...I mean, your adoptive mother..." He scratched his head. "Shit, what should I call her other than a rotten, crazy kidnapper? She's been part of your aunt's operation for a long time."

"Lisa was always nice to me," Ashley said sadly. "I just can't believe she could do what you're saying."

Earl pursed his lips. He seemed bored with the conversation. "Since this might be our last time together, we shouldn't let it go to waste," he said, saliva oozing down his chin.

Ashley bit her lower lip, thinking. "What's Sally going to say when I tell her you raped me?" She noticed his hesitation. He was thinking but kept unbuckling his belt. He was about to reply when a female voice startled him.

"What would I say?" Sally said, her fists on her hips, scowling. She looked at Ashley, then at Earl. Her eyes widened as Earl dropped his pants. Sally noticed the prominent bulge under his tighty-whities.

Earl tried to respond. "Sally, I was just joking around."

Sally cut him off. "What the hell is wrong with you? Where is the girl who was watching the children?"

Earl's eyes reflected that he had once again done something stupid as he pulled up his pants. "She tried to get away. I had no choice. She's hidden somewhere in the woods. No one will find her for months, and we'll be long gone by then."

Sally knew when Earl lied, and with the white-caked stains on his jeans, she knew what had happened. "You just can't keep your cock in your pants for one simple job. You're a fucking idiot." She pointed to his pants. "You must have left your DNA, you moron," she said, throwing her arms in the air and walking outside. "Earl, follow me," she ordered.

Simone watched the two of them arguing. "I trusted Sally all these years," she told herself. "Will I ever see my brother before I die, or will I find him with this Pied Piper?" She heard the two of them screaming at each other.

Outside, Sally raised her voice. "What am I going to do with you?" Her face twisted with disgust. "Don't reply," she cut him off, her hand in his face like a traffic cop. "You were supposed to pick up Lisa an hour ago. Where is she?"

Earl bit his lower lip, shrugging his shoulders uncaringly. "She's probably taken a vial of her pills and is sleeping off her depression," he said coldly.

"I want her here with me. We meet up with Piper after midnight at the pier to hand off the children. He's got our new identities, passports, and one-way tickets to Argentina. That's going to be our home for a while."

Earl looked befuddled, raising his voice. "Argentina? I thought we were going to some tropical island."

"Argentina is a safe place for us. They don't have any extradition treaties with the United States. I've already transferred our money from the Cayman Islands account." Palmer had no more patience for her brother-in-law. "Just get Lisa here. If you don't want to come, then stay and face the consequences."

Earl turned without a word and jumped into Sally's car. He hated how she talked to him.

* * * * *

Earl saw Lisa's car in the driveway. "She's home," he sighed. "Maybe she's wasted and won't notice…" He was still excited, thinking about Simone. He shook his head. "Shit, even wasted, she notices everything."

The front door was unlocked, and he pushed it open slowly. His eyes widened when he saw Lisa's twisted body lying at the bottom of the steps. He began to shake.

"Oh boy…oh boy," he said nervously. "Sally isn't going to believe I didn't do this. Oh boy," he moaned. He slowly shuffled over to her body and saw the note pinned to her chest. He pulled out his cell phone and tapped his foot anxiously. "Pick up," he mumbled. He got her answering machine. He ripped the note off his wife's chest and was inside his car, heading back to Solana Beach.

* * * * *

"It looks as if it's working," Seymour said, giving Blanchard a high-five slap. "Hope they're both stupid enough to take us to the drop-off point."

Earl was in the van, backing out of the driveway of Palmer's rental property in Solana Beach. He proceeded slowly onto Highway 101. He was heading south. Seymour and Blanchard watched patiently.

"We should have gone into the warehouse and checked for Ashley," Seymour said, his voice cracking as a lump formed in his throat.

Blanchard squeezed his partner's neck assuredly. "If we were wrong, we'd never catch all of them red-handed. If she's still alive, we'll find her, I promise you," he said.

"Can you be a little more sensitive? Leave out the 'ifs' until we know for sure," Seymour reprimanded his partner.

"Sorry. Call Evans and let him know we're heading downtown. He needs to have San Diego PD ready to roll when we find the exact location.

Chapter 91

Luis dropped by unannounced at the Solana Beach location with Michelle Arnold in tow. "Palmer, Piper wants you to hold on to this pain in the ass until tonight. We're too exposed where we're staying. Someone might see us with the girl. We killed two more FBI agents to get her, and now San Diego is flooded with FBI and police. Do you have all the children that were ordered?"

Sally shook her head. "Earl will be here shortly with the rest of the children. Does Guzman have all my papers and the money?" Palmer asked cautiously.

"You'll get everything you need tonight once you fulfill your end of the deal. Don't be late," Luis threatened.

Thirty minutes later, Earl pulled up to the warehouse, where Sally was waiting. She looked pissed as she tapped her finger on her watch. He knew instantly that she'd explode when he told her about her sister.

Earl jumped out of the truck, his eyes looking down, unable to face Sally. "You're not going to be happy with the news I have," he blurted out.

Sally looked at the passenger side of the truck and didn't see her sister. "By the shitty look on your face, what did you do to Lisa?" she demanded.

Earl handed her the note. "I found this pinned to her chest. She was riddled with bullets."

Sally read the note, crumpled it up, and tossed it across the warehouse. "It doesn't make sense. Why would Piper kill my sister?" Sally pondered, swiping a tear from her cheek.

"Maybe he's not keeping his end of the bargain. We should be careful. Let me cover your back when we get there," Earl said.

"We'll see. He still needs my services for a while longer," she said, pulling her revolver out of her purse.

* * * * *

Luis drove south on Interstate 5 toward the pier. He had his brother Herman on his cell. "How did it go with Palmer's sister?"

"I'm confused. When I found her, she was already dead."

"How?"

"Three bullets to the chest. She had a note pinned to her, signed by Piper," he said nervously. "Did Piper tell you he was going to do that?"

"He didn't do that. I'd know. I'll bet it's our FBI friends who think they're smarter than us. They must be following her husband, Earl. Piper's going to love how perfectly his game is playing out. They're walking straight into his trap. It's just too easy," Luis chuckled. "Soon we'll be rid of everyone, including the FBI."

* * * * *

At an undisclosed location, Guzman paced wildly inside a warehouse located near the Naval Base south of downtown San Diego. "Are we ready?" he asked Luis.

Luis and his brothers were finishing up by placing a large plastic tarp and four folding chairs in the middle of the warehouse. "We're ready. The tripods are in place, and the Russian knows what he has to say. I have some good news for you, boss."

Guzman looked at his watch. "Tell me later. Our guests should start arriving any minute now," he said, rubbing his hands, a feral grin on his face. He backed up into a darkened corner, waiting for all the excitement to begin.

The first person to arrive was Senator Jarvis, followed by Director Jenkins.

"Why are we meeting here and not in a public place? Your note made no sense," Jenkins said sternly.

"Doctor Kane said he had something important to tell us about the Pied Piper, and I thought it would be a feather in your cap if you could finally close your case."

Jenkins remained silent. His instincts told him something was not right when he saw the four chairs and the plastic tarp in the middle of the warehouse.

A voice from the darkness startled both men. Jenkins drew his gun, his hand shaking.

"I'll tell you everything in short order. We'll be getting a visit from the Pied Piper any minute," Dr. Kane informed them. "Now, put your gun away and have a seat." He briskly walked over, shook both men's hands, and pulled Senator Jarvis to the side of the warehouse.

Jenkins took a seat, nervously fondling his weapon. He knew he shouldn't have come alone, but Jarvis, whom he knew was a traitor, made it clear that Kane wanted him there or he wouldn't talk.

The Russian who had entered with the doctor excused himself, his tone overly anxious. He walked slowly backward, watching Kane talk to the senator. He noticed Jenkins eyeing him and gave a half-hearted wave before fading into the darkness, away from the three men. Piper had Luis and Herman escort Ivan outside.

Dr. Kane whispered to Jarvis out of Jenkins's earshot. "Tonight, we're going to free ourselves from the Pied Piper's claws. He's just moments away from arriving. He will finally feel the pain he has caused thousands. Tonight, he's going to die along with Jenkins. The Russian has everything under control. Then we can get back to our businesses."

Jarvis stammered. "This seems too easy. I don't like it."

Kane, in a low, harsh whisper, looked Jarvis in the eyes. "You're an idiot, senator. He's been eliminating everyone who has done business with him. He wants to retire, but with nobody around that could identify him."

Jarvis would not stop ranting. "He's not that stupid. You think he'll come here... let himself be so exposed. You're the fucking idiot," the senator barked. He stood and started to walk out when a voice from the dark called out to him.

"Senator, come back and sit down," Guzman said. "What the good doctor has said is true," he added confidently.

Jenkins stood holding his gun when Luis pushed him down and twisted the weapon from his hand. Kane turned white when it sank in that the trap was for them. "Ivan, you're a pig," he shouted.

"Now, Doctor Kane, did you think I wouldn't find out about your half-hearted plan to kill me? You should have stayed in your laboratory in France."

Guzman was wearing his jester's costume and mask. He giggled, enjoying the anxiety on everyone's faces. "I don't want to kill any of you...well, not yet. I have a non-negotiable deal you should consider."

Jenkins stood. "What the fuck is going on here?" he shouted at the Pied Piper. It was the first time he had ever seen the sociopath in his costume, and he tried not to laugh. He knew the man behind the mask was crazy.

"In due time. Now sit down and watch," Miguel said politely.

Luis was holding a laptop with its wireless antenna at attention.

"I want the two of you to wire all the money you've earned from my services over the years. Every penny must be transferred to my bank account tonight. I have taken the liberty of notifying your respective banks to expect your orders."

Kane stood and screamed. "Piper, you're nuts. I'll never do that," he said furiously.

Without warning, Guzman fired one round into Kane's knee. The doctor fell to the plastic tarp, screaming in pain.

"Senator, do you want to negotiate?" Piper said coldly. "I don't have much time... so what will it be, my dear friend?"

Jarvis was the first to enter his password and transfer codes. Thirty seconds later, one hundred fifteen billion dollars was in Guzman's account.

Herman helped Kane into his chair.

"What will it be, doctor?" Piper asked, pressing the hot barrel against Kane's temple, causing him to scream again.

"All right. All right," he cried, holding his bloodied knee. It took almost three minutes for the transfer to be completed.

"Wow," Miguel said. "Seven hundred and twenty-five billion. I guess the organ business is very profitable," he mocked.

Luis closed the laptop and faded into the blackness. Herman rolled in a Sony fifty-seven-inch digital widescreen TV. On top was a DVD player.

"Jenkins, this is for your pleasure. I want you to enjoy a walk down memory lane with your fraternity brother who's helped me kill a few of your agents. You have to see what kind of experiments Doctor Kane has been conducting. I've kept a wonderful chronicle of our relationship and thought you should have this as your last memory of me. After tonight, the work of the Pied Piper is over."

Luis had returned with shackles that he strapped to each of the men's ankles, connecting them to a long, thick anchor chain looped through a metal ring drilled into the concrete floor.

"Gentlemen, enjoy your last minutes together," he laughed.

Chapter 92

Blanchard and Seymour switched off their headlights and coasted to a halt five hundred yards from where the van had stopped. Eddie radioed Evans.

"I want everyone to hold their positions. The children are our priority. Until we know we can safely remove them, no one moves. Is that clear?" Seymour barked.

With his night-vision goggles on, Blanchard watched Earl Mathews and Sally Palmer inside the truck. They appeared overly anxious.

"Maybe pinning the note wasn't such a smart idea," Blanchard said nervously. "They might bolt or even kill the children and run."

"No," whispered Seymour. "She wants her freedom and will do whatever it takes. That's who she is. Once they clear the van, we move in and secure the area. We still need to know which warehouse she was supposed to meet the Pied Piper at. This will work. I know it," he said tentatively.

Palmer and Earl were briskly walking toward warehouse number 97. The instant they were inside, Seymour ordered the SWAT team to take their positions around the warehouse. Eddie's heart pounded as he waited for word that Ashley was on board and safe.

He was out of the car, racing toward the van, his gun at his side. He skidded to a halt as the SWAT team leader came over his radio.

"We have sixteen children, six infants, all safe. One teenager… young lady, state your name, please," the officer asked. He repeated the reply. "We have one Ashley Seymour. Agent Seymour, she appears to be unharmed. We also have Michelle Arnold on board, unharmed."

Evans was immediately by the truck's back door. He saw Michelle standing by Ashley Seymour, hugging her. "Michelle, I'm so happy you're safe," he told her as he embraced her. "I promise that no more harm will come to you. You have my word."

"I hope so," Michelle replied. "I've been told this before."

"I'll make it up to you, but I've got to capture the Pied Piper and all of the other bad men and women who hurt children." Evans nodded. He waved over one of the officers and ordered him to watch the two girls.

Ashley noticed about a hundred yards from her a man fall to his knees, sobbing. She looked at Evans. "Is that my brother Eddie?"

Eddie, for the first time since his parents had died, began to cry. "She knows who she is?" he sobbed.

Agent Blanchard was by his partner's side, lifting him up. "Get a grip. We have to get the Pied Piper, or we're fucked," he shouted.

Seymour stood and wiped his moist cheeks. He radioed Evans to send in the rest of the team. He and Blanchard were running hard toward the warehouse, weapons at the ready.

"Take no prisoners," Blanchard yelled.

They approached the warehouse from the south end, while SWAT positioned themselves from the north. To Blanchard's surprise, they were followed by Deputy Director Evans. He looked at him, surprised. His vest was outside his shirt. He was ready to fight.

"You didn't think I'd let you guys have all the fun, did you?" he grinned.

They busted through the metal door, their eyes trying to adjust to the darkness. In the distance, they saw a widescreen TV and four men sitting in chairs, watching a video. They did not turn around when the metal door crashed open.

Palmer and Mathews seemed confused, spinning wildly, surprised to see the FBI agents approaching. Then an explosion of floodlights blinded everyone. Before they could react, a barrage of bullets came at them.

Seymour, Blanchard, and Evans began shooting back, but they fired haphazardly. They could not determine the location of the men firing at them. Evans went down first, a bullet grazing his forehead.

Then Seymour felt his chest explode with pain. A bullet had penetrated his vest.

Blanchard fell to the cold cement floor, covering the Deputy Director. He felt for a pulse on Evans, fumbling nervously. "I can't find a pulse," he screamed. He looked to his left and saw that Seymour was down and not moving.

His rage was getting the best of him. He wasn't about to lose again to the Pied Piper, but Evans and Seymour needed attention fast. The barrage of bullets stopped as quickly as it had begun, leaving a deafening echo in his ears. He dragged Seymour outside and ripped off his vest; blood was everywhere. "Officer down," he shouted three times into his transmitter, "south side building entrance." He pressed his hand hard against the wound. "You hang in there, Agent Seymour. You have a sister to meet, and I'm not ready to lose another partner."

Once Blanchard secured his partner with a medic, he ran back into the warehouse for Evans. A smile exploded on his face when he saw Evans sitting up, blood dripping down the side of his face.

"Thought you were dead," said Blanchard. "I couldn't find a pulse."

Evans shrugged his shoulders. "You never could find a pulse during your training, so why should this be any different?"

Blanchard tried to speak, but his voice was garbled. "What the fuck just happened in there? Where was SWAT?"

"Not sure. There are too many bodies inside to know what happened. The Pied Piper set a trap. How I, for the life of me, can't figure out, but he beat us again," Evans said despondently.

* * * * *

The medics could not stabilize Agent Seymour, and he was airlifted to Scripps La Jolla Trauma Center. He was unconscious with shallow breathing. His condition was listed as grave.

Evans was sitting on the back of the paramedic truck, along with Ashely Seymour and Michelle Arnold, his head wrapped in gauze. A light red stain was oozing through the bandage where the bullet had grazed off his skull. However, inside the warehouse, another scene altogether unfolded.

Doctor Kane, Senator Jarvis, and FBI Director Jenkins had been riddled with bullets, chained to their chairs. The twisted bodies of Sally Palmer and Earl Mathews were lying ten yards from them. On eight heavy-duty commercial tripods were automatic rifles that had been fired by remote control. The Pied Piper was nowhere to be found. The only thing left by the large TV screen was his final mocking note.

To President Webster:

It's over. I will not be a headache for you any longer. Sorry that so many of your people had to die, but what was a son about to do when your country had my mother killed? Please don't come looking for me, or you'll lose more people. I hope you've learned that I am unstoppable, I am the Pied Piper.

* * * * *

With Agent Seymour in surgery, Evans was still convinced that the Pied Piper and Miguel Guzman were the same person. His career didn't matter to him at the moment. He just wanted to arrest Miguel Guzman.

The Coast Guard and Deputy Director Evans had boarded the Ship of Hope near Point Loma. Miguel was relaxing in black silk pajamas, visibly surprised to see the Deputy Director standing before him.

"Is there a problem?" he said calmly and in control. "You realize this is an invasion of my privacy?"

Evans had a pounding headache and was in no mood for small talk from the sociopath he was staring at. "You're in United States waters, and I'm the FBI, and I'll do whatever I want," Evans said venomously.

"Do as you please," he waved his hand dismissively.

Miguel Guzman opened his cell phone. He dialed the president's private number, which he had received months earlier.

He woke President Webster and demanded that the persons responsible for detaining him be punished.

Evans stood there with a befuddled expression on his face. One of his agents had returned from searching the ship. He told Evans that Guzman's Ship of Hope is just that, a floating hospital ship.

He looked at Guzman and closed his eyes, unable to handle the situation. "Not again," he muttered.

Chapter 93

Ashley could not stop sobbing. "Is he going to be all right?" she asked Blanchard, who wore a vacant expression.

"Eddie's a fighter," Blanchard responded.

"Have you known my brother a long time?" she asked. "I know nothing about him," she said, fighting back tears.

Ted Blanchard swallowed hard. "I've known him since he became an FBI agent. We just became partners a few weeks ago. I did know your father a long time ago," he said sadly. "He was my first partner out of the academy."

Ashley was lost in thought. "I have no memory of my mother or father. I hope that when things settle down, you can tell me all about them," she implored.

"It would be my honor to tell you everything about your parents and your brother. You know that Eddie told me he had never stopped looking for you." He paused, thinking of all the letters Eddie wrote to his sister on her birthdays. "I think Seymour…I mean, Eddie should tell you all about it himself."

Blanchard remembered that she had just had her birthday. "Oh, by the way, happy birthday. It was yesterday, right?"

She had a puzzled look on her face. "No. It's not for another few weeks. Are you telling me that my birthday is another lie?"

A doctor in blood-stained scrubs walked toward them, stopping in front of Ashley. He knelt and placed his cold hand on hers, his tired eyes about to deliver news she did not want to hear.

"Your brother fought hard in the OR," the doctor said, unemotional.

"Is he dead?" Ashley shuddered, her eyes fixed on the doctor.

"The bullet shattered muscle and bone. We were able to get most of the bullet out. He lost a lot of blood."

Ashley gasped, unable to catch her breath. "Are you saying he's dead?" her voice rose.

The doctor remained unemotional, only adding to her panic. "I said he's a real fighter. He'll be out of recovery in about two hours. You can see him then. He's a lucky man," the doctor said, standing and walking away.

Blanchard could not believe the doctor's callous demeanor and grabbed his arm roughly. "We've just been through hell, and this young lady deserves a better answer from you," he reprimanded.

The doctor had a startled look on his face. He shook off Blanchard's tight grip, his face beet red. "I've just pulled two twelve-hour shifts and lost a patient before your friend was brought to the operating room. I'm sorry for my attitude. There's no excuse for my behavior. What I meant is that he's going to be just fine. He's a real fighter. Now I've got to go. I have to work on a gang member who's just been shot." With that, the doctor briskly turned and walked away, shaking his head.

Ashley did not know whether to laugh or cry. She chose to cry, burying her head into Blanchard's shoulder.

After a few minutes, she lifted her head, her eyes red and the tip of her nose pink. "I can't stop thinking that just two days ago I had a mother and father and an aunt. Now I find out that they were all criminals, and I have a brother who's an FBI Agent."

"You can't imagine everything that's happened over the last few months," Blanchard said somberly.

"I guess it's going to take some adjustment to allow reality to set in," Ashley admitted.

"You'll do just fine. Eddie's a great guy, once you get to know him.

* * * * *

A day after the massacre in San Diego, Miguel Guzman held a satellite press conference that was televised worldwide. With the sincerity and charm that had made him beloved around the world, he explained how embarrassed he was to be associated with Senator Jarvis, Sally Palmer, and Doctor Thomas Kane. He apologized to the world and to the governments that had supported his work for not realizing how his three friends and associates were using him and taking advantage of his goodwill. Before ending the press conference, he looked deep into the camera lens, his eyes moist, and spoke with the sincerest emotion.

"I hope all of my friends around the world still believe in me and the work I continue to do. I am not the Pied Piper, and my offer of fifty million dollars for any information that leads to the capture of this hideous man is still good. It is always sad when the media accuses an honest person of a crime before all the facts are known. This has now happened to me, and for the record, I want the press to know I forgive them and the FBI agent who was doing their job. I hope I can once again gain your trust. Thank you for allowing me to talk to all of you."

Evans was fixed on Guzman's eyes. He heard his words, but the eyes told the true story. The bastard was lying. He knew, but couldn't do anything about it, at least not at this time.

* * * * *

Miguel and Luis sat out on the open deck at the stern of the ship, smoking cigars, sipping whiskey, and laughing. The sun was beginning to rise over the Baja Coast as his ship sailed at a comfortable eighteen knots on its way home through the Panama Canal, then on to the Belize harbor.

Miguel loved the sunrises over the ocean. They thrilled him more than sunsets. It was his home away from home, and the morning orange glow meant another day of power awaited him.

His face tightened as his mood shifted. His mind was lost in thought. His demeanor grew restless, like a caged animal sensing a storm brewing. He took a deep breath. His eyes narrowed before he spoke to Luis.

"So, did you like my little speech?" Miguel asked.

"Piper," Luis said cautiously. "The speech was perfecto."

Miguel scowled. "It's Miguel... Miguel Guzman. Never call me that name again," he said, his tone menacing.

Luis's face flushed, and he apologized. "Miguel...I'm sorry. It has been so many years. It will stop right now. I will tell my brothers to remember," he said anxiously, wanting to say more.

"You have something else you care to say?" Miguel probed.

Luis nodded. "We have yet to deal with the Russian and the hospital staff on the other ship. If the Pied Piper must vanish..." he swallowed hard, "They all must disappear."

Miguel smiled. "It is being taken care of as we speak. The United States Coast Guard should have received a tip that a ship was leaving San Diego Harbor with children aboard. The Pied Piper will die on that ship," Guzman said coldly, waving his friend away. "One other thing. I guess your prophecy didn't pan out, Luis. My birthday has come and gone. I'm still standing," he mocked. "You should tell Maria that she is a fraud."

Luis disagreed with his boss. "Maybe it wasn't supposed to be this birthday," he countered. "I'm not so sure Evans and his team won't try to seek their revenge when you least expect it."

Miguel ignored his remarks with a caustic laugh. "Let me know as soon as the news broadcasts the story about the Pied Piper's death. I have won the last game," he whispered, expelling a large plume of smoke.

Guzman's words did not satisfy Luis. He had not seen Evans, Blanchard, or Seymour's bodies lying dead. He still needed to find the traitor on the ranch. He shrugged his shoulders and leaned back, puffing wildly on his cigar, feeling his mood turn jovial once again. "Well, maybe you're right."

Chapter 94

It had been five days since the massacre at Pier 97. The evidence the Pied Piper had left on the DVD, inside plastic storage boxes, along with photos of hundreds of missing children, had helped close over three hundred and seventy cases dating back twenty years. Every detail about Doctor Kane and his house of horrors painted a horrifying picture of how he had experimented, mutilated, and created an infant organ farm using each of his young victims. The Pied Piper had made sure to connect Dr. Kane's work to his father's work during Hitler's Third Reich.

The Austrian and French governments vehemently denied any knowledge of Kane's activities or of ever condoning his experiments. Sally Palmer's network of caseworkers and foster care parents, spread across the United States, had all been arrested and were awaiting arraignment.

Senator Jarvis's four factories, two in Asia and two in Africa, had been closed, and the children, mostly teenagers and some who were now young women, were returned to their respective countries and to their families, if any could be found. Those without families were placed back into their country's poorly managed child services agencies.

Deputy Director Evans had served as the interim FBI Director until President Webster could appoint a more suitable candidate.

Rumors of a scandal began to surface. The President's staff frantically tried to douse the flames. Their efforts failed, and the scandal was affecting Webster's re-election campaign.

In the meantime, Evans was ordered not to speak to the press about his team or their investigation. The president needed time to assess the potential fallout, if any, for him. Political survival had become the president's number one priority, not the welfare of the children the FBI had recovered.

President Webster's poll numbers had dropped by twenty points. His appointment of Sally Palmer to his Federal Foster Care Department was a failure he couldn't run away from, bringing his inept administration to the surface.

Agent Edward Seymour had been released from the hospital, and he requested a six-month leave of absence to recuperate and get to know his sister. During the five days he was in the hospital, Ashley had instantly connected with him. His mother had been right when he was a little boy. Ashley hadn't forgotten him.

He arranged for Ashley's urn to be exhumed from the cemetery and for her birthday letters to be removed. Each day, he read her the letters he had written, sharing his experiences from those years. They cried together; however, it was Eddie's stories about their parents that Ashley wanted to hear most of all.

On the day Eddie was released from the hospital, he had scheduled Doctor Harding's funeral. Ashley cried, not over his death, but because she could never thank the man who had cared so much for her brother.

"He sounds like he was a great man," she had said, holding her brother's hand tightly. "I only got to know him briefly…in a doctor-patient sort of way," she said somberly.

"He was. I could not have asked for a better surrogate father. Much of what I know about our dad comes from Philip's memory," Eddie told her, unable to hold back his tears. "They were best friends. I have an album he gave me with pictures of Mom and Dad when they were young. He also gave me photos of Mom, pregnant with me, and then with you. You won't believe how funny I looked as a kid. You were always beautiful. You look like Mom… you know that, right?"

"I just wish all of this had never happened. It's still hard to wake up now and realize those eighteen years of my life were a lie. Promise me you'll keep telling me more stories," she begged.

"That's an easy promise to keep." As they got into the limo, he kissed her cheek. "I have a surprise for you," he said sheepishly.

"Tell me," She giggled. His eyes welled up, hearing the laugh he had missed for so long.

"Philip has kept our family home all these years. I could not live in it by myself, but with you back in my life, I was wondering if you'd feel comfortable…you know…being a family there?"

Ashley gasped. "That sounds wonderful!" She hugged him tightly.

Eddie could barely breathe as she squeezed hard, but he realized that God had given him a new beginning that he would never take for granted.

* * * * *

Evans was on a mission to bring everything out into the open. He needed closure, and exposing the corruption was the only way he knew would allow him to sleep at night.

He had prepared a detailed report on what had happened leading up to the Pier 97 incident. Senator Jarvis's involvement with the Pied Piper reflected poorly on President Webster, even though he had tried to distance himself from everyone. Sally Palmer's actions were blamed on the Secretary of Health and Human Services, whom the President immediately fired.

Evans was determined to continue his quest to find the Pied Piper; however, President Webster had ordered him to stand down until after the election. When he received an anonymous tip that a freighter leaving San Diego Harbor was heading toward Guatemala with a large number of children, he could not obey the president's orders. Before he turned in his resignation, he had one last job to do.

With the Coast Guard leading the way, Evans was ready to board the freighter when an explosion rocked the harbor. The ship carrying the children was engulfed in flames and sinking rapidly.

Evans was in shock. Why would the Pied Piper, if this were his ship, kill himself in this manner? Was Enrique Ramirez really the man he had been chasing for two decades? He knew he wouldn't know for sure until they recovered all the bodies.

* * * * *

A week later, President Webster announced that, thanks to the dedicated work of the Coast Guard and the FBI, the Pied Piper was finally dead. Forensics could not get enough DNA from the charred remains of the captain of the ship. However, they were able to match up the missing severed ear they had when Enrique Ramirez was a young man with the body they found on board. That was all President Webster needed, and the case was closed.

For Evans, it wasn't. He was furious. He knew whoever died on the freighter was neither Enrique Ramirez nor the Pied Piper. He hated Washington politics and that President Webster took full credit for ending the world's largest human trafficking cartel.

Ted Blanchard was promoted to Deputy Director. He was determined to find his niece and kill all the men associated with his sister's murder.

Chapter 95

Six Months Later

After Robert Evans resigned from the FBI, President Webster, for selfish political reasons, ordered the DOJ cover up the scandal in his administration. FBI Director Jenkins was praised as a great American who lost his life while trying to capture the Pied Piper.

Miguel Guzman received a formal apology from the president on the White House lawn. He was also given another ten-million-dollar check to continue providing healthcare to all poor children around the world. Guzman's link to the Pied Piper was completely cleared.

The official word about Sally Palmer was that she had died of a heart attack. Her Federal Foster Care Agency had been disbanded, and all the cases she was involved in were returned to their respective states without further explanation.

Webster's election was twelve months away. His ratings were now higher than ever. All the polls showed him leading his opponent, an up-and-coming young Democrat from California, by twenty percent.

Oscar Weidman's son, Rudy, had taken control of the San Diego Union Press and made Evans an offer he couldn't refuse.

Evans petitioned for full custody of Michelle Arnold, hoping to settle down. He became the managing editor of the San Diego Union Press, with the sole task of finding the man who murdered Oscar Weidman. Neither man believed the Pied Piper was dead or that Miguel Guzman was the humanitarian everyone portrayed him as.

"I know how to draw the Pied Piper out into the open," Evans had told Rudy. "I just need to get a team in place first. It will be dangerous. I just hope you're ready to soil your father's newspaper's reputation," he said.

"My father never worried about his paper's reputation. He printed the news as he saw fit, and so will I. I haven't slept well since my father's murder. Whatever you want this paper to do, I'll do it. You will have unlimited funds and the freedom to print whatever you want."

Evans smiled. "That will work just fine," he laughed. Now the game will be played by my rules, he silently boasted, rubbing his hands together. A big smile spread across his face.

He wasted no time and was on the phone. "Ted, I have a favor to ask," Evans said sheepishly.

"Does it have to do with the Pied Piper?" he said skeptically.

"Yes. I need Seymour, too. Can you talk to him? If we could meet tomorrow, that would be great. I have an idea, and for it to work, I need you and Seymour. We have to act quickly."

* * * * *

Blanchard arrived at Seymour's house in Carlsbad as Ashley and Seymour were getting into their car. Ted jumped out of his SUV and waved.

Eddie's eyes widened. He couldn't believe what he was seeing as he looked at his partner. "Did someone stick a pin in you? I always knew you were full of hot air. Man, you've lost a lot of weight," he complimented him.

Blanchard ignored his remark with a playful scowl. "I've got a lot to tell you about the last six months. But that's not why I'm here. Evans wants a sit-down. I think you'll like what he has to say."

"Sure. When?"

"Tomorrow at his new office."

Eddie looked at Ashley and then back at Ted. He whispered in her ear, and she nodded. "Come join us. We're heading to the zoo — something neither of us has ever done together. What do you say?" Eddie hadn't noticed the woman and the young woman sitting inside the SUV.

"I'm with someone. We don't want to intrude," Blanchard replied.

"Bring them along. New girlfriend?" Seymour asked.

"No…well, it's a long story. Teresa…we were a thing way back when. I screwed it up twenty-five years ago. With all the Pied Piper stuff happening, I thought it was time to clean up my past so I could have some new tomorrows."

Eddie and Ashley quickly walked over to Ted's car. The windows rolled down, and a beautiful woman extended her hand.

"You must be Edward Seymour. I'm Teresa Harper," she said, smiling. "I knew your father and Philip back when we were all young and idealistic. This is our daughter, Tina."

Seymour's jaw dropped four inches. He looked at Blanchard, puzzled. "You never told me you had a daughter," he said.

"I never knew I had one until I reconnected with Teresa. It's another long story," he said, blushing.

"We're going to the zoo," Ashley said. "Oh, excuse me," she said, embarrassed. "I'm Ashley," she added, extending her hand to Tina. "And hello to you, Principal Harper," she giggled.

Tina smiled warmly at Ashley. "Great to finally meet you. I've heard so much about you from my dad," she said, her eyes fixed on Eddie. "Mom," Tina said, tapping her mother's shoulder shyly. "I'm free, and the Zoo sounds great."

The day at the zoo went by too quickly, especially for Eddie, who wanted to talk more with Tina, but his attention was on his sister, trying to remember what they had missed a long time ago.

Eddie was captivated by Tina's charm. She was twenty-four, a psychologist, and breathtakingly beautiful. He wondered what his ex-partner would think if he asked his daughter out.

Chapter 96

In an oversized rocking chair, Miguel Guzman sat with his daughter, Anne Marie. It had become their morning ritual before breakfast. The day began exactly as it had every morning since he had returned to Isabella and the ranch.

The deep blue sky, with its white puffy cotton-ball clouds, was tinted with a light pinkish glow as the sun rose over the jungle that surrounded his home.

"The sunrise is the best time of the day, my love," he said softly, his tone gentle and calm. He pointed to the playful horses in the green pasture. "A new baby colt was born yesterday. It will be your pony—a birthday present next month."

Isabella arrived, closely followed by one of their servants. She was singing, her happiness unmatched since they were first married. She was radiant. She was five months pregnant with a boy, something Miguel was not too pleased about. He never wanted to bring a child into the world with his messed-up DNA.

"Breakfast is ready, mi amor," she said sweetly. "Give me Anne Marie and go eat. Will you go into town with me today? The puppeteers will be there, and your daughter loves them."

Miguel had not left the ranch since his return. He had no desire to be around crowds. His blackouts had become more frequent, and he was afraid he'd do something he'd regret.

"Not today, my love. I have some papers to work on. The ship still keeps me busy. You have fun." It pained him to see her disappointment, but he knew it was best if he stayed home.

After Isabella and Anne Marie were gone, Miguel was hard at work at his desk. He turned on CNN as he did every morning, but the news being broadcast left him rigid in his chair. Robert Evans was talking about the Pied Piper. He could not believe what he was hearing. He threw his coffee mug across the room, shattering the large mirror over the fireplace.

Luis had come running into the office. "Miguel, you all right?" he asked.

"Evans is tarnishing the Pied Piper. He's making all my work out to be… he's said I am a child molester, and that bastard called me a cannibal. He's making me out to be a pedophile and a psychopath. He can't do this… he's called me revolting," he screamed.

Luis took a deep breath. "You're not the Pied Piper anymore. He died, remember? It doesn't matter what anyone says. You won your game. Miguel Guzman's a free man, well loved and respected by billions of people around the world. Turn off the TV and let us take a nice long walk," he said.

Miguel scowled. "It does matter. Evans, Blanchard, and Seymour did not die that evening. I didn't really win the game. They're not dead, and they should be," he said angrily.

Luis took a deep breath. "It doesn't matter. Let sleeping dogs lie."

Miguel had not been this agitated since returning home. The old fury, the Pied Piper's demeanor, was surfacing, and Luis was worried.

"Evans is teaming up with Blanchard and Seymour," he paused, taking in a trembling breath. "I know I should have made sure they died that day. I have to do something about this," he said, his eyes red with fire.

Luis wondered whether the prophecy had not yet ended. He had to see Maria one last time for her wisdom.

* * * * *

Guzman's foreman, Jorge Ruiz, grinned after hearing the anger return to Piper's voice. He rushed out toward the barn, his cell phone to his ear.

"Mother, the prophecy has begun. It's time. My sister's kidnapper will finally be punished the only way that could hurt him, with shame."

Maria Ruiz had been waiting patiently for this day to come. She recalled how arrogant Luis had become six months ago when he accused her of fraud. Today, God will allow me some peace before I go to heaven, she told herself.

"Jorge, send the package to Robert Evans using one of your email addresses, the way you attach things. He must know that Guzman must not leave his ranch. He has to see his life and reputation destroyed before his eyes. I need to stand over him and see the same pain in his eyes that he put into mine twenty-one years ago."

Chapter 97

Evans beamed when he saw Blanchard and Seymour walk in. "Thanks for coming," he said, extending his hand. Sitting on a couch next to a big picture window was a man dressed in a light brown tropical suit.

Blanchard pointed to the man on the couch. "Who's this?" he said curtly.

Evans smiled. "Boy, nothing gets by you. You're as sharp as ever," he joked. "Gentlemen, meet Inspector Frankel."

Blanchard seemed puzzled. "Isn't he the guy who helped protect Michelle Arnold?"

Frankel interjected, his face unemotional. "I'm sitting right here, and you can ask me yourself."

"Ted, do the warm-fuzzy stuff later. We need to get started. Now that I am with the San Diego Union Press, I have started a series of news pieces about the Pied Piper. None of them will be too flattering. I will keep them coming until he comes out from under his rock."

Blanchard rolled his eyes in disbelief. "You really think he's that stupid…if he's still out there?"

Evans took a deep breath. "I am on a mission. I can't rest, knowing in my heart he's still out there. Every night, I listen to Michelle as she sleeps. She wakes up screaming from her nightmares. She still believes Miguel Guzman is the Pied Piper and that he'll come after her one day. I believe her. I have to do this so she can find some peace."

Seymour appeared confused. "But the President said the reports said the Pied Piper's dead. The only lead we had was Miguel Guzman, and President Webster and the media vindicated him. Could we have been that wrong?"

"The Pied Piper and Miguel Guzman are one and the same...I'm certain of it. I don't believe the charred body found on that freighter was Enrique Ramirez. It was just a dead body. No DNA, no nothing. Whatever evidence they had, they processed too quickly, on orders from President Webster. Back then, what didn't happen was us dying in the warehouse. Do you really believe that after all these years the Pied Piper would give up that easily?" Evans shook his head.

Blanchard was chewing on his lower lip. "I've never believed it was him on that ship either. I've been trying to get clearance from President Webster to visit Guzman's ranch and meet his new daughter, but all I'm getting from his Chief of Staff is to let it drop. That's bullshit. I've got to see for myself that it's not Megan," he said angrily.

Evans forced a sincere smile. "He's killed too many FBI agents... my friends," he paused, taking a deep breath. His eyes had become glassy as he tried to control his emotions. "Let's not forget all the children he kidnapped and sent to their slaughter. It seemed coincidental that there were two ships, and that after so many years of eluding capture, the Pied Piper just kills himself. I don't believe in coincidences."

"I don't live a day without thinking about the animal, but what good will it do to give him the publicity he got off on...if he's still alive? He had thrived on having it in the first place?" asked Seymour.

Evans opened a thick file and stared at its contents. "The one thing I do know about the Pied Piper is that he always reacted irrationally when the media printed horrible stories about him. The notes he left behind after a negative article or televised news report reflected a man obsessed with his image. If he's really dead, we'll never hear from him, but if he's not, he'll come looking for me."

He believes he's a legend, a fabled hero, in his criminal world, but gentlemen, he's about to play a different game. I made the mistake of following the law when I was part of it, but now the gloves are off.

Blanchard put his feet on a glass coffee table, his hands clasped behind his head. "What do you need from us?"

Evans handed Seymour and Blanchard a copy of an email. "I received this yesterday. It appears someone in his organization wants to talk. He says he has proof that Miguel Guzman is the Pied Piper." Evans paused a moment for Blanchard's reaction to the last paragraph about his niece.

"Is this true?" he said, sitting up straight. "Megan's at the Guzman ranch?"

"The information has not been confirmed. What I do know is that he and his wife, Isabella, introduced their new daughter around the same time Megan was kidnapped. A CIA friend of mine is trying to get a photo so we can ID her. I believe it's Megan."

Seymour put his hand on Blanchard's arm. "If it's Megan, we'll both go down and bring her back," he said confidently. "We're still partners, right?"

Evans interrupted. "The person who sent this email sent another one two weeks ago. He told me that the Guatemalan authorities have the old file on Frederick Ramirez." His eyes fixed on Blanchard. "You remember the day at the house?"

Blanchard nodded. "Yeah. That day I saved your life. You were just a rookie and almost got yourself killed."

Evans blushed. "Don't remind me," he frowned. "I was sent the original file a week ago. Remember the mess we found at the Ramirez house?"

"Yeah. Frederick Ramirez and his wife were dead. It looked as if Frederick had killed his wife and servants and then put the gun to his head."

"For an old guy, you still have your memory. Do you remember the partial ear we found at the crime scene? Well, President Webster returned it to Guatemala, and it's back in the case file there, preserved in a jar. President Webster did not compare the DNA from the ear to Guzman's DNA. He was so happy to close the case that he had the FBI's forensic unit rush to a conclusion. I had the DNA tested, and it's a perfect match to Guzman's DNA."

"Are you telling me that we have actual proof that Guzman is Enrique Ramirez and the Pied Piper?" Blanchard said, excited. "Boy, will this piss off Webster."

Evans had a big grin on his face. "Miguel Guzman is Frederick Ramirez's son, Enrique Ramirez. It turns out that the young boy who got away that day in Santa Catarina was Enrique."

Blanchard had turned white as a ghost. "You mean to tell me he's been holding a grudge that long?"

"It appears so. I never could figure out why he hated you and me so much. It all makes sense now. He's blaming us for his cousin's death and whatever else happened to him when he returned home. I'm just guessing, but I'll bet you a buck that his father cut off part of his ear, so he'd remember that day."

Seymour's face turned ashen. "Are you telling me that my the three of you were the cause of all of this?"

"Your father was…um…the lead agent. All I can guess is that for Enrique, he could blame himself for his screw up," Evans said fretfully. "He needed someone to blame, and we were his logical choice."

Eddie's jaw clenched at Evans's remarks. "So, your fuck-up thirty years ago caused my parents' deaths and my sister's kidnapping!"

"It's water under the bridge. We were doing our jobs. I'm sorry for how you feel, but that's not why I wanted you all here today," Evans told him coldly. Guzman's foreman feels we need to move quickly. Miguel has taken my bait and now wants to finish what he started…" Evans swallowed hard. "He wants the three of us dead and most likely the people close to us."

Eddie was livid. "You have a lot of nerve getting me and my sister involved in your harebrained scheme. He's been smarter than all of us put together, no matter how much confidence you've had in each of the traps you've set for him." Seymour leaned against the couch pillows, his arms folded tightly across his chest. "You're a bastard, Evans. You know that?" he cursed. "You've once again put my life and my sister's life in mortal danger."

Blanchard's face had gone pale after hearing Evans's words. Realizing he might be able to get his niece back was all that mattered at the moment. "I want Megan back more than anything, but I have a family now. I can't put them in danger."

Seymour, his eyes little slits of anger, stared at Evans. "If the Pied Piper, Miguel Guzman, or whoever the fuck he is has started mobilizing again, we're already in danger," he said. "I'm not happy, but I agree with you. We need to flush him out and strike before he makes his move. Does your insider have a way to get us close to him?"

Evans nodded, biting his lip nervously. "He wants us to meet him in Guatemala City. He has certain terms and conditions we have to agree to, or he will not cooperate."

Blanchard punched his palm. His face had turned beet red. "Conditions? What damn conditions? Is he playing a fucking game? Maybe it's the Pied Piper setting us up once again, and this time we'll be in a foreign country, unprotected."

Evans shrugged his shoulders. "He didn't say. I have four plane tickets to Guatemala. I'm leaving tomorrow with Frankel, and I'm going with or without you guys," Evans said. A knot formed in his throat as he tried to hold back his emotions.

Seymour looked at Blanchard, then back at Evans. "I'm in. The bastard killed my parents and kept Ashley away from me for eighteen years."

Blanchard remained silent. He was lost in thought. "Count me in," he said. "I want him dead for what he did to my sister and her husband. No trial, just our own form of revenge."

Evans clapped his hands. "I knew the two of you wouldn't pass up a chance to get payback. I've hired a team of ex-Army Rangers to assist us. A CIA friend in Guatemala will coordinate everything for us, and Inspector Frankel has a team from Interpol in place that wants the Pied Piper dead as much as we do."

"What about our families?" asked Blanchard.

"I've arranged for around-the-clock security for everyone while we're gone."

"Do we have enough evidence this time to nail his ass?" Seymour asked. "He's made of Teflon."

Evans tossed him a bundle of photos he had gotten from his contact in Guatemala. "If this doesn't convince you, then nothing will. We're not going to arrest him. If you're in on this…he's a dead man walking."

Seymour's eyes widened with shock as he flipped through the pictures. He passed the photos to Blanchard.

Blanchard's blood drained from his face. He was looking at the Miami promenade. Then Miguel Guzman was holding Megan. It kept getting worse. He was looking at photos in his sister's bedroom, Guzman still donning his Pied Piper costume, acting like a hunter taking a photo of his trophy after a kill.

"I have first crack at that bastard," Blanchard screamed.

Evans had given Seymour and Blanchard ID photos of their respective security guards. "They should already be waiting at your homes when you return. Pack light. The game is on, and this time we're going to be the winners."

Chapter 98

The four men landed in Guatemala City, where they were greeted by Evans' CIA friend, Todd Jackson.

The greetings were kept to a minimum as they were swept toward a small village near Lake Atitlan. The two-and-a-half-hour ride through lush jungles walled in by the high mountains and volcanoes that made up the country's tropical topography went by quickly.

They were dropped off at a hillside ranch that overlooked the large volcanic lake. Other than its beauty, the lake was known for the twelve villages around its base, each named after one of the Apostles.

Inside the one-room rustic ranch house was a large, warped wooden table resting on a dirt floor. The room smelled of mold and feces. Sitting at the table in front of a laptop was a stocky man in his mid-thirties. He was clean-shaven, wearing a multicolored cotton shirt and baggy pants, typical attire for the millions of Indians who lived throughout the country.

Jorge stood and introduced himself. In a dark corner of the room sat an elderly woman with deeply etched wrinkles on her face, forcing a sad smile that revealed her decaying, twisted teeth.

"I'm Jorge Ruiz, and this is my mother, Maria. Thank you for coming. We need to act quickly. Senor Guzman is preparing his men to leave for the United States, with one thing on his mind... harming all of you and your families," he said, his English perfect.

Evans wanted to know more before they got started. "How are you connected to all of this?" he asked, his tone skeptical. Once again, everything was playing out too easily.

Jorge nodded, indicating he understood the doubt in Evans's voice. "I can understand why you are cautious. You've been close so many times, and each time you lost both men and your pride. I, too, lost something over twenty years ago… my sister was kidnapped the day you and your partners captured Enrique Rameriz's cousin. I had hope that my sister was still alive until I read the bastard's log of all his kidnappings. My mother's been plotting her revenge all these years," he paused, craning his neck and nodding at his mother.

"Why didn't you go to the Guatemalan authorities with this evidence?" Evan asked.

"Like I told you earlier. Indians in this part of the world are not considered human and would have imprisoned me for slandering a man like Miguel Guzman."

"I'll ask again, why now are you asking for our help?" Evans inquired.

"I promised her that when I was a man I would help her put down this animal, but the authorities in Guatemala do not see their Indian population as human. I could not kill Guzman without putting my entire family at risk."

"Understand my doubts about what you're telling us," Evan told him. "How can I be sure you're not setting a trap for us?"

"As you already know, timing is everything with the Pied Piper. You were always restrained by your laws, but now you aren't. Once we learned what you were doing and saw how upset Miguel was getting, the timing was right to destroy him."

Evans was not buying everything Jorge was telling him, but he needed to hear more and let the young man explain his evidence.

Chapter 99

Guzman was unable to control his temper as he read the latest newspaper story about the Pied Piper. "They are all going to die," he screamed. He paced like a caged tiger, growling at every word he read.

Luis tried to calm him down, but he was beyond reason. "Let my brothers and I go and kill these horrible pigs. You need to stay here and let us do our jobs."

"Bullshit. I am the Pied Piper and can't be stopped. I will personally kill their families first, one by one, while they watch. I'll start with the Arnold girl, then with Blanchard's new family, and end with Seymour's sister. Then, when the three of them realize their lives are over, I will make each one beg me to kill them quickly. But that won't happen, I promise you, Luis. They will die slowly, painfully, screaming for my mercy on my ship of hope. I will cut off their limbs and feed them to the sharks. Then, I will cut out their organs while they watch," he laughed.

"But, sir," Luis tried to argue, but Miguel raised his hand to quiet him.

"Make yourself ready. We leave in one hour. Everything has been arranged."

* * * * *

Jorge guided the assault teams through a safe part of the jungle to the back of the Guzman ranch. The six ex-Army Rangers took their positions on the eastern and southern sides of the ranch. Frankel's men covered the west side.

Evans, Blanchard, and Seymour were going to storm the house from the north, hoping to catch Guzman by surprise.

It was time to move. Everyone, especially Evans, was nervous. Again, everything was happening too fast and too easily. But it was different now. He was responsible for Michelle, and her fragile mental state did not need another tragedy. Nevertheless, he gave the order to rush through the front door. Once they were out in the open, exposed, ten men, all carrying automatic weapons, ran out of the barn. The area around the house exploded with gunfire.

Between the Rangers and Frankel's men, Guzman's guards were felled before they could empty their first magazine.

Seymour kicked in the front door, his gun at the ready. What he found was a hysterical woman holding a small child. Evans grabbed the baby, and Blanchard patted the pregnant woman down for weapons.

"Give me back my child," she screamed. "Who are you, and what do you want?" she ranted. "When my husband returns, you'll be sorry. He's a very powerful man." The second she saw Jorge, her foreman, standing under the front door archway with a menacing grin, she stopped screaming, a puzzled look on her face.

"Señora Guzman, where's your husband? These men want to speak with him."

"What's going on?" she said calmly, her eyes darting around the room at the men carrying automatic weapons.

Blanchard spoke first, holding his niece, Megan, who was cooing in his arms and hugging him tightly. "We're here to arrest your husband. He's a murderous pig," he said, his tone serious.

Isabella shook her head. "Give me back my daughter," she pleaded. "Miguel is not here. He left for the United States four hours ago on business. There must be some misunderstanding. My husband is a humanitarian. He's loved around the world for his charity work."

Evans interrupted her. "He's the Pied Piper. You can't tell me you haven't known what kind of man your husband is and the pain he's brought to thousands of families around the world with his gruesome acts."

"That can't be true," she argued, sobbing, her hands cupping her face.

"It's true, Isabella," said Jorge calmly. He had taken Miguel's laptop from the den. He brought up a screen listing all the records of the children the Pied Piper had kidnapped over the past twenty years. Her face turned white as she looked over the details of the list.

"This has to be a mistake," she said, her eyes wide with disbelief.

For the next hour, Jorge helped Evans locate all the evidence needed to convict Miguel Guzman.

Isabella sat in shock, unable to speak. Once she realized what her husband had done to give her Anne Marie, or as she was told, Megan Morgan, she ran into the bathroom, retching.

Blanchard was hugging Megan but did not seem happy. "Guzman will be landing…" He looked at his watch. "I'll bet he'll be in California in about an hour. We need to get back home before we come back to…I don't want to think about what he's still capable of doing."

Within the hour, they were aboard a Gulf Stream flying back to California, courtesy of the CIA. Evans had called Rudy Weidman with his story. The evidence and photos had been emailed.

The following story, which was going to be on every newscast and in every newspaper, was that Miguel Guzman is the Pied Piper.

Evans emphasized to Rudy that he had to ensure that Isabella Guzman's face was plastered across every media outlet and that she was captured by Blanchard, Seymour, and Evans. The article needed to make clear that she was being transported back to the United States. He knew it was their only chance to give their families time to survive.

Jorge and Maria Ruiz were on their first plane ride, sitting huddled together nervously.

Jorge stared out the window, lost in thought. "Mama, do you think Evans will keep his word so Enrique will feel the pain he's caused us?"

"That I cannot say. These men have a great deal of hatred for the man they've only known as the Pied Piper. God has his own justice, and I have a good feeling about this," she whispered.

Chapter 100

Rudy Weidman and his wife, Nancy, had just settled down for a relaxing dinner. Married only nine months, they had not yet returned from their honeymoon, spending night after night enjoying romantic dinners, planning their future, and the family they both hoped to raise one day.

The doorbell had disrupted Rudy. "I hope it's not one of those charities selling candy for delinquent children," he moaned. He glanced at his watch. It was nine-thirty, and he was noticeably upset as he marched toward the incessant ringing.

"I'm coming," he shouted. "Stop ringing the damn bell," he yelled. He looked through the peephole and immediately recognized Miguel Guzman.

He moved away from the door just before it was kicked in.

Guzman had a gun pointed at his forehead.

Luis and Herman ran through the house, checking every room.

Beth Weidman rushed in from the dining room. She screamed when she saw the man with long hair pressing a gun against her husband's head.

"What's going on?" she screamed. "You want money and jewelry. Take whatever you find. Please don't hurt us," she pleaded.

Miguel, with a sweeping blow, planted his gun against Rudy's head, knocking him down. Beth ran to him, holding him tight in her arms. She trembled as she rocked her dazed husband.

Luis and Herman had returned. "The rest of the house is clear."

"You've made a big mistake by ruining the Pied Piper's good name. You and Evans should have let sleeping dogs lie. Now all of you will be punished."

Rudy's words were slurred as he spoke. "I guess you haven't seen the news. "You've been exposed. Your wife is in custody, and the three men you want dead are on their way back from your ranch with Megan, the little girl you kidnapped. They said they've come to 'fulfill the prophecy'," Weidman said arrogantly.

Luis' face was ashen upon hearing those words. He turned to Miguel. "How could they know about the prophecy?"

Miguel wasn't listening to Luis. His eyes were focused on the scared editor. There is no prophecy, but the one I'm about to fulfill on all of you," said Guzman in a cold, sinister tone. Luis, my friend here, is very superstitious."

Luis interrupted. "Sir, what if the world actually knows you're the Pied Piper? There will be no place for us to hide."

Miguel slapped his friend hard across the cheek, a crazed look on his face. "You must have known that one day my disease would consume me as it did my father. I expect to die young, but I will not go the cowardly way my father did. I have only one destiny that is real…the Pied Piper will go down in history as the most famous criminal the world has ever known. All that matters now is that the closing act of my story can be completed."

Luis, his anger controlled, responded. "If we must die, then let it be on our terms."

Guzman bent down and lifted Rudy to his feet. "I want you to call Evans and get him to your house as soon as they land. Luis, you take Herman and the men…," he paused, massaging his temples. A severe headache throbbed. He winced.

Miguel walked over to Weidman's wife and hit her with the barrel of his gun. He then walked over to Rudy and lifted him by the hair. "I want to know the location of the Arnold girl, Ashley Seymour, and Blanchard's new wife and daughter."

Before Rudy could respond, Luis grabbed his wife by the throat and began choking the life out of her. Weidman let out a helpless cry. He knew he had no choice.

"Good decision," said Miguel. "Luis, bring all of them to me now. I want them here before the three Musketeers arrive," he ordered, his face flushed with fury. "This time, it will be done right."

"What about Isabella? She's carrying your son," Luis said nervously. "What if they hurt her?"

Miguel thought for just a brief moment. "Let them think she's leverage. It doesn't matter now. They won't hurt her... Americans have a conscience, and Evans is a coward."

* * * * *

Rudy had finally gotten a hold of Evans on his cell phone. He was spewing Guzman's instructions when the phone was yanked from his ear.

"I thought..." Guzman was breathing hard. "I told you... the damn game was over," he stammered. "You... you lost. You're being a poor sport," he shouted like a spoiled child. "I was going to live happily ever after, and now you've ruined everything."

Evans waited until there was silence on Guzman's end. "I never said the game was over. In fact, it has just begun," he said boldly. Then the color drained from his face when he was told that the Pied Piper had Michelle again.

Blanchard saw the change immediately. His eyes widened with curiosity. "What's happening?" Evans leaned back in his seat, his shoulders slumping.

He cupped the phone's mouthpiece. "He's got Michelle," he whispered. "Michelle, honey, don't cry. You'll be all right. I'm coming to get you," he calmly told her. Michelle's cries had faded.

"Tell Seymour and Blanchard the people they love are with me too. Now, who is controlling your little amateurish game?" Guzman laughed. "Here are the new rules. You will come to Weidman's house, just the three of you. Don't call the FBI. I'll know. And don't think San Diego's finest will help either. I still have friends there. If you play by the rules this time, you'll save your loved ones. If I see any men other than the three of you, everyone will be dead before you reach the front door. I'll be gone, this time for good. Trust me."

Blanchard ripped the phone from Evans. His face had a fury Evans had never seen. "Hey, nutcase, this is Agent Blanchard. I have someone here who wants to speak to you."

"Miguel," Isabella cried. "Stop this madness. I don't care what you've done. I want our child to have a father. I don't want to be alone. Please listen to their offer."

Blanchard was back on the phone. "If you love your wife and the child she's carrying, you'll do as I say. If not, I guarantee you'll be hunted for the rest of your life while your wife rots in federal prison and your child is tossed into foster care, maybe even an orphanage in Guatemala or Honduras. You do know what happens to those children, don't you?" He could hear Guzman's heavy breathing. "Good, you understand. Don't be foolish and let your competitors take your new child."

"You fucking animal. I should have killed you the night I killed your partner... You fat son-of-a-bitch. You harm a hair on my wife's head, and I will see that your daughter and girlfriend take a long, unpleasant cruise on my ship. I know you know what I'm capable of."

Blanchard remained calm and in control. "You're in no position to issue ultimatums. Just release everyone and turn yourself in. Then we'll send your wife home to have your child. Take it or leave it. I'll call you back in ten minutes with your answer," Ted said, slamming down the phone.

Seymour could not believe his ears. He stood, grabbing Blanchard by his shirt and pulling him up. "Are you nuts? He's going to kill everyone. What were you thinking?"

"He's going to kill them anyway. I'm hoping to give us some more time. Something we need right now. Trust me on this. The guy loves games, and he won't end the game without seeing us suffer," Blanchard told him as he shook off his partner's grip. "We can't show him we're intimidated. If he senses fear, he'll think he's won."

Eddie pushed Blanchard away, throwing his arms up in frustration. "You're trying to reason with an irrational psychopath," he shouted, his eyes moist. "What if your gamble doesn't work? I don't want to lose Ashley again."

"I have just as much at stake as all of you. He's got Teresa and my daughter, Tina, too."

Evans leaned forward, whispering something to Inspector Frankel. When he finished talking to the inspector, he waved his friends to sit down. "Ted, I've always known you had balls, but I didn't know they were that big. Frankel and I have a plan that might work."

Chapter 101

Guzman was furious. "That asshole hung up on me," he bellowed at Luis. His body began to tremble wildly. No one had ever backed him into a corner, and he was struggling to cope.

He lifted his gun and pointed it at Blanchard's terrified daughter, who was huddled with her mother. "You're going to be the first to die, and then we'll see how brave your father is." He smiled when Teresa stood to shield her daughter.

"Please don't hurt her," she said, her lips quivering, clearly frightened.

"It doesn't matter to me who dies first," he howled. "Blanchard will suffer one way or another for his insolence."

Guzman's face twisted with pain, and his headache had worsened. He pushed Teresa with such force that she stumbled to his left and fell helplessly to the floor. He inched closer, his adrenaline pumping faster as he watched Blanchard's daughter realize she was about to die. He did not appreciate that Tina closed her eyes. He had to see the eyes. They had to meet his eyes to satisfy his fetish: to see death escape from his victim.

He pressed the barrel of his gun hard against the girl's forehead, the hammer cocked. "Open your fucking eyes," he shouted. "I want to see you accept your fate," he ranted. His mood had exploded into another dimension. He was acting out of character. The Pied Piper was no longer in control.

Luis grabbed his arm abruptly. He knew the risk, but he had to take it. Miguel spun around, the gun's barrel resting on his friend's cheek, his eyes empty pools. A new creature had emerged.

"Don't ever touch me again. You hear?" he screamed. His words sounded like his father's on the day his mother died. "I'm the Pied Piper…"

Luis stood his ground. Miguel stopped yelling, his eyes wide with disbelief.

"Miguel, you do this now, and they've won the game," he said patronizingly. He was talking to his boss like a parent talking to a child. "Don't you want to see Blanchard's pain? If you do this right now, you will not have the satisfaction you've waited for all these years."

Guzman was blinking rapidly, digesting Luis' words. His eyes rolled back into his head. The room fell silent as everyone watched in horror at what was happening.

Guzman's body began to flail. His gun fell to the floor, and his head arched back, his chin raised to the ceiling. In an instant, he collapsed, dropping hard onto the carpet. He was convulsing wildly.

Luis and Herman were by his side. They had never seen this before. Miguel's men were distracted and did not notice Rudy reaching for the gun that had fallen three feet from where he sat with his wife.

Rudy's wife pulled at his shirt as he stretched his arm for the gun. He swatted her hand away.

"Do you even know how to use the gun?" he asked himself. His fingertips felt the cold barrel as he leaned further. *Just another inch,* he rooted himself on. It was short-lived.

Luis had seen movement from the corner of his eye and immediately swung his gun toward the brave editor. "That would be a foolish thing to do," he said calmly, kicking the gun away. "Everyone, stay calm, and maybe we can reach a good resolution to this situation."

Rudy spoke nervously. "Let us go and take your boss back to where you came from. He needs medical treatment. Tie us up, rip the phones from the wall, and take our cell phones. Go while you still can. You don't seem to have your heart in murdering us," he acknowledged. He was nervous, trying to reason with the one man who seemed to control Guzman.

"Shut up," Luis screamed. "Let me think." He whispered something in Spanish into his brother's ear.

Herman stood. "No," he shouted. "Maybe we should go. Miguel is going to get us all killed. We have an opportunity now. Let's take it," Luis' brother pleaded with him.

Luis nodded. "But we can't leave him here. Let's put him in the van. We can figure out what to do with Piper later," he said, startled when Miguel popped up fully alert and grabbed a gun from Luis' waistband.

"What happened?" he asked, his voice low and raspy.

Luis looked puzzled. "You just collapsed for a few minutes. What's going on with you?"

Miguel ignored his comment, staring blankly through his friend. He answered Luis' original question as if he had never blacked out. "I think your idea has merit. It's better if I wait and watch them suffer."

Chapter 102

Six hours later, the Learjet landed smoothly at Palomar Airport in Carlsbad. Evans did not like Blanchard's plan. It was risky, but under the circumstances, they had no other choice if they wanted to save their families.

Blanchard dialed Weidman's house in Rancho Santa Fe. It was the ideal location for what they had planned. After one ring, Guzman picked up the phone.

"Blanchard, have you made your decision?" Miguel asked. His tone had become overconfident.

Ted did not respond to his remark. "Here's the deal. You release all the hostages and turn yourself in."

"What about my wife?" Guzman asked in a cold monotone.

"Isabella will be released and flown back to your ranch only when my people know you've kept your end of the bargain."

There was a long silence before Guzman responded. "That's not going to work," he said. "I'll trade hostages only if you, Seymour, and Evans take their place. Oh, one other thing. You have to come unarmed."

"That's bullshit," Blanchard shouted. "This is our deal…take it or leave it," he said, controlling his emotions. He knew that if his bluff failed, everyone in Weidman's house would die.

Guzman was breathing heavily and fast. He sounded like a man hyperventilating. "You're playing a high-stakes poker game, and I'm calling your bluff. Kiss your friend Weidman goodbye," he said.

Blanchard's eyes opened wide with terror as he heard Rudy's wife scream in the background. Then a loud explosion erupted. The ringing hurt his ears. He could hear cries in the background.

"Now, you've been called. Are you going to raise me or fold?" Guzman said with confidence.

"You're dead," Blanchard screamed. With his cell phone pressed against his chest, he whispered to Evans, "He just shot Rudy. He said he'd release the hostages only if we took their place."

Seymour grabbed the phone from his partner. "We'll be there in forty minutes. You harm anyone else, and I'll personally chop up your body and feed it to the sharks you've been calling your friends for so many years."

"Ah, my good friend, Special Agent Edward Seymour, you've made a sound decision. Don't be late. The three of you come alone, or everyone dies," Guzman said, his voice becoming calm again.

* * * * *

A half mile from the Weidman's house, Evans, Blanchard, and Seymour said goodbye to Inspector Frankel. "If I don't return…" he hesitated, his voice cracking. "Give this letter to Michelle...tell her I'm sorry."

Watching the three men leave, Inspector Frankel was upset with the plan they had chosen, but he knew he would have done the same thing if the tables had been reversed. He watched the SUV head toward the long serpentine driveway that started at Del Dios Highway and wound its way toward Weidman's twenty-thousand-square-foot house nestled on ten acres in Rancho Santa Fe. Trees and wild grass framed the entire property.

He and his men had to run through unfamiliar territory and set up their positions in less than five minutes. His sniper, a four-time Gold Medalist at the Olympics, was running ahead of all of them, hoping to get the best vantage point for the one shot that would end it all.

* * * * *

Herman was the first to see the SUV pull up the driveway. "They're here," he called out to his brother. "There are only three of them."

Luis began gathering the hostages. "Miguel, let's get this over with," he said nervously.

"Not so fast," Guman said. "They have to see their loved ones die before their eyes," he whispered, as if he were talking only to himself.

"What about Isabella and the baby?" Luis argued.

"What about her? She'll be collateral damage if it comes down to it," Miguel said unemotionally. "This happens in a game like this. Remember, life is a sport, and winning is the only thing worthwhile," he ranted incoherently again.

Luis had become enraged. "Isabella is innocent. She's trusted you for all these years. What about your son she's carrying?"

Miguel put his gun in his shoulder holster and cupped his friend's face in both hands. "You know what's happening to me. I would eventually kill them like my father killed my mother. I'm having a son. He'll be cursed anyway. I want to go out a winner," he said in a low whisper.

"What about my brothers and me?" Luis asked.

"You once told me you'd lay down your life for me. Have you changed your mind? A promise is a promise," he reminded him, his eyes empty black pools. "Do I see betrayal in your eyes?" Miguel whispered. It was a rhetorical question for him because he had already grabbed his gun and fired it into Luis's chest without a second thought. Then, without hesitation, he pivoted with the speed of a hawk snatching its prey and fired at Herman, who stood there in shock. When Luis's two remaining brothers rushed into the living room, they too were shot with point-blank accuracy.

Guzman stood over his fallen men, a satisfied smile on his face. "Mother, I'll be with you soon," he whispered, his eyes red with fire.

Chapter 103

Michelle Arnold had not taken her eyes off the Pied Piper throughout the entire killing spree. He was no longer Miguel Guzman, but a monster. She remained calm and cool. She didn't understand why or how, but she was in survival mode. She wanted to live and enjoy her new life with her adoptive father. Just as she had when escaping from Dr. Kane's cement fortress, she was not about to die today.

When Guzman started shooting his men, she had grabbed Ashley's arm and whispered into her ear.

"If you want to live, follow me." She then signaled to Teresa and Tina, using perfect hand signals that would have made a SEAL team proud to follow her. Rudy's wife sat, rocking back and forth, still in shock and not looking at Michelle.

Michelle was once again fighting for her life, but this time she wasn't alone. She had others to save. She was the only experienced person who had been under fire, and what she was doing seemed natural.

She put her finger to her lips and began crawling toward the kitchen. She looked back and waved for the women to follow. Like ants following a designated trail back to their nest, the women crawled after their young leader.

* * * * *

Guzman had picked up the weapons from his dead crew, men who had been loyal to him for over two decades. He showed no emotion. His illness had fully blossomed. Then he turned, looking for his hostages. They were gone. He bellowed like a wounded wolf. He scanned the living room and saw them crawling toward the kitchen.

He bounded into the kitchen like a tiger corralling his next meal. "Where the fuck do you think you're going?" he shouted, waving his gun. He was so enraged that he fired wildly into the kitchen, a bullet ricocheting off the stainless-steel refrigerator. "Stop before I shoot again. This time I won't miss."

* * * * *

Inspector Frankel had taken his position with his men. Each one of them had a good view of the front, back, and sides of the house. The sniper had positioned himself, his rifle aimed at the large bay window that looked into the living room. His eyes were wide with fear as he watched Guzman kill his men. He knew the hostages were next. He jumped up and ran toward Frankel's position by the kitchen window, hoping he'd not be too late.

Inside the kitchen, Guzman made the women line up against the large sub-zero refrigerator with Michelle in the middle. His automatic weapon was pointed at them. He was ready to fire when he heard the front door burst open.

Seymour skidded to a halt when he saw Guzman's men lying dead in the living room. His heart pounded against his chest. He knew he was too late. "Guzman, you mother fucker, where are you?" he screamed.

Evans and Blanchard heard Eddie's scream and stopped before entering the living room. They could see Guzman's shadow. Using hand signals, they told Seymour he was in the kitchen.

Guzman shouted, "My dear friends, your women are still alive, but not for long. Throw your weapons into the kitchen and enter in a single line, your hands locked behind your heads, or I'll start putting bullets into them one at a time." When they did not respond, he fired a round into Teresa's shoulder.

The three men took a deep breath as they listened to Tina scream for her mother.

"Mom, wake up…please wake up," she sobbed.

"You motherfucker," Blanchard shouted. His legs had turned to rubber.

Guzman gave them one more chance to do as he had said. "Do it now, or they will all die. Believe me… I will kill all of them before you reach the kitchen."

Three guns skidded by Guzman's feet, and the three men walked slowly in, their arms stretched high above their heads. Their eyes were locked on the man they hated, defeat etched on their faces.

Blanchard panned the room and saw that Teresa was conscious and being rocked in Tina's arms. He breathed a sigh of relief and returned his focus to Guzman.

"Very good," Guzman said. "I want to make this quick. Now get down on your knees and face your loved ones." Miguel walked behind Evans and Blanchard, his gun pointed at the backs of their heads. "I've waited so long for this moment," he said calmly. "The day the two of you…" He spat on Blanchard and Evans, "…ruined my life. I received the worst beating of my life." He pushed back his hair that covered his deformed ear. "I've had this to remember that day. If you had left us alone, my mother would be alive today. Maybe even the Pied Piper would have remained a children's fable, but as you know, life is never that simple."

Eddie looked at Ashley and mouthed that he loved her and was sorry. Blanchard did the same toward Teresa and Tina. Evans was surprised to see Michelle staring into the middle distance, not paying him any attention.

Rudy's wife was sobbing. In their eyes, the women knew they were all about to die.

Guzman laughed. "I never thought it would happen this way. I guess all good things happen for a reason," he said, his voice calm. "Which of you ladies wants to go first? Let me see a show of hands, please," he said, laughing.

Seymour tried to jump up, but Guzman hit the back of his head with the butt of his gun. Eddie slumped forward, moaning. Ashley gasped and fell to the floor to comfort her brother.

Michelle had not stopped staring outside. She was riveted on the men with rifles, all of whom were pointing at them.

Inspector Frankel touched his two-way. "Do you have a shot?" he asked his sniper.

"Sir, the Arnold girl and Blanchard's daughter are too close for a clean shot."

Frankel kept waving his arm at Michelle, but she did not seem to understand what he wanted her to do. "We can't wait. Take your best shot and pray."

Michelle kept watching the man in a brown suit signaling her to fall to the floor. Something clicked, and without thinking, she shouted, "Duck!", grabbing Tina's arm. She hoped that the other women would stay down on the floor.

Michelle watched Guzman react to their movement as his finger squeezed the trigger. One shot exploded from the barrel of his gun, just missing Michelle. She saw Miguel attempting to reposition himself.

The sniper had a clear shot that would have blown a hole through the back of Guzman's head. When his target started to move, he had to take the percentage shot. He knew that if he missed, more would die inside the house.

Before Michelle could react, she heard glass shatter, and an explosion echo through the kitchen. Before Guzman could get another shot off, he was struck in the back and fell forward, landing on top of Seymour.

Frankel and his team burst through the double French doors, taking up defensive positions and searching for the rest of Miguel's men.

Seymour pushed Guzman's lifeless body off him while Evans and Blanchard formed a protective blanket over the sobbing women with their bodies. They did not move until they heard Frankel shout: "House secure."

Maria Ruiz and her son, Jorge, hobbled into the kitchen. She walked over to Guzman's body and spat on his face. "Now the Prophecy is complete," she said, crying.

One of the ex-rangers found Rudy Weidman tied up in the laundry room. He was alive.

Evans thanked Inspector Frankel and the ex-Army Rangers for their help. "I'm glad it ended this way. You never know what our justice system would have done if Guzman had gotten himself a good legal team."

Seymour wanted to make sure the Pied Piper was dead. He felt for a pulse and, to his surprise, found one. He looked at Blanchard and then back at Evans. "The bastard's still alive," he said, his eyes wide with disgust. He pointed the barrel of his gun at Guzman's chest.

"One more bullet wouldn't hurt, right?" Seymour muttered.

"God has one sick sense of humor," Blanchard said. "Call an ambulance. It looks like he's going to trial."

EPILOGUE

Six months later

Miguel Guzman suffered a stroke in the hospital and combined with the sniper's bullet that shattered his spine, he was paralyzed from the neck down. The doctors believed he could hear and see, but that was about all he could do.

President Webster decided to transport Guzman back to Guatemala and let the authorities there handle him. He did not want to put a paraplegic on trial. Guzman was already a prisoner in his own body.

Maria Ruiz and Jorge took up residence at the Guzman ranch, ready to help Isabella with her newborn baby boy. In the meantime, Maria wanted to tend to Miguel's constant care needs.

The prophecy had come true for Maria. Miguel Guzman, the Pied Piper, was suffering the worst form of punishment a man like him could face. Every day, when his diapers had to be changed, when he had to be fed baby food, or when he tried to doze off to sleep, Luis's clairvoyant read him all the stories told about him as the repugnant Pied Piper and how everyone loathed him.

A year after moving to the Guzmans' ranch, Maria Ruiz died in her sleep. Miguel's son was now three months old.

Isabella did not want to believe the negative rumors circulating about her husband. She tried to remember only the man she loved, who had done wonderful charitable work. She named her son Frederick in honor of the Ramirez tradition. Each day, she'd read her son the story of the Pied Piper, which she believed made her husband happy, blending her husband's accomplishments around the world into the fable.

Maria Ruiz's son continued Guzman's mental torture until Miguel died ten years later.

Guzman Enterprises, worth over $350 billion, had been liquidated. After a small trust fund was set up for Isabella and baby Frederick, the rest of the money was divided among all the families who had suffered from his heinous acts as the Pied Piper.

The Federal Government mandated that foster care programs nationwide ensure that every child placed, either temporarily or permanently, in a foster home be fingerprinted, photographed, and have a DNA sample collected to protect them better.

Civil rights groups protested, but their complaints fell on deaf ears. The House and Senate wanted tracking devices on every child, but they couldn't get it passed and backed off, hoping that the other safety measures would improve foster care programs nationwide.

Evans officially adopted Michelle and continued his work with Rudy Weidman at the San Diego Union Press. He exposed President Webster's cover-up, which eventually cost Webster his re-election bid by over 25 percentage points. It was the most significant defeat for an incumbent President.

Ashley Seymour inherited everything Sally Palmer, Lisa, and Earl Mathews owned, totaling $26 million. She gave half of it to her brother for all his suffering. Eddie resigned from the FBI and began writing a book.

Eddie had started dating Ted's daughter with his permission. They both had become very serious and were planning a future together.

Ted Blanchard married Teresa Harper and moved to La Jolla. He became the new Director of the FBI, heading up a new division to help combat human trafficking globally. He and Inspector Frankel became an unbeatable international team.

The only broker who survived the Pied Piper's early termination plan, Mary Lynn Rose, had resurfaced in Guatemala. Rumor had it that she was living with Isabella Guzman and her son, Frederick. Human trafficking continued to thrive without the Pied Piper, keeping the FBI and Interpol busy.

Thank you for reading this book! Please take a few moments to leave a review at:www.https://www.amazon.com/dp/B07NSPZJZ6

Please check out my other suspense thrillers at www.aweaveroftalespress.com and sign up for first release notices.

www.ingramcontent.com/pod-product-compliance
Lightning Source LLC
Chambersburg PA
CBHW051532250626
47157CB00001B/9